"This worldbuilding reminds me of a taste of China Mieville's New Crobuzon, a dose of the scheming Universities in Paul McAuley's Confluence novels, and an air and aura of mystery and thriller in the bargain. A gaslit quasi-Victorian underground city, though, in the end, is something new under the sun, and having two female protagonists as our leads and views into the city even more so. Patel gets high marks for trying to bring something new, and wandering the boundary of science fiction and fantasy to do it."

Skiffy & Fanty

"This is one of the fastest paced books I've read in a long time. Patel wastes no time with excessive description or extraneous scenes, but still manages to convey a full sense of the world and its underlying implications. The stakes are always clear, transitioning effortlessly from scene to scene, and I found the story impossible to put down. Fans of fast-paced narratives should definitely give this one a look. The ending is perfectly set up, but only in retrospect: I didn't see it coming, and the world is left completely upturned. In short, *The Buried Life* is a fantastic start to Carrie Patel's new series, and this one is going straight onto my 'Buy Sequel Immediately Upon Release' list."

Fantasy Book Critic

"Carrie Patel has conceived of a dark steampunk-esque yet futuristic world filled with anachronisms that, despite that, work well together. It's as if this world has been cobbled together from past cultures and times, which is not as unusual as it may sound, to make for an underground claustrophobic world that you can almost feel pressing down on your head and soul. And there's a library to die for – what bookaholic could resist? This is Book #1 in a new series and I'm really looking forward to Book #2!"

Popcorn Reads

CARRIE PATEL

The Song of the Dead

ANGRY
ROBOT

ANGRY ROBOT
An imprint of Watkins Media Ltd

20 Fletcher Gate,
Nottingham,
NG1 2FZ
UK

angryrobotbooks.com
twitter.com/angryrobotbooks
Unearthed

An Angry Robot paperback original 2017
1

ISBN 978 0 85766 609 3
EBook ISBN 978 0 85766 610 9

Set in Meridien by Epub Services.
Printed and bound in the UK by 4edge Limited.

For everyone who dreams of a better future.

CHAPTER ONE

THE EXECUTION

Liesl Malone marched through Recoletta's surface streets toward Dominari Hall, surrounded by an escort of twenty guards. It was a flattering number, though Malone suspected they had come not to keep her from escaping, but rather to keep the angry onlookers from getting to her before the hangman.

From the volume of the shouting and the glimpses Malone caught between the guards, she guessed half the city had shown up to enjoy the spectacle of her death.

She turned her eyes instead to the sky above.

It was midday, and the blue sky was laced with thick clouds. It was odd to think that she'd used to avoid looking up at it – as a city-dweller, one got used to having something over one's head. On the surface streets, people didn't think much about it, but they did nothing to remind themselves that they'd left the protection of layers of stone. One of the many polite fictions of civilization.

It was a breathtaking spectacle, though, once one got past the vertigo. Yet all of these people were staring at her, hair matted and clothes rumpled from four days' imprisonment. She wished she could tell them to gaze up, where the view was much better.

"The hell's so funny?" said someone next to her. One of her guards.

She didn't realize she'd been laughing. She thought about

trying to explain it, but the man's skin was filmed with the sticky sweat of fear. He was probably expecting a riot to break out any minute now.

So Malone just shrugged and shook her head.

The first time she'd really been out under the sky it had terrified her. Left her with the sense of something impossibly vast, waiting to swallow her. It had been on her way to the Library, where she'd first met Sato. She hadn't previously realized the difference that Recoletta's stone outline made on the wide expanse above.

As they approached Dominari Hall now, it was a gallows that marked the city's skyline.

It was taller than she would have expected, with a platform that was almost comically wide and an L-shaped beam that reached higher than some verandas. Everyone needed a view, she supposed.

And just when she thought the damn thing couldn't be any larger, it grew bigger and bigger the closer they got.

She looked past it and focused on the sky instead.

Malone had never given much thought to what happened after death, probably because she'd never expected to die before. She'd faced plenty of dangerous and violent situations, but death to her had always been a thing that either would or wouldn't happen, which wasn't the same thing as thinking that it might. She'd never been in the habit of pondering the inevitable, anyway.

But now, she felt her own impending death like a cold hand on the back of the neck. No longer in the realm of wouldn't or might, it simply was.

Which was strange, because if she ever had given thought to how she would die, she never would have guessed it would happen like this.

She fell forward, and a hand grabbed her arm. She hung suspended, her nose a few inches from wooden steps, before her escort hoisted her back on her feet. Steps. She'd reached the gallows already.

She climbed the stairs to the platform, not moving especially quickly or slowly. They'd certainly built the thing high – maybe that's why they'd burned three days on her trial, to get the damn thing finished.

She idly wondered if a jump from the platform would kill her, and if that would deny anyone the satisfaction of a proper execution.

It seemed like an admirable sort of defiance, but it would also be a messy one, and Malone had always hated mess.

She reached the platform. It was fifteen feet on each side, big enough to hang her as well as the Qadi, Lachesse, and the rest of their inner circle.

Perhaps there was something to hope for, after all.

"Are you all right?"

It was probably the dumbest question Malone had ever heard, and she'd worked with her share of rookies. She looked at the young man who had asked. He seemed familiar, like he might have been someone she'd known in the Municipal Police. He wore a guardsman's uniform and a solicitous frown. She wondered if he really minded what was about to happen to her or if he was just anxious about watching someone die.

She fought a brief but powerful urge to sink to her knees and beg for mercy. But if she fell now, she knew she'd never get up again.

Instead, she licked the sweat from her lip and said, "Fine," in a voice that almost fooled her.

Skies above, this platform was huge, and she felt tiny on it. Perhaps that was the point.

Something swatted at her nose, and she flinched. The rope thudded onto her chest, then drew up around her neck as someone tightened the noose. She wiggled her fingers, just to be able to move something.

Lady Lachesse stood next to her and was saying something to the crowd, but over the blood rushing through Malone's ears, her voice was nothing more than a long hum with no pauses and no consonants. Hundreds had packed into the plaza surrounding Dominari Hall, their faces too distant to be anything more than blank. Malone wanted to warn them not to trample the garden, but then she remembered it had withered months ago.

There was a moment of relative quiet in which Lachesse turned to regard Malone. Malone realized that this was the part where she was supposed to say something.

But if nothing she'd said over the last four days had made a difference, nothing more would now.

"Get it over with," she finally said.

She looked up at her city and then beyond it. That was what she regretted most, really. Not that her death was a farce, but that it would leave the city she'd loved in the hands of Lachesse and her cabal – people she wouldn't have trusted with pocket change. She'd done all she could, but it hadn't been enough. Not for Johanssen, not for Sundar, and not for Recoletta.

Pressure tightened around her neck. She was hoisted off her feet.

In agony, she realized this was going to be a slow way to die.

Her eyes rolled skyward, away from the crushing pressure on her neck. Every muscle in her fought for air, even as her thrashing, kicking body burned through its reserves. She knew struggling would only make it worse, but her spasming muscles were beyond all control.

The sky was a blue blur smeared with white. And her view of it was fading, narrowing.

And moving.

Malone thought it might have been a specter of her failing vision, maybe a burst blood vessel in her eye. But no, something was passing through the sky, darker and heavier than rainclouds, and it was coming toward them.

Fast.

Malone tried to shout, but she didn't have the air. She tried to jerk and gesture, but her body was already flopping and shaking, her hands tied behind her back. She hopelessly willed the crowd with everything she had to stop looking at her and just look up.

Her head fell forward, and she found herself eye-to-eye with the sympathetic young guard. But before she could try to blink or roll her eyes at him, he shuddered and turned away.

And then he looked up.

Everything on the platform stopped, and then everything moved very fast.

Malone felt the shouts and screams more than she heard them. Out of the corner of her dimming vision she saw people clearing the plaza, fleeing for shelter in the city below. Some of the guards were guiding them, others were joining them.

They had all forgotten about her.

The world grew darker. It could have been the shadow descending from the sky, or it could have been the light leaving her eyes.

CHAPTER TWO

A VERY SMALL ROOM

Jane Lin sat on a wooden crate, hugging a scratchy blanket around her raw and tender shoulders. She knew she was supposed to feel scared, but she just felt sick.

The man staring back at her was sitting on a larger crate, which she supposed was meant to make him appear more important.

To her, he just looked uncomfortable.

She'd been sitting in that room for what felt like a long time. Long enough to get hungry, lose her appetite to nausea, and then start to feel hungry again.

But company had shown up a few minutes ago, and he hadn't brought any food, so Jane expected it would be a while yet.

And not before this guy got whatever answers he'd come for.

He had bronzed skin that was sallow in the lamplight and dark, kinky hair that grayed around his temples. The two of them were crammed together in what she assumed was a storage room – given all of the stacked crates – close enough that their knees were almost touching. Close enough that she could smell his sticky odors of salt and sweat.

"Perhaps you could just tell me what you want," Jane suggested.

The man stiffened. She wasn't sure if she'd offended him or if that was just the way someone used to sitting on crates moved. "You passed at us. Conossed where to be, no?"

She was still getting used to the strange dialect. It was just familiar enough that she could usually get the meaning, but foreign enough that it took her a little longer.

"Well, sort of," she said.

He took a familiar purse and emptied a handful of coins – gold, with square holes punched through their middles – onto the floorboards between them.

"So you conossed o no? Which ess?"

Jane sighed. "Yeah, I 'conossed.'"

He grunted, as if this proved some vast theory. "Then who sent? Ee what for?"

"No one sent me. That's what I'm trying to–"

The man leaned forward, boring into her with his squinty stare. "Then how'd you pass here?"

She'd had more productive conversations with dirty laundry. "I came from Recoletta. My city. You know the cities?"

He grunted again, which could have meant anything.

"You certainly know about the Library," she said.

He narrowed his eyes to slits. Jane imagined that he'd had a lifetime of practice with that look, squinting at all sorts of bright glares that a citizen of Recoletta – or one of the other underground cities – rarely experienced. He was very good at it.

"So what for they send you? You spy for them?"

"No! I was running from them. Fleeing." That anxious feeling – the one she thought she'd just escaped – was uncoiling in her gut once more.

He sat back and nodded to himself. "Then a criminal."

"I'm not," Jane said.

He searched her with those flinty eyes. "But you got the culpa."

Guilt. Yes, she had plenty of that.

"It's not that simple," she said, ignoring the tightness in her stomach.

"Never ess." He leaned forward again, propping his elbows on his thighs. "So deemay how you come to pass here."

A story. It always came down to telling a good story that highlighted the right detail and omitted the inconvenient ones.

Fortunately, Jane knew a thing or two about that.

This story started in Recoletta, in another small room.

After she'd killed Augustus Ruthers, Jane had spent eighteen hours locked in an office in Dominari Hall while the Qadi's soldiers waited to see how she would be punished. Those hours had given Jane plenty of time to contemplate the blood that had been shed over Recoletta – Freddie's, Ruthers's, and that of the thousands who had died in the two takeovers.

She fully expected hers would be next.

After eighteen hours, the door finally opened.

"Miss Lin," the guard on the other side said. "Time to go."

She must have stood there, frozen in place, because the guard finally cleared his throat and blinked at her.

"We've got to get this office set up for the new deputy treasurer. If you could please clear out, we'd be much obliged."

And like that, Jane went from prisoner to free woman.

No one stopped her as she walked through the same corridors where she'd hidden and crept less than a day ago. The guards who had chased and shot at her were clearing offices, moving furniture, and bustling with orders, paying her no mind. If she'd dared return to the room where she'd shot Ruthers – or the hall where the guards had killed Freddie – she all but knew she'd find the bodies cleared and the bloodstains cleaned up, and she didn't think she could stand it.

Her cheeks were hot and wet, and she couldn't tell if it was relief, fury, or something else.

She wandered before she knew where she was going. After several minutes, she found herself in front of the room where she'd last seen Roman Arnault, locked up and awaiting whatever fate the Qadi's forces had in store for him.

Jane tried the handle. The door swung open.

Roman was gone. An exhausted guard stood alone in the

room, scrawling in the margins of a roughly used notebook.

"Where is he?" Jane asked.

"Down at the Barracks. Being held for trial." The guard squinted. "What are you doing here, anyway?"

But Jane turned and ran. No one gave chase.

Jane had found the Qadi holed up in a small office away from the main hall and its bustling foot traffic. Four Madinan guards watched over the office, their faces still but their eyes squinting and roving as if expecting the halls themselves waited to swallow them up. They'd stopped Jane at the door until the Qadi herself called for them to let her through.

As she moved past them, Jane felt their eyes on her back.

The Qadi sat behind an oversized desk, fortified by stacks of papers and a massive kettle of tea. She poured two cups as Jane sat down.

"I'd thought you'd have gotten yourself far from this place by now," the Qadi said.

"Is that why you let me go? So I could run?"

Consternation flickered behind the Qadi's veil. The look wasn't quite as satisfying on her as it was on Lady Lachesse, but it was close.

"Why have you come here, Miss Lin?" the Qadi asked, placing one shallow cup of tea in front of Jane.

She felt a sharp reply on her lips, but she bit it back. She needed the Qadi's help, after all.

"I'm here about Roman."

"His trial is in five days." The Qadi raised her teacup behind her veil, sipped, and grimaced as the wide brim caught in the fabric. "If you really want to attend, I suppose I could reserve a gallery seat for you, though I wouldn't recommend it."

"But what is he being tried for?"

The Qadi scraped at the bottom of the sugar bowl and found two meager lumps. "Treason. Conspiracy to murder. All his work bringing Sato to power, all those murdered whitenails? Someone must pay."

Jane's hands felt numb. "You're going to execute him."

"That depends," the Qadi said in a firm, too-measured tone.

"No. This is a sham, and you know it." Anger washed over her and filled in all the spaces that grief, exhaustion, and hunger had left empty. "And why? Sato's the man you're after."

"Sato's dead," the Qadi said, and Jane found that she wasn't surprised.

She was furious. "Then why kill an–"

The Qadi set her sugar spoon down with a clatter. "Because, Miss Lin, your personal affections aside, Roman Arnault is guilty of the crimes with which he's charged. He helped Sato come to power, resulting in a catastrophic loss of life and the near-destruction of this city's infrastructure. And as part of that undertaking, he furnished Sato with the information and resources to assassinate certain members of Recoletta's political structure."

"Never mind that a few days ago, you were planning an armed invasion of Recoletta."

The Qadi's smile was an infuriating twitch behind her veil. "And now I am an honored guest. Roman, however, is still a traitor."

She was right, of course. And yet there was more to it. Roman had done what he could to curb Sato's extremes, but he'd been caught between his conviction that the corrupt Council was on its last legs and his premonition that a revolt like Sato's was, for better or worse, inevitable. He'd hardly been the blood-soaked renegade that the Qadi seemed to imagine. If he was trapped now, he'd been no less so then.

Not that Jane expected the Qadi to find any of this especially convincing.

"If you were to try and execute every crooked or desperate person who ever helped Sato, you'd have an awful lot of blood on your hands," Jane said, thinking suddenly of Ruthers. She suppressed a shiver.

"That is exactly what I'm trying to avoid."

Jane opened her mouth but found that the words had dried up on her tongue.

The Qadi stirred her tea until a smooth vortex sucked at the liquid. "I know this is mob justice, Jane Lin. But it is the only kind of justice fit for Recoletta now. People need to see someone – someone living – held accountable. And if one man's blood will cool their anger and paranoia, I am happy to spill it."

Jane was caught between horror at what the Qadi was saying and envy at the woman's clarity.

The Qadi tapped her spoon against the rim of her cup and set it aside. "I see judgment in your eyes, Miss Lin. But you were in Madina long enough to understand why I wear the veil. People like us – Father Isse, Chancellor O'Brien, your long-dead councilors, and I – we've never had the luxury of your moral high ground. We've been charged with mankind's survival. And we've had the Catastrophe at our heels for hundreds of years."

She thought of Roman, the trapped and defeated man he'd been when she'd spied him on her way to Ruthers. He'd been wrong to support Sato, but he didn't deserve this. She'd seen goodness in Roman, and she'd always hoped it would have the chance to come out.

Jane's mouth still felt dry, but she knew what she had to do. "Then take me," she said. "I'm the one who killed Councilor Ruthers."

As the Qadi maneuvered the teacup behind her veil, Jane caught a glimpse of the woman's lips, twisted in distaste.

"That is exactly why we cannot touch you." She sipped her tea, then pried the cup from behind her veil once more.

Jane swiped a dry tongue over her lips. "What do–"

"Haven't you been outside? You're a hero." The Qadi spat the word like the vilest of curses.

"Me?" A lot had happened in the last twenty-four hours – Freddie's death, Ruthers's death, Roman's imprisonment – but none of it had made her feel heroic.

"Word of Ruthers's death had spread halfway across the city

by the time we returned from the Library," the Qadi said. Jane cringed to hear her crime spoken aloud. "We couldn't very well admit that a laundress had thwarted us, could we?"

But it made sense. In the warped, conniving way of everything the Qadi and the other politicians did.

"You had to save face," Jane said, putting it together. "Or no one in Recoletta would have accepted your authority."

The Qadi tugged her veil and smoothed it down. "It wasn't terribly difficult. Rumors had already begun that Sato and Ruthers had been in league from the beginning. That Sato had released Ruthers and executed the other councilors on his orders."

Jane's laugh scratched at her dry throat, but she wasn't amused. She was horrified. "That's absurd."

The Qadi acknowledged this with a tilt of her head. "It improved our standing considerably when people learned that you had found refuge in Madina."

Jane wanted to argue with the woman, but her tongue stuck to the roof of her mouth. Out of everything that had happened to her and the people she cared about, the worst was the notion that it had all been twisted to serve the interests of the Qadi and her ilk.

"I know what you're thinking," the Qadi said, scraping again at the sugar bowl. "But for now, people have a hero, a villain, and a story with pleasing symmetry, all of which are more satisfying than the truth. And, your moral objections aside, you've no right to deny them what little comfort they find after two wars."

As Jane watched the woman scratch a thin crust of sugar from the empty bowl, she reflected that perhaps the Qadi was right. And perhaps she had also given her the key to securing Roman's release.

If the people of Recoletta needed a hero and a villain, then she could furnish them with a few of her own.

A rattle of disgust drew Jane's attention. She looked over to see the Qadi drop her spoon in frustration.

"Is there no sugar in this whole wretched city?"

Jane pushed herself back from the table. "You were supposed to send trainloads of food." That was how the Qadi had tried to sneak her own forces into Recoletta before chasing down Sato at the Library. Jane stalked out of the room before the older woman could respond. The guards didn't stop her.

She stalked down the hall, numb with anger. It beat aching with grief and guilt, though.

Especially when it gave her something to do.

She realized that she could tell the Qadi about the vault, the coveted repository to which Roman was the key. No one knew that Ruthers had taught her the code before he died, and if anything would stay the hangman's noose, it was the promise of pre-Catastrophe weaponry.

But for Roman, that would be worse than an execution. Held captive and used to open the one thing he feared above all – that was a mercy even she could not inflict upon him.

She would find another way. Or burn Recoletta trying.

CHAPTER THREE
CHECKS AND BALANCES

Malone awoke to pain.

Her whole body felt as though it had slowly been pulled apart, each joint and limb tugged by an unseen force. If it weren't for the stiff ache in her back, she might have thought she was still hanging.

She opened her eyes and saw two hazel ones staring back at her.

A woman with auburn hair and a long, straight nose was bent over her. She was saying something, but Malone couldn't make out a word of it.

Her throat burned. "Water," she said. The word felt like gravel in her neck.

A man's voice rose with a few sharp syllables – more words Malone couldn't make out. The woman backed out of her field of vision.

Malone tried to rise, but the effort shot pins and needles through her body, and that ripped an agonizing gasp from her throat. Her blood was resuming its proper course, but it filled her veins with fire.

Strong arms gripped hers and pulled her upright. She shut her eyes against the pain and the urge to vomit. When she opened them again, she saw a man watching her, standing at the end of the table she was sitting on.

He was about a head shorter than she was, with oiled black hair, a meticulously cropped goatee, olive skin, and eyes that narrowed in the corners, like Jane's and Sato's. Yet the most distinctive thing about him was the scar that curved across his left cheek, ending just under his eye. He was dressed in a silky black and crimson uniform that hung a little too loose on him. The woman was wearing something similar.

The man bowed at the waist, not in the manner of Recolettan whitenails, but lowering his head with the rest of his body.

He said something else that she didn't understand.

"Water," she said again. Malone didn't recognize the room she was in, but it looked like a small office, just big enough for the table. Light filtered in behind her, casting warm hues on the pale wood paneling of the walls.

The hazel-eyed woman returned, bearing a flimsy tin cup before her.

Malone took it. She'd never tasted anything so good.

The man cleared his throat before he spoke again. Slowly, this time. "I am very much regretting to seem brute, but we must spreck. I am Geist."

Malone slowly wiggled her arms, legs, fingers, toes. They were all there, and they all hurt. "Where am I?"

"We are still in Recoletta, of course. Conzentresse, please. You are comprending me now, ya?"

Malone nodded. She didn't catch every word, but she got his meaning.

"Goot. I am cherching for some persons who I estimate are living here boocoo yars. Perhaps you are knowing them." He unrolled a thick sheet of paper with two gray pictures: one of a family of three, and the other of a young man. The images had an eerie, spectral quality, as if the people in them were corpses. Except for the lack of color, they were more realistic than any painting Malone had ever seen, but they made her skin crawl.

The family included a man, a woman, and a small boy, all with dark hair and serious, unsmiling expressions. She didn't recognize them, but there *was* something familiar.

The young man in the second image was Augustus Ruthers. He couldn't have been more than twenty in the image, but the proud, aquiline face was unmistakable.

"Augustus Rothbauer," Geist said, pointing to the image of the young man. "Und Ilse et Jean Arnault mit their son, Roman." He drew the last syllable out in a way Malone had never heard before. "You know them?" he asked. It was barely a question.

Malone laughed. It felt like sandpaper in her throat.

"This is funny?" Only his raised eyebrows told Malone this was a question.

"You're five days late," Malone said. "The man you're calling Rothbauer is dead. And Roman left town."

The hazel-eyed woman had been busy with some cups and a pitcher on the table near Malone's feet. She dropped one of the cups which shattered on the floor, spilling a brownish liquid too dark and thick to be tea.

"Merd, Phelan!" Geist said. "Sortay, sortay!" He shooed her away, and she backed out of the room, head low.

"You're from somewhere else," Malone said, trying to clear the fog from her brain. "Same place Arnault's family first came from."

"Und Rothbauer, ya. The Continent."

"Why are you looking for them?"

"They are having something that belongs to us." He said "*us*" with an expansive lifting of his brows. He was talking about more than just the people on this ship, likely the whole of the Continent. And if he was being this vague, then there was no sense in asking him what that "*something*" was.

"Then why are you asking me?"

This time, Geist laughed. "Because you were the sole person in the platz remaining to be asked. How are you thinking you are here? The others, they flet." He made a little flapping motion with one hand.

The gesture took Malone back to a moment she wasn't ready

to revisit – the agony, the crowds, the shadow–

"In plus," Geist said, "the last person to be seeing him before his evanoosment was you."

The surprise gave her a much-needed jolt. "If you already know–"

"What I am not knowing is which plass he is going to next."

Malone watched Geist, wondering how much else he knew. His expression betrayed nothing. "He didn't say. That's the whole point of disappearing."

Geist pulled a chair out and sat at the table. "Then perhaps you commence by telling me the history. Perhaps we comprend it together."

But there was nothing she would rather do less – Arnault and his damn history had gotten her into this mess in the first place. Malone swung her legs over the table. "No. I'm done. Find Roman Arnault on your own – I'm going."

"Going where?"

"Away." To the farming communes – where she should have gone as soon as the peace deal had gone through – away from the intrigues and the politics of the city. "Far away–"

She broke off when she saw the view outside.

A round, metal-buttressed window curved from floor to ceiling in the little room. All she could see was sky.

It was only when she moved closer that she could see the city below her. Far, far below her.

The verandas looked as small and insubstantial as trash on the pavement, the surface streets between them like lines of mortar. She could see the shapes of the different districts below her – the sprawling gardens of the Vineyard, the ramshackle mess of the factory districts – but it was small and distant.

Geist gestured to a chair. "Please, setz. Consider it un faveur." He tapped a finger on his neck and gave her a smile that was perfectly symmetrical and perfectly empty.

Malone took the nearest chair, moving as carefully as she would around a coiled snake.

"Now," he said, "you were to be telling me about Roman Arnault."

But if she was going to tell him about Roman, she might as well tell him the rest. "The first thing you ought to know is that Roman isn't the one you're searching for. She is."

He raised his eyebrows. "She?"

"Jane Lin."

It started with a bad decision made for the best of reasons.

After the assault on the Library and Malone's elimination of Sato, Malone and the others had followed a night of battle with a long, cold morning of verbal conflict that was no less perilous and no less exhausting. But after hours of haggling and horse-trading, the farmers, the powers from the north, and the new leaders of Recoletta had finally reached a deal.

After that, they needed to get away from each other as fast as possible, before somebody had cause to regret the terms.

She had bid farewell to Salazar as the sun broke the horizon. The farmers had been the most energized of all, even with several days of marching behind them and still more to go.

But when Salazar shook her hand and gave her a rare smile, she understood well enough. Theirs had been a victory of progress. According to the newly inked treaty – what everyone was already calling the Library Accord – they would have joint ownership of the crops and goods they produced for the cities. Their quotas would be relaxed, and they would engage in annual rotations in which some of their brightest would go to the cities to learn while doctors, educators, and engineers came to live in their communes.

Best of all, they would have an advisory seat when the Council of Recoletta was reconstituted along with the governments of Madina, Underlake, and the Hollow.

Malone was almost surprised to see Salazar returning to the communes instead of claiming one of those seats himself. Until she remembered that he wasn't that kind of leader.

"There'll be meetings, then the votes, then some more meetings. With any luck, we'll get around to making a decision after that," he said. "But someone's got to make sure the whole process moves forward. I'd hate to see all this fall apart over squabbles back home."

The trains for the cities were already being loaded. Malone felt the high, sharp steam whistle in her teeth.

"Come with us," he said. "You know the cities as well as anyone. Be useful to have someone of your experience in the coming weeks."

She watched the trains, belching and chuffing as the last of Underlake's soldiers boarded.

"Like you said, someone's got to make sure this doesn't fall apart," Malone had said.

They made their farewells, and Malone had turned to the trains, trying not to dwell on the image of the burning carriages and screaming soldiers she'd last seen in Recoletta.

At least she'd be able to get some sleep. If recent events were any indication, it would probably be her best opportunity for the foreseeable future.

As she reached the tracks, she glanced over her shoulder for one last glimpse of the farmers, exhausted but triumphant. She would be welcome in the communes. There, she would be the hero who had brokered the compromise in their favor.

In Recoletta, she would be one of the last remnants of two fallen governments. And anyone wanting to discredit her would only have to point out that she had failed – or betrayed – them both.

Salazar looked back at her in final invitation, but only for a moment. They both knew she'd made her choice.

Malone boarded the train while a falling star streaked across the sky in the distance.

Back in Recoletta, Malone had reclined behind her desk – a desk, at any rate – with her feet up, but it felt like she was still marching. When she closed her eyes, fire and musket blasts seared her vision.

The door swung open with an undignified groan.

"Not now," Malone said, her eyes still closed.

"Lady Lachesse would speak with you," said a voice. Young, male, breathless. Inexperienced. Like most of the guards and inspectors these days.

"Not now." As long as the politicians weren't actually killing each other again, Malone wanted to stay as far from their intrigues as possible.

"Councilor Ruthers has been assassinated, Chief. And Roman Arnault is in custody."

Her eyes snapped open. The bright light from the hall was blotted out by a regal shape with wide skirts and a crown of coiffed hair.

Young, male, and breathless fidgeted by the open door behind Lady Lachesse.

"You can go," Malone told him. He disappeared behind the closing door. "So. Assassinated," she said to her visitor.

Lady Lachesse seated herself on the other side of the desk. For decades, the whitenail matron had been one of the quiet powers behind Recoletta's ruling Council, and more recently, she'd been one of the chief architects of the Library Accord. Trouble followed her like a cloud of musky perfume. One could tell when she'd had her hand in something because it always stank.

Malone took a deep breath and braced herself against the odors of licorice and amber.

"It doesn't bode well when the chief of the Municipal Police is the last person in the city to learn of a crime," Lady Lachesse said.

"I've had a busy couple of days," Malone said. Something about this was odd. Why had Lachesse come to harass her personally? People like her paid others to do that sort of thing.

Lachesse sniffed. "Not busy enough, I see."

"So. How did Arnault get to Ruthers?"

"He didn't. He's in custody." Lady Lachesse blinked her painted eyes.

Malone held a swell of annoyance in check. "You told me he assassinated Ruthers."

The whitenail sighed. "I told you Ruthers was assassinated. And that Arnault is in custody."

Malone kicked her feet down from the desk. She was too tired to spar with the old woman. "Then who–"

"Will you just listen?"

The tension in Lachesse's voice snapped Malone back into the moment. For the first time, she realized that the color in the woman's cheeks was too splotchy, too low to be rouge. Lachesse was agitated.

Malone leaned slowly forward, the way she'd learned to do when questioning a suspect. "I'm listening."

"It was a nobody. An exile," the whitenail spat. "A laundress by the name of Jane Lin."

Malone knew the name. But she was experienced enough to hide it.

"We apprehended her and Arnault together," Lachesse said. "In Madina. But she escaped and found Ruthers."

"How did she escape?"

Lachesse looked up, eyes narrowed. "You aren't nearly upset enough by all of this."

She wasn't, if she was being honest. And, under the present circumstances, she wasn't sure if assassinating one of the most corrupt politicians in Recoletta's history was any different from assassinating the demagogue who had followed him. With Sato's blood on her hands, she had little room to judge.

But she chose her words carefully. "I spent my last night in old Recoletta jailed in the Barracks, thanks to Ruthers," Malone said. "But that doesn't mean I don't want to bring his murderer to justice."

"I said nothing about justice," Lady Lachesse said. "I'm talking about a prudent response."

This was just the kind of political nonsense Malone had been hoping to avoid. She felt a headache coming on. "Just tell me what you want."

"Jane Lin is a hero," Lachesse said. "And if you don't stop her, she'll destroy the peace we just shed so much blood to attain."

"What? Where is she now?"

"The Qadi had to release her. But that girl is dangerous." Anger burned in Lady Lachesse's eyes and smoldered in her voice.

It was suddenly clear. "You're mad because she got around you. This is personal," Malone said.

The whitenail shook her head.

"Then tell me." And quickly, she hoped.

"She'll ruin us trying to save him," said Lachesse.

"Who?"

"Roman Arnault."

Malone nodded. If she'd had her notepad, this would have been the part where she closed it and gave Lachesse a long, steadying look. There was nothing here but an old woman used to seeing shadows. "Then perhaps you should speak with the Qadi," Malone said after a considered pause. "I'd need the Council's authority to open an investigation without clearer evidence."

Lachesse shook her head again. "There is no Council without Ruthers."

"Then who—"

"That's why you will step in as interim governor."

Malone blinked. She was searching for a way in which she might have misheard that. "No."

The old whitenail leaned forward and spoke slowly. "Recoletta needs stability. Someone strong needs to fill that role."

Malone heard herself laugh. "There's a long line of people who'd be happy to occupy it."

Lachesse closed her eyes. "And all of them are wrong for it. Ruthers is dead. The rest of the old Council is dead or missing. Sato's other advisors and governors are tainted by association." She laid a finger across the desk, the immaculate, four-inch nail pointing at Malone. "You have survived both governments. And ended one."

"That's a qualification?"

"People need to see a familiar steward in power. Someone who knows when to play by the rules and when to break them. Just until a new Council can be selected."

At which point Malone would be all too ready to give up her new position; which Lachesse must have been counting on.

"Find someone else," Malone said. The last thing she wanted, after the skulduggery she'd experienced as Sato's chief of police, was to find herself wedged even deeper in the political machinery.

Lady Lachesse clasped her hands on the desk with a clatter of rings and clicking of nails. "I've already put your name forward with the relevant parties. I'll be surprised if you aren't confirmed by the end of the day."

Heat flared beneath Malone's collar. Lachesse was used to moving other people around like pieces on a board, but Malone had no patience for it.

Malone took another deep breath of the woman's musky perfume and expelled it in one forceful sigh. "Find someone else," she repeated, her irritation mounting.

Lachesse smiled and made a row of Xs with her crossed nails. "And whom would you recommend?"

No one, of course. Almost no one in Recoletta had the experience or profile for the job, and the few that did were as venal and power-hungry as Lachesse.

"We paid dearly for this peace, Malone. Don't throw it away just because you don't want to get your hands dirty."

She remembered her parting with Salazar and her promise to keep the peace intact. She'd known there would be trials, she just hadn't expected so much this soon.

The room was suddenly stifling, and Malone felt like she was going to choke on the thick, over-perfumed air. Lachesse had found just the place to dig her nails in, and there wasn't anything Malone could do about it.

Lachesse rose, an infuriating smirk on her painted lips. "Expect your confirmation this afternoon, Chief. In the meantime, I'd suggest you get ahead on your investigation of Jane Lin."

CHAPTER FOUR
THE PRICE OF A DRINK

The interrogator sat back on his crate. It was impossible for Jane to tell if he was bored, unconvinced, or just testing her.

Or if that was just the way his sun-beaten eyes always looked.

Still, it felt good to be the one in control of the story. Or it had until her mouth went dry.

She peeled her tongue from her teeth and swiped her cracked lips with it. "Could I have some water?"

The interrogator waited and stared at her long enough that she knew he was just trying to make her nervous. If she hadn't been so hungry, thirsty, and exhausted, it might have worked. But she was already at her threshold for discomfort.

He banged on the door with a fist. "Companyero, some sweet." Moments later, the door opened, ushering in a gust of cool, moist air.

And a hand with a metal cup of water.

The interrogator gave it to Jane. She took it and drank, feeling the first swallow trickle down her throat and into her gut.

"They let you go, ess what it sounds like," he said. "You fled, that's what you say. Which ess?"

She was still gulping the water, thankful for the excuse it gave her to stall. The tricky part about spinning a story was keeping straight the parts she'd told and the ones she'd recalled but kept to herself.

She'd mentioned Roman by his first name only, but she hadn't said anything about the vault. She hoped that would be enough detail for her interrogator.

Jane wiped her mouth with the back of her hand. "I didn't leave right away. I told you, it's not that simple."

"So set it out," he said. "You had parley with the jefe-lady, ee then what? Still looks like culpa to me."

He didn't know the half of it.

"I'm just getting started," Jane said. "There was another parley."

After her discussion with the Qadi, Jane had quickly made her way out of Dominari Hall. She hadn't known what to make of the Qadi's story about her strange pardon, and it made sense to get out before anyone got a different idea.

And after all that had transpired there, she'd be glad to never set foot in it again.

The tunnels outside were chaos. Protesters clogged the cavern, demanding food, justice, an audience. All things they'd never get in Dominari Hall.

During Jane's time in Madina, stories had spread about the horrors people had suffered under Sato's authority – food shortages, violent riots, whole districts turned over to crime. Watching the angry crowd, Jane could believe it.

She didn't envy whoever got the job of putting it all back together.

A phalanx of guards stood against the crowd. Reflexive panic surged in Jane at the sight of the crooked row of men and women until she remembered that they weren't after her now. Not that they were in any condition to go after anyone – their uniforms were worn, torn, and barely fit. Many of them looked too young or too old, and their darting eyes and hunched shoulders betrayed their fear and inexperience.

This was a dangerous place to linger.

Jane ducked her head and moved past them. She was almost clear of the place when a hand grabbed her arm. She spun, fist raised, to see a bespectacled man with lank hair and olive skin.

He flinched and let go of her arm.

"Please, I just want to talk," he said, hands raised to shield his face. "Couldn't get your attention."

"You have it now," she said, still wary.

"My name's Burgevich. I believe you also know Fredrick Anders."

Freddie. "Knew," she said. Her voice was thick in her throat.

Confusion and concern fluttered across his face. "Can we talk? Not here," he said, casting a swift glance at the guards.

She wasn't sure about this twitchy stranger, much less about sharing memories of Freddie.

But at that moment, it was better than being alone with those memories. And with the memory of Ruthers, falling before her gun.

"Let's get out of here," Jane said.

His smile was quick and boyish. "I know a place. Best whiskey you ever had."

Jane and Burgevich took the main streets below ground. She could have sworn they were heading toward the Vineyard, the once-wealthy part of town where some of Jane's clients had lived, but she didn't recognize any of it. Or maybe it was her memory of the place that had changed.

But no, she was certain this had once been the jewel of Recoletta, with broad, skylit tunnels, working gas lamps, and moss flowers hiding the smooth walls.

What she saw now was like a bone sucked of its marrow.

Doors and windows had been smashed, or else barricaded with splintering boards. Statuary had been toppled over and left to lie in trampled gardens of leaf-bare twigs. Anything that was not bolted down to the tunnel walls or floor – and indeed, many things that were – had been ripped up and rooted out. The murals that had once decorated the passages were scarred and stained with crude etchings and all manner of filth, and the area reeked of stale urine and standing puddles.

She was just starting to doubt the wisdom of coming to this place when Burgevich pointed to an intersection where the gas lamps had been ripped from the tunnels. "Almost there," he said, turning to her with that sunny schoolboy grin.

Then she really got suspicious.

But she let him continue in front, still trying to remember how Freddie had mentioned his name, and he said nothing, not until they'd reached a wooden door with soot- and oil-fogged windows. The light seeping through was warm and buttery, and the music coming from inside was the hum of quiet conversation and the tinkle of glassware. So when Burgevich opened the door, she allowed him to usher her inside.

The bar was small but full, with tall, wooden tables just large enough for two or three people to crowd around. The patrons themselves huddled over flickering candles, cradling glasses of whiskey that glowed in the firelight. It was difficult to tell who they'd once been – some wore wide-brimmed hats and jackets with the lapels pulled up, some wore the coarse uniforms of the factory districts, and others wore silks and satins that must have once cost a fortune, now roughed up with dirt and wear.

Burgevich found them a spot at the bar, where an older man with a tangled, white beard and a face full of wrinkles filled and refilled the mismatched glasses.

"Two, please, Mr Petrosian," Burgevich said, sliding onto one of the stools.

The older man nodded, setting a squat tumbler and a tulip glass on the bar.

Burgevich leaned in. "The Chau gang's desperate. They've been cutting their flour with clay dust to meet demand, and even they can't get salt into the city."

Petrosian nodded thoughtfully, like a man savoring a morsel of fine food, and poured two fingers of whiskey into the tumbler.

Then, he turned to Jane. "And for the lady?"

"I've got her," Burgevich said quickly, giving Jane a conspiratorial wink. "Word has it two of the Qadi's men were caught looting in the Vineyard."

Petrosian held the bottle motionless, frowning at Burgevich. "I've heard that one thrice since yesterday. I expect better from a newspaperman."

Now Jane recalled where she'd heard Burgevich's name. He'd been a colleague of Freddie's at the paper. In fact, Freddie had complained about him snapping up the Vineyard murders assignment just as the mess with the Council, the Library, and Sato had gotten started.

Realization must have shown in her expression, because Petrosian was regarding her with placid curiosity. His face looked as though it were held together by all the wrinkles and lines.

Burgevich coughed in embarrassment. "Well, did you know they've got a berth reserved on the next train back to Madina? Seems the Qadi doesn't trust Recolettan justice."

Jane shivered. She could hardly blame them.

The older man droned appreciatively and filled the tulip glass for Jane. She murmured her thanks and tasted the whiskey. It was as smooth as oil.

Petrosian acknowledged her pleasure with a nod before moving on down the bar.

Burgevich leaned forwards. "Petrosian trades in secrets. Has since the early days of the Sato regime. Though, with a new government in town, everyone is wondering if his prices are about to change." He tilted his head at the busy tables around them.

"You've been coming here for a while."

"It pays to know where the good information is. And Petrosian's stock is unmatched."

She regarded her glass. "Can't imagine there was much of a paper under Sato."

"Not exactly. But there was still a lively trade in words." He sipped from his tumbler.

"And you think that's about to dry up?"

"Hard to say. That depends on who's running the show now."

He peered at her out of the corners of his eyes.

"And I'd thought we were here to drink to Freddie."

"This," Burgevich said, raising his glass, "is exactly what Freddie would be doing if he were here."

"No," Jane said. "He'd be running." And he'd be right to.

Burgevich bit his lips and asked his next question slowly. "How did it happen?"

Jane hesitated. The superstitious, animal part of her brain believed that saying it would only make it real. But the rest of it knew that Freddie deserved to have his story told. "He came to my rescue. Followed the Qadi's forces back to Recoletta and broke me out. One of the guards shot him while we were making our escape."

Burgevich watched her through his small-framed glasses, his gaze steady and unwavering. "And then you turned back and shot Ruthers."

Someone plunked a glass down hard on the bar; it sounded like a gunshot. Jane flinched, snatching her hands into her lap.

Burgevich looked on, candlelight glinting in his lenses.

She was beginning to see why Fredrick had disliked this man. Burgevich's keenness and energy would've been bright lights and sirens on many a hungover morning, and his simmering ambition would have seemed like duplicity.

"The whole city knows what I did," Jane said.

"But nobody knows why," Burgevich said with a wry grin.

Because Ruthers had been Roman's jailer. Because he was supposed to be the last man with the code to the vault. Because she and Roman would have been free if she'd shot him the first time she had a gun.

Or because Sato and Ruthers had been working together, as the Qadi and her allies were now saying.

"That's going to cost more than a few tidbits about local crime," she said.

Burgevich smiled over the rim of his tumbler. "Fredrick told me you were sharp. What do you want?"

That was easy. Whether or not he could help her was another matter. "I want to get Roman Arnault out of the Barracks."

He raised his eyebrows. "There's a secret all of its own." He scanned the huddling, whispering patrons and lowered his voice further. "Unfortunately, that's not the kind of help I can provide."

Jane sipped her whiskey and tried to hide her frustration in the bottom of her glass. It had been a long shot, anyway.

"But someone connected to the old Council might be able to help. Roman used to work for them, you know. And now that Sato's gone, some of them are finding their way back into power." He knocked the rest of his whiskey back. "And you ever decide you want to talk, you know where to find me." He pushed back from the bar and thunked his empty glass onto it.

As he left, Jane was surprised to note that she had almost finished her drink, too. She was watching the spirit shimmer and flare in the candlelight when a hand appeared and tipped another shot in.

She looked up to see Petrosian eying her, clearing Burgevich's empty glass with one hand and refilling hers with the other.

"On the house," he said. "In honor of a mutual friend."

He'd spoken more like a conspirator than a mourner. "You know Roman," Jane said.

"A man who appreciates good information as much as good whiskey." Petrosian raised a glass of his own from somewhere behind the bar.

"This seems like the sort of place he would like," Jane said, regarding the wavering shadows and the creaking wood with a new sense of appreciation. It was a comfort, if a small one, to share a pleasant memory with a stranger. But one thing she knew was that Roman didn't have friends. He had associates. "I suppose he spent a lot of time here over the last few months."

"Long before that. Back when Recolettan silver was worth something," he said, running his surprisingly elegant fingers over the bar top. His nails, she noticed, were clean but trimmed short.

But he moved his hands with such care and delicacy that Jane was sure his nails had once been long. Many whitenails in Madina and Recoletta had begun cutting their fingernails to avoid the unwanted attention they attracted.

"Maybe it will be again soon," she said, considering the carefully dispersed crowd.

"Coin's only as good as the place it comes from, and a place is only as good as the people in it." He frowned at the motley crowd.

"Things could change. With Sato gone. And Ruthers, too." Jane took another drink before she could dwell on the thought.

But Petrosian shook his head. "Hasn't been much good in Recoletta for a long time. Men like Ruthers rotted this place to its core. All Sato did was kick us around and shake us out."

"What about Roman?"

Petrosian's laugh was like wind through dry grass. "I said I like the boy. I never said he was good."

Jane wanted to rebut and tell him about the violence Roman had tried to prevent, but she didn't suppose Petrosian had stopped by to debate Roman's goodness. In fact, she was becoming more interested in why he had approached.

Likely as not, he was hoping to pry loose the same secrets Burgevich had wanted.

The whiskey merchant raised his glass to his lips, and his smile was gone as quickly as it had appeared. "The way things are going, he won't be with us much longer."

"You sound awfully certain of that," Jane said, trying to ignore the chill creeping along her back.

"Roman Arnault's fate rests in the hands of a foreign premier who sees Recoletta as little more than a firebreak for her own city, a whitenail who's been awaiting her rise for the last six decades, and a chief of police with more power than she knows what to do with."

The Qadi, Lady Lachesse, and –

"Chief of police?" Jane asked.

Petrosian stopped himself short with a kind of mock surprise. "Ah, yes. That much is still news, at least." He gave her a sly look, glancing from the bar back to her as if he were tallying her tab in his head. "Liesl Malone, formerly of the Municipal Police, will soon be appointed interim governor of Recoletta." He drank again, smacking his lips. Enjoying himself.

"Meaning what, exactly?" Cold prickled at the back of Jane's neck.

"Meaning she'll be a Council of one until a true Council is appointed."

Jane mulled it over. It certainly sounded as though there could be worse outcomes. Worse people for the job. But she remembered Malone as she'd met her in the old Council's final days, dogged and striving against Ruthers. Something about the woman's transition to the very nest of power she'd once despised sat uneasily with Jane, though maybe she was seeing malice in every shadow and corner now.

But Petrosian appeared as though he'd made up his mind already.

"You don't think she's good?" Jane asked.

"She thinks she is. Nothing makes a person more dangerous."

"I met her once or twice. She seemed reasonable."

"You met her before the city collapsed. Before she became Sato's chief of police." He leaned in. "Before she became a friend to rebels and farmers."

This was also news to Jane, but she tried not to let it show. "You're saying she's changed."

"I'm saying she believes in something now. And Roman Arnault's trial and death may allow her to save it."

Jane took it all in with another sip of her whiskey. The old man was trying to goad her into something. She could feel it in the way he kept dangling Roman before her, and yet she could feel her resolve giving way. Her throat burned and her head swam, and it was hard to tell how much was the alcohol and how much was the deluge of new information.

Petrosian was talking again, and she had to make a concerted effort to focus on what he was saying.

"Malone could perhaps be convinced that Arnault is not her biggest problem. But you'd need rare information, and to find that, you'd need to know where to search," he said. "That will cost you." His falsely avuncular manner had all but faded.

She knew she shouldn't ask. Because she knew that whatever he asked for, she would give him. "What do you want?"

He placed a heavy key on the table. Jane had seen keys like it before, back when she'd worked for the rich and powerful whitenails. "I'm offering you a treasure trove of information. In exchange, I'll need a powerful and important secret." Petrosian was regarding her with a gaze that could have pried the lid off a jar.

"What makes you think I have something like that?" Jane asked.

Petrosian smiled, but only with his lips. "Think about it, Miss Lin. I've got glasses to refill." He disappeared to tend to other customers, leaving Jane with her almost-empty glass and a view of stained wood and crowded shelves.

She stared at the key and tried to think of something useful, anything to avoid telling him about the one secret she had promised herself never to tell anyone.

But what could she say about the Qadi, or Lady Lachesse, or even Roman Arnault that he wouldn't already know? What could she tell him when he had already shared Malone's rise to power like idle gossip?

In the panicked minutes after Ruthers had told her the vault code, she had privately sworn never to breathe a word about it. If the Qadi, or Lachesse, or any of their allies learned the code then Roman – and even she – would never be free of it.

Yet if Roman died, none of her earnest efforts or noble intentions would matter.

Petrosian was circling back, the bottle in his hand nearly empty and the smile on his face as satisfied as if he'd drunk it all himself.

She could lie to him. Make something up. But a man like him didn't become an information broker without learning to tell good information from false.

Petrosian returned.

"What did you do before everything?" Jane asked. "Before Sato and the fall of the Council, I mean."

"Much the same," Petrosian said. "Though my shop was nicer and the clientele better dressed. And most paid in coin."

He didn't say it with any particular longing, and yet she had no doubt that Recoletta was full of whitenails trying to claw back as much as they could. "Is that what you want, then? To return to those days?" Jane asked.

"There's no such thing as a return. And at my age, I'm beyond hoping for one. I merely want to know which way we're headed."

That was encouraging. Perhaps he'd be content with something less than the vault code itself. But she needed to draw that out of him, just to be sure.

"You're saying you'd rather keep secrets than use them?" she said.

"Meddling is a messy business," Petrosian said. "And the very best secrets are like fine wine. Exposing them diminishes their value considerably."

"Then knowledge of a thing would be just as useful as the thing itself."

Interest kindled in Petrosian's eyes. "Presuming we're talking about something of sufficient value."

He held the bottle over Jane's glass, a question in his eyes.

Petrosian had little reason to be interested in the vault. No, he wanted rare and valuable information, something to ferret away with all of his other secrets, and perhaps to barter for another rarer and more valuable secret in the future.

But by the time he did that, Jane planned to be long gone with Roman. And if she wasn't, this indiscretion wouldn't change much.

"Roman Arnault is the key to an ancient vault of wonders," she said.

Petrosian tilted the bottle back a degree. "That's hardly a secret to me."

"But the code to the vault is," Jane said. "That much was a secret to everyone but Jakkeb Sato and Augustus Ruthers." She paused. "And me."

His wispy eyebrows shot up. "You have the code?"

"Ruthers told me before he died."

His eyebrows rose even further, and he inclined his head toward her.

But she had him trapped. "Just a moment ago, you agreed the knowledge of the code would be as valuable as the code itself."

A defeated smile quirked at the corners of his mouth. "But how am I to know whether you're telling the truth?"

"Even if I gave you the code, you'd never know if it was the real one. Besides, this would be a very foolish secret for me to invent since it would likely send Lachesse, the Qadi, and Malone after me if they got wind of it." And by Petrosian's meticulous logic, it would then be of little value to him.

At last, he nodded and poured a thin stream into her glass. "The estate of Augustus Ruthers," he said, pushing the key toward her. "May you find something there to distract our dogged governor."

"What exactly am I looking for?" Jane asked, sliding the key into her pocket. The metal was cold but as smooth as polished wood.

He pressed his lips together. "Without having been there myself, it's hard to say. But rest assured you'll find something, and you'll know it when you do."

"That's less specific than I'd hoped," Jane said.

"I offered you an opportunity, not an answer. But go and look around. If you feel I've shortchanged you, I'm sure we can come to another agreement." He bowed and departed to look after the rest of his patrons.

CHAPTER FIVE
THE HIDDEN

Geist sat back. "Keska say? I was not knowing that I was speaking to the gouverneur of Recoletta! Marveyoo."

Malone probed the tenderness at her neck. "Safe to say I've been deposed."

Phelan returned, bearing a new cup. She placed it before Malone and filled it, then gave another to Geist.

It looked like tea, but darker and thicker. Malone sipped hers and nearly gagged – it was as bitter as a bad memory.

Geist winced in apology, his scar shriveling on his cheek. "Myself, I prefer it warm, but the gas is most volatile." He lifted his face up toward some indeterminate presence above. "We must avoid unnecessary flamme while aloft."

Malone couldn't imagine that anything less than a gallon of water would improve the taste, but she kept that to herself.

Meanwhile, Geist enjoyed his drink with obvious gusto, closing his eyes and humming with pleasure. It seemed to revive him. "So," he said, "this Qadi, you say she wears a masque?"

"A veil. It's common among Madina's wealthy."

"Hmm." Geist exchanged a thoughtful glance with Phelan, who was picking up fragments of the broken cup. He craned his neck to peer out the window behind her. "And alles that you are telling me, it is happening below, in the refuge?"

"The what?"

He blinked. "The bunker. Soo-terr. Underground." For the first time, he appeared just as confused as Malone felt.

"You mean the city?"

"Ya, of course." He sipped his drink quickly. "But you were about to be telling me of this Jane Lin. She is who?"

"Like I told Lachesse, she was nobody."

Geist's eyes focused on her. "Everybody is somebody."

"She became somebody, all right." If only she'd seen it sooner.

"Tell me," Geist said, while Phelan knelt to mop up the spill.

Once Malone had gotten official word of her appointment, it hadn't taken long for the crises to roll in. Half of Dominari Hall's administrators and all of its whitenails had accosted her on her way out, attempting to extract various promises that she would punish or reward someone or the other. Fulfilling all of those requests would have meant promoting and then firing nearly everyone in a position of influence at least once.

Malone had the sneaking suspicion that the rest of Dominari Hall had known about her appointment even before she had. Which, given the way politics ran on gossip as much as paperwork, made sense. Worse, with the exhausting influx of requests, demands, and entreaties, she was also beginning to suspect that Lachesse had appointed her merely to wear her down and get rid of her.

And after her first day, she was well on her way to offending or displeasing nearly everyone in a position of influence.

Not that this had ever bothered her before.

But this time, it wasn't just her future at stake, but the future of Recoletta, the farming communes, and two other cities as well, and the very idea of that weight on her shoulders when she'd returned from the battlefield less than twenty-four hours ago made her head ache.

It also reminded her that she needed a bath, a meal, and sleep on a proper horizontal surface.

She could get at least two of those things at her apartment, provided it was still there.

After a few failed attempts at leaving, Malone finally managed to sneak out of one of the back exits. It was a long way home, made longer by the fact that none of the railcars were running – they hadn't been for months – and no carriages were out. Not that their wheels could have handled the cluttered ruin that many of Recoletta's streets had become, anyway.

Worse, the food stalls were all gone and the few cafes she remembered either looted or shuttered. She wished she'd thought to scrounge for something in Dominari Hall's kitchens, but that would have been another hour of delays and interruptions.

At least her unit was still there, her key still fit the lock, and when she opened the door, everything was just as she'd left it, her tea kettle on the stove and her clothes scattered across the bed.

There was even some food in the cupboard – a loaf of bread that crunched between her teeth and a wedge of sheep's cheese with a thin rind of mold. She considered scraping it off. Instead, she ate it quickly.

Her eyelids were heavy as she washed off the sweat and grime of the last few days. She pushed her scattered clothes to the edge of the bed and slept.

It was midmorning when she'd finally awoken – hours after she would have started her day at Callum Station in other, quieter times. Yet she didn't feel rested. Rather, she felt as if she'd spent the night escaping and returning to the same dream about burning trains, burning fields, and burning cities.

Whatever the day held, she wasn't ready for it.

Dominari Hall had already been in crisis mode by the time Malone returned, though the place hadn't left crisis mode in months. There was much to do, but she couldn't feel anything more than preemptive exhaustion.

Not until she saw Farrah stomping down a gilded and mirrored hall toward her.

Farrah was a capable administrator. She had been Chief Johanssen's secretary under the old Council and Malone's secretary under Sato. Malone secretly believed that Recoletta would never fall so long as Farrah, cool, efficient, and pragmatic, was seated behind a desk somewhere, reducing its crises to ink and pulp.

Whatever problem Malone brought to Farrah, she always got the sense that the secretary was only humoring her to take a break from something larger and more important.

Which was why the sight of Farrah's long strides and bloodless lips gave Malone a shiver of apprehension.

"The hell have you been? I was about to send out a search party." Farrah was already walking past her.

Malone had no choice but to follow, back the way she'd come and out the grand double doors of Dominari Hall.

"What's the problem?"

"Not here." Farrah flashed her a warning expression and pointed at a waiting carriage.

Malone tugged at her chafing collar. The streets and districts that were still traversable by carriage had become minefields of horse shit.

"Someone's got to get the damn railcars working again," Malone said.

Farrah shot her a look. That someone, of course, was her.

"Hurry up," Farrah said. Even the two mares tethered to the carriage were stamping and snorting their impatience.

Malone pulled herself into the carriage next to Farrah. No sooner had she shut the door than the thing rumbled into motion.

And something thudded on top of the carriage.

"Guards," Farrah said. "Local ones."

"Want to tell me where we're going now?"

"Merchant district. Near the old market."

"The main road's a mess," Malone said. "It's faster if we walk." Not that she wanted to clean muck off her boots later.

The SONG *of the* DEAD

"Not a good idea. Besides, there's no point in making this a bigger spectacle than it needs to be."

Malone left the question on her face, and Farrah sighed her acknowledgment.

"Three of the Qadi's guards were murdered early this morning. Outside a tea shop, of all places."

Malone was still vaguely surprised there was anything of the sort still standing in Recoletta. "Do we have suspects? A motive?"

"Why do you think you're here?" Farrah asked.

For the first time in ages, Malone felt the old thrill in her blood. "A case."

Farrah looked at her, something unreadable in her eyes. "Remember, you're just here to check around."

It took the better part of an hour of bumping and rattling along the pitted and potholed streets to reach the market district, and by the time they did Malone's nerves were thrumming. Her senses were alive to everything – the smell of decay and excrement, the patterns of garbage shoved against the tunnel walls, the shadows painted beneath the fogged skylights.

This was what she had risen early for, once upon a time.

The carriage pulled to a stop at the corner, pointed – Malone couldn't help but notice – down the wide mouth of the tunnel. Ready for a quick escape.

Their escort clambered off the back of the carriage, sweeping the tunnel with searchlight glares. Six other plainclothes guards patrolled the scene, too skittish to seem official and too stiff to blend in. Malone wondered if they were dressed so to avoid a spectacle or if the street clothes, like the guards themselves, were simply all that was available.

Farrah took in their surroundings with a businesslike scowl. "Let's make this fast," she said.

Malone climbed out after her. The street was quiet. Not the way you'd expect on a regular Thursday morning, but nothing had been regular in a long time.

Most of the shops here were boarded up or smashed in, too.

Commerce had largely moved into the black market – and its ambulatory bazaar, the Twilight Exchange – but a new, secret life had replaced the old, like fungus growing on a tree stump. If Malone looked for it, she knew she'd find signs of that life everywhere – piles of rags where people had taken to sleeping, clusters of holes where the temporary residents removed and replaced boards to cover up their shelters. Old bloodstains and bullet holes that no one would have bothered to clean up.

But none of that life was here now.

Malone stopped in front of the bodies. They were lined up against the wall, bloodstains like skid marks showing where they'd been dragged. Someone had left them here. Hoping they'd be found.

She squatted, knees popping as she balanced her buttocks on her heels. How had she gotten so much older in the months she'd been away from this work?

And how had the victims gotten so young?

Malone peered into their faces. None of them could have been more than twenty-five. And here they were, one with his throat slit, another with her head bashed in, and the last weeping from a dozen different gashes.

All three victims were wearing the loose, crisp uniforms of Madina.

All three were wearing empty holsters.

Malone patted down the bodies and checked the ground around them, even though she knew it was futile. Someone had taken the weapons, though whether it was a statement or simple opportunism, she couldn't yet say.

But perhaps the victims could.

She inspected the bodies, lifting their hands and probing their limbs as carefully as if they'd been alive. She found twisted limbs, raw knuckles, lacerations along the forearms. They'd fought, all except the first man, who'd had his throat slit before any of them knew what was happening.

And the others had been disarmed shortly after that.

Odd, the three of them venturing this deep into town. Odder still for them all to have left their guard down, especially after two of their fellows had been caught looting – Malone had heard that bit of gossip a dozen times over.

Movement flickered at the far end of the tunnel. Someone passing by and hurrying on. The two guards watching that direction looked from Malone to the tunnel mouth and back again, nervous.

"Almost done?" Farrah asked. Malone could hear her speaking between her teeth.

"Still checking," she said.

Blood spattered and trailed for several yards, dragged along by a few partial boot prints. Only two or three different pairs of shoes as far as she could tell, but smaller than she expected.

No, not smaller. Finer.

One print narrowed where the sole tapered into a pointed toe. Another vanished in a high arch and reappeared in the stamp of a heel. A third, similar to the first, was mottled with something like a cordwainer's mark. Only expensive shoemakers bothered with that.

Malone stood back and regarded the tracks and streaks of blood. There had likely been more than three assailants from the way the corpses looked, but she couldn't get a read from the prints.

All this for a tea shop. The Qadi's people must be getting just as desperate as Recolettans.

Malone took a lantern from the carriage, lit it, and pushed the door. It swung open with the slightest pressure.

The room smelled of dust, wood, and the musky and floral aromas of tea. Most of the shelves were empty even though the scent lingered. Dust motes floated in the glow from Malone's lantern.

She scanned the grimy floor, searching for footprints.

What she found instead was a two-inch length of fingernail, jagged where it had snapped off.

"Malone, we should hurry," Farrah said.

She left the shop and turned back to the tunnel where Farrah waited, her face ashen in the gray light filtering in from the skylight. The woman kept glancing to either end of the tunnel as if she expected someone to materialize there at any moment.

Let her stew. Malone had a job, and for now, it was one she knew how to do.

She regarded the smeared blood, the bodies propped up against the wall. The scene was beginning to take shape in her mind, almost as if she could see the whole thing play out in reverse. Three Madinan guards had come to the market district – off duty, most likely – for tea? For something else? At the invitation of a third party?

They were taken by surprise. Caught off guard not only because they were young and inexperienced, but also because the attack had come from an unlikely source.

"Whitenails," Malone said, half to herself and half to Farrah. "Or one at least, but definitely the fancy crowd."

Farrah whistled through her teeth. Out of the corner of her eye, Malone saw the waiting guards converge on the bodies, unfolding canvas sheets.

"They murdered them here, and they knew they were coming." If they were still wearing fancy shoes and keeping their nails long, then they weren't living on the street yet. "Might have even lured them here." Sato's coup had not been kind to Recoletta's privileged whitenails, and some had taken up arms in response. But this was an odd time to go hunting for trouble, especially when the old guard – Lachesse and her peers – was returning to power and the leadership was reinstating the Council.

Which had always been run by whitenails.

The guards rolled the corpses into the canvas sheets.

"Who would gain from angering the Qadi?" Malone asked.

"Ponder that one later," Farrah said. "We need to go." By now, she was stamping and fidgeting as much as the horses.

The guards were loading the bodies into the cargo compartment of the carriage.

"Tell Dr Brin to see if the same blade was used on the two men," Malone said. "And ask him–"

"They're not going to the morgue. And Brin's been missing a month," Farrah said sharply.

Malone felt a sting of guilt. "Then where–"

"It's better you don't know, Malone. Officially, you're not here. None of us are. I'm going to handle this as quietly as possible, and with a little luck none of this gets back to the Qadi, or Lady Lachesse, or anyone else who might raise a stink."

A couple of the guards kicked garbage over the bloodstains. Malone wanted to stop them, but what was the point now?

"Pay off whoever you want, but I need to ask around."

Farrah scowled at her in disbelief. "Your job is to keep Recoletta from another breakdown, not chase killers."

Frustration and disappointment swelled in Malone's chest. "Hard to keep the city stable with murderers running around."

"They've been here a long time. And they will be until the shops are open, the railcars running, and the markets full of food."

Malone knew Farrah was right, but that didn't make any of this easier to hear.

"You need to keep the peace between the Qadi and local forces, and you need to make sure that Recolettans accept the Qadi's people. That they know they're peacekeepers, not occupiers."

Farrah pointed to the cargo compartment, which the guards were shutting and latching on the three wrapped bodies.

"That is what we're up against," Farrah said. "And we're not going to beat it by lining up the facts, because the facts don't matter. The story does. That's why you need to make deals. Compromises. Speeches."

Skies above. Malone's mouth tasted sour.

"And you're going to smile and shake hands with the politicians you hate, and you're going to show up early every day to do it, because that's what it will take to keep the peace we all bled for."

Malone just had a chance to see the color in Farrah's cheeks before the other woman turned away.

She sighed. She'd known that it was too good to be true, that she couldn't put off the job she'd never wanted for the one she still loved. But it had felt good to pretend for a little while that she would be able to solve her problems the one way she knew how.

She would have loved to thrust this responsibility onto Farrah. The other woman certainly understood what was required. But she was the one who had inherited it. More importantly, she thought as she watched Farrah issue orders, Farrah was the one who could move bodies without asking questions.

CHAPTER SIX
DISORIENTATION

Jane's backside was numb, her throat was dry again, and her nausea had only gotten worse. The little room, which had been fairly calm since the interrogator arrived, rocked and swayed.

She wanted a meal, even though she knew she'd probably only vomit it back up. She wanted to gulp pitchers of water and sleep in a nice, steady bed where she could forget about Recoletta and Ruthers and the rest of it for just a few hours.

Mostly, she wanted to see the sky. She was sure that a breath of fresh air and a long, steadying look at the stars – or the horizon, if it was still day – would do her good.

But she was stuck here, telling stories about things she'd rather forget, and trying to keep straight in her own mind what she'd revealed and what she'd kept to herself. She hadn't mentioned Roman's surname or the vault, that much she knew.

The interrogator shook his head and sighed. The room was small enough that she could smell the fish and pepper on his breath.

"You conosse the problem?" he asked. "Of your buried cities?"

Jane could think of plenty, but she was reasonably sure the interrogator had something else in mind.

"You inhabit sujeira," he said.

This one was beyond Jane. "What?"

The interrogator spread his hands toward the floor. "Basura. Sordor."

"Filth?"

His white teeth gleamed. "Ess. You escave holes ee live there, in proxima your own filth."

Despite the way she'd described Recoletta, she wanted to explain that it hadn't always been that way. But her years as a laundress for Recoletta's elites had taught her the difference between a debate and an assertion.

"You seem to know an awful lot about the buried cities," Jane said.

If he recognized sarcasm, he gave no indication. "Always they've been asi. Place of corruption. Equal to the Continent." He sat straight and forward, his voice forceful with passion.

"Then it's a good thing you figured out how to avoid them both," Jane said. She could tell she'd hit a sensitive subject, and she was working around it as carefully as she could.

"No ess civilized to live interred by filth. O acircled by the dead. Repugnant, equally. People must clean away the corruption. Every dia, every generation." He sat back and relaxed a little. "What did you encounter next? After the whiskey man?"

"Corruption," Jane said.

The morning after Petrosian's, Jane had awoken to a roaring hangover.

She felt something wrong as soon as she opened her eyes. She ached with hunger, thirst, and nausea, but every twitch and movement sent pain rattling through her body.

It was not a good day to have urgent errands waiting.

Jane wondered if this wasn't the real price of the information she'd bought the previous night.

She also wondered where exactly she'd found herself. When she could move her head without tipping the world on its side, she rolled over and looked around.

She was in a bedroom. She didn't recognize it.

But the sheets beneath her were soft and thick, and there were pillows all around her – under her head, on top of it, and nestled in the crook of her body.

Jane remembered leaving the bar. She thought she remembered heading towards her old apartment. But that was on the other side of town, near the factory districts, likely with a couple of miles of blockaded or gang-run streets in between. And who knew who had claimed it in the months she'd been away from Recoletta?

Much like she'd claimed this place. Wherever it was.

"Hello?" she called. "Anybody there?"

Silence. Maybe she really had just stumbled upon this place by herself.

And now that she was fully awake, she realized that her bladder was bursting and her mouth was dry as cotton. Time to figure out where she was.

She sat up, still wearing the previous day's clothes, and closed her eyes against the sudden reeling of the world. She opened them only when she was certain she'd contained the worst of the nausea.

The bedroom was large and colorful in a tasteful way. Tapestries, baroque in their intricacy, hung from the walls. They looked mostly faded, though – a pale sky hung over rippling hills and waves of grass that had turned a deep blue. She glanced away when her head started swimming again. An odd decoration for a city-dweller to have.

There wasn't much else of note in the bedroom. One door led to a bathroom, another to a messy storage room, and a third to the hall. The walls were smooth and high. Someone with money lived here – or had, once. Strewn around the floor and among the blankets and pillows next to her were a man's clothes. Dark trousers, a dark jacket, and a few rumpled white shirts. All dirty. Something about them was familiar, but she'd probably seen and washed dozens of other similarly nondescript articles before.

Her throat was burning now. She pushed herself up from the bed and spread her feet wide, wobbling like a foal to keep her balance. At least the rug under her feet was thick and soft.

Luxurious like the tapestries, she guessed. She wasn't going to risk looking down.

She made her way to the bathroom, and after she'd relieved herself and vomited, she felt better. Well enough to do something about the old whiskey taste in her mouth, for sure.

Jane stumbled back through the bedroom and out into the parlor, and that was when she recognized the place.

She was in Roman Arnault's apartment.

Another wave of unsteadiness washed over her again.

She must have made her way here on instinct last night and found the door unlocked. She was relieved to note that she'd had the sense to lock it behind her, at least. It didn't seem like the place had been looted. Roman, of course, had probably still been living here until his final trip to Madina. Either he'd left in a hurry or he'd left it open for someone else.

Jane made her way to the kitchen in hopes of finding something to drink. She felt a little guilty searching through his cabinets and cupboards, even though she was sure he wouldn't have minded. Her stomach heaved at the sight of a few half-empty whiskey bottles. Eventually, she found a carton of black pine tea and set a kettle to boil. At least his place still had gas.

She gulped three glasses of water while she waited. By the time she'd suppressed the urge to vomit (again), the tea was ready. She held a cup of it under her nose, breathing in the bitter vapors while she thought.

That had been stupid, getting drunk the previous night. She only had four days to save Roman; she couldn't afford to waste any of them feeling sick.

Jane played back through the events of the previous night. After Burgevich had left, she'd talked to the proprietor of the whiskey shop, Petrosian. He'd claimed to be an old acquaintance of Roman's, and for a price, he'd offered to give her something that might help their mutual friend.

In return, she'd confessed that she knew the code to the vault. She hadn't told him the code itself, and he hadn't asked – that much she remembered. Perhaps he thought her information was valuable enough as it was. More likely, he didn't want to risk finding himself in the same position as her and Roman. After all, Roman had been running from that sequence his whole life.

The tea had a kind of aromatic astringency that left her mouth feeling dry but cool. She gazed around the living room as her senses came alive. The first time she'd come here, Roman had caught her rummaging through his files, searching for clues about the whitenail murders. He'd caught her, of course, and thrown her out. She hadn't known at that time whether he was a killer or a victim.

But he'd had information, and it had led Liesl Malone to the Library. If his blood was the key to the vault, he might have something on that, too. All she'd heard was that it was a cache of powerful weapons from the Catastrophe. If they were both linked to the place, she might as well learn what she could about it.

She picked through the shelves crowded with books. Nothing remarkable here, even among the hidden files and papers where she'd found the map to the Library. She considered the mantel, the cabinets, the exotic bric-a-brac. She didn't know what she was looking for, but she didn't think it was here.

Jane returned to the bedroom, thinking of the storage room.

No, she realized when she'd crossed the bedroom and dialed up the gas lamps. Not storage. A study.

An oversized escritoire stood against one wall. Papers and books were clumped in careful heaps about the room, and a trail of notes led a merry chase from one corner and pile to the next. Jane had seen this kind of deliberate chaos in the homes of certain clients once upon a time, enough to recognize that this was the room in which Roman had really lived.

For people like him, disorder was merely another form of organization. She just had to figure out the pattern. Unfortunately, the irregular and secretive work he'd done as the Council's hatchet man and Sato's spymaster would make that difficult.

She skimmed the nearest stack. Something to do with a whitenail's scandalous affair. She tried the next. Chronicles of another whitenail's embezzlement of the Bureau of the Treasury.

She tried to remember what Roman had told her about the vault. Unfortunately, he'd claimed to know little about it, said that he'd refused to learn the code she now knew...

Of course. Roman had wanted nothing to do with the vault. Anything he might have about it would be in the place he was least likely to search.

Jane scanned the office, the escritoire against one wall, a fireplace against another, bookshelves next to the door, and papers scattered throughout.

It was all a careful mess. Every flat surface was covered in papers, parcels, or envelopes. The escritoire groaned as she rifled through its drawers, and she reflected that she didn't even know what she was really looking for. She sighed, and a draft whispered from the fireplace.

The top page on the nearest stack rustled, but Roman had kept the space around the hearth clear, luckily. Something about the tidy little fireplace seemed odd, and it took Jane a minute to register what it was.

No cinders had blown over the hearth. In fact, there didn't appear to be any ashes in the firebox, and barely a specter of soot on the lintel. Just logs as thick as a grown man's thigh, stacked neatly on the grate. Entirely too tidy.

Roman couldn't have used the fireplace in years.

Jane knelt and pulled the topmost log aside, and it clunked onto the brick hearth. She tore another from the stack. Black lacquer shone beneath the grate. Jane reached under and worked a wide, squat box from the grate, its surface gray with dust.

People didn't hide nondescript little boxes without good reason. Whatever Roman kept here, it was obviously important. Or personal. He certainly didn't handle it often. She tamped down the last of her guilt with the reminder that, if it was important enough, it might be able to save them both. If not, it probably wouldn't matter anyway.

She wiped the dust from the lid and tried to raise it, but it was locked.

The key was most likely buried somewhere in the escritoire if Roman wasn't especially careful. Hidden in one of the bookshelves if he was. If he was anything like her wealthy, eccentric former clients, the key was somewhere in the study.

That was the problem, of course. Roman wasn't like anyone else.

After a moment's thought, Jane pulled one of the logs from the fireplace and smashed it on the box's tiny latch. She lifted the lid.

Inside were a handkerchief, a pocket watch, and half a dozen coins. Personal tokens, but nothing that would explain the vault, and certainly nothing that would ease Roman's plight.

Jane picked up a couple of the coins and examined them even as her heart sank. They were small and copper, dark with age. But they didn't look like any currency she'd ever seen. Each had a strange, boxy symbol on one side and a square hole punched through the middle.

She glanced at the watch, suddenly wondering what time it was. The thing probably hadn't run in years, but Jane felt the hours evaporating around her like air from a sealed room. She'd been here too long already.

She wrapped the coins in the handkerchief and tucked it and the watch into her bodice. As she did, her hand brushed something else.

The key Petrosian had given her. She recalled their exchange the night before and Petrosian's offer of access to Ruthers's manor.

The last thing she wanted was to visit the home of the man she'd murdered. But if it held the means to Roman's freedom, then she had to go.

•••

Councilor Ruthers's manor wasn't far from Roman's neighborhood. Jane had never been there, but she'd served enough clients in the area to know where it was.

And, even with the gas lamps shattered, the gardens trampled, and the overpriced storefronts trashed, it was difficult to mistake the spacious, arched tunnels of the Vineyard.

Jane passed estates she'd known, where she'd once accepted and delivered laundry for the wealthy and powerful of Recoletta. Now, these places were either neglected or vandalized, with creeper vines growing over smashed or rusted gates. From what she'd seen since Madina, their former residents weren't faring much better.

She reached Ruthers's manor after a fifteen-minute walk. She would have known it even if Petrosian hadn't described it.

The tunnel she'd been traveling, wide enough to accommodate the broad facade of an estate and an entryway garden on either side, opened into a small cavern. Steps, wide and low, rose through an arbor. Two carriages could have clattered along side by side, all the way to the facade, which was an imposing masterpiece a hundred feet wide and just as tall, framed by heavy pilasters and stone monsters carved in relief. A skylight poured afternoon sun onto the scene, and faded radiance stones nestled along the cavern walls.

This was where the most powerful man in Recoletta had lived until she had killed him. Jane felt her cheeks grow hot, as the morning's nausea returned to her in a rush. She looked up at the diamond windows and gray stone and around at the shaggy garden, reminding herself that these were all just pieces of a place, none of which could hurt her any more than Ruthers could.

Besides, it was what lay inside that mattered.

Jane climbed the shallow steps to the door, a heavy thing of wood and wrought iron, and used the key Petrosian had given her. The door swung open more easily than she would have expected.

The hall inside was dark and cool, with tall, marble-paneled arches reaching up – probably above the surface – to pull a pale glow down from the clouded skylights. The floor had been swept clean, though she supposed Ruthers would have arranged for this in preparation for his return.

She suppressed a shiver.

Jane had been in enough houses like this to guess that the rooms nearest to her would be sitting rooms and parlors. The bedrooms would be at the back and down the stairs that she could just see like shadows in the darkness. Kitchens, laundry, servants' quarters, and other functional but unsightly places would be scattered behind the walls and stitched together by a network of narrow, bare-stone corridors. Ruthers's library and office would be somewhere removed, away from the busy main hall and unconnected to the servants' tunnels.

At least that was the normal design of estates like this, for powerful men and women who balanced delicate matters of state with busy social calendars. Jane had never been in one quite this big, though.

She headed down the central hall, each footfall a thunderclap, checking the rooms as she passed them. Mahogany tables inlaid with opal, velvet-cushioned settees, wall drapes thick and soft as down blankets, all of it priceless and pristine. It was a wonder any of it still remained, but Ruthers had always cast a long shadow.

Jane continued until she reached a grand staircase at the end of the hall. It split halfway up the wall, twin arms winding up and around to two balconies along the hall. She could see the tops of arches on either side just beyond the balustrade, and she guessed that long galleries lay beyond, big and spacious enough that drafts whispered from above.

A gentleman of Ruthers's station wouldn't keep anything important so close to the surface.

The staircase also curved down in two wide arms that met on a darkened landing. Whatever she needed had to lie in that direction.

She took a radiance stone glim from the side table and proceeded down the stairs.

She descended to a rotunda that was wider and almost as tall as the hall above. Three smaller corridors radiated from it, one straight ahead and one to either side. On a hunch, Jane followed the hall to the left.

Cool drafts prickled at the back of her neck. Even though Ruthers was as cold and still as his manor, she couldn't help but feel dread at snooping around uninvited. She didn't believe in ghosts, but something intangible lingered in this place, and it made her want to leave it as quickly as possible.

Halfway down the hall, she smelled something dry and musky. She recognized it as the scent of old books.

She followed a twisting, carpeted passage – the kind most guests would have ignored – until she reached a heavy wooden door with a darkened brass lock. It creaked open at her push, and she gasped.

For a man who had spent a significant portion of his career hiding an ancient library from the rest of the city, Ruthers had an impressive collection of books where most whitenails would have kept their wine. Jane didn't realize her hands were shaking until she noticed the shadows jumping behind the rows of bookshelves.

Something groaned in the distance behind Jane. She spun but saw nothing besides the thick shadows painting the hall.

So she turned back to investigate the library. It seemed like the best place to start.

There must have been a dozen shelves, each holding a couple of hundred books. She couldn't tell what they were about from a quick scan of the spines, but if the heavy lock on the door was any indication, they pertained to matters of the utmost secrecy.

Pre-Catastrophe history, in other words.

A locked room like this would also be a perfect place for storing records of the excavation. Correspondences with foreign city leaders. The kinds of records that might exonerate Roman Arnault.

Pre-Sato history, in other words.

She looked around and past the shelves, hoping to find a desk of some kind. That was the likeliest –

"Stop right there," a voice said from behind her.

Jane did. She heard a metallic click.

"Turn. Slowly," the voice said.

Jane turned.

In the glow from her radiance stone, she saw five – no, six – people standing near the door. The woman in the lead wore regal, outdated attire – a heavy silk dress with the seams torn at the shoulders and a few badly matched patches sewn at the elbows. There was something familiar about her. She pointed a gun at Jane with one hand and held her shoes with the other.

"It's poor manners for someone like you to enter a house like this uninvited," the woman said, looking Jane up and down with evident disdain.

The haughty, cultured voice was also familiar, but it was the woman's four-inch fingernails, immaculate despite her attire, that jogged Jane's memory.

"Madame Attrop," Jane said. "This is hardly the sort of welcome I'd have expected from you."

Confusion clouded the whitenail's brow and cleared with a sudden lift of her eyebrows. "Jane Lin. Forgive me, but strange times have bred caution." She kept the gun raised.

"If I meant you harm, I certainly wouldn't have come like this," Jane said, holding the glim aloft and keeping her other hand conspicuously open.

"Yet you have come. And with a key, no less."

Jane tried to keep her expression neutral. She didn't know the nature of the relationship between Attrop and Petrosian, but she'd always prided herself on discretion.

"I came for information," she said.

Attrop tilted her head to one side.

For the first time, Jane considered the people standing around

Attrop. She didn't recognize any of them, and they wore a strange assortment of clothes – tailored, pearl-buttoned blouses over heavy factory workers' trousers and long, woolen cloaks on top of threadbare shifts.

It was impossible to tell what they'd been before Sato, but it seemed telling that Attrop was here, in tattered finery, rather than in Dominari Hall with Lady Lachesse. Perhaps she'd be willing to help.

"The Qadi of Madina tried to send a trainload of soldiers into this city barely a week ago," Jane said. "Strange that she's taken up residence in Dominari Hall, no?" She was fishing for a reaction – some sign of where Attrop stood in relation to everything else.

An invisible thread tugged Attrop's lips taut for a split second. "Strange, indeed. You've come to an unusual place to stop her."

There was a challenge in Attrop's eyes. The woman was smart enough to know Jane was feeling her out, and now she was daring her to lie, to tell her what she wanted to hear. "I'm here to save Roman Arnault," Jane said.

The man next to Attrop shifted, his lantern jaw elongated in a frown.

"So you know him," Jane said, looking at the man.

He remained silent. She didn't recognize him, but something about the way he held his shoulders suggested he'd be offended if he knew that.

Attrop almost smiled. "Mr Arnault has a certain effect on most people. Though I see he's had a very different effect on you." She cocked her head as if jostling a memory back into place. "Yes, I remember a certain attachment at the city's last gala, months ago." The inflection with which she said "last" seemed to mean "final" as much as "previous."

"And I remember you were keeping different company then," Jane said. "With Lady Lachesse in particular."

Attrop kept her face still, but the light that flashed through her eyes was unmistakable. Jane's suspicions had been correct.

But then the whitenail thumbed back the hammer and

extended the gun toward Jane.

"As I hear it, she's become your ally," Attrop said. "Your compatriot and confidante in Madina. And now, your liberator in Recoletta."

Jane saw her miscalculation as clearly as a loose seam in a jacket. Attrop was on the outs with Lachesse and the very people who had just released Jane. The whitenail's companions shuffled and squared their shoulders, dogs chafing at the leash.

She was aware of her own arms stretching forward, as if she might force them all back with her glim and flat palm.

"Lachesse and the Qadi," she said slowly, "released me because they had no choice. Because they would rather make me part of their plan than admit that I foiled it."

Someone in the back of the group snorted.

"But Lachesse is the one who turned us over to the Qadi and brought us back here," Jane said. "Roman and me. She's the reason Roman's locked up now. She's no friend of mine."

It was a simplification, but only a minor one.

"So," Attrop said, "you're telling me Lachesse got close to you, used you to bargain, and then sold you out when the price was right?" She watched Jane with eyes as hard and sharp as flint.

"Basically," Jane said.

Attrop lowered her gun. "That does sound like her."

Jane heaved a sigh and brought her arms down. She hadn't realized she'd been holding her breath.

The younger man next to Attrop was still scowling. "We don't know–"

"I know," the whitenail said, cutting him off without looking over. "The question is, what is Miss Lin doing here?"

"If you've been following me, you already know," Jane said.

Attrop's eyes widened in surprise. "Following you? My dear, we live here."

"But how–"

"We saw you coming from the windows over the garden. And even if we hadn't, you made enough noise to announce yourself to the factory districts." Attrop seemed offended that Jane could have believed otherwise.

It certainly explained a few things. Like how well the place had been kept up. As big as Ruthers's garden was, this place was probably pretty easy to defend –

Jane glanced up at a dry, hissing sound to see Attrop glaring at her in impatience.

"I was told I'd find information here that proves that Ruthers, not Roman, was behind the excavation of the Library, the death of Sato's parents, and–"

"And you think any of that is going to save your gallant?"

Jane said nothing. She'd known it was thin, but at least it was something.

"Even if you prove that Ruthers was as bad as he was, even if you somehow convince people that Roman was merely his pawn, none of that is going to loosen his shackles one bit. You know why?"

Jane couldn't bring herself to do more than shrug.

"Because all of that was months ago. Years, in some cases. All that matters is what's happening today."

Jane swallowed a lump. It had felt good to hope. More than that, to try something. "Is that why you've been hiding out here?" she asked. "Holding court in the ruins of the Vineyard and wearing priceless silks that have gone to rags?"

The people gathered around Attrop frowned and looked between one another. The lantern-jawed man took a step forward and growled – actually growled. Jane made another mental note; he was the one to watch out for.

But he stopped at Attrop's humorless chuckle.

"Miss Lin, I'm afraid you've missed the point. The last thing Lachesse and her new allies want is for Recoletta to think about the last week, let alone the last several years. That's why they're giving people something else to think about."

Jane met Attrop's expectant glare as it all fell into place. "Roman's execution," she said.

"Is a sideshow." Attrop nodded. "And if we want to drain it of its power–"

"We give them something bigger," Jane said.

Attrop's grin showed all her teeth.

"You still haven't told me what you're doing here," Jane said.

"We," Attrop said, inclining her head to include the as-yet nameless men and women with her, "have been working on something bigger."

Jane didn't wait to think about it. With Roman's execution days away, doing anything was better than doing nothing. "Then I want to help."

Attrop barked her humorless laugh again. "My dear, I wouldn't let you leave this place if I believed otherwise. But let's continue this discussion somewhere warmer, and where we can all sit. Dalton, fetch the brandy." She set her shoes on the floor and stepped into them with uncanny grace.

As she held one hand out for balance, Jane couldn't help but notice that one of her carefully kept nails had snapped off.

CHAPTER SEVEN
UP AND RUNNING

Geist nodded, eyes wide. "Ach, but you are having such an interesting series of professions! A detectif, a politiker, and now an criminal. Phelan, you are still cleaning?"

The woman was running a rag over the spill for maybe the hundredth time. She looked up sheepishly.

Geist jerked his head at the door, and she left.

Malone thought she was starting to get a read on her strange host. The way he sipped at his drink – his caffee – when he was excited or tugged at his goatee when he was mulling over something.

But there were still many details she hadn't figured out. Like what – exactly – Geist and his people wanted from Arnault. Or how they'd known to search in Recoletta.

Or why they were trusting the word of a woman they'd cut down from the gallows.

Geist sighed through his nostrils as Phelan's footsteps receded down the hall. He shook his head and turned his attention back to Malone.

"You are telling me that this Jane – the waschergirl – did the assassinat of the ausland guards? Most imposant."

"She didn't kill anyone," Malone said. "Not beside Ruthers." What Jane Lin did was far more destructive.

"Then I am hoping you are arriving at the point rasch," he

said, tenting his fingers and tapping the tips together.

"You said you wanted the history. I'm giving you the history." Malone waited a beat, just to make her point. "This is where it started to fall apart."

The trim black ensemble that Farrah had commissioned for Malone looked almost like her old uniform, but it was far too nice. Polished black boots rose to her calves, too tight to conceal a weapon. The toes were pointed rather than blunt, and the heels were ever so slightly elevated: just enough for Malone to notice, but not enough to reasonably object. Farrah was a shrewd one.

Her slim slacks were tailored. Holding them up, Malone hadn't expected them to fit, and she was surprised to find them as pliable as a second skin. She could walk, sit, turn, and crouch as comfortably as she ever had, only the fabric was so smooth and expensive that she worried about doing any of those things in it.

The shirt buttoned all the way to her neck. It didn't appear drastically different from the dozens of black shirts she'd always worn; only, like every other piece of her new outfit, it felt finer and costlier. She forced herself to stop fidgeting with the buttons when she realized that she didn't really want to know whether or not they were real pearl.

The high collar on the wool coat was excessively dramatic, but the only thing worse than wearing fancy clothes was bothering to complain about them. At least it was black. And it was thick enough to hide a gun holster at the small of her back. Farrah was shrewd, indeed.

She almost looked like an inspector. Which was something to be thankful for, because she felt less and less like one every day.

She picked up the last piece of her ensemble – a gold pin, some kind of meaningless curlicue studded with small blue gems. It was ostentatious, and Malone's excruciatingly trained animal brain rebelled at the idea of wearing something designed to draw attention, but Farrah had insisted.

Perhaps because she still looked and felt too much like a cop.

Against every desire and instinct, she pinned it to the flaring lapel of her coat and left the office before she saw herself in the mirror again.

Farrah was waiting outside. She looked Malone up and down with a small, approving nod.

"Where are we headed?" Malone asked, ignoring it.

"Maxwell Street Station." A surreptitious smile colored Farrah's voice.

As they swept through Dominari Hall, clerks, petitioners, whitenails, and strangers made way and watched them with gaping, incredulous expressions.

That was what it felt like, anyway. Malone felt the tips of her ears growing warm.

"Remind me," Malone said, "what are we doing at a transit station?"

Now Farrah gave her a long, incredulous glare. "Restoring railcar and trolley service, Governor."

"Don't call me that."

"The sooner we get Recoletta running, the sooner I can stop, Governor."

"Do you have to do that?"

Farrah spun her head to stare her down again. "Did you even read my report, Malone?"

"When was I supposed to do that? As soon as I got back yesterday, I had a line of whitenails and bootlickers down the hall, all circling and bickering because none of them wanted the others to know they were even coming to me! Just when I was getting through the first half of them, you shooed them all away to bring that tailor in."

Farrah nodded with satisfaction. "Half of them would sell their own children for one of Mr Jalbani's suits. With any luck, everyone in Dominari Hall has heard that story twice by now."

A thrill of anger tickled the back of Malone's stomach. "And they'll think I'm as corrupt and decadent as every other bureaucrat who's held office in there."

Farrah blew an exasperated sigh through her nostrils. Malone thought she could almost see smoke. "They'll think your time is too valuable to waste on petty squabbles and power grabs." She wagged a finger in Malone's face. "Figure out how to get rid of them on your own, or next time I'm commissioning a ball gown."

Malone bit her lip, feeling the steady clack of her new boots on the tile. "Can I use these?" Malone asked, bringing one foot down hard.

"Why do you think I gave you heels?"

Good humor trickled back into her bloodstream like the warmth of a strong drink. She was fortunate to have Farrah as an ally. And Salazar, wherever he was now. She'd worked with a lot of loyal, resourceful people.

Like Johanssen, her dead chief. And Sundar, her dead partner. They would have known how to play this, and Recoletta would have been safe in their smooth, capable hands.

Her good feeling vanished as suddenly as it had crept up on her.

"It shouldn't have been me," Malone said to herself.

But Farrah looked up and scowled. "Like I said, the sooner we get the city sorted out, the sooner you can go back to being anonymous and inconsequential." She said it with a vitriol that sounded too forceful to be real.

They passed through the high double doors and into the subterranean plaza in front of Dominari Hall.

Malone frowned. "Farrah. Didn't you say we got the railcars working again?"

"So you were listening."

"Why are we taking a carriage? It's faster if we just–"

Farrah seized her elbow and dragged her towards the waiting coach, and Malone fought back a wince at the iron grip on her expensive sleeve.

While they rumbled toward the Vineyard, Farrah rattled on about appearances and presentation and public confidence, and

Malone listened just enough to catch the salient bits – flip the lights on, make a show of it, and hope the sweeps had gotten around to cleaning Maxwell Street Station up a bit.

Given the musty smell of manure in the tunnels, Malone was not especially hopeful on that front.

The rest of her was watching the detours they were taking around barricaded tunnels, the rubble that had been swept into piles but not cleared, all of the things that a few working railcars wouldn't fix.

"– about distraction," Farrah said.

"What distraction?" Malone turned back to her.

Even in the semidarkness, she could see the irritation smoldering in Farrah's eyes. "Skies above, have you been paying any attention?"

"I was planning our escape route."

Farrah was silent for a few seconds, probably trying to decide whether or not she was joking. She wasn't certain herself.

Finally, the other woman made a noise of disgust. "It's a ribbon cutting, Malone. The worst you'll have to deal with is boredom."

"You weren't here last time," Malone said, recalling the visit she and Arnault had made only weeks ago, when Maxwell Street Station had been temporarily transformed by the mobile black market known as the Twilight Exchange.

The carriage pulled to a stop. A few guards in Recolettan uniforms flanked the arched entrance to Maxwell Street Station, and a dull roar rose from within.

Malone's stomach twisted. She'd always hated speeches.

Maxwell Street Station had been the transit hub of the Vineyard in the old Council's day. Under Sato, it, like the rest of the Vineyard, had become contested territory between the shifting influence of criminal gangs and insurgent leaders.

Whoever had cleaned the place up had done a better job here than in the tunnels.

Maxwell Street Station had always been the functional gem of the Vineyard, a place where grandiose aesthetics met functional design. It used all three spatial dimensions in the finest tradition of subterranean architecture, spinning steel bridges and loading stages over railcar platforms bordered by long, wide steps, all beneath a great dome of softly reflective tile.

Today, it was actually polished to a mirror shine.

Even without the benefit of a skylight, the station was one of the brightest corners of Recoletta. Pillars of white flame rose behind panels of glowing, frosted glass. Fresh radiance stones studded the underside of the dome and the arched entrances to the railcar and trolley tunnels, and the distant girders that clung to the dome like strands of a spider's web gleamed. Every tile and light-reflective inset had been polished, and a crowd of a couple of hundred spectators stood around, their eyes bulging from hunger-lean faces with awe and suspicion.

Even Farrah seemed to have forgotten her irritation. "I didn't think they'd have time to fix the gas lines," she said, her voice soft with wonder.

Something was tingling in Malone's skull like the first sign of a cold, but she couldn't yet tell what.

"Well, what are you waiting for?" Farrah muttered, pointing to the nearest platform. A single railcar sat in the middle of the platform like a beast awaiting slaughter. The brass had been polished and the wood varnished to a luster it probably hadn't had since its first voyage across town. The throng standing before it watched as if they expected the thing to come to life on its own.

"What am I supposed to say?"

Farrah gave her a gentle shove. "Next time, read the report."

Malone climbed the steps to the stranded railcar and waiting crowd. She was halfway there before she realized that she didn't know how far the railcar lines had been repaired, let alone where this one was going.

She found herself at the top of the platform, facing a gathering of people who looked as uncertain as she felt.

Sundar would have been good at this. She'd watched him

charm stone-hearted bureaucrats and belligerent thugs alike. Whatever the situation, the former actor had always found the right words. Almost always.

She cleared her throat.

"Citizens of Recoletta. Thank you for the confidence you've put in your government." That she didn't feel it herself made it even harder to say.

Her listeners blinked back at her. Coughed into ragged sleeves.

"Recoletta is a great city," she said, realizing too late that she'd put the emphasis on "city" rather than "great." Or maybe it should have gone on "Recoletta." What was it about big speeches that seemed to confound every word?

"A very noble city," she continued, "with a glorious and noble history–"

She broke off to clear her throat, realizing she'd just said "noble" twice. Nothing to do about it now but keep going and hope no one else noticed. She tried to recall Sundar's calming presence, his natural ease with words. The thought did little for her.

The onlookers twitched with movement – impatiently shuffled feet, murmurs to neighbors, picking under fingernails.

"We have prevailed over, um, sinister forces, and now we thrive together," she said to the ragged, hungry gathering.

Someone sneezed. A man near the front of the group shook his head.

How had Sundar managed when she felt like she had a mouthful of pebbles? It wasn't just that he'd been good at reading people, he'd been good at empathizing with them. When he spoke, it felt as though he meant every word.

Malone suddenly realized why her own speech was going nowhere. She didn't believe any of it herself.

She needed to try something else. At least she knew this couldn't go much worse than it already was.

"Listen," Malone said, "you don't need me to tell you how bad things have become. We've all lost people. We've all lost our city."

The people below looked at her with hard, wary eyes, but at least they were looking.

"Your leaders failed – I mean, we failed you. We gave you over to tyrants and cowards, and we became those things ourselves.

"But this is still our home. And it won't be easy, but we've got to build it back up together. And we've got to be patient while we do it. I won't lie – it's going to be a long, hard process. The healing always takes longer than the wounding. But we won't get there if we're still tearing each other apart." The words were tumbling out of her, faster and heavier than she'd intended, but she feared that if she stopped, she'd choke on the ones still welling up inside her.

"I wasn't ready for this. I'm still not. I can't make any promises about when things will return to normal, or if we ever will. But I promise I'll do my best to do right by you."

The crowd was rapt now, a couple of hundred pairs of eyes fixed on her. She hoped that was a good thing.

"Our ancestors came together and hollowed this place out of the Catastrophe, didn't they? We'll get some dirt under our fingernails, but we'll fix it together." Something in the temperature of the room was changing – it was a spreading warmth in the others, a rising and swelling in her own chest.

"Let's rebuild Recoletta together, starting today," she heard herself say. She couldn't think of anything else to add, so she flipped the switch before she could bungle the speech again.

For three terrifying seconds, nothing happened.

Then, Malone heard the sizzle of electricity and the groan of metal, and she saw victory in the faces of the cheering assembly.

She turned, and sure enough, the railcar was moving, crawling along the tracks with a slow but steady pace. Relief bloomed in her chest.

Then the two windows at either end of the railcar slid open, and two men unrolled a banner that spread the length of the vehicle.

It read: "DOWN WITH FOREIGN CORRUPTION. STAND WITH JANE LIN."

Malone was just confused enough that she almost missed what happened next.

But the commotion from the throng rose like a wave, and Malone followed its energy up, almost impossibly, toward the ceiling, where the empty trolley tracks hung.

At least, they had been empty before.

Now a trolley slid along one of the middle tracks with an oiled grace that put the railcar's wheezing progress to shame.

Then the door slid open, and Jane Lin emerged from the bank of seats. Even from this distance, Malone recognized her face and the pale, stony terror etched on it.

"Citizens of Recoletta," Jane called, "you have been crushed too long under the heel of invading despots and their hired friends." Jane pointed down.

At her, Malone realized.

"They tell you to wait for a better future. To submit to them again. And what do they offer but empty promises? Does she look like she's been thrown from her home? Has she waited hours for half a portion of gruel?"

Malone felt the onlookers' gaze on her again, but their warmth had become a blaze. She wanted to explain that it wasn't as simple as Jane was telling it, but that was a hard case to make in a brand new suit with pearl buttons.

Jane's face was whiter than ever and rigid with conviction. Or fear. "Show them you've had enough! Cast off their yoke and stand with us!"

The station rumbled underfoot, and thunder shook the walls. For one terrified moment, Malone remembered the bombs that had inaugurated Sato's reign.

Then, railcars and trolleys burst from the tunnels. They filled the tracks with cars stuffed with chanting, cheering men and women. Malone couldn't make out what they were saying until she heard it echoed behind her.

"Jane Lin. Jane Lin."

Malone turned back in time to notice that the chant was

coming from no more than a dozen people at first. People scattered throughout the crowd yet chanting the very same thing at the very same time. People who had been ordered to wait for this moment.

And their chant was spreading.

Malone saw it as much as she heard it, saw fury and purpose kindle in their faces amidst the rising din of voices. She saw them looking, fever-bright eyes searching for an outlet for their rage.

They settled on her.

Malone glanced up again. Jane Lin was still standing in the open trolley, yelling something, but it was lost to the mob's chant.

The mass of people moved like a snake coiling to spring. Farrah was nowhere to be seen.

Malone assessed her options quickly. The rabble blocked most of her exits, and they were rapidly filling the space between her and the arch through which she and Farrah had entered. There were pedestrian tunnels and railcar shafts behind her, but she didn't know how far they'd been cleared.

Or whether the mob's organizers had another contingent waiting there.

Malone cursed under her breath. She hated the idea of running blind through the maze of destruction at her back, but it beat running straight into the mob. They'd tear her to pieces. They were just waiting for her to move first.

Suddenly, the horde lurched forward.

Malone's heart jumped into her mouth, but they weren't coming for her. Not yet.

Commotion spread from the back of the crowd and rippled forward. Someone had taken up a new cry, and it was slowly building into a dissonant harmony.

Fire.

Smoke and flame rose from the back of the gathering, where one of the glass flame guards had been shattered. Malone's police instincts kicked in, and she was trying to figure out what was burning when she caught movement under the arched tunnel.

Farrah, waving frantically by the exit.

The fire had thrown the mob into confusion, and the collective animal hadn't yet decided whether to focus on Malone or the fire. But they would soon.

Malone ran.

The crowd's ragged edge boiled behind her, but the way ahead was clear, and Farrah had already taken off. Malone almost ran into her where she'd stopped in the tunnel just outside the station.

The carriage was gone. So were the guards who had been standing by the arch. Hearing the frenzy rising from the station, Malone couldn't blame them.

Malone retraced the route they'd taken to get to the station, avoiding the blocked tunnels and dead ends she'd noted on the way over. Farrah followed close behind, but Malone was too winded for a told-you-so.

The tunnel curved and twisted. It was just enough to keep them out of sight of their pursuers who, with any luck, would tire soon.

Malone darted around a corner and past a rubble-choked tunnel. The sounds of the mob were fading behind them.

"Hear that," Farrah panted behind her. It was a question, but the woman was too winded to give it the inflection.

"Listen. Ahead," Farrah said, and then Malone noticed it. Shouting voices. Running feet. The mob – or some portion of it – was preparing to cut them off.

Another corridor branched off twenty feet ahead. Malone was almost certain it was a dead end, but it was something. She swerved into it and heard Farrah stumble in behind her.

Half a dozen doors lined either side of the corridor. It ended in a barricade of lamed wagons, broken furniture, and one half of a set of double doors. Malone rushed to the barricade and began pulling at shelves, table legs, and anything else she could get her hands on. Behind her, Farrah rattled one doorknob after the next.

"Locked," Farrah muttered. "Locked..."

A howl of fury rang from the main tunnel.

"Shit!" Farrah twisted another knob, hurling herself against another locked door. Malone listened to the painful thuds that followed while she kept tearing at the barricade. It was deeper and sturdier than she'd expected – for every chair or cabinet she dislodged, another would shift into its place. The screaming, stampeding crowd sounded like it was just around the corner.

Her grip slipped around a tabletop, and she realized her hands were slick with blood.

Malone heard a yelp from halfway down the hall and looked back in time to see a door slam shut. Farrah was gone.

And shadows were licking at the mouth of the corridor like flames.

She cursed and dove through the window of the wheel-less carriage, feeling seven different places where she'd have bruises. If she survived the day.

She sat up and tugged at the corner of the curtain. The figures at the other end of the corridor were little more than shadows in the gloom, but she counted three. No, four. They advanced along the corridor toward her, heads swiveling and voices barely intelligible growls.

"– they go?"

"Try that side. I'll–"

"– get my hands on–"

One of them was checking the right side of the hall. Two were checking the left – where Farrah had disappeared. Malone hoped anyone else on the other side of the door at least had enough self-preservation instinct to maintain a peaceful silence while the mob was outside.

Of course, someone could have pulled Farrah in just to slit her throat and check her pockets. No noise in that.

Malone was halfway to her feet before she realized she was moving.

And the fourth pursuer was headed straight toward her.

Malone forced herself to slide back down, below the window.

But the woman hadn't seen her – not yet. She was probing the other side of the barricade, searching for a way through. The carriage creaked and groaned.

Malone twisted her arm to the small of her back and drew her gun, slowly enough to feel the barrel scraping the stitches in the leather. She watched the tattered curtain. When the woman found her here, Malone could probably crush her windpipe before she called to her companions. As long as they weren't looking, she might have time to squeeze off a shot or two before they noticed her. And the noise from the main tunnel had gotten loud enough that perhaps no one else would notice.

It was a good lie.

The other three were still moving down the hall, their pounding muffled through the blanket of noise. The nearby woman's exploratory thumps and curses were getting closer. Malone braced herself.

She could feel the sudden stillness as the woman stopped what she was doing. And then –

"Ha, wounded! Got you now."

The blood. The other woman knew she was here.

"Hey, stop! Stop!" A man's voice, coming from further down the corridor. Near Farrah's door.

Malone sprang to the window just in time to see the woman sprinting away. And then she lost her in the flood of people rushing into the corridor.

She ducked again, the hairs on the back of her neck becoming needles. The screams and shouts had taken on a different pitch now. The people in the mob were fighting. Killing. Dying. And over what, they probably didn't even know.

The good news – if she could call it that – was that her pursuers had likely forgotten all about her and Farrah.

She made herself as comfortable as she could against the gutted cushions on the floor of the carriage and remembered the riot at the train station just before Sato's flight to the Library, when a starving, frustrated crowd had turned into a frenzied horde and killed a third of the inspectors awaiting the food shipment. The crowd had turned in a matter of moments – almost as quickly as the group in the tunnels outside had. It was as though Recoletta's people, like the city itself, were changing their substance, becoming malleable and reactive. She wondered just who they would be when the dust settled and what kind of city would have hardened around them.

Malone rested her arms on her knees and kept her revolver pointed at the door, though a part of her realized that if the time came to fire it, she'd do just as well to turn it on herself.

Having nothing to do but wait for that moment was the worst of it.

Malone tried to ignore the sounds of violence and the aches of her abused joints, tried to forget the roars of the food rioters and the screams of her fellow inspectors, and counted.

She'd reached seven hundred and forty-three when the last footsteps died away. The shouting had stopped around six hundred and eighty, so it stood to reason that the last of the mob had moved on. Still, she waited for an even nine hundred before she dared to move the curtain again.

Almost a dozen bodies lay in the corridor. There would be more in the tunnel beyond, but under the circumstances this wasn't as bad as she had thought. It had sounded much worse.

Thankfully, most people were bad at killing. They didn't really want to do it and weren't generally sure how. A few of the people on the ground were already stirring. Some would stumble away before help arrived and do their best to forget this.

This hadn't been a planned massacre so much as a clumsy and spontaneous upwelling of violence. That was better for the obvious reasons, but in another sense it was worse.

A door creaked open. Malone spun, gun raised, to see Farrah standing at the threshold and mirroring her own surprise.

Before Malone could say anything, Farrah rushed over and threw her arms around her neck.

"You look like horse shit," Farrah said into her collar. "Smell like it, too."

Malone felt her own body rigid with pain. And shock. "What happened?"

Farrah drew back and surveyed the small passage with professional detachment. "My guess? Someone feels left out of the reconstruction effort."

That wasn't what Malone had meant, but she could already see Farrah's mind working and knew better than to derail it.

"Though it appears things got out of hand," Farrah said, chewing her lip. "You've been talking with some of the dethroned bureaucrats."

More than she could count. It felt as though she'd done little else since her appointment, and every pompous whitenail and lowly clerk she dealt with was either offended by someone else's advantage or indignant about their own lack of one.

But this wasn't the work of just any disgruntled politico. This was someone who had power and knew how to mobilize it.

"Attrop," Malone said. The woman had spent a lifetime building and destroying dynasties. She'd been a whitenail under the old Council and infamous "Bricklayer" under Sato. And she'd made it clear the night they'd destroyed Sato that she expected a seat at the table.

Farrah balked. "If that's where we are, things are worse than I thought."

Malone remembered the sounds of chaos and violence. Attrop was a fool to think she could control that kind of juggernaut.

Or she was a fool not to have seen it coming.

Malone shook her head. "Much worse."

Farrah's wide eyes prompted her on.

"Attrop wanted a demonstration. Not a murder," Malone said, testing the idea out. "Definitely not a massacre."

Farrah's eyes widened further. "If she's not controlling them…"

"They did this on their own," Malone said, looking at the

bodies. Trying to focus on the ones that were moving.

Farrah cursed under her breath. "This is what I was talking about. We need to get at the source of her power."

"How? I don't even know where she—"

"Not like that," Farrah said, biting off each word and closing her eyes. "The battleground is politics. We don't need to flush her out, we just need to give people something bigger to stare at."

"Then let's get some more trains going."

Farrah laughed humorlessly, her eyes still closed. "Even if it were that easy, nothing stops Attrop from doing this again. We need something big, Malone. Something she can't interrupt and can't take credit for."

"Next week—"

"And we need it now." Farrah opened her eyes and turned them on Malone, daring her to offer up another useless idea.

Malone felt sick to her stomach before the idea even took shape in her mind. "I could move up Roman Arnault's trial." She'd barely stopped herself from saying "execution."

Farrah nodded and licked her lips. "That could work." Her skin was especially pale.

Malone stood there a moment, waiting for Farrah to give her a reason not to. She knew she wouldn't. They both knew anything was better than the mess around them.

"I'll set trial for the day after tomorrow," Malone said. "Can you get everything mobilized before then?"

Farrah looked offended.

Malone threw up her hands. "Fine. Just tell me what to do."

"You'll need to make an announcement." Farrah looked her up and down, taking in her ripped and bloodstained ensemble. "Good thing Jalbani has your measurements."

Malone glanced down, feeling something squish under her boots.

Horse shit.

CHAPTER EIGHT
TRADING WORDS

"Culpa," the interrogator said. "So I say from the commenso."

The guilt was there, all right, gathering like a gallstone in Jane's gut, even edging out the nausea. But not for the reasons the interrogator thought.

"No space aki for perturbers and rowdies. Need discipline. Orden. O we cast 'em out."

"Just calm down," Jane said. "You wanted to know how I got here, and I'm telling you everything." Or as much as she dared. Everything but the vault and Roman's full name.

The motion outside picked up, tossing the little room about. A few sharp jolts almost knocked Jane from her crate.

The interrogator raised his eyebrows. "What I hear ess you make problems. Maybe we cast you out now. Prevent more problems."

"Let me finish," Jane said, steeling her voice with a confidence she didn't quite feel. She wanted to brush the stray hairs from her face, but she didn't dare let the interrogator see how clammy her palms were, or how badly her hands might shake. "That was a mistake. But it's not even what I got into trouble for."

"So what ess?"

"Telling the truth."

•••

"You told me we would stir up trouble. You didn't tell me anyone would get killed," Jane had said to Madame Attrop the day after the ordeal at Maxwell Street Station.

"My dear, you didn't ask."

They had returned to Ruthers's mansion. Jane stood with her back to a smoldering fire. They'd retreated as soon as the crowd had chased Malone out of the station, and now Attrop sat in an overstuffed armchair in a parlor that seemed absurdly large for her little band of spies and schemers. The lantern-jawed man – Dalton – paced the door as if he were waiting for someone to come down the stairs after them. Hoping for it.

Jane shook her head to clear the first furious response that flashed into her mind. "The point was to outdo Malone. Not to–"

"No, the point is to unseat Malone, the Qadi, and their bogus government by any means possible." The high back of the chair scooped the old woman up, and the arms rose around her like cresting waves. She looked thin-boned and fragile in it. She fluttered a hand. "Though, if it makes you feel any better, Malone and most of the fools who chased after her walked away in one piece."

"How comforting."

Attrop cocked her head, a wry smile painted on her lips. "I wonder, are you angry that our gambit turned to violence? Or just that people were chanting your name when it happened?"

"That's not fair," Jane said. Yet something burned in her chest. She pushed Ruthers out of her mind in a way that had almost become routine. "Especially when you didn't do the talking."

"Oh, but if I had your clout, I would have. You're the woman who ended a dynasty with a single shot. That's power, Jane." Attrop's eyes shone.

The burning sensation dropped from her chest into her stomach. She opened her mouth, half-expecting to wretch. "It's not," she said instead.

"I beg your pardon?"

Jane took a steadying breath. "That's desperation." It felt good to admit it.

Attrop flinched. Jane felt the gesture like a tug on the thread of a spider's web.

"You're stirring up a mob you can't control." And she herself had been desperate enough to go along with Attrop. She felt guilty and foolish all at once.

The old woman scowled over her clasped hands. "Be careful, Jane. There's still plenty I do control."

By the door, Dalton had stopped his pacing and was watching her with his arms folded.

"If people want blood, they'll have it," Attrop said. "But we can choose whose they spill."

Before Jane could argue further, footsteps clattered down the stairs and along the hall at a swift jog. She waited, listening to the echoing steps for what felt like a long time. The emptiness of this big, lonely house rekindled the ache in her chest.

Dalton craned his head into the hall and nodded back at Attrop, all professional solemnity.

A young woman dashed into the parlor, panting but trying to cover it. She blinked between Jane and Attrop.

Attrop sighed. "If you're going to let your mouth hang open, you might as well form words with it."

"Sorry, madam," the messenger said. "I've just come with news from Dominari Hall. Roman Arnault's trial has been moved up to tomorrow."

Jane wasn't certain if the room went quiet or if that was just the rushing in her ears. She put a hand on the mantel to steady herself.

She looked up at Attrop when she was certain the room wouldn't spin out from under her.

"I'm sorry, Jane," she said. She almost sounded like she meant it. "I could organize another demonstration."

"It wouldn't be enough," Jane said. And if it was anything like the last one, it would be too much.

Attrop nodded. "As I told you, this is a war of distractions."

Something withered inside Jane, just as it had when Attrop

had caught her here in the midst of another fruitless errand. But this time was worse, because more than her feeble hopes had died.

And if she was honest with herself, perhaps that was the worst part of all of it. That everything she'd done for most of the past year had only made matters worse. Cooperating with Malone had painted a target on her back. Sparing Ruthers had set the snare for her and Roman. Killing Ruthers had trapped them again, but in different ways.

Her last card was the truth about the vault code, but she realized that she was even further from playing it now. Beyond Roman's own fears about the vault – and about being used to open it – there wasn't a person in Recoletta she would trust with it. If the two revolutions had proven one thing, it was that the people who seized power were the last ones who should have it. Perhaps that was what she had come to admire about Roman – he had the sense to fear the power other people craved. As for the others – Ruthers, Sato, Lachesse, Malone, Attrop, the Qadi – they were all the same. Same bad news, just sung to a different tune.

Something about the idea stuck in places she didn't expect. When she realized what it was, she laughed out loud.

"Miss Lin, I do hate to be the last one in on a good joke," Attrop said.

There was still one last thing she could do. And even if it didn't make matters any better, it certainly couldn't make them any worse. Not any worse than they deserved to be, anyway.

"Enough, Jane. What's so funny?" Attrop asked. Seeing the old woman at a loss spread a kind of trickling warmth through Jane's blood.

"I need a drink," she said, ignoring Attrop and shoving past Dalton at the door. She kept moving, up the hall and up the stairs, pushing forward before anyone could think to stop her and before she could second-guess herself. It felt good to have a plan.

•••

Jane found Burgevich sitting alone at one of the back tables at Petrosian's bar, almost as if he'd been waiting for her. He looked up as she crossed the room, and it was impossible to tell if his expression was surprise or just an effect of the shivering candlelight.

"I'm glad to see you so soon," he said, as she slid onto the tall chair opposite him.

"It's been an eventful couple of days," Jane said.

"So I've heard." Burgevich leaned forward, his expression hungry. "I've been hoping you could tell me more."

A growling rumble sounded from behind her. Jane glanced over her shoulder to see Petrosian standing behind the bar, two glasses on the countertop. He plunked a bottle down next to them.

"I believe I bought last time," Burgevich said.

"What I've got for you will more than make up for it."

The shadows around Burgevich's smile deepened. "I'll hold you to that, Miss Lin."

He rose to fetch their drinks, and Jane screwed up her courage. What she was about to do felt right. It felt like what she'd wanted to do from the beginning. She just hadn't understood how powerful the truth might be, and even if she had, she wouldn't have been ready for the consequences.

But if Recoletta was doomed to be stuck between corrupt bureaucrats and power-mad demagogues, then perhaps she was doing everyone a favor.

Burgevich set a clouded glass in front of her. She took a drink to seal her resolve.

Across from her, Burgevich swirled and turned his glass. "You were saying?"

Jane let the whiskey sear her throat. This was right. She tried not to let herself consider that she was out of options – and nearly out of time – anyway.

"I'm going to tell you what nobody in Dominari Hall wants you to know. But you've got to promise me something," she said.

He raised his eyebrows.

"You've got to promise me that you will run this story first thing in the morning."

"Why?" But he was already spreading his notebook on the table, licking his thumb to flip to a blank page.

"Does it matter?" Jane asked. "Do it, and by this time tomorrow, no one will be talking about anything else."

He considered this, rolling his first sip of whiskey around in his mouth before he nodded. "Let's hear it."

Jane told him everything. From her escape to Madina to the conspiracy between the Qadi, Chancellor O'Brien, and Father Isse to conquer Recoletta. She explained that Sato had never intended to spare Ruthers, much less work with him. On the contrary, Ruthers had been working with the Qadi to reconquer Recoletta the whole time. It was only her assassination of Ruthers that had changed the story and Arnault's leak that had foiled the initial invasion.

Their new leaders – Malone, the Qadi, and Lachesse – weren't saviors so much as the last people standing.

It was an ugly truth, but it felt good to tell it. Even if she wasn't entirely sure whether she was cleaning the blood off her hands or just adding more to them.

As Jane told her story, Burgevich's pen never left his notebook. When she'd finished, he gave her a few beats of silence before speaking.

"Even if people do believe this, it'll drive them to riot," he said.

"They'll believe it because Malone and the others have been feeding them nonsense," Jane said. "And if they're going to get drawn into a riot, they might as well see who's holding their strings."

Burgevich closed his notebook. "I wish you could have given this story to Fredrick."

His name was still a painful reminder of all she'd failed to do, and she wasn't sure any amount of truth-telling would ever change that. Jane forced her wince into a smile. "Me too."

"Of course, he would have been too hungover to meet your deadline." Burgevich tossed back the rest of his whiskey. "I should go if I'm going to have this ready for tomorrow morning. And you should get to a good hiding place. Or some powerful friends."

"Know where I can find some?" It was almost a shame she'd burned those bridges.

He laughed as he shrugged into his coat. "If I did, I sure wouldn't be here. Good luck, Jane Lin."

He drifted into the shadows, and Jane returned to her whiskey glass. It was nearly empty. She had just begun to wonder how it had gotten that way when another slid in front of her. She looked up at Petrosian, who nodded at the door.

Burgevich gave her a quick salute as he slipped out.

"The lady runs a hard bargain," Petrosian said, refilling her glass.

"Not nearly hard enough." She glared at Petrosian, thinking about the useless information he had sent her to Ruthers's to find, and the cabal she'd discovered in its place.

His eyebrows rose in mock surprise. "I should hate to leave a customer dissatisfied. After all, I live and die by my reputation."

"Oh? And what did you leave me with?" She was angry she'd told him about the vault code, and all the more because she should have known better than to trust him. But she hadn't seen another option.

Petrosian tsked and topped off her glass. "Exactly what I promised – a means to distract Malone from Roman Arnault. The execution timetable aside, she's very much focused on you now."

Sudden realization hit her. "You knew I'd find Attrop there."

"Suspected." He squinted and pursed his lips as if tasting the word.

"You wanted me to find her." She was still angry at herself, but also a little impressed at him. "But you told me you don't meddle."

"No, but I very much wanted to know what our former crime boss was up to. She's kept uncommonly close counsel of late, so finding someone she might talk to has been... challenging."

"You might have told me," Jane said.

"That would have cost extra." Petrosian lowered his voice and angled his gaze down at her. "And as I recall, you held something back as well."

The code, of course.

He corked the bottle. "And if Mr Burgevich dances to your tune, then you'll get what you want anyway, won't you?"

Jane felt some warm coal of frustration smoldering within. "This isn't how I wanted to do things."

He chuckled again. "Miss Lin, if we could all accomplish the goals we desire through the means we prefer, we'd see more wealthy painters."

She looked at the level in her glass. The memory of her hangover was fresh enough to bring bile to her throat. "No more."

"You'll need a clear head, won't you?" He nodded. "You've got to run."

"Do you know—"

"I know you've been talking to Burgevich for an hour straight, and he barely touched his whiskey until just now. You either gave him a story or a scare, and if he bought you a round of my best, I can guess which."

Jane considered the fresh glass in front of her.

Petrosian shrugged. "If you're going to run for your life, you might as well enjoy it first."

But where and how? "Then maybe you can point me to a good hiding place. After all, you owe me," she said, keenly aware that she had little reason to trust him. Still, it would be nice not to feel wholly responsible for every bad idea floating in her head just now.

"I'll give you something better," Petrosian said, placing a revolver onto the table.

Ice shot through Jane's veins. She glanced around, but no one else seemed to notice.

"You're on the verge of making a lot of enemies. So get yourself someplace where you'll be uncomfortable enough to remember that, while you wait to see whether your scheme works out. Then, get ready to run."

Jane sipped her whiskey, just to give herself something to do. It was as flavorless as water.

Petrosian shrugged. "It's your decision. But at least take this. You've become one of my best customers. I'd hate to lose you."

He was gone before Jane could see whether he was smiling or sneering.

Only her whiskey glass and the revolver remained on the table.

She didn't want to take it. She hadn't held one since shooting Ruthers. The cold metal barrel, the grip as rough as a factory man's language, raised gooseflesh on her arms.

But she eyed the cartridges nestled in the chamber and slid the gun into her pocket. She'd never known how to refuse a courtesy.

CHAPTER NINE
STRANGE MERCIES

Geist leaned forward and sipped his caffee. Phelan had just returned with a fresh pitcher.

Malone had barely touched hers, but after so much talking, her already-abused throat was dry and raw. She gulped her caffee and immediately regretted it.

Geist seemed to misread her expression. His scar twisted in sympathy. "Dreckt. This waschergirl made boocoo difficulties."

Jane Lin had certainly done that. Malone wondered if any of them might have been avoided if she'd been able to talk to her.

Of course, first she would have had to catch her.

"She made another difficulty," Malone said, watching Phelan refill her cup. "Very boocoo."

Geist nodded appreciatively. "Und then you were travailing to assassinate Roman, ya?"

Phelan gasped as the pitcher slipped from her hand, spilling the muddy brown liquid all over the table.

Geist snarled something incomprehensible at her.

"Pardon, pardon!" Phelan said, cringing as she bent over the mess.

Malone sneezed against the woman's musky, bittersweet aroma.

"Continue the history, please," Geist said, winding his hand at Malone.

"Like I was saying, things only got worse from there."

•••

Malone hadn't imbibed since her visit to the farming communes, but her skull throbbed with each step. Come to think of it, she'd barely had anything to eat or drink in the last twenty-four hours, which was likely part of the problem.

She'd also overslept again. But between the disaster at Maxwell Street Station, the liberal pawing she'd suffered from the physician (at Farrah's insistence), her announcement of Arnault's accelerated trial, and the subsequent deluge of petitioners, she'd endured more than enough to earn a decent night's rest.

Not that anyone else – least of all Farrah – was likely to see it that way when she finally made it to Dominari Hall.

And the transit station mob, as it happened, had only been the beginning. By the time Malone had gone home last night, Dominari Hall had been surrounded above- and below ground by chanting protesters demanding everything from her resignation, to trials for all whitenails, to Jane Lin's appointment on the new Council.

It was that last part that gave her pause.

Whatever disruption Attrop, the former Bricklayer, had planned, elevating a common laundress like Jane to the whitenail enclave of the Council couldn't have been part of it. And given the cold terror on Jane's face at the train station, Malone didn't think she was crazy or foolish enough to want that position.

Which meant that the agitated masses had come up with this on their own.

Malone was so lost in her thoughts that she reached the plaza in front of Dominari Hall before she realized how oddly quiet it was. After yesterday's uproar, the plaza and surrounding tunnels should have been chaos.

Instead, a contingent of guards blocked the entrance. The sight of their scuffed boots and poorly-sized uniforms, all forming a crooked line, wedged a bolus of dread into Malone's stomach.

She approached the man with the largest and shiniest pins on his jacket. He was standing just off from the others, eyeing them while they watched the deathly still plaza.

"What's going on here?" she asked.

His shoulders straightened. "Not a thing, Governor. All quiet since the shift started this morning."

"That seem odd to you?" The words came out sharper than Malone intended but just as sharply as she really meant them. She much preferred being chief of police.

The guard gave her a dead-eyed look and waited just long enough for his disdain to register. "Not after the midnight shift's demonstration."

A thunderclap pealed in her skull. "The what?"

"Fired a few warning shots to clear the mob. No one was hurt, Governor."

As if that somehow made it all reasonable. Malone hadn't realized how accustomed people had become to life under Sato and all of the fickle brutality that came with it. She'd always thought Recolettans would pick up the old standards and routines like the refrain in a familiar song.

"What idiot ordered these 'warning shots'?" Malone asked.

He blinked back at her. Were all of the guards this bad?

"Lady Lachesse, Governor."

That explained a few things. None of them good.

"Next man or woman who discharges a weapon better be under immediate threat, or I'll show them a demonstration. If your people can't handle a few mouthy protesters, I'll find someone who can." Though where, she had no idea. This was already the bottom of the barrel.

"Governor–"

"Anyone tells you differently, you send them to me."

Surly compliance ossified in his jaw. "Understood, ma'am."

Malone left him in the plaza and continued into Dominari Hall, letting the adrenaline carry her to the real challenge.

Farrah would have advised her to summon Lachesse to her office and to cool down in the meantime. But the old whitenail would find an excuse to put her off, and she didn't want to wait.

She marched down the main hall, wide and pristine while many of Recoletta's tunnels were still vandalized or clogged with debris. Her feet sank into the thick carpet. It felt like stomping through mud.

When she reached the door to Lady Lachesse's office, the page standing vigil stepped aside and blanched.

Malone opened the door without knocking.

Lachesse glanced up sharply, and Malone savored her expression as it melted from indignation into quiet forbearance. She was seated behind her desk, one hand raised in gesture and the other in her lap, speaking to a man sitting across from her. Malone couldn't recall his name, but she was certain he'd been a clerk of some kind under the old Council. The two of them sat still, watching Malone as if she were a shape in the shadows that would disappear if they searched long and hard enough.

"You have time," Malone said. It wasn't a question, and she didn't phrase it like one.

Lachesse nodded to the man. "I'll send for you." As if she didn't expect this to take long.

Malone waited until he'd left and shut the door behind him before taking his seat and pulling it to the edge of Lachesse's desk. "We need to discuss a few things," she said.

"At your pleasure, Governor." Lachesse's face was carefully neutral.

"You've been ordering the guards around."

Lachesse's eyebrows arched. "Yes, well, something had to be done about the protesters. And you seemed preoccupied elsewhere."

"Any use of force comes at my discretion alone. Do you understand?"

Lachesse assumed a mask of innocuous surprise. "Of course, Interim Governor." She sharpened the word "interim" into a threat. "I would note, however, that it is not wise to let enemies gather on your doorstep."

"Better on my doorstep where I can see them than in the shadows where I can't." As if Malone didn't know she was surrounded.

Lachesse smiled. "You know best." She looked away from

Malone and tidied her desk with hands crowned by impossibly long, perfect nails.

Watching her, Malone wondered again if she hadn't been appointed merely to dirty her hands on Lachesse's behalf.

The whitenail tapped her desk in an admirable impression of someone just remembering something. "Since you've raised the regrettable situation with the protesters, I suppose we ought to discuss how you mean to handle Jane Lin."

If Lachesse was raising the issue, it was only because she'd already decided how to handle it. "I've got enough to arrest her now."

"It's a bit late for that," Lachesse said, tilting her head forward.

Hairs rose along the back of Malone's neck. "Meaning?" Of course, she knew what Lachesse meant. But she didn't like leaving important details to suggestion. Perhaps that was still the detective in her.

"Goodness, but I didn't realize you were such a squeamish little thing." Lachesse snapped her fingers and their long nails like a paper fan.

"You chose me for this job because you wanted someone to restore Recoletta to order," Malone said.

"First, I need you to keep it from falling apart."

Malone shook her head. At least Sato had spent a few months organizing parades and making nice speeches before he'd reached this point.

"The problem runs deeper than Jane Lin and Roman Arnault. Killing them won't fix it," Malone said.

"For a detective, you have remarkably little imagination. Executing Arnault lets people crush the last of the old regime. Executing Jane squashes their ambitions for a new one."

Malone felt herself maneuvering around Lachesse, but she wasn't even sure what game they were playing any more.

"You're talking about symbols when people are talking about food, shelter and safety," Malone said. "Getting rid of Lin and Arnault won't change those things."

Lachesse laughed and pointed one sharpened nail at her. "Changing appearances changes everything, Malone. The people of Recoletta are not unhappy because they live in small homes, but because they used to live in larger ones. Or because they did not, but the people across town did. Your job has always been to give them something more substantial to focus on while the rest of us remake the city. Do you understand?"

"And here I thought you appointed me for my good looks," Malone said.

Lachesse clasped her hands and spoke slowly. "I appointed you to give you permission to do what needed to be done. To pacify Recoletta with all available speed and force. I've read your reports from the Municipal Police. You've never lacked the will to make hard choices. You just need a reason."

Malone waited for outrage and disbelief, but they never came. All she felt instead was a sudden, startling clarity.

"You're right," she said. "I'll get rid of Lin and Arnault."

Lady Lachesse smiled like a woman used to obedience. "I'm so glad we see eye to eye."

The tunnels to the Barracks had been cleared. Which was convenient for Malone's purposes, but an ill portent for the city.

The Barracks had been the headquarters of Recoletta's city guard and a jail since the time of the old Council. It was a maze of tight, twisting corridors with no symmetry and no apparent order. It was the kind of place that seemed to change around a person, though maybe that was just the disordered, early-era design. It was rumored to have been one of the first places built by Recoletta's pre-Catastrophe founders and, like most of those places, it felt like a tomb.

The passage opened into a tall, wide cavern. Even from the outside, the Barracks was an imposition on the eyes. It rose the height of the cavern like the cocoon of some burrowing worm, tumored with lumpy towers and ramparts. The builders had been careful to leave a wide cavern around the Barracks to give its guards a clear line of sight and to prevent anyone from tunneling into it through a wall.

The windows and doors that pocked it looked ready to swallow her whole. Malone wiped the sweat from her palms and reminded herself that she had every authority to be here.

Of course, it was getting out again that worried her.

At her approach, the guards stationed at the front nodded and opened the doors.

A serious young man stood in the lobby. The stone walls were bare and rough – the builders hadn't even bothered to file down proper corners. Even the writing table in front of him was little more than a thick stalagmite with the top sanded flat. The logbook perched atop it appeared to be growing into the stone.

The young man glanced up. He had the anxious, queasy expression of a student hoping the teacher wouldn't call on him.

"I'm here for Roman Arnault," Malone said.

The young man swallowed. The lump in his throat looked painfully swollen against his thin neck and shoulders. Either he was younger than he seemed, or even the guards were on rations. "He's in the isolation wing – cell row D. Take the first corridor on the left. No, right. Then, go up one... two levels. There's another lobby with a bunch of passages. Take the second on your left, and follow it around the first curve. One more flight of stairs and you're at the prison cells."

"Right," Malone said.

"If you get lost, just keep making your way down. You'll find the way out eventually." He said it as if getting lost were an inevitability.

Malone took it as a challenge. "I'll keep that in mind."

She headed off. Already, her brain was mapping the place out like hostile territory, flagging potential escape routes and dead ends. It felt good to occupy herself with something, if only to distract from the notion that she was burrowing deeper and deeper into an anthill.

Heavy footfalls and murmuring voices carried from the

corridors around her. The cadence of patrols and office chatter. The twisting, looping corridors, the places where the walls between them thickened and thinned, all made it hard to tell where the sounds came from.

Malone fought the urge to glance over her shoulder. Nothing would have been guiltier.

She reached the branching passages the young man had described. One led off toward a quiet burr of distant voices and rustling papers. Offices, perhaps. Another split into a series of storage rooms. Two more curved and twisted far enough ahead that she wasn't sure where they led.

The last should lead toward the prison area. Malone followed it and continued up the stairs to a short hallway with a row of cells.

The guard behind the desk at the head of the row saluted her. His accent was unusual but not uncommon – like many of the soldiers and clerks these days, he had the vague sound of coming from "somewhere else." And like a lot of those people, he sounded like he was trying to cover it. Badly. Which meant he was probably one of Sato's. Malone had a grudging admiration for those people, wading into a quagmire and sticking it out.

"Here to see the prisoner, ma'am?"

As if there was only one. Yet the hall was silent. And as much as Arnault knew, Lachesse and her ilk would want to keep him alone.

She nodded.

But for the creak and squeak of the guard's boots, everything was quiet. Malone began to worry that they'd beaten or starved the strength out of Arnault. That would make things considerably more difficult.

The cell row was different from what she remembered. It was only five cells long, and the rooms she glimpsed through the bars looked smaller than the one she'd sat in – ideal for detaining a handful of prisoners who needed to be kept apart. But memory worked its own illusions on architecture and besides, it was possible she'd been on a different floor and in a different area completely. In fact, that seemed more and more likely as she let the details around her sink in.

A pity, because she still remembered the exit from the other cell row.

The guard banged on the second to last door. "Governor Malone to see you." He retreated back to his desk.

The laugh on the other side of the door resonated with droll scorn. At least she knew that much of the man was intact.

Which was good, because she might not have recognized him otherwise.

Arnault's perpetually ill-fitting jacket hung loose. He'd always been a large man, but he looked thin – even gaunt. Had they starved him so badly in the last few days? Or had the final weeks of Sato's rule diminished him, too, so slowly that she hadn't noticed until now?

He sauntered over to the door and gripped the barred window. Only then did she see the patchwork of bruises and welts covering his face.

His sharp blue eyes and mirthless smile were the only familiar parts.

"You've done well for yourself," he said. His voice was a dry croak.

Malone glanced at the guard. He was waiting by his desk, barely twenty feet away. "I need to speak with Mr Arnault in private," Malone told him.

He shifted nervously. "The prisoner is not to be left alone."

"He won't be as long as I'm here." Malone fixed him with the cool glare that had brought junior inspectors to tears and sent senior bureaucrats into apoplectic fits.

But he held his ground. "My orders were to remain," he said, the slightest quaver in his voice.

Arnault said nothing, but Malone glimpsed his smile of amusement out of the corner of her eye.

The sense of powerlessness before the indomitable bureaucracy of the Barracks was all too familiar to Malone as an inspector. But she remembered then that she wasn't an inspector, she was a governor. And if she was going to be stuck with that position, she might as well make use of its advantages.

"Your accent," she said. "You came to Recoletta with Sato."

The guard's audible swallow was answer enough.

"Curious that you are so reluctant to leave the traitor's side," she said. It was brittle logic that could have just as easily been turned on her, but she had the benefit of rank and a Recolettan pedigree.

And the hapless guard recognized that much. "Madame Governor, that's not–"

"Then perhaps your sergeant will explain to me what it is. Because there will be plenty of room on the gallows for any of Arnault's conspirators."

The guard looked at his feet. "I'll leave you to question the traitor, Madame Governor." He gave her a hurried bow. Malone watched him scurry down the stairs with a mixture of remorse and relief.

"You always did have a way with the defenseless," Arnault said over her shoulder.

"We don't have much time," she said, turning back to him.

"Yes, and I have you to thank for that." He was watching her with the derisive amusement she knew too well.

Malone bristled despite herself. "And Jane Lin. Ask her about it when you see her."

The sneer fell from Arnault's face. "She was supposed to go free. That was the deal. If you–"

Malone held up a hand. "Whatever deal you're talking about, you need to explain it. Right now."

He licked his lips. Weighing the risk of talking with the risk of staying silent. "Lachesse and the Qadi wanted information. You're allies now, right?" He was watching her for a reaction.

"If I knew what you were talking about, I wouldn't be here," Malone said.

"The vault." He waited, still watching her.

But she was tired of games and deceptions, and besides, they didn't have time. "I came here to release you, Arnault. Don't make me change my mind."

He blinked away surprise. It was hard to say if he believed her, especially beneath the injuries distorting his face. Malone guessed not, but she also guessed he had little left to lose.

Arnault leaned in, his voice low. "There's an old place, built before the Catastrophe. Very far from here, and very dangerous."

"So what do they want with it?"

"They think it holds an ancient weapon."

"But you don't," Malone said. Holding Arnault to a straightforward answer was like carrying a handful of oil – he always slipped through your fingers before you could get anywhere useful.

He shrugged and shook his head at the ceiling. "It doesn't matter what I think. The whitenails believe it will protect them from another Sato. So they'll have it, or they'll see that no one does."

It all sounded fantastical, and Malone preferred concrete facts and realities to speculation and symbolism. There wasn't time to straighten the latter into the former, but whatever the vault was, she didn't trust it in the hands of Lachesse and her people.

"So how do we make sure none of them get it?" she asked.

Arnault's smug grin looked painful on his split lips. "They won't."

Malone waited.

"They can't open it without me," he said. He glanced away, fidgeting. At first, Malone thought he was lying, but no, he was squirming. "They'd also need a code that only Sato and Ruthers had, and they're both dead." He met Malone's gaze again and smirked. "So you might as well finish what you came to do." He nodded at her hip.

At her gun.

She should have been insulted, but Roman was a man of few compunctions. She could hardly expect him to see them in someone else.

Malone retreated to the guard's desk, where the keys were hung. She took them and unlocked his cell.

He stood in the open door, slack surprise on his face. He was even thinner than she'd realized.

Arnault stared back in bewilderment. "What are you–"

"We need to hurry," she said.

He swallowed, making a dry, clicking sound in his throat. "Governor or no, they're not going to let you walk me out of here."

"If I can sneak four dissenters through a mob, one shouldn't be a problem."

Arnault didn't seem convinced, but it didn't really matter. All he had to do was move. "That was all Farrah," he said as he passed her. He stretched his arms and rolled his broad shoulders as he scanned the hall. It looked like the guards had locked him up in his own clothes. It smelled like that, too. At least he still had his shoes.

"Stay five feet behind me," Malone said, moving toward the corridor that had brought her here. The same one the guard had taken.

Arnault laid a hand on her shoulder as she passed. She resisted the urge to shrug it off.

"I need a gun," he said.

"We're not shooting our way out of here."

"We might need–"

"If it gets to that point, we're already done." She pushed on, and he didn't argue further.

She heard voices up ahead, their sharp, angry syllables ricocheting down the hall. They passed the final bend to the hall where the tunnels met. Malone held up her hand and strode ahead to scout it.

Two men stood in profile, arguing. No, one was scolding and the other withering. The latter she recognized as the guard who'd been watching Roman.

The scolding man loomed over him. "– orders, and that

certainly does not include a filthy Municipal."

It was a relief to see that she wasn't the only one keeping the old grudges alive.

All of this was lost on the hapless guardsman, however. "Sir, she's the gov–"

"I don't care if she's standing arm in arm with a resurrected Sato and Ruthers. You stand guard until one of your commanding officers relieves you."

"Yes, sir."

"Follow me, Constable. I'll show you how this is done."

They were coming her way. Better to meet them here and stall for time. She only hoped Arnault didn't do anything foolish.

Malone stepped out of the hall and into the lobby. The surprise on the commanding officer's face was worth whatever was about to happen.

"Is there a problem, officers?" she asked.

The senior officer – a lieutenant, by the insignias on his jacket – struggled admirably to recover his bluster. "Madam – Governor – my colleague tells me that you ordered him away from his post."

She mustered an expression of affront. "I did no such thing. I merely ordered him to give me a moment of privacy with the prisoner."

The lieutenant flushed. "Governor, I–"

Malone renewed the attack. "Arnault's trial has been advanced to tomorrow, so I don't have time to deal with your ineptitude. If you can't keep your watch under control, I'll speak with General Covas about finding someone who can."

Of course, Covas had probably not yet forgiven her for her surprise visit the night of Sato's assassination, but this lieutenant had no way of knowing that. His face darkened with embarrassment.

"That won't be necessary, Governor."

"Good. Then check in with the watch officer about increasing patrols in the Vineyard. I want them on the streets before another mob forms."

The lieutenant opened his mouth in protest and snapped it shut just as quickly. "Yes, ma'am," he finally said.

With that, he sulked off toward the offices, and the first guard turned back toward the cells. Toward Arnault.

"You there," Malone said. She didn't know what to say to him, but she needed to keep him away from the hall.

The guard stopped and regarded her. She folded her arms and took a deep breath to stall for time.

"Tell me about the staffing here," she said. "I want to know which of our exits are the most vulnerable."

He frowned.

That had come out sounding more suspicious than she'd hoped.

"The next few days will be delicate," Malone added. "If Arnault or his allies mean to try something, it will happen during the trial."

The guard gave her a serious nod. "There's no need to worry. General Covas has personally approved the shifts guarding the prisoner, and we'll be doubling up starting tonight." His back was to Arnault's hall now. Another corridor corkscrewed away over the guard's other shoulder, at ten o'clock to Arnault's hall. If she could just distract the guard long enough, perhaps Arnault could make it.

Malone cleared her throat. "From where I'm standing, that all looks good." She spoke loudly and hoped Arnault was listening.

But if he did, he didn't show. Meanwhile, the guard waited, tugging at one too-short sleeve.

Nothing to do but try again. "Listen," Malone said, her voice still raised, "you could get around the problem."

The guard blinked. "Ma'am?"

"Just thinking aloud," she said, watching for Arnault from the corner of her eye. What was keeping him? He was supposed to be good at sneaking and subterfuge.

"If you're done with the prisoner, I better get back to my post," the guard said. He started to turn.

"Not yet," Malone said, a little too fast. "He's losing his voice. I need some water before we continue." Anything to buy a little more time.

The young guard pressed his lips into a thin, angry line. "I'm sure one of the duty officers can help. But like you said, I shouldn't have left my post. Excuse me."

He headed down the hall before she could frame a reply. Not that he looked open to another excuse, anyway.

She tried to think of something as she watched his back recede.

And she was surprised to find her hand on the grip of her pistol.

She snatched it away. She couldn't.

So she followed him, hoping she'd think of something to say when they inevitably ran into Arnault.

But they didn't. Not as they rounded the bend, not as they returned to the row of cells, Arnault's still hanging open –

Someone grabbed Malone from behind. Her first instinct was to pull the attacker over her back and onto the floor, but she felt the cold steel of a gun barrel against her cheek.

And she felt the familiar weight absent from her side.

"Into the cell or I execute the governor," Arnault said.

The poor young guard was ashen and trembling. But he was backing down the row towards the open door.

"Put your gun on the floor. Slowly," Arnault said. The guard did, holding his pistol out like a dirty sock. He was too scared and too inexperienced to try anything else.

"Now kick it over to me," said Arnault.

The young man obeyed.

"That's it. Into the cell. Malone, lock him up."

Malone took the keys and locked the door, careful not to say anything and not to look at the young guard in any way that would give away the bluff.

Well, she hoped it was a bluff.

"Count down from one hundred," Arnault said, taking the

fallen gun and motioning toward the exit. "Quietly."

When they were out of earshot, he turned to her. "Told you I needed a gun."

They jogged back to the hall. It was too risky to go back the way she'd come in – the front entrance was too well-guarded – so Malone pointed down one of the mystery tunnels, watching for a way down.

It all reminded her of her last trip to the Barracks, when one of Arnault's associates had released her. She could only hope they were both headed toward a better outcome than last time.

The way was clear so far. Malone kept her pace brisk but natural. Maybe the alarm hadn't gone up yet.

"Which way?" Arnault asked. He looked – and smelled – even more of a wreck out of his cell, but hopefully that wouldn't be her problem much longer.

"Down," she said, remembering the lobby guard's instructions.

"I thought you had a plan."

She let her disgust rattle out of her throat. "It's still working out better than yours."

They came to a stairway at last. Muttering voices and the patter of footsteps carried through the tunnels, but the strange architecture of the Barracks made it difficult to tell where they were coming from. Malone led them down the stairs and to another branching hall. She instinctively turned left, which felt further from her original entrance and closer to another outer wall, but Arnault grabbed her arm and pulled her in the opposite direction.

"Guards. Listen," he said.

Sure enough, the echoing thuds and voices resolved into the sound of several troops moving their way. Malone and Arnault ducked down another corridor just in time.

She caught scattered bits of conversation from the group as they headed up the stairs.

"– from the detention cells."

"– thin along the east wall, so–"

"– cut him off above."

When the guards had disappeared up the stairs, Malone and Arnault darted back into the hall. She went right. He made a left.

This time, she grabbed his arm.

"They said east," he whispered.

Malone pointed off to the right. "East."

He thought about this, then shrugged and motioned for her to lead.

As they continued, Malone found herself oddly grateful for the Maxwell Street Station riots. After that ordeal, most of the guards were out on patrol rather than prowling around the Barracks.

By the time they reached a T-junction at a rough-hewn wall, Malone could feel freedom like warmth in the air.

She rapped the wall. "Solid. We're home free if we can get to the other side."

"And get past the patrols." Faint light glowed to their left. Arnault led the other way. They soon found a low passage burrowing through the wall and a door framed by slitted windows just a few inches wide.

"No guards?" he asked.

"One-way door," she said. The outer walls of the Barracks were designed to keep people out rather than in. Once they left this way, there'd be no getting back in. Which was just fine by Malone.

She pressed her nose to the slit windows but didn't see any movement outside. "Let's go."

They eased the door open and scanned the cavern. The outer walls rose a hundred feet away. Somewhere out there was a tunnel that would take them deep into the city. Safety felt so close, but the muted sounds of patrols reminded Malone that they weren't free yet.

"Behind us," Arnault whispered.

She leaned back into the hall and heard guards approaching. No time to hesitate. They slipped out the door together.

Malone tried to ease it shut, but it still closed with a loud clank. Arnault tensed, ready to run, but she shook her head and pressed herself against the door, just out of view of the slit windows. He grudgingly did likewise.

The marching footsteps came to a stop somewhere on the other side of the door.

"Did you hear that, sir?" asked a voice.

"Hear what?" said another.

"The door–" A faint shadow flickered across the slit of light on the ground. Malone wanted to press herself further into the door, but she didn't dare move. She held her breath as a single pair of footsteps drew closer.

"What is it?" asked another voice further back.

"I don't know, but I–"

"You're going to get us all in trouble if we're late. Let's go."

The footsteps retreated with a crunch of grit and swish of fabric. Malone didn't move until her thudding heart had quieted enough that she was sure of the silence.

Arnault's particolored face glistened with sweat. He slicked a damp lock of hair back from his forehead and nodded to Malone.

With the one-way door at their back, they had the protection of short walls to either side – just enough to protect a party leaving the Barracks as they assembled beyond the door. It gave them a chance to check the rest of the cavern in relative safety.

Arnault crept along the wall and peered around the edge.

"Two guards patrolling forty yards away, backs turned," he said. He pointed to a tunnel in the cavern wall that Malone had to lean out to see. "That takes us straight to the Bureau District." Which was empty enough to provide some hiding spots – the administrative district had been the first to go. "We run, we can make it," he said.

"Too risky."

"If they see us, they'll give chase."

"Especially if they see us running."

His sigh was a growl. "First alarm, I'm taking off."

"Just keep pace with me. We'll walk fast."

After a silent count of three, they stepped away from their hiding spot and marched toward the distant tunnel with brisk, regular strides. It couldn't have been more than a hundred and twenty yards away. Malone tried to focus on that steadily decreasing number and on the drumbeat-regular pace of her steps. Anything to keep from looking at the patrol to her left, Arnault to her right, or the battlements behind her.

She could feel Arnault resisting the same urge.

"As long as we don't make any sudden movements, we'll blend in," she said. More to convince herself than anything.

Arnault grunted.

By the time she brought her attention back to the exit, they were almost halfway to it. They'd been out of cover for twelve seconds. If someone was going to come after them, chances were they would have already done so.

Malone heard a shout come from somewhere behind her.

She didn't run. Not yet. Next to her, Arnault bucked like a skittish horse. Malone resisted the urge to place a restraining hand on his arm.

Another shout, quickly followed by a peal of laughter. Relief puddled in her veins. Arnault let out a whooping sigh.

Malone's hands shook with adrenaline as they slipped into the tunnel and away from the Barracks. The sluggish calm of relief and post-adrenaline exhaustion swallowed her along with the high, narrow tunnels of the Bureau District.

They found a quiet corner next to the abandoned Census Directorate. Most of the people who would have worked in the district were holed up in Dominari Hall, trying to rebuild their structures and organizations the same way soldiers and sweeps were clearing the tunnels. She'd always hated the bureaucracy here and the petty men and women who managed it, but now the thought of something so dependably predictable was a strange comfort.

Besides, it might fall to her to rebuild it in the coming weeks.

She could only hope the new Council formed sooner rather than later.

Arnault leaned against a tunnel wall that was polished to a flat shine. The whole district was wrought from a hard, angular kind of beauty that brought to mind a maze of mirrors.

"What now?" he asked, panting.

"Get Jane and go. Anywhere as long as it's far from Recoletta." She didn't expect she'd need to tell him twice.

But his eyes narrowed. "Why?"

"Because you two are trouble, and people won't be happy until there's blood."

"No, why are you helping me?"

They were wasting time. Malone didn't want to talk about this. She didn't know how. "Easier to sleep on than knowing I put a noose around your neck."

Arnault was quiet a long time. She wished he'd just go, before this got more awkward.

"I'm not the good guy, Malone." He sounded hoarse, and just as uncomfortable as she felt.

"You're a piece of shit," Malone said. "Doesn't make killing you like this right. Besides, Jane won't go without you."

She could almost feel the heat in Arnault's cheeks. "You thought about coming with us?" he asked. It wasn't exactly an invitation.

Malone laughed before she realized she'd opened her mouth. "I thought we'd had enough of each other."

"Being governor doesn't mean you're safe. It just means you'll get the blame when things go wrong."

She knew it. She just didn't want to think about it.

"The way I remember it, you pulled a gun on me back there. I just had to go along." If she kept saying it like that, maybe she could make it sound true. "Besides, someone has to put Recoletta back in order."

He looked pained. "Doesn't have to be you."

She only wished there were someone else she could trust with the job.

"Just get yourselves out of the city so I can rebuild it. Before someone else knocks it down."

Arnault grunted.

"I'm serious. Jane's trouble." Malone had meant to say "in trouble," but she didn't correct herself.

"You won't see us again," he said, and he stuck out his hand. She stared at it for a second, her confusion building, before she realized he was offering it.

She took it.

"Thank you," he said.

Geist sat back. "Und remarking present conditions, I am thinking the other politikers did not esteem your innocence in Arnault's evasion."

Malone shook her head. The young guard locked in the cell was probably the only person they'd fooled at all. Lachesse and the others had figured it out rather quickly, and from there it had just been a matter of waiting through the sham of a trial.

But that was all behind her. What concerned her now was how Geist had seemed to know much of her story already.

"Who else have you been talking to?" Malone asked.

Geist smiled. Phelan returned to clear the cups, and Malone smelled the familiar musk again. Amber and licorice.

Lachesse.

"Of alles your compatriots, she never flet. Valiant, no? Und I am thinking that if I comprend the same history from a woman in richesse and a woman on the gibbet, then it must be vert, ya?"

He was smirking – so like Arnault had – but everything else in the room was blurring and fading into a bruised, red-and-black haze. "Let me off this place," she said.

"This is being imprudent," Geist said.

Now that Malone recognized the musky perfume, she couldn't smell anything else. It felt like she was going to choke on it. "You'll have to throw one of us over."

Geist ran his fingers over his goatee and exhaled a long breath. "You are stark furious. I comprend this."

Phelan withdrew to the safety of the hall, her eyes cast down and her ears reddening.

"Wass do you regard here?" he asked, rising and smoothing one hand over the table. The overlong sleeve almost covered his fingers. "Here?" He touched the blond wood paneling behind him. "There?" He pointed out the window behind Malone.

"I've talked enough," she said.

"The Continent constructed this wunder, und we forty-three voyaged very far to retrieve Roman Arnault." He circled over to the window and looked down at Recoletta, his hands clasped behind his back. "What are you thinking mine compatriots will do if they apprend that you exiled him? Or esteem him dead?"

"There are other airships," Malone said. Her tongue tasted like a lump of ash, dry and bitter. She was too numb for horror, but it was only a matter of time.

Geist laughed. "Boocoo, yes. And boocoo persons to occupy them. You will not be finding them so indulgent." He turned away from the window and took a seat next to her, close enough that she could see the veins crackled across his eyes and smell the sour, bitter odor of the caffee on his breath. "You sacrificed to conserve your city. Recount where Roman went. Or do you resign alles now?"

Malone knew he was right, even if she didn't have the energy just now to piece all of the implications together.

"He found Jane, and she must have taken them someplace far from Recoletta." Which could be just about anywhere.

"Her direction?" Geist asked.

"I don't know where she would have gone."

"Perhaps no. But you comprend her, and you comprend him. Better than any others, I am thinking. So you will assist." He smiled with something he probably intended as reassurance. "But goot to do something, ya? Besides, you will encounter this a goot place for maladapts."

CHAPTER TEN
ON THE RUN AGAIN

The interrogator held his chin in his hand. Now his eyes were starting to look a little bloodshot. "So you tell your relato to the bellman, ee he tells it to the public. Then you escape. To pass aki."

Jane could only assume he was referring to Burgevich as the bellman, but at the moment it was beside the point. "Well, you seemed to know a thing or two about escaping," she said.

The interrogator stiffened. "Ess different."

"It always is," Jane said.

But he wasn't amused. His eyes burned, and his sun-beaten face withered into a frown. "Ess different. The Catastrophe was your castigo."

That was interesting. He was using almost the same word that Recolettans did for the mysterious disaster that brought civilization to a halt hundreds of years ago. She listened, trying not to let her surprise show.

"Ess the problem – your public can't layer. So many livros left to decay. They conosse nothing."

Jane wasn't entirely sure what he meant, but she'd worked for enough temperamental whitenails to know not to interrupt, question, or argue. She kept quiet and listened.

He kept talking. He was on a tear now.

"Your terrens ee the Continent ulcered of corruption. It consumed you. This ess your castigo." He jabbed a finger at her.

"We did not escape. We passed here to be liber of your corruption. Aki where the salt preserves us."

Jane could only hope. Her skin still stung from where she'd been bathed and scrubbed down with the stuff.

"Aki we guard ee maintain pure until the salt cleanses the sujeira from both terrens."

Jane waited until she was sure he had finished. She didn't completely understand his story, but it was something she could work with.

"Then I suppose I'm lucky I found you," she said. "Because after I spoke about all the corruption I saw, I couldn't stay."

The trick was to tell him the rest without mentioning the vault.

Jane had left Petrosian's after midnight with only a gun and the grim satisfaction of having set her vengeance in motion. Returning to Roman's had been a reflex as much as anything.

The last thing she'd expected was to find him there, surprise on his bruised and battered face.

"Roman!" she said, her heart pounding. "What...? How did you–?"

He drew her close and planted a kiss on her forehead. Not the kind of greeting she'd hoped for, but one look at his face told her there were other things on his mind.

"We have to leave," he said.

Jane looked past him and saw two traveling bags already stuffed with supplies. "What exactly is going on?"

"Malone broke me out," he said, turning from her to stuff some bundled shirts into his bag. "But they'll be looking for both of us." He glanced back at her long enough to give her a mischievous smile that turned her insides to warm molasses. "I hear you've been making trouble."

"Nothing you wouldn't do," Jane said. "But what's this about Malone? I thought she was rushing your execution."

"Whatever she did before, she risked herself to get me out

now." He fastened one of the bags and dropped it at her feet. "And you, Jane. I don't know what you did, but it put you on the chopping block."

Cold dread replaced the warmth in her belly. She wished she could take back her interview with Burgevich. But even if it wasn't already going to print, he didn't seem like the type to let a good story go.

Roman fastened the other bag. "She's not a monster, just a bureaucrat. And a reluctant one." His face tensed with some private pain – Jane supposed he was thinking about his own role in the last couple of governments. "But once we're out of the city – and once the trouble you stirred up dies away – things should quiet down for her, too."

Jane very much doubted that would be the case, but there was no point in discussing it now.

"We'll have to head to the farming communes," Roman said. "One on the outskirts. I don't know that the cities will ever be safe for you." He gave her a look full of apology.

"What about you?" Jane asked. So far, nothing about this reunion was turning out as she would have envisioned.

"There's something I have to do." He spoke stiffly, as though he were still trying to accustom himself to the idea.

"I think we're past secrets, Roman."

He nodded, the hint of a smile on his lips. "It's the vault. I always thought – like my parents did, I suppose – that Recoletta lay far enough from its shadow." He swallowed. "Recent events have proven otherwise."

A sense of foreboding tingled at the back of Jane's neck. "What, then? Where else is there to run?"

He shook his head. "I'm tired of running, Jane. I'm going to destroy it."

A thrill of fear and exhilaration shuddered along her spine. This wasn't the same man she'd seen locked away in Dominari Hall days ago.

"How do you mean–"

"I don't know," he said. "I'll have to figure it out when I get there. But I'm going to make sure it can't be used against anyone else." He looked her in the eye, his resolve as stark as the bruises on his face.

Affection and admiration bloomed in her chest. If he was ready to stand for something, she wouldn't let him stand alone. "I'm coming with you," she said.

He winced. "I'm going to the Continent. It's not–"

"You said yourself I'm not safe here. Besides, you may need me."

He gave her a smile she remembered well from clandestine meetings in Madina. "I don't doubt it, but this isn't your burden."

"I'll decide that." Jane laid her hand on his. It was surprisingly warm. "Besides, I know the code."

He fell silent, his face slackening in surprise.

"Ruthers told me. Just before I..." She stopped. The memory was still a fresh wound in her mind. "I never meant for you to know. But under the circumstances, it seems useful. Besides, we're past secrets. Right?"

He nodded slowly. "Let's hurry."

They took to the surface streets, where the ornamental spires and pavilions of the underground city cast dark, jagged shapes against the reddening sky. They passed through the quietest parts of the city, communicating with nods and glances as they looked for empty streets and kept an eye out for patrols. Working with Roman felt easy and natural, even as they kept silent. After navigating so many intrigues with Lachesse, the Qadi, Petrosian, and Attrop, she had forgotten how good it felt to be around someone she trusted.

But as they left the cobbled streets and marble verandas for loamy soil and towering trees, Jane found herself thinking about Malone, wondering just what Burgevich's article would mean for the woman.

She realized belatedly that Roman was talking to her.

"– keep out of the nearest communes and wait until we've

made some distance."

"Great," Jane said, speaking a little too quickly.

He'd realized it, too. "Something's on your mind," he said, a sly smile playing at his lips.

She tried to deflect. "You're right. They're likely to search the nearest communes first."

He wasn't fooled. "We said no secrets."

But wondering about Malone's fate felt like ants crawling under her skin. She couldn't bring herself to talk about it, much less to add it to Roman's worries. Not when he looked like he'd been starved and beaten for a week straight, not when he finally seemed so hopeful and purposeful.

"It's not like that," she said, searching the fallen leaves for words. "The last few days were strange. I just need time to sort out what happened. What it means." She looked up at him. "Do you understand?"

Roman nodded quietly and said no more about it.

They stayed just out of sight of the train tracks, hiking until their feet were sore and until the evening dark forced them to stop. Neither of them dared start a fire, so they nibbled stale crackers and cheese and unfastened their bedrolls with fingers tingling from the cold.

They huddled together for warmth. "I'll take first watch," Jane said.

"We should both rest." His voice was already thick and slow.

But try as she might, she couldn't sleep. Every time she closed her eyes, she only saw Ruthers. Or Freddie.

Or Malone.

Dawn found her just as exhausted as when she'd first lain down. Still, she was eager to move on.

They took the first few miles as fast as they could. The ground was reasonably level and the undergrowth light. The crisp morning air and Roman's easygoing irreverence made for an invigorating combination.

As the day wore on, Jane's legs grew heavy and her feet sore with blisters. Biting flies stung at her neck, and the pack left her back sweaty and aching. It felt like a penance.

With darkness came howling winds. They spent the night in the lee of a rock, but it did little to shelter them from the cold. Jane sat up to watch the forest – she still didn't expect to fall asleep any time soon.

The next day was worse. Jane's exertions left her legs knotted and spasming with cramps by noon. She didn't want to slow them down, but Roman was looking pretty ragged, too.

"How are you doing?" she asked.

"Wishing I'd brought a bottle of Petrosian's finest," he said.

The mention brought back uncomfortable memories of the darkened bar and the secrets she'd traded there.

Some of her unease must have shown on her face because Roman cocked his head at her. "Everything all right?" he asked.

"Just tired," she said.

He nodded, but he didn't seem to believe her. "Let's take a break," he said.

Jane set her pack down. Her muscles shrieked with relief, even as she lowered her aching body onto the hard ground.

"We're far enough away that Recoletta will have to make a wide sweep – and some good guesses – to find us," Roman said. Jane noticed he'd simply said "Recoletta," because of course there was no telling who was leading the city right now. "Been thinking we'd spend the night in the communes. A real bed and a full meal would do us both good."

"What if the farmers report us?"

He shook his head. "They prefer to keep the cities out of their business. But we'll keep our heads down."

Jane didn't really want to argue against a hot meal and a soft bed. After they'd massaged some feeling back into their muscles, they angled over to the train tracks, where the ground was more level and their passage quicker. They only encountered a couple of trains, but the columns of smoke and the distant rumbling gave them time to duck into the bushes.

No need to take unnecessary risks.

The sky was just beginning to darken when the forests flattened into fields and the loose contours of a commune appeared on the horizon. By happy accident, they reached town under the cover of early evening dark. Jane hoped that made their approach less conspicuous.

Of course, their first order of business was finding room and board for the night.

The commune looked different from those she'd passed through months ago on her journey to Madina. It was busier. Livelier. As she and Roman followed the crowds to a cluster of buildings and a cobblestone plaza, she could have sworn she heard a Recolettan accent once or twice. She kept her head down.

"Big crowd," Roman muttered.

"These places get busy after sundown," Jane said. "Like Turnbull Square, except the whole town gathers in one place."

Roman raised his head, craning his neck around for a few quick seconds. "Looks like more than the whole town. Like more people than this town was made to hold."

The thought of another night outside made Jane's back ache. "Could make it hard to find a room."

"But easy to blend in," Roman said.

They wandered until they found a two-story building that was taller and wider than the rest. From what she remembered, it was like the kind of place with rooms for travelers.

In the underground it was hard to get more than a vague sense of a place's size and shape just by seeing it from the outside. In that regard, at least, the communes were much easier to assess.

Inside was a dining room with long wooden tables, about half full with laughing, talking patrons. On the right, a hallway and a staircase led away – to guest rooms, she supposed.

And from the left came a smell, rich and savory, that woke a rumble in her stomach and moistened her parched mouth.

Roman was already heading toward it.

He ladled a dark, rich-smelling stew into two bowls and nodded to a quiet table in the corner. Two men and a woman, their faces pink with sun and their rough clothes mottled with dirt, crowded around one end, but there was room at the other for Jane and Roman both to sit with their backs to the wall.

And no sooner did they sit than they tucked into their bowls, heads down and silent.

The stew was delicious. Each spoonful was as thick as gravy and rich with the salty flavors of some kind of game meat. Jane was eating so quickly that she nearly swallowed a chunk of potato, but the morsel melted into pulp on her tongue.

She forgot about Roman, forgot about their flight, forgot about why they'd come here. For a few moments, she lost track of everything and everyone but the bowl and spoon before her.

Until she looked up and saw a pair of legs in grease-spattered trousers, standing on the other side of the table.

The woman wore a coarse and unfortunately pale shirt flecked with bits and blobs of what appeared to be stew. Her light hair was tied back in a messy but effective ponytail, and her folded arms were red to the elbows – the way Jane's used to get after working over a tub of hot water.

The woman was looking at Roman, and Roman was looking back at her, his face carefully blank.

"Just passing through," Roman said. "Need to stay the night."

"One room?"

"Yes," she and Roman both said. They regarded each other and shared a quiet chuckle. Jane felt heat in her face and saw it in the tips of Roman's ears, too.

"No trouble here, got it?" the woman said, pointing at the mottle of bruises on his face. "But I'll see if we got something."

"Busy night?" Jane asked.

Suspicion flickered into her gaze. Then, a loud crash from the kitchen jarred it loose. The woman spared a backwards glance before turning back to Jane and Roman.

"Committee from some of the other communes. Working

through some new deal with the cities." She shrugged, as if the political business was beyond her.

Roman looked to Jane, his alarm only visible in his eyes. He raised his eyebrows a fraction of a degree. The woman hovered over his shoulder.

"You gonna pay or not?" she finally asked.

"Sorry, how much?" asked Jane.

"Six grays. Room and meals."

Roman pulled a ten-mark note from his pocket and held it out to the woman. She examined it without taking it.

"That's no good here," she said.

"It's city money," said Roman.

"We aren't in the city." She pointed to the door before Roman could argue. "There's a whole caravan of farmers and city folk in town. Either find someone to trade out your money or I'm giving the room to the next one of them comes asking."

The woman turned to go, and Jane felt the cold and aches of another night outside creeping into her bones. Of course, trading Recolettan marks would draw the very attention they were trying to avoid. That was certainly how it had played out months ago when she and Freddie had fled to Madina.

Then she remembered the coins she'd found at Roman's. She found one and slapped it on the table.

"Will this do?" Jane asked.

The proprietress picked up the coin. She ran her fingers over the boxy symbols.

"Where'd you get this?" The question came from the proprietress and Roman at once. The former was watching Jane with careful calculation, the latter with blank horror.

"Does it cover us or not?" Jane asked.

The other woman tucked the coin away and produced a large brass key. "Second floor, third room on the right. No trouble." This time, she directed the comment at both of them.

As she left, Jane regarded Roman. His face was ashy beneath the bruises. "What was that about?" Jane asked.

But Roman kept his head down and his eyes on his rapidly dwindling stew. "I'll tell you later. We should get to the room soon."

Jane ate quickly – that was easy enough.

Their room was small and sparsely furnished, but it had four walls, a roof, and a bed, which was enough. Roman latched the door and wedged one of the two chairs beneath the handle. The lamplight from the plaza outside was bright enough to reach the room. Jane drew the curtains, then settled into one side of the bed.

All of her illusions of a long soak in a hot bath vanished in a mound of cotton and feathers.

She turned to wish Roman good night and saw him sitting in the other chair, facing the door.

Sleep was already weighing on her eyelids and thickening her tongue. She considered the tiny, hard chair beneath Roman with dread. "We trading watch?" she mumbled.

He shook his head.

Jane sat up and saw that he was pointing a gun at the door. "What are you–?"

He held a finger to his lips. "Waiting."

"What for?"

There was a knock. Roman stood and backed away, his footsteps careful and silent. Adrenaline and urgency jolted her awake. She slipped out of the bed and tiptoed toward the window, pulling back the curtain.

On the ground below was a woman holding a torch and looking back up at her. The woman waved.

Jane gasped and backed away.

"I just want to talk," called a voice on the other side of the door. It sounded vaguely familiar, but Jane couldn't place it.

Roman was as grim and still as stone.

The knock sounded again. "Come on, let's do this face to face."

Whoever the stranger was, he knew they were in here. If he'd wanted trouble, he probably could have gotten a spare key. Or come in shooting.

Whatever this was, they might as well get it over with.

Jane put her finger to her lips and motioned to Roman for calm. He pressed his mouth into a hard line but nodded back.

Jane moved the chair, unlatched the door, and opened it. The face on the other side was just as familiar as the voice, with a thick, black beard and a penetrating stare.

"Salazar," she said.

He didn't seem surprised. Just tired. He jerked his thumb at the door. "Your man's on the other side with a gun pointed at my head, isn't he?"

Jane nodded.

The farmer rolled his eyes. "Come downstairs when you've got him settled. We'll talk somewhere we can have a drink." He turned to head down the stairs.

Roman lowered his gun as the footsteps retreated. "How well do you know him?"

Jane shrugged. "He didn't kill me the last time I wandered into one of his communes."

He tilted his head in question.

"Before. On the way to Madina," she said. "Freddie and I ran into him in a place called Meyerston."

"Then he's a long way from home, too," he finally said.

"Probably here working through that new deal."

Roman grudgingly tucked his gun away. Jane let out a sigh of relief she didn't realize she'd been holding in.

There was still a lively crowd in the dining room downstairs, which was comforting. Salazar was sitting in the same corner she and Roman had occupied, and the other patrons had left a wide ring of privacy around him. That was comforting, too.

Before Salazar were three glasses of a coppery brew. Jane took a seat across from him and accepted one of the glasses as he pushed it toward her.

"Wrong season for cider, I'm afraid," he said. "But lucky for you, the proprietress brews some of the best ale in any of the communes."

Jane sipped hers appreciatively. Roman sat down next to her and peered into his glass as if expecting to find a fly in it. He folded his arms on the table.

Salazar tilted his own glass toward Jane. "The last time I saw you, you were fleeing Recoletta. Headed toward Madina." He took a drink. "What are you running from this time?"

Roman grunted. "Who says we're running?"

Salazar frowned, eyeing Roman's bruises. "That face-painting of yours, for one. So, what is it this time? And what's it got to do with this?" He laid the strange coin on the table like a bad hand of cards.

Jane felt queasy. She was beginning to regret digging through Roman's things.

"What do you know about it?" Roman asked.

Watching the two men trade questions and stares was like observing a poker game in which each player raised the ante to determine what the other already had.

Her money was on Roman.

Salazar folded his hands on the table. "I know men from the east carry them."

"Other farmers? Or citizens?" Jane asked.

Salazar shrugged. "Folk that bring strange devices and strange tales."

"What kinds of tales?" Jane asked.

"About the end of the world," said Salazar.

Jane wasn't sure what to make of this, or even if Salazar was being serious.

Roman, apparently, didn't think much of it. He snorted. "How many of these 'men from the east' have you seen?"

"None," Salazar said. "But they've seen a dozen, all told." He gestured behind Jane and Roman. Jane turned and looked at the other patrons, noticing the furtive whispers and nervous glances the other men and women cast their way, as well as the expanding perimeter around them. She could have drawn a line across their toes and it probably would have formed a perfect half circle. She suppressed a shiver.

Even if this sounded like nonsense, they believed it.

Salazar continued. "They slip among some of the communes every few years. Usually demand some sort of tribute – food, leather, fabric, maybe. But the farmers that meet them say these men watch us. That they're searching for signs of our doom."

"Why didn't you say something to Recoletta?" Jane asked.

"Oh, we did. Generations ago. Whoever was on your Council then thought we were just trying to dodge our quotas." He shrugged. "Besides, these people only robbed a few of us once every few years. Recoletta was robbing us all the time." His voice was raw and sharp with irritation. Even the new deal hadn't healed all the old wounds just yet.

"But if they're taking goods from you, where are they coming from?" Jane asked.

"From the edge of the earth," Salazar said.

Roman thumped the table and burst out laughing.

Salazar glared at him in irritation. "You citizens think we're a bunch of sun-addled clodhoppers, I know. But you're the ones living with your heads buried in the sand. There's something foul out there," Salazar said, gesturing toward the door. "You all hide from it, but that doesn't make you safe."

"What is it?" Jane asked. Even if he was spinning her a yarn, it was an interesting one.

"All I can tell you is what I've seen," Salazar said. "The rusted bones of dead cities rising from the ground. A great, poisoned lake washing over them."

"You make it sound like a children's story," Roman said, derision curling his lips.

"Then tell me one I can believe," said Salazar

Roman was silent for a long time. He took the first sip from his ale. "Is that why we're here? So we can invent a new superstition around the Catastrophe?"

Salazar gritted his teeth. "We're here so that you can tell me whether my people are in danger."

Roman took a longer drink. "You've more to worry about from the cities and their scheming politicians than whatever devils rise from the east."

Salazar was watching Roman, trying to discern whether he really meant this, and Jane was watching Salazar because his expression was a little easier to read.

"Suppose that answers what you're running from," Salazar finally said.

Roman raised his glass in toast. "Way I hear it, they're your problem now."

But Salazar was onto something, and he wasn't letting go. "Because if you came from Recoletta, you're heading away from any other city you might find shelter in. You're heading east, and there's nothing out east."

Roman waved his hand like someone conducting a familiar chorus. "Except poisoned lakes, ghost towns, and strange men. Tell me, when did your people last see one of these strange easterners?"

"Two days ago."

Roman's face went slack.

"They went sniffing around the Library after the bodies got cleared out," Salazar said. "Folk spotted them again a few days ago, almost directly east of here."

Salazar's mouth twisted into a smirk, but there was no humor in his eyes when he turned to Jane. "You brought war the last time we crossed paths, Miss Lin. Are you about to plunge us into the fire again?"

She was starting to worry that she and Roman had done exactly that. If Burgevich's story and Roman's escape had caused as much of a stir as she expected, it wouldn't be long before the combined forces of Recoletta and Madina began searching the communes for them.

A dozen apologies, excuses, and questions rose like bile in her throat, but she forced them down. "You asked me for information. What you did with it was your decision."

Roman leaned forward and squinted at Salazar. "You're the one that sent the list of demands to Sato, aren't you?"

Salazar nodded, proud and defiant.

"That makes you one of Malone's new friends," Roman said.

"She's an honorable woman," Salazar said.

Jane's stomach squirmed. She buried her face in her glass, lest she give something away.

"But her other friends aren't," Roman said, "and that's who you should be worried about. Not boogeymen from the east."

Salazar inclined his head. "There's trouble already?"

"If there isn't, there will be soon."

"Puts us in an awkward position," Salazar said, turning his glass in his hands.

"And the easiest way out of it is to send us on our way first thing in the morning." Roman's voice was even, but tension pulsed in his jaw.

Salazar tilted his head. "Some might say we should host you longer. Until our mutual friends in the city stop by."

Jane bit her tongue and willed herself – and her terror – to remain invisible.

Roman matched Salazar's stare. "Some might say that. But not a friend of Governor Malone's."

Jane took another drink. A long one. She was staring at the bottom of her glass before she realized she'd finished it, and Roman and Salazar were both watching her.

Salazar broke the tension with a sigh that came all the way from his toes. "I'll have a pair of horses ready for you by first light – assuming Miss Lin doesn't find herself at the bottom of too many cups tonight. Keep a good pace, and you should make it to Redhill by midday. You can trade out your horses there and ride past the end of the railroad to a village so small even we don't have a name for it." He frowned under his heavy brows. "After that, you're on your own. But you won't have far to go."

Jane imagined a horde of faceless men rising from a ruined city and chasing them into a lake that melted her flesh from her bones. Based on Salazar's expression, it looked like he was imagining the same thing.

Roman nodded. "You won't hear from us again."

"I've no doubt," Salazar said, almost laughing. "That's why you're leaving the horses somewhere we can get them later."

Jane picked up her glass before she remembered it was empty.

"You said you're a friend of Malone's," Salazar said. "So consider this a favor to a mutual friend." He gulped the rest of his ale, watching her and Roman. "And if you're lying, well, I guess it's like you said. Better you leave before we get tangled up in your mess. Again." He cast a quick glance at Jane.

"Thank you for the hospitality," Roman said.

"Hospitality's easy. It's cleaning up after company that's hard." Salazar pushed back from the table and his empty glass. "Take your time. Have another drink. Your horses will be ready at sun-up." He gave them a curt nod and sauntered through the watching crowd.

Jane stared at her hands on the table. She was afraid to move them, lest their shaking give her away.

Then one of Roman's large and surprisingly soft hands covered hers.

"Are you all right?" he asked.

"Fine," she said, quickly enough that it fooled neither of them.

"Do you want to talk? Because we–"

"No," Jane said. Because speaking about her betrayal would have made it more real, and because she still couldn't bring herself to put that on Roman's shoulders, too.

He opened his mouth and closed it again. "I'll get us another round," he finally said.

Perhaps it would at least help her sleep.

The next morning, Salazar was waiting outside with a pair of horses, both saddled and ready. He handed Roman a folded piece of paper.

"If you have any trouble, just show this wherever you stop."

Jane had never ridden a horse before, though she'd been in

plenty of carriages. Her perch on the animal's back felt higher off the ground than she would have expected and all too aware of her precarious balance.

Arnault set off at a trot, and her mount followed.

The miles passed quickly, and they reached Redhill around midday and changed horses. Jane's legs ached from the ride, but the groom said they were more than halfway to the tiny village. They hurried on.

Past the railroad tracks, the path was uneven and progress slower. Dark clouds gathered on the horizon, and Jane felt a mirrored sense of foreboding welling up inside her. Whatever it was, Roman seemed to have caught it, too – he grew quiet and pensive, his conversation more sporadic.

She'd lulled herself into a silent reverie by the time the last settlement snuck up on them. Salazar had been right – it was barely big enough to be called a town. And the people there were as brusque and reserved as if Salazar himself had ridden ahead with warning of their arrival.

It was no matter. They surrendered the horses, ate a quick dinner, and retired to the room their hosts had cleared for them, sleeping side by side on a lumpy mattress. Roman smelled like sweat, leather, and horses, but it was a comforting reminder of his presence through the night.

Dawn glowed gray in the windows all too soon. Jane knew they were coming to the end of a road without quite knowing what lay there. Dread gnawed at her stomach like hunger, but she also felt a vague sense of relief. Wherever they were headed, they would get there soon, and Jane could leave her doubts and fears about Recoletta behind.

The path faded to a patch of trampled grass, and the shape of the land changed underfoot. Dark, smooth scales of ancient roads rose and sank beneath the dirt. Jane got the feeling they might be crossing an old bridge, but whatever had been under it had long since dried up. The last hint of the path disappeared, and they picked their way through the trees.

Then they emerged, and Jane gasped aloud.

A city of rust rose in the distance. Defiant beams and girders rose from crumbled heaps of stone. Streets wider than any in Recoletta wound like rivers between islands of rubble. Whatever strange, massive verandas had been here were mostly scattered chunks, but even the fragments that remained standing dwarfed any building Jane had ever seen.

Roman took her hand and gave it a gentle squeeze.

"That's from before the Catastrophe," she said.

He nodded.

She took in the unreal proportions of the remains on the surface. As large as the verandas were, she wondered how much bigger it might have been – might still be – underground. It was enough to make her forget about Freddie, Malone, and Ruthers for a while.

They kept going, approaching the dead city without quite walking toward it. It swallowed the horizon in a way that left Jane feeling that she could turn around only to see it rising behind her.

"Is it dangerous?" she asked.

"Not any more."

The texture and shape of the ground changed. Jane looked down and saw crumbled stone and twisted metal poking up from the grass and realized that, even here, she was walking on the bones of the ancient city.

She wondered what else lay beneath her feet, and quivered with horror and wonder.

They continued this way for several minutes, the dead city looming larger and surrounding them by degrees. Roman barely gave it a passing glance, yet she felt his anxiety in the gentle pressure of his thumb on the back of her hand and in the cool dampness condensing in his palm.

If Salazar was to be believed, the end of the world lay ahead.

The land before them flattened out. Something like glass shimmered on the horizon.

Roman laced his fingers through hers.

They drew closer, their steady steps belying her racing pulse. Her animal brain figured out what she was staring at several seconds before she found words for it.

"That's water," she said.

And more than she had ever seen. Jane had heard of lakes, and she'd glimpsed natural ponds and pools on her overland journeys. But she instinctively understood that the expanse before her was something else entirely. It was alive with movement. Foam-flecked waves surged and grabbed at the land. Its vast surface swelled and undulated, and Jane tried to imagine what manner of monster or machine could disturb it so.

"This is the sea," Roman said, as matter-of-factly as if it were a tunnel, or a railcar, or anything else a person might expect to see on a morning walk. "I'm sorry. I wanted to tell you, but..."

But she had dodged his every attempt, had shut down his revelations for fear of making her own.

"I know," she said, squeezing his hand back.

She remembered the tapestry in his apartment, the broad sky over rippling hills of blue.

Jagged silhouettes blurred the distant horizon. The sight of land was an unexpected relief. "It must go on for a hundred miles." The words sounded ludicrous even as she said them.

"Thousands," Roman said. He looked back at her, waiting for the information to sink in. "This is just where it begins."

Not the end of the world, then.

Jane examined their surroundings. There was nothing but the sea, the ancient ruins, and the trees staking their claim in between. "I thought we were going to the vault."

He nodded. "To get there, we've got to cross it."

Jane heard herself laugh. "How?"

"Salazar said his eastern men passed this way days ago. They should be out here somewhere, scavenging."

Yet everything about the landscape, with its crumbled skyline and hungry sea, felt dead. "How are we going to find them?"

"Oh, I expect they'll find us." A tremulous note of dread shook his voice.

Jane took these last quiet moments to scan it all – the ancient city, the forest, and the stretch of land beyond – trying to memorize these last details of home one last time.

Not long after, Jane heard a buzzing noise. Something was moving, racing from behind a speck of land in the middle distance. The term "boat" sprang to mind as yet another thing that she'd read about but never understood. It sped toward them, looming larger than any carriage.

Shouting voices rose over the thrum and spray. The people gathering at its front had the stiff, ready posture of men and women preparing for action.

Roman held both of her hands and turned to face her. "In a few moments, they're going to take us with them. At some point, they'll probably separate us and ask us questions – who we are, how we knew they were here. Tell them everything, only do not mention my surname, and do not mention the vault." He gazed at her long enough to make sure she understood.

Suddenly, Jane regretted all the opportunities she'd let slip to hear his answers, his explanations, and even just the comforting sound of his voice. Of course, then she would have spent the days of their journey dreading the waterborne monster bearing down on them now.

"Roman–"

"You're strong, Jane. You survived in Madina. You'll find your way here, too." He tightened his hands around hers. "The crossing should take around three weeks, depending on the route and–"

But she couldn't bear the thought of an indefinite separation with her guilt unconfessed. "I need to tell you something," she said. "Before we left Recoletta – before I knew Malone released you – I may have made a mess." She told him as quickly as she could about her escapade with Attrop, her final tell-all to Burgevich, and what it might mean for Malone and for Recoletta.

He listened and said nothing, and by the time she was done Jane couldn't bring herself to ask him whether he forgave her, or whether what she'd done could be forgiven.

As if in answer, he leaned down and kissed her.

When he pulled away, the boat was almost upon them.

It swerved as it reached them, and a group of six men and women splashed into the shallows. They each held something high over their heads.

Guns.

Jane stood perfectly still as a woman with a dirty blonde ponytail approached, her shotgun pointed at them.

"Perdido?" the woman asked. "Disoriented?"

"Just waiting," Roman said. He might as well have been discussing the weather.

The woman grunted. "Pakay?" Her fellows spread out around them. Jane heard two of them behind her, muttering in their strange, half-intelligible language.

"We're seeking passage to the Continent."

The woman looked at Jane for the first time. "Depend on the segundos. No promessas."

"We'll take our chances," Roman said with a confidence Jane wished she felt.

The woman nodded to the others from the boat. "'Vestigate 'em."

Jane felt hands on her shoulders and stiffened.

"Calma," said a voice behind her as its owner raised and straightened out her arms. Two strong hands ran along her arms, torso, and legs with a thorough but professional efficiency. It was over before Jane could get flustered enough to blush.

Roman was receiving similar treatment while two of the other boat people disemboweled their bags. They found the guns – Roman's and the one Petrosian had given her – and set them aside.

When the men and women were satisfied, they led Jane and Roman toward the lapping water. Toward what Salazar had called "the poison lake."

But it couldn't be poison, because she had seen these men and women jump into it before, and now they were wading deeper and scooping up big handfuls of the water, rubbing them over their necks and faces.

Even so, dread shivered in Jane's stomach when she stepped into the waves.

Or maybe it was just the cold.

She waded deeper, until the water reached her thighs, gasping with each step and each splashing wave. With mounting terror, she realized that she didn't know how to swim.

"Ablute," said the man next to her. "Purify." He was splashing water onto his chest and ladling big handfuls of it onto his head, rubbing his bare skin vigorously.

Jane understood that she was expected to do the same, so she did, suppressing the urge to shudder at what amounted to taking a cold bath with a handful of strangers.

Evidently, it wasn't enough. Someone grabbed her shoulders, and before Jane could protest, dunked her backwards into the water. It was just enough warning for Jane to close her eyes and hold her breath.

She was pulled back up, panting, and found herself staring into the eyes of the woman with the ponytail.

"Grace ee bendictions," the woman said, pulling Jane back to her feet.

Jane tasted salt on her lips and spat into the water.

It was up to her shoulders by the time they reached the boat. She held her fear in check with deep breaths, bracing herself against the waves that sloshed into her face and threatened to pull her off her feet. She was suddenly grateful for the ponytailed woman's hand on her arm.

The people waiting on the boat lowered a rope ladder and hoisted Jane, Roman, and their sodden captors into the boat and distributed blankets. Once they were all aboard, ponytail hauled up the rope and the boat sped away.

Jane stood at the side of the boat and gripped the rail with one hand and Roman's arm with the other. Even with the blanket around her shoulders, the breeze was cold enough to leave her shivering. Still, the cold was a welcome distraction from the discomfort building in her gut. She kept her gaze fixed on the dead city as they sped by. The ruined buildings stretched on even longer than she had imagined.

Then, they ended, and she saw nothing but distant miles of flat sea.

Jane heaved her head over the railing and vomited.

She felt Roman's hands on her neck, pulling her hair away from her face. When she was done, he put one arm around her shoulders.

She gazed into the sea beneath them. Muddy green and so deep it was opaque. A spray of water splashed her face, and she flinched.

Even though her stomach was as empty as the horizon, Jane felt another wave of sickness roiling inside her.

"It helps to look at a fixed point on the horizon," Roman said.

"There's nothing," Jane said, and the realization washed panic over her.

But he pointed over her shoulder.

She turned. The mass on the water was too far away to be more than a dim shape, but it spread across the horizon like the islands they'd left dwindling in their wake.

"Salvage," Roman said. "The city of ships."

Jane leaned over the railing and vomited again.

"Asi you pass aki," the interrogator said.

Jane nodded. She was all out of words. All that remained was to see if he'd bought them.

"Tu companyero with the injured face, who ess?"

"I told you, Roman's a bureaucrat who was working for the wrong side. Not important enough to spare, just important enough to punish," she said, keeping her voice carefully even.

CARRIE PATEL   139

"No, who ess pa' you?"

Jane hesitated. She'd been so busy – first trying to free him, then running with him – that she hadn't had much opportunity to consider who they were to each other besides collaborators.

"I guess it's complicated," Jane said.

He gave a dry laugh. "Always ess. Ee what can you realize?"

"Beg your pardon?"

"If you stay, you gotta function. Make labor. So, what can you realize?"

Jane understood what he was looking for. "I can clean," she said. "Purify."

His grin was so sudden it was startling. "In that caso, bienvenido to Salvage."

CHAPTER ELEVEN
THE FLYING PRISON

The inspector in Malone couldn't help but admire the *Glasauge*. As a police officer, she realized that few prisons were more effective than one floating hundreds of feet above the ground. Even while her hosts insisted she wasn't a prisoner, she had no place to go, and no choice but to trust them to bring her down safely.

Yet while Malone the cop commended it, Malone the captive abhorred it. She hated knowing that she was suspended aloft by nothing more substantial than bags of air, and her knees wobbled every time she remembered that there was no solid ground under her feet, only wood and metal and a vast expanse of empty space. She hated the way her stomach lurched when she looked out the window, and she hated even more that everyone else on the *Glasauge* could read her weakness.

But worse than being carried away from Recoletta in a floating prison was being stuck in it with Lady Lachesse.

Yet to Malone's astonishment, the old whitenail didn't seem to mind the airship one bit. Malone would catch her sitting in the aft lounge – where metal-ribbed windows curved from the floor to the ceiling, angled down over the landscape – staring out as if she were regarding nothing more than a pretty picture.

A couple of days had passed since her aborted execution, but she'd spent most of them in the cabin Geist had assigned to her, hiding from his men, from Lachesse, and from the oppressive reminder of her own vulnerability. Dominari Hall had been stifling, and the few days she'd been there as interim governor, she'd ached to get out, to bury herself in the investigative work she knew and loved. Here, however, she felt even more trapped, with nothing to do and nowhere to go.

So when she roused herself and went to wash up, she gasped at what she saw in the mirror. The wound under her neck had puckered into a red, blistered scar. Her neck still ached, and the mark on it stood out on her pale skin like a brand. More surprising than that, though, was everything above the scar. Her hair was a tangle of greasy clumps, and her skin was pasty. Malone had never been vain about her appearance, but she hardly recognized herself.

She poured some water into the basin and splashed it onto her face, combed it through her hair. After several minutes, she almost looked like herself again.

When Malone opened the door, Lachesse was standing in front of it, waiting.

"Finished?" she asked with an arch of her eyebrow.

"All yours." Malone shouldered past her and headed back down the hall.

"I'm not talking about the washroom, Inspector," Lachesse said. Malone kept going. "I'm talking about your moping. Hiding."

Malone stopped. Her hand was already on the door to her cabin, her mind on the rest she might squeeze from the hard cot.

"You've been in there two days, Malone."

She turned the knob. "Then I'll see you in another three."

Lachesse clucked. "I wouldn't have thought the woman who survived her own hanging could be defeated so easily."

Malone knew it was bait, but it stirred her up all the same.

"Have Geist dangle you over the side by your neck. Then we'll see how you feel."

Lachesse fluttered a hand. "Yes, I know you've been recovering from your ordeal," she said as though they were talking about a head cold rather than an interrupted execution. "And I've seen the way you clam up at the first sight of a window. But you've shut yourself in that room because you failed and you can't stand to face it."

Malone had never punched anyone as old as Lachesse, but if she wasn't still worried about Geist tossing her overboard, she would have been sorely tempted to do it now.

"You left Recoletta almost as broken as you found it," Lachesse said. "You were endowed with the governorship of the city..."

The old woman lied as easily as most people breathed, but even for her, that was incredible. Malone took a step toward her. "You installed me because you needed a scapegoat."

The old woman laid a long-nailed, ring-bedecked hand over her chest. "A scapegoat for what? You brought trouble on yourself when you released a known traitor."

"I had to get Lin and Arnault out of the city as fast as possible. And without some farce of a trial." The recent memory of her own stung more than she would have expected.

Lachesse smirked. Malone realized her mistake.

"Yes, well done," the whitenail said. "Even after seeing the unrest that had built for months under Sato's rule, you still couldn't quell the dissent brewing right under your nose."

"I didn't know Lin would publish that story!"

A crewman flattened against the side of the corridor to squeeze past Malone, his too-tight uniform pressed against the wall so cleanly that he never touched her. Lachesse maintained a tranquil silence as she waited for the man to pass.

"You might have if you'd talked with her," Lachesse said as the crewman disappeared around a corner. "Instead, you used every excuse you could find to go sleuthing around the city, avoiding the political responsibilities with which you'd been entrusted."

"I never wanted to be a politician!" Malone said. Her voice felt loud and painful in her throat, but Lachesse was ignoring how little control she had actually had. And how much responsibility Lachesse herself had for engineering the situations that had led them both here. "I never claimed to be good at it. You foisted this on me because you needed a distraction. A spectacle."

Lachesse blinked back at her, as cool as ever. "So?"

"So?" Anger burned in her aching throat. "How can you blame me for–"

"Because it was your responsibility, Inspector Malone. You helped bring Sato to power. And then you helped topple him. You don't get to walk away from either of those things just because the cleanup wasn't on your terms. Of course I 'installed' you as governor. I told you – people look to you, whether you like it or not." She scoffed. "And whether you deserve it or not."

Malone's argument dried up on her tongue.

Lachesse pressed on. "You make excuses for yourself as if you're the first leader to ever take charge of an angry and broken people. Yes, your job was to distract and placate Recoletta while I made these deals you find so distasteful – deals like the one that kept the Qadi and her allies from invading. And perhaps if you'd worked with me instead of turning your nose up, you might not have failed."

Rage boiled up in Malone, as bracing as a steaming hot bath. "I failed?" she said. "I killed the madman who would have left Recoletta in ashes. I forged peace with the farmers who feed our city. I made your little deal with the Qadi and her allies possible." She pulled at her collar to expose the scar on her neck. "I survived you. And I'm not done yet."

Without realizing it, she'd brought herself almost nose to nose with Lachesse.

The older woman smiled with feline satisfaction.

"That's the spirit, Inspector." Lachesse turned down the corridor, heading toward the observation lounge. "Now, if you're ready to keep fighting, come with me."

Malone stifled her annoyance and followed. She was starting to realize that she wasn't tired anyhow.

Their deck – with cabins along either corridor, a mess at one end, and the lounge at the other – was fairly quiet most of the time, when the majority of the crew was on duty elsewhere.

So Malone was glad that there was no one to see her tense up as she entered the lounge and laid eyes on the floor-to-ceiling windows, the glass spiderwebbed with black iron cames.

"Sit, Malone."

She realized with a start that Lachesse was already across the room, nestled comfortably enough in a padded chair next to the center window.

Another chair sat empty across from her.

Malone clenched her hands into fists and began the long walk over to it.

It felt like the slowest she'd ever walked in her life. As irrational as it was, she couldn't stop imagining that the malevolent forces of gravity would reach through the window and pull her out of the ship. And yet trying not to think about it only lodged the thought more firmly in her mind, so she focused on the one horror that, perhaps, disturbed her more: the idea of giving Lady Lachesse the satisfaction of her discomfort.

By the time she sat down across from the whitenail, her clenched fists were clammy with sweat and her legs were shaking. Whether it was fear at the view or fury at Lachesse for forcing her to endure it, she didn't know.

And Lachesse herself only sat there in companionable silence, as unruffled as if they were back in her office in Recoletta.

"It was never personal, you know," the whitenail finally said. She was still gazing out the window – Malone wouldn't have even been sure the woman was talking to her, except there was no one else in the room.

"Easy to say when you were the one holding the rope," Malone said.

"I know you think I'm a corrupt, amoral, and heartless old crone with no love for anything but power." She smiled thinly. "I suppose that must make it easier for you."

Malone knew the old woman was waiting for her to ask the follow-up, and while she didn't want to play into her script, it gave her something to think about other than her fear.

"Easier how?"

Lachesse contemplated the view for several long seconds, making Malone wait for her answer.

"Easier for you to see yourself as the hero."

Malone stared at the empty lounge. Her stiff bunk was starting to seem appealing once more.

Lachesse sighed. "It's just a picture, Malone. And you can make up any story you need about it."

It took Malone a second to realize that Lachesse was talking about the view again.

"What's yours?" Malone asked.

"That I see farther than anyone in the history of humanity. And that this is all I will see if Roman Arnault falls into the wrong hands."

Malone steeled herself for a glance. What she saw surprised her so much that for a moment, she forgot her fear.

A brown waste stretched out below them for miles. Malone couldn't see a single patch of color – no trees, no grass, no water.

"Where are we?" Malone asked.

"South and west," Lachesse said, as though that explained it. "Geist believes Roman would have fled this way, away from Recoletta and the allied cities."

"I told him it's Lin he's chasing," Malone said. If it were up to Arnault, he'd likely have been holed up in some dive in the factory districts.

"Perhaps you should remind him," Lachesse said with a sidelong glance.

The fear was creeping back, but it was of a different type. It was the fear an animal instinctually feels at seeing death, the frantic buzz that still crept into Malone's mind whenever she saw a corpse.

And this was a corpse of the land. Hills rose and fell like mounds of dead flesh, ruptured by craters like bullet holes. Rocks and blocks of carved stone – or something like it – littered the landscape like shattered bones.

"What happened here?" Malone heard herself ask.

Lachesse shrugged. "The Catastrophe."

At that moment, the stairwell just outside the lounge thundered with rushing feet. Lachesse glanced toward the commotion with disdain.

"Flying ships and uniforms that look like badly fitting pajamas," she said. "One wonders what the situation on the Continent is really like."

Malone realized she hadn't been wondering about that enough. Nor had she been paying enough attention, because the old whitenail seemed entirely too pleased with herself.

"You know something about the Continent," Malone said. She might still be following Lachesse's script, but it didn't bother her as much now.

Now, she had questions that needed answers.

Lachesse, meanwhile was transforming into a different woman. A much smaller, younger one. "I thought they were just stories."

"Tell me," Malone said.

Lachesse took a deep breath, like a thousand troubled witnesses before her. "It was something I heard a long time ago, from a man who had recently arrived in Recoletta. At the time, anyway." She licked her lips. "He mentioned someplace very far away, on the other side of the sea, where people lived very differently. In a way similar to how they had before the Catastrophe."

"Before the Catastrophe? What does that mean?"

Lachesse shrugged with her eyebrows. "I wasn't certain, and my companion didn't offer to explain." She paused. "There was a generous quantity of wine involved."

"Who was this companion?"

"Augustus Ruthers."

It was the confession more than the fact that surprised Malone. After all, Lachesse and Ruthers had run in many of the same circles, and Ruthers had been a relation of Arnault's. It seemed only natural the story would lead there. "How did he come to tell you something like that?"

The whitenail gave her a mischievous smile. "We were intimate."

Malone hid her surprise behind pressed lips. Perhaps she should have seen that coming too.

"As I said, this was long ago, when we were still young enough to boast to our lovers. He had arrived in Recoletta less than a year prior, and he quickly proved himself an ambitious man of uncommon means. At the time, I assumed he was simply eager to make and impress new connections." Lachesse flashed a sly smile. "Not that I minded."

"But you said you didn't believe him," Malone said.

"In my experience, the more impressive the tale, the less of it is true," Lachesse said. "But he never raised the issue again, and I couldn't coax another word of it from him. I made no assumptions about it until young Roman Arnault and his parents arrived amidst rumors they had also come from beyond the sea."

"And what did they say about it?" Malone asked.

"Absolutely nothing. And they made no greater association with Ruthers than anyone else in our circles, so I hardly thought of the matter again." Lachesse cast her eyes toward the door, as if expecting someone there. "People move between cities more often than one might think, but rarely without dire need. Yet when they arrive with the kind of resources that Ruthers and the Arnault family had, one learns not to ask questions."

It was a bare story, and hardly worth the time it took to hear it. Yet Lachesse had deemed it worth telling, and the woman's restless movements and darting eyes told Malone she was afraid of something.

And she was waiting for Malone to ask the right question. "What do you think we'll find on the Continent?" Malone asked.

Lachesse smiled again. "That's what we've got to find out

now. But first, we've got to help our host find his fugitives, or we may wear out our welcome."

Malone could agree with that much. Besides, Jane Lin would have to answer for what she'd done in Recoletta.

She took a longer, steadier look out the window. She saw the dead landscape now without the fear sinking its claws into her heart.

There was no way Jane Lin would have traveled out here.

"Where are you going?" Lachesse asked.

"To tell our host he's chasing the wrong person."

Malone was searching for Geist when she found Phelan – or rather, Phelan found her. Malone had found herself able to understand Geist and a few of the other crew members when they spoke slowly and carefully, but Phelan was still a blur of awkward smiles and syllables.

Which was a shame, because Phelan seemed to be the one person on the *Glasauge* who didn't press herself against the wall just to avoid contact with Malone.

But Phelan understood her just fine, so when Malone asked for Geist, she found herself escorted to the mess hall and plied with caffee. Perhaps the one thing Phelan didn't understand was how much Malone loathed the stuff.

But Geist appeared a couple of minutes later, his oversized uniform rumpled. "You are coming aus of your cabine? Goot. You must be ameliorating." He gave Malone a professional smile and sat across from her, waiting.

"Yes," Malone said.

"Goot. Because I am requiring your assistance. We voyage days, and yet." He spread his hands in the direction of the window behind her and gave her an imploring frown. "I am stark hoping you are comprending something new."

For a man who barely found his way to the end of a sentence, there was nothing subtle about Geist.

"That's the tricky thing," Malone said. "While we're looking,

Lin and Arnault are running. And the radius of places they could be grows wider."

Geist turned his caffee cup in one hand and stared back at Malone with hard, flat eyes. "Ya."

She was enjoying this more than she would have thought possible. "The problem is, I don't know where they are."

Geist's upper lip twitched, yanking his cheek and its crooked scar along with it.

"But I can point you to someone who probably does."

He blew out a sigh of relief. Or maybe exasperation. "Recount it, please."

"We've got to go to the farms." Jane had passed through them on her first clandestine trip from Recoletta. They'd be a natural and necessary place for the pair to rest up, resupply, and orient themselves. And if Jane and Roman had indeed made any stops, Salazar could almost certainly find out about it.

Geist's expression fell. "Farms?"

Surely even the Continent had these. Malone tried to think of how to describe a farm to someone who didn't know the word. "Big open spaces. Lots of surface land, big views of the sky. They provide our food and other raw materials."

Geist was clutching his hands together, his fingers quivering and wiggling like spiders' legs. "Absolutely no."

"What?" Malone asked. Two days ago, he'd been willing to try anything, to fly untold distances just to find Roman.

"These farms, they are seeming very insalube. Of mal hygiene." He squirmed and wrung his hands as if he were trying to wash himself of the very idea.

Oddly enough, his attitude wouldn't have been at all out of place in Recoletta – or any of the underground cities – where grass-stained trousers or sunburnt arms ruined reputations. In Recoletta, the unsavoriness of the outdoors was something of a superstition, but with Geist, it was more.

She didn't know what to do with it right then, but she filed it away for later.

"You realize that we've all eaten food from the farms? That I've been to them?" It was a risky angle – after all, Geist's people could easily throw her overboard if they deemed her a "contaminant" – but she needed familiar ground under her feet.

Besides, if they kept wandering around without finding Roman, they might throw her overboard anyway.

Geist, however, was deep in thought, turning his cup in his hands again.

"You are esteeming they comprend where to encounter Arnault?" Geist's face was still scrunched with doubt and disgust.

"If he's been through any of the communes, Salazar'll know," Malone said, watching Geist's face for a sign of surrender. If she could just get to Meyerston and Salazar, she might be able to get away from Geist, Lachesse, and the *Glasauge*. Then she could pursue Jane and Arnault on her own terms.

Geist took a deep gulp of his caffee, watching her over the rim of the cup. "I apport the navigator. You will recount the route."

CHAPTER TWELVE
THE FLOATING CITY

Jane learned several important things in her first days on the floating city. The first was how to walk on constantly swaying ground while keeping her food down. The second – and only marginally less important – was that her new home was called Salvage, and the locals meant that name literally.

Salvage was a flotilla of interconnected, pre-Catastrophe ships that had been repurposed and retrofitted to serve as a mobile, waterborne city. The residents spent their lives eating, sleeping, and working in the kind of proximity that made Recoletta's factory districts seem spacious. Most of them, she learned, had never set foot on dry land.

She was assigned a berth on a ship called the *Lazy May*. It wasn't much bigger than a supply closet, and yet two bunks had somehow been stacked inside. The sleeper on the lower bunk groaned and turned from the door. Jane's escort pointed to the upper berth and told her she was fortunate to have one to herself. She shuddered to think of what it meant to be crowded here.

She had also wondered why a newcomer like herself would get a bunk all to herself. At first, she thought it made it easier for Salvage's leaders – the almirante, the capitans, and their segundos – to keep an eye on her, assuming they still had doubts about her story. She soon decided that it was more likely a question of corruption.

Salvagers had an obsession with corruption – a moral and physical filth that they believed collected in dark corners, grew on the undersides of hulls, and was secreted by those who did not wash often or thoroughly enough. Jane would have called these things grime, rust, and sweat, but they meant something much more to the people around her. And as best she could tell, the origins of all such corruption were the muddy, heathen lands on either side of the sea.

When she considered it that way, it made sense that no one wanted to bunk with her. Besides, she was happy for what privacy she could get.

It also explained a lot about her job. After her interrogation, she had been assigned to Salvage's army of cleaners – people who swept, scrubbed, and polished every inch of the city every single day.

It was unpleasant, but it was something. And it gave her an excuse and opportunity to observe the city and its people.

Unfortunately, she hadn't been able to find Roman yet. They'd been separated as soon as they'd come aboard Salvage. Jane's interrogator had told her he'd be assigned to the *Albatross*, one of the handful of engine ships that moved the city. The information, however, was less helpful than she might have hoped – by all accounts, thousands worked the *Albatross*, and in three or four shifts throughout the day. Worse, directions on Salvage were practically unintelligible, even when she could get past the accent. Everything was leeward or windward of some ship or another, none of which Jane knew in the first place. All she could tell was that the *Albatross* was far from her usual rotation. Given that she barely had the stomach to cross more than a couple of the ever-bobbing decks and swinging gangways before queasiness overcame her, it might as well have been back in Recoletta.

She could only hope he wasn't having as bad a time of it.

In the absence of better company and happier thoughts, she tried to focus on keeping her head down, her ear to the ground, and her nausea in check.

The last part might have been easier if she hadn't been assigned to clean one of the messiest boats in Salvage. She supposed she had her inherent "corruption" to thank for that, too.

Despite the daily cleaning routine, she could usually smell *Nossa Senhora*'s ammoniac musk from a deck away. And in the early hours, when the wind and waves were quiet and the masses crowded in their bunks, she could hear the trilling and cooing from even farther.

The cabin and the upper portion of the *Nossa Senhora*'s hold had been modified and fitted with rows of pigeon coops. The birds inside roosted on perches, huddled in nest boxes, or strutted and pecked along the floor.

All of it was covered with bird droppings, and all of those droppings had to be scraped up, collected, and carted off to Salvage's floating farms.

With a sigh, Jane took a handkerchief and trowel from the supply cabinet, tied the former around her nose and mouth, and started cleaning.

No one had bothered to explain what the pigeons were for, and she had gotten the distinct impression that she shouldn't ask. As far as she could tell, they ate, shat, and took short flights across Salvage. The only other person who worked the *Nossa Senhora* was Leyal, a short old man with skin the texture of calluses and eyes so pale they looked faded by the sun. He said little to her, but he nannied the pigeons as if they were his own three hundred grandchildren.

The work left her arms and back sore, but it added routine and regularity to her day. She could usually guess the time by how much progress she'd made along the coops. And how many times she'd gone out to vomit.

It was midmorning when her gut lurched within her the first time.

Jane rushed out of the cabin and onto the deck, taking deep gulps of salty air. After she'd retched most of her breakfast overboard, she started to feel better.

Three weeks of this, Roman had told her. And only three days had passed.

She was leaning over the railing with her eyes closed when a hand, rough and dry as sandpaper, fell on her shoulder.

Jane spun with instincts tuned by paranoia. Leyal stood before her, a gray pigeon on his shoulder and something yellowish and shriveled between his fingers.

"Toma," he said.

It took some gesturing on his part before she understood she was supposed to eat it. She took it and tried a bite. It was sweet and spicy, not in a way that burned her tongue, but in a way that left her head feeling clear. She chewed the rest of it and relished the clean, tart taste.

Leyal nodded in satisfaction. "Gingiber," he said. "Pa' aki." He patted his belly.

"Thanks," Jane said.

"Any mal, you say something. O it aggravates." He stroked the bird's slate-colored back. Something on its leg glinted in the light.

"Maybe I should say something about getting a new assignment," she said. One that didn't clog her nose and fog her head with the stench of birds.

Leyal laughed. "No, no. Only you aki."

"I know, I'm already covered in corruption," Jane said. The private berth almost made up for it.

"Ess the mensages," he said, tossing the pigeon up. It took off toward the other end of Salvage.

"The what?"

He gave her a pitying look and clucked. "You don't conosse? Palomas transport notices. Relatos. The segundos send you because you don't layer."

It suddenly clicked into place for Jane. The interrogator had said something similar to her. Something about decaying "livros" and all the things her people didn't know.

They thought she was illiterate.

"Yes," Jane said, testing her theory. "Few in the buried cities can even write their own names."

"Claro, everyone conosse this." Leyal was still watching the bird as it disappeared.

Now that Jane understood the purpose of the pigeons, she started noticing a lot more about them. She got to know the schedule by which they came and went. She kept track of Leyal's rotation around the coops. She noticed the little metal canisters that so many of the birds wore.

She noticed, after a week cleaning the *Nossa Senhora*, that one of them was red.

The bird in question had found its way into one of the few empty coops from the trapdoor outside. In all her time working there, she hadn't seen any red canisters or any birds in that specific coop. What was more, she was in the middle of the quiet morning hours when the birds almost never arrived. And Leyal was on the upper deck, fussing with the pigeons there.

She knew she was supposed to keep her head down and avoid drawing any attention to herself – or Roman – until they got close enough to leave for the Continent.

And yet this mystery was just sitting here, preening its feathers. A question begging to be asked.

Besides, red was the universal color of trouble. And if trouble was brewing on this strange city where she understood so little, it would be better to know it now.

Floorboards creaked overhead, and the rusty melody of Leyal's singing drifted down to Jane.

He never started a song unless he was distracting himself from a long, mindless task, which meant he'd be busy for at least a couple of minutes. Probably.

Jane opened the coop, wincing as it clanged. The other birds cooed and trilled, bobbing their heads in little stop-start motions to watch her.

The lone pigeon only fluffed its feathers, settling deeper into its perch.

But when she reached into the coop, a rough wave knocked her to the side. The bird flew out of the coop and over her shoulder.

Jane cursed as the little creature flapped to the top of the supply cabinet. The damn thing was almost twice as tall as she was.

She cursed again as the floorboards near the ladder squeaked and Leyal's humming grew louder.

His feet appeared on the topmost rungs.

Jane eased the coop door shut just as his shoulders came into view.

The errant pigeon was still perched quietly atop the cabinets.

"The palomas greet for repast." He dusted his palms on his trousers, which looked dirtier than his hands could possibly be.

"Sure," Jane said. She was trying to keep her voice light and airy, but it just sounded high.

He jerked his thumb toward the ladder. He hadn't noticed the stray pigeon yet, but if Jane opened the cabinet to get the feed, he almost certainly would.

She needed a distraction. She thought of the one thing that was sure to grab his attention.

"The droppings in the last cage smelled off," Jane said, pointing to the row of coops beyond the ladder. "The black-and-green one seemed… sick. I think there's something wrong – something mal – with it."

"Ah-ah!" Leyal cried, loudly enough to startle Jane. Thankfully not the roosting fugitive. "Something mal with?" He watched her, his faded denim eyes wide and bright.

It took Jane a moment to understand what he was asking. But then she remembered that his pigeons were never "it."

"With her," she said at last. It was a guess, and apparently a good one.

"Which ess her nome?" Leyal recited the pigeons' names

at least twice a day, chanting them in his rough singsong and often prompting Jane to repeat them back. It had always felt like a frivolity, but she'd made a career once upon a time out of humoring frivolities.

Fortunately, Leyal was so eager to see her get this one right that he was practically mouthing the name himself.

Jane put on her most patient smile and followed along. "Tea-um. Teodora."

He raised three fingers. His eyebrows climbed up his forehead.

"Teodora III," Jane said. Most of the pigeons had a number of some kind affixed to their name. As old as Leyal looked, and as many pigeons as he'd likely been through, she supposed he'd had to start recycling names at some point.

"Splendido!" he shouted, nodding vigorously. The cooped pigeons stirred and warbled, but there was nothing from the cabinet behind Jane. Yet.

"I will see her. You bring the repast," he said, already turning his back to her.

Jane looked back at the cabinet. Her fugitive sat there still, peering at her in profile.

Holding her breath, she eased it open. The bird pecked crossly at the door and scooted to the edge while she wedged the bag of feed out of the cabinet.

But as the pellets and seeds rattled inside, it trilled with interest.

Jane glanced over her shoulder. Leyal was still absorbed with the cage at the end of the row.

The runaway pigeon cooed again, hopping to the front of the cabinet. Jane waved an arm at it, and it retreated back. She hurried toward the ladder before the little creature could get any more ideas.

Ahead of her, Leyal was holding Teodora III in one cupped hand and stroking her with the other, murmuring softly. She had to draw him away from the deck if she hoped for a chance to read the message.

She balanced the food sack on her shoulder and started up the ladder. The fugitive bird was still perched atop the cabinet. As she watched it, it ruffled its feathers and shat.

The birds on the second deck were pleasanter company. They cooed their appreciation as she doled seed into their troughs. They hopped and flapped toward her, staring back with black, barely blinking eyes.

Meanwhile, Leyal's song was winding to a close.

He thumped around below. The squeal and rattle of metal signaled that he was shutting the gate. Heading to the supply cabinet.

There wasn't much time to think. Another big wave rocked the deck, and Jane dropped the bag of seed. She threw open the door to the nearest coop, waving her arms to scatter the pigeons inside.

The panicked birds flitted past her, dispersing throughout the deck. Jane could have whooped with relief. "They're loose!"

Leyal's rough work boots clomped toward the ladder. His head rose from the hatch, twisting and swiveling like one of his birds' as he took in the empty coop, the seven escaped birds, the spilled seed bag, and Jane's fervent display of panic.

"I'm sorry," she said, "the deck pitched, and I grabbed the coop, but I–"

"Shh," he said, hoisting himself onto the deck. "Never chant them panico. Always calm with the palomas."

Jane heaved a sigh. "Sorry. I–" She grabbed at the ladder as the deck rose and fell again. "I think I'm going to be sick." It was probably true.

He shooed her toward the hatch. "To the gingiber."

"Thanks," Jane said, but Leyal had already turned from her to soothe his birds. As she climbed down, she grabbed a handful of spilled feed.

The cause of her trouble was still waiting for her on the cabinet. Jane approached and dropped the feed on the floor, watching the bird as it noticed the prize on the ground. It hopped to the edge of the cabinet but no further.

Jane took one slow step back. Then two.

She'd taken a dozen before the pigeon descended to its peace offering. It pecked away at the seed, raising its head at every third or fourth tap to make sure she wasn't taking any liberties. Leyal, meanwhile, continued his singing and sweet-talking upstairs. The pigeons trilled along with him.

She took an exploratory step forward, and the bird stopped pecking. It looked up at her.

"Shh," she whispered. "It's okay, bird."

She felt foolish, but the pigeon cocked its head and cooed back.

She took another step forward. "I just want to see what you've got." Another step. "Friends?"

The bird hissed and puffed up its feathers.

Jane swore. She was still too far to grab the bird, especially with the deck rocking under her. And if Leyal heard the damn thing start flapping and screeching, he'd be back in seconds.

She was almost level with the fugitive's empty coop. Close enough to read the names hanging from the side.

Maybe there was something to Leyal's manner with the birds, after all.

"Flavia?"

The bird shifted on its little gray feet, squaring off against her.

"Angelo."

It gave a desultory peck at the pile of seed, watching her still.

"Goo... ah. Gyoo-seepay?"

Nothing but another half-hearted peck. Whatever the name was, she'd have to hope it wasn't that one.

"Carmela."

The pigeon raised its head – her head – and cooed.

"Carmela," Jane said again, stepping closer. The bird cooed again and resumed feeding. By the time Jane was close enough to grab her, she climbed willingly into Jane's hand and suffered herself to be picked up.

Jane stroked her soft back as she listened for Leyal. He was still singing upstairs, but this would all be for nothing if he returned to find her holding one of his pigeons and reading the message it carried.

So she steadied herself with splayed elbows and a wide stance and carried Carmela outside.

The bird gave her a cranky trill as the sea breeze blew the door shut behind them. Jane shushed and stroked her, looking around to satisfy herself that she wasn't being watched.

For now, the decks of the ships immediately downwind were clear. For once, Jane was grateful for the *Nossa Senhora*'s stench.

Jane examined the red capsule and hesitated. Some part of her brain was nagging at her, telling her she shouldn't be doing this. After all, hadn't her snooping gotten her exiled from Recoletta in the first place? And arrested in Madina later?

That was only half true. In Madina, she'd been able to warn Roman about the Qadi's impending invasion. And the fact that the Qadi and her allies had been after Roman – well, perhaps that was something she could have learned if she'd had more information.

And that was all she was taking now – information. What could be the harm in knowing more about what was happening in Salvage?

She'd made up her mind. Holding Carmela close to her chest, she fumbled at the capsule around the bird's leg until something came loose between her fingers.

The paper that slid out was coarse and rugged like old cloth, and rolled into a tight spool. It unrolled and expanded quickly, soaking up the damp ocean air.

Even so, she had to hold it close to her face to read the message flapping in the breeze.

"Kennedy agitates. Refuses petition to interrogate the bounty. Demands privilege of salvage. Avise."

Jane read the message two more times, forcing herself to slow down. The words were all familiar but obscure, like so much of what was said on Salvage. She couldn't be entirely sure of their meaning, but several of them stood out nonetheless.

Agitates. Demands. Interrogate.

She didn't know for sure that the message referred to Roman, but she couldn't pry the notion from her head, either.

If they were going to be stuck in this floating city for another two – or more – weeks, she needed to warn him. And she needed to do something about the message.

She couldn't let it fall into the hands of Leyal or the capitans. Whoever had written it might send another, but she could at least delay its receipt and whatever consequences it would set in motion.

After reading it one more time to commit it to memory, Jane wadded it up and dropped it into the splashing, lapping water between the hulls. It disappeared in the foam.

The only question that remained was what to do about the bird.

She couldn't let the bird return with an empty message capsule – Leyal would know someone had tampered with it, and she would be the obvious suspect.

Maybe she could remove it.

Yet several seconds of wiggling and tugging produced nothing but kicking and squirming from Carmela and a mounting sense of dread in Jane.

Even if she could remove the capsule, no one would believe it had come off on its own. And Leyal would recognize a new pigeon, no matter what coop Jane put her into.

Cold sweat moistened her palms.

Carmela wriggled against her chest. Somewhere across the still-empty decks, voices rang out in laughter and conversation.

There was little time.

She stroked Carmela's back again. "I'm sorry," she whispered.

Jane twisted the bird's neck before she could reconsider.

She dropped the pigeon into the churning water. It landed with a splash, its gray feathers mixing with the dirty foam and, somewhere, the remnants of the message.

Jane swiped at her eyes, swallowed the queasy feeling rising in her throat, and turned back toward the cabin of the *Nossa Senhora*.

Leyal was waiting inside, his sun-dried face creased with irritation. "What ess this corruption?" He pointed at the pile of feed on the floor.

"I told you, I was feeling sick." She knew she should apologize, but she just wanted to get away from the *Nossa Senhora*. She went to the cabinet and took a few slices of gingiber.

"You did sujeira," he said, thrusting a broom toward her.

"I'll make a bigger sujeira if stay," Jane said. She popped a piece of gingiber in her mouth and prepared to journey across Salvage's rolling, swaying decks.

CHAPTER THIRTEEN
CIVILIZED PEOPLE

Geist's westward survey had taken them far enough out of the way that it was another day before they reached Meyerston. The sun was low when the borders of the commune crept over the horizon. Fields of grain shimmered in the late afternoon breeze, sewn onto the landscape in tidy squares and patches. Figures were already gathering in the distance below.

As the *Glasauge* made its slow descent, its crew chattered and fretted amongst themselves. Geist waited on the lower deck like a man preparing to go behind enemy lines. He was no more pleased about the plan now than he had been when Malone had first suggested it, but there was no other way to find Arnault.

It had been decided that a small escort would accompany him and Malone into town to look for Salazar. Lachesse and the rest of his crew would wait on the airship, prepared to flee at the first sign of trouble.

Malone imagined she was supposed to feel bad about leaving Lachesse behind, but she couldn't muster up anything more than a vague relief at being free of her and having solid ground beneath her feet. Besides, the old whitenail had apparently chosen to board the *Glasauge*.

The *Glasauge* set down with a thump that almost knocked Malone over. Geist and his escort gasped and flinched.

But then the outer hatch opened, and the rich, wonderful

musk of the farm greeted Malone like a warm kiss.

She was almost free.

The ship had landed in a field just beyond the village, and a crowd of half a dozen had already gathered there.

Salazar was waiting at the head of it, his eyes narrowed in the same stern gaze he probably used to appraise bushels of wheat or inspect sick goats.

His surprise only showed when he set eyes on Malone.

He looked to the scar on her neck. "Wasn't expecting to see you so soon."

"Me neither," she said. "I hear you've been all over lately."

He grunted. "Nothing like a couple of weeks on the road to set your back aching for your own bed." He regarded Geist for the first time. "And you are?"

Geist's face was ashy, his expression rigid. "Geist."

Salazar held out his hand. "Welcome to Meyerston."

Geist considered the proffered hand as though it were a dead rat. He bowed instead. "Plaisure."

Salazar met Malone's gaze over Geist's bent shoulders. One eyebrow quirked in question.

"Let's head in," he said. "Can't welcome guests without a proper meal."

As they continued toward the village, Malone glanced back at the *Glasauge*, stranded in the tall grass like a wounded bird. A handful of guards had taken up posts around the exterior to discourage any undue curiosity. Malone thought she saw Lady Lachesse's face in one of the windows, ghostly pale with the heavy powder she always wore.

She spun away quickly. It could have been her imagination. Though the sudden pang of guilt in her gut said otherwise.

As they headed into town, Salazar turned to Geist. "Some of my people saw your flying cart." He jerked his head toward the *Glasauge*. "This is the part where you tell me where you're from."

Geist coughed delicately. "You were sprecking something about making welcome to your gasts with a 'proper meal.'"

Salazar's feet found the well-worn grooves in the path. "I was talking about Malone."

Geist said nothing, but Malone watched his face go pale.

The dirt path hardened into a cobbled street, and houses and meeting halls rose to greet them. The farmers were staring at them and muttering to one another with the same combination of wonder and suspicion that Malone remembered from her first visit.

Only now, she saw among them a handful of city dwellers, their cheeks sunburnt and with borrowed farmers' flannels loose around their shoulders.

"We did good work," Salazar said next to her.

Malone hadn't realized she'd been smiling.

But then the evening breeze blew, and all of that was lost in the aromas of cook fires.

Salazar led them past a porched building off the town square – the same building, Malone remembered, where they had first met and negotiated. He guided them toward the epicenter of the meat and smoke aromas, the inn with the ridiculous sign of the pig holding a sheaf of wheat.

Geist hesitated at the threshold, looking like he had something stuck in his throat.

"We'll have some privacy upstairs," Salazar said. He continued on, and after a quick glance around the square and its crowd of onlookers, Geist and his escort followed.

Up the stairs and away from the guest rooms was a small parlor. Two of Salazar's people busied themselves opening the windows and clearing some of the derelict dishes. Salazar himself took up a position in the middle of the table, dug his elbows into the wood, and surveyed his guests. "Might as well make yourself comfortable," he said. "Food'll be up shortly."

Malone sat across from him, and Geist, taking a place beside her, gave her the tiniest expression of annoyance.

But Malone hadn't enjoyed a proper meal since before Sato's death. Probably since the last time she was among the farmers.

At that moment, she could think of nothing but the hot, fresh feast on its way.

So it took her several long seconds to realize that Salazar and Geist were both staring at her in curiosity and impatience, respectively.

She turned to Salazar. "We think Roman Arnault and Jane Lin may have passed through one of the communes recently. I was hoping one of your people might have reported two Recolettan fugitives." It was all she could do to ignore the aroma of roasting meat.

A smile played around Salazar's lips. "Saw them myself. Not even a week ago."

The pleasing scent evaporated from Malone's nostrils. "You – you did?"

"Up in Ashbury. They looked to be in a big hurry. The – ah, food's here."

A scruff-haired young girl arrived with a tray piled with cuts of something – a roast lamb or goat, perhaps – still sizzling from the cook fire. She set it down while others laid tureens of roasted and buttered vegetables on the table.

It took every last ounce of Malone's willpower to wait until the dinner plates had been passed around. But once Salazar gave the go-ahead nod, she pulled a hunk of flesh from the tray and tore into it. It was hot enough to burn her mouth, but she hardly cared. The crisp skin crackled between her teeth, and the tender meat melted on her tongue.

And the blood roaring through her ears drowned out the drone of voices at the dinner table.

But after a few moments of ecstasy, the sound of her name called her back like an alarm bell.

Geist was speaking, his plate empty but for a few stray parsnips. "– und Malone will be aiding us to cherch for Arnault."

"No," Malone said around her mouthful of goat. She didn't care how rude it was.

Geist blanched. But he had to have known this was coming.

Salazar's people were chewing their food with slow, careful motions. They held their knives and forks up as though they expected to use them on the people at the table. Geist's, on the other hand, were pushing beans and cauliflower around their plates like children listening to the grownups argue.

"We'll be glad to have you," Salazar said.

Malone savored the flavor of the goat and the unquestionable rightness of the moment. Why hadn't she gone with Salazar in the first place? The food was better and the people were hardworking and straightforward in a way she'd always admired. Here, she was the hero who had brought their new compromise to the cities. And here, she wouldn't have to play the politician.

What had Recoletta offered to make her stay in the first place?

"You promised to aid us." Geist sounded genuinely wounded.

"After Salazar tells you what he knows, I'll have fulfilled that promise."

Geist had no answer for that, but his eyes and mouth narrowed with accusation.

"You have an airship full of people. Hell, you have an airship," Malone said. Even though she owed Geist nothing, she felt the sting of his disappointment at her failure to finish the job. "What do you need from me?"

"You are a detectif. I was hearing you were a goot one," he said. It sounded like a reproach.

"And who would've told you a thing like that?"

He raised an eyebrow. "Your Lady Lachesse, of course."

She laughed, to cool the steaming carrot in her mouth as much as anything. "You should learn to approach her with some healthy skepticism."

"My friend's said her piece," Salazar said, polite but firm. "So why don't you help yourself to some cabrito."

"I have little appetit," Geist said. Sure enough, he was still harassing the same bit of parsnip with his fork. None of his crew had eaten anything on their plates. None of them had taken any goat.

Well, that just meant there was more for her. Malone sliced herself another helping.

"Then I'll get right down to it so you can be on your way," Salazar said. With that, he told them about Roman and Jane's visit to Ashbury and their hasty departure.

"But certainment they were having some destination," Geist said. "Where were they directing?"

Salazar gave Malone the barest of glances, but she took his meaning clearly enough.

"I'm done protecting those two," she said.

Salazar shrugged. He was fidgeting with something under the table – Malone could see the movement in his upper arm. "They were headed east, so I gave them a pair of horses and directions to Redhill."

"Wass is in this red hill?" Geist asked.

Salazar's smirk was tight. Tense. "More horses. Redhill was just a stop."

"Wass was their ultimate destination?" Geist asked.

"I was hoping you could tell me." Salazar leaned forward, resting his arms on the table. Malone couldn't see what he had in his hand, but she could see his fingers working furiously around it. "Only thing I know of out east is a dead, pre-Catastrophe city and a poison lake stretching far as the eye can see."

Now it was Geist's turn to smirk. "Un superstition. I sure you it is not poison."

Salazar bristled. "Try drinking from it and then tell me."

Geist answered with a placating smile and held up his hands. "Malone sprecks they were abandoning an instable politique in Recoletta. Did they recount anything such?"

"'Bout the only thing they did tell me that's looking to be true." He scowled and slid something – a small metal disk with a hole punched through the middle – onto the table. He was watching Geist, whose face was as still and rigid as a mask.

"Thought you might recognize it," Salazar said. "Because the farmers in the easternmost communes see these from time to time, and the folk what carry 'em aren't farmers, but aren't city folk neither. So I'm hoping you can set a few things straight for me."

Geist licked his lips. "It is alles complique."

"Then let me make it simple. We've got you surrounded. That flying cart of yours is big, but not big enough to carry more than a hundred souls, tops. And since you're enjoying hospitality at my table," Salazar said with a pointed glance at Geist's mostly empty plate, "how about you give me a few answers."

The Continental gave him a thin, perfunctory smile. "There are being two gran lands. The Continent und this place."

Salazar shook his head. "This place – you mean Recoletta and the communes?"

"Und more. More buried cities, more empty lands."

Salazar was still chewing this over. "You said 'this place.' Surely your folk have a name for it."

Geist folded his hands beneath a pained expression. "It does not translate."

Malone had spent enough time in politics to know an evasion when she heard one, but she decided not to press the point just yet.

"What about the Continent?" Malone asked. "Is it like this place – big and scattered with cities and farms?"

He laughed at this. "The Continent is plus bigger. Und our cities. Most of them are–" he broke off and meshed his fingers together. "More linked."

"So how did your spies get here?" Salazar asked. "I'm thinking a flying ship like yours would've been noticed long ago."

Geist blushed. "Ya, those are nouvelle. Entre your lands und the Continent is the sea. The poison lake." He smiled, but Salazar did not.

"So how do you cross it?" the farmer asked.

"On a city of boats, naturalleesh. This is Salvage."

"So that's how your old spies – people like Ruthers got here," Malone said. "But not any more."

"It was imprudent to be still relying on Salvage for such voyages." Geist's tone and expression were carefully neutral.

Malone recognized this from her politicking days, too. "You had a falling out with Salvage," she said. "And a big one if it pushed you to develop something as expensive as your airship. The question is, what was it over?"

Geist winced. "We digress."

Salazar jumped in. "Only so much a bunch of boats can make for themselves. Must be why they come round to the eastern communes every few years asking for tribute."

The Continental blanched. "We advised against this."

"But I'm guessing you weren't supplying them, either," Salazar said.

Malone turned to Salazar. "How long has Salvage been taking tribute from the farms?"

He shrugged. "Longer'n I've been around, that's for sure. But they don't have much of a schedule – one day they show up, clean a portion out of your storehouse, then they're gone. It'll be years before they hit the same place twice, which is a long time for tempers to cool. Especially when we were already used to paying tribute to the cities."

"The cities were supposed to protect the farms."

Salazar laughed. "How do you expect that conversation went? The few times they tried to report it, the city folk thought they were making it up to shirk their quotas." He shrugged again. "Just got easier to pay up."

Geist was listening quietly, seemingly happy at having been forgotten.

Malone pushed her plate away. "So we've got two lands, and in between is Salvage, friend to neither."

"Exactly so," Geist said.

"And if Arnault was heading east, then you think he's on Salvage now."

"I fear such."

Despite herself, Malone had gotten the scent of the hunt.

"What's he doing on Salvage, then? Staying, or making his way to the Continent?"

Geist scratched the back of his neck. "Also I am wondering this. Salvage is not an easy place for one not accustomed to it."

"Then it's safest to say Lin and Arnault will end up on the Continent, right where you want them." Malone regarded Geist, whose expression might as well have been chiseled from stone. "Except that's not what you want, is it?"

"Roman Arnault possesses something imposant." Geist straightened his lapels to mask his irritation. "It is regrettable for the wrong people to encounter him first."

Malone suspected he was talking about access to the vault, but she wasn't ready to tip her hand just yet. Let Geist believe she knew less than she did.

But Salazar wasn't yet satisfied. "What's Arnault got that you all want so badly?"

Geist plucked at the end of his goatee. "A key. To a gran cache. It is difficult to explain, but you would not desire the wrong persons to be having it."

"Who are the wrong people?" Malone asked. For all she knew, Geist was one of them.

"Persons who detest you. They would destruct you simply because you are different. Und because their histories demand it."

"For all we know, you could be one of them," Salazar said, thinking along the same lines as Malone.

"Then I would not trouble myself to avise you of them. Und I certainment would not waste my time on civil conversation." He smiled.

"Why do you care?" Malone asked.

He turned a sharp gaze on her. "Why did you? You continued in Recoletta."

He was right. Worse, she felt the old conviction kindling inside her.

Salazar folded his arms and leaned back in his chair. "If you're saying there's a foreign army looking to invade, know they wouldn't find it so easy."

Geist laughed bitterly. "I arrive to you in an airship. You illume your homes with candles. How hard do you esteem it will be?"

Salazar snorted. "You'd still have to get your people over here."

"Und as you observed, we have been doing that for a very long time." He folded his hands. "We must find Roman Arnault, und we must do it in avance of our rivals."

"You already know where he's going," Malone said.

He dabbed at his forehead with his napkin. "The Continent is stark big. It is easy to lose someone."

"So we follow Salvage. Watch where they make landfall." That much was obvious.

Geist gave her a smile – a real one. Salazar was shaking his head.

"What?" Malone asked.

"We," Geist repeated.

The hunt for Roman Arnault was still her case. She wasn't sure when, but at some point during dinner, she'd realized that much. And as much as she hated to admit it, Lachesse was right – the mess they were in now was her responsibility as much as it was anyone's. And she couldn't leave it to Geist, whom she hardly trusted, or Lachesse, whom she trusted even less.

She looked around the table, surrounded by honest friends and good food.

It had been a lovely dream.

Salazar sighed. "I'll see you're well provisioned. Sounds like it'll be a long time before we see each other again."

"Most kind," Geist said, again with the uncomfortable smile.

Malone realized something else, too. She'd been aching to get out of Dominari Hall and to sink her teeth into a case again. And now, she had the greatest manhunt of her life before her and a warm trail leading her across the sea.

CHAPTER FOURTEEN
DECKS

A combination of Jane's own grit, Leyal's gingiber, and directions from a few dozen strangers had finally brought her across the maze of Salvage to the *Albatross*. She'd arrived with painfully warm skin, a dry mouth, and a thrice-emptied stomach, but she arrived.

And she'd done so with feet that were surer on Salvage's rocking decks and an ear that was growing better attuned to the floating city's strange patois. She hadn't realized how much she'd been avoiding the confusion of human interaction until she began asking directions of nearly everyone in sight.

It felt good to have her bearings again.

The *Albatross* was a big ship, sitting low in the water and belching thick clouds of smoke into the sky. Moorings lashed it to its neighbors on all sides, but only three wide gangways led from it to any of the adjacent decks. A whistle shrieked, marking the shift change. She waited, observing the flurry of activity and looking for Roman. The workers leaving the *Albatross* were covered in grease and soot, yet none of that obscured the qualities that made Roman distinct in her mind. She watched for the rhythm of his limp, the cut of his hair, his prowling way of scanning a crowd with his chin pointed down.

The workers cleared, the shift change ended, and Jane settled in to await the next one.

She watched the natives navigate their city with catlike grace and listened to the bellmen as they marched across the decks, ringing their namesakes and calling out the day's news. Once or twice, she caught a glimpse of something on the horizon – distant behemoths that leapt from the waves only to disappear beneath them again. No one else seemed to pay any mind.

The sun beat down overhead, warming Jane's scalp and shoulders past the point of anything pleasant. Her skin and clothes were filthy from the tide of workers brushing past her. But she waited.

When the whistle squealed again, she was ready.

The men and women pouring out of the *Albatross* looked the same as those from the previous shift. They trudged forward, exhausted but eager to leave.

Some were a little taller, some broader in the shoulder. Some moved faster, and others were too tired. The minutes ticked by, and they all still looked the same.

All except the one coming down the far gangplank, walking with a poorly disguised limp.

She tightened her grip on the railing and held herself there a few seconds longer, until she was sure the down-angled chin and prowling gait could belong to no one else.

Then, she took off.

The flaw in her plan, which she was just beginning to appreciate, was that Roman was almost off the gangplank before she recognized him. He would just now be stepping onto the next deck, which was still two decks away from her, and there was no telling where he would head afterwards.

Jane squeezed and elbowed her way through the crowd. Unfortunately, workers disembarking from the *Albatross* were just as determined to leave the place as she was to approach it.

But she squirmed, darted, and apologized her way down the gangplank and across the next deck, where of course Roman was nowhere to be found.

It was hard to stand still among the workers, most of whom stood head and shoulders above her. She was pushed toward another gangplank and swept along it to another broad deck, where the workers began to disperse.

She heard a man's voice behind her. "Too small to be an oiler, she," he said. "But all covered in corruption just the same."

It struck her then – Roman couldn't have gone farther than the nearest salt ship. All she had to do was follow his shift mates headed in the same direction.

"Where's the salt ship?" Jane asked, turning.

Four workers all pointed in unison. If there was one thing any Salvager knew, it was where to get clean.

"*Conestoga*, she is called," said another man. "No offending, but you're gonna need the bottom deck." The others nodded.

"Graces," she said, hurrying ahead.

She continued up the gangway, through the plodding, creaking, chattering afternoon traffic. She reached the deck of a long ship. "Conestoga" was painted on the side.

Sure enough, three figures were hauling buckets up the side of the boat, their sun-darkened necks glistening and bent under squeaking pulleys. Jane continued past them and into the hold below.

The floors were slick and the air heavy with the musk of the bathers. The hold was a wide open space filled with sloshing troughs and strung with makeshift privacy screens – stained canvas sheets and tasseled silk hangings. They swayed with the movement of the boat, warping the shadows of the people moving behind them.

Jane found an unattended basin and splashed water over her arms, careful to let the runoff drip to the floor grating rather than back into the basin. When she wiped at her face, she was surprised to see her palms come away black.

This would be a bigger task than she'd expected.

She grabbed a handful of sand from a bin next to the basin and scoured her arms, face, and neck. It stung her sun-abused skin. She would never have believed something like sand could make her feel clean, but it beat the soot, grease, and sweat she was scraping off herself. Besides, there was something about a little discomfort that made both washing and penitence feel all the more effective.

Clearing her skin seemed to clear her head, too. As she patted her face and arms dry on the cotton sheet hanging next to her – trying not to think about how many other bathers had already soiled it today – she looked down at the grating between her feet and saw movement. Reaching limbs and sodden hair, flashing in the light filtering through the floor.

Jane returned to the stairs and descended another level, keeping a careful grip on the railing. The steps were slick and streaked with black, and a heavy odor rose from the lower level.

Suddenly, the comment about the bottom deck made sense. That was where all the oilers and engine ship crew cleaned up.

The light was poorer on the lower deck, filtered through the hatching of the grates above and through the scores of people moving across it. Which was just as well, because the men and women washing up here stripped themselves almost – in some cases completely – to the nude, scrubbing themselves with the quiet concentration born of ritual and exhaustion.

The deck was crowded – much more than the one above, especially since no one seemed that concerned about privacy screens. With any luck, Roman would be down here.

Jane hoped he'd be easier to recognize when he wasn't covered in soot.

She squeezed past the dripping bathers, trying to scan the room without being too obvious. If she knew anything about Roman, though, he'd have his back to a wall and his eyes on the crowd.

So she made her way toward the wall on her left and began working her way back.

She'd almost made it halfway across the deck when a voice behind her rose above the splashing and muttering. "Oye."

Jane pretended not to hear it.

"You. Companyera," the voice came again, louder and more

insistent. The bathers in front of Jane ignored her and continued their ablutions.

Meanwhile, footsteps, heavy and wet, plodded behind her.

Jane turned. In front of her was one of the tallest women she'd ever seen, naked but for a thin white undergarment around her waist, and that was nearly transparent with water. She crossed her arms over a chest like a carriage front. Jane couldn't help but notice that her head was almost level with it.

"Deck's for oilers. You wanna clean, go arriba," the woman said.

Jane glanced around, searching for any focal point but the muscled breasts in front of her, and sorely wished she had a coating of soot to hide the blush that was surely rising in her face.

Something squelched next to her, sounding like the fear welling in her chest. But it was only a man kneading his dirty shirt in the basin, frowning into the gray, opaque water.

He plunged himself in to the elbows, and some of the water spilled out, slopping onto Jane's shoes.

"I'm checking the water," Jane said. "Gonna need some fresh."

The big woman grunted. "I always tell 'em so. We go through it double-fast."

"Naturally," Jane said, already backing away.

"Ee get us some fresh," the woman said.

Before Jane had a chance to ask what she meant, the woman bent – giving Jane a sudden and surprising view – and hoisted an armful of filthy towels and sheets.

Which she dropped into Jane's arms.

And what was an armful for the larger woman was several for Jane – it piled up to her face, and she had to hold it to her chest to keep it from spilling onto the floor.

The woman folded her arms again and smiled.

"I'll see what else needs collecting," Jane said, averting her face from the foulness. She left before the other woman could get any new ideas.

The bundle of fabric smelled like week-old goat's milk and looked like it had been trampled by half the population of Salvage, but at least the other bathers parted way for her.

She tried to tell herself she'd handled worse before, but she knew that was a lie. So she focused on the faces in the crowd, and the accents in the murmuring voices, and the cooling drip and splash of clean water from the grating above.

Jane found him in the corner. He was scrubbing his shoulders with handfuls of sand and watching the crowd through a curtain of wet hair.

Gray rivulets of water ran down his arms and torso, crossing pink welts and red lines. In the week since they'd been picked up, he'd started to return to himself, filling out the expanse between his broad shoulders once more.

She was suddenly grateful for the cooling splash of water dripping from above.

Roman glanced up. His eyes found hers around the armful of filthy towels, and his smile was both sudden and surprised.

"If you'd told me you were coming, I would have cleaned up sooner," he said. A charmingly ridiculous smile played at the corners of his mouth.

"I wouldn't want to impose," she said. She was starting to think she'd arrived at just the right time, anyhow.

He gave her a quick up and down. "I take it you're not here for a salt bath."

Remembering her actual purpose sobered her up. "Actually, I came to talk," she said as casually as she could.

His grin faded as though he heard the worry in her tone. "Two minutes," he said. "Meet me topside."

Jane headed back toward the stairs, clearing her path with the armful of towels. She left them by the stairs in what felt like a small but satisfying act of defiance.

He emerged into the afternoon light after a couple of interminable minutes. His ragged shirt – the same one she'd last seen him in, she was sure – was already stained and torn from his brief time on Salvage, yet he was looking like himself again. The bruises on his face had mostly faded away, and even his patchy beard did little to disguise him.

It was all she could do to peel her gaze away from him to scan the decks for anyone else watching.

"Already?" he asked, following her eyes.

The message Jane had intercepted had her paranoid about who might be watching, but there was no such thing as privacy on Salvage – not when bathing was a communal activity. The best she could hope for was to disappear into the crowd. Fortunately, a galley was as good a place for that as any.

Galleys, at least, weren't hard to find. One simply had to follow the aromas of frying fish.

They found one just a couple of decks over from the salt ship. It didn't have a cabin, only a series of rippling canvas sunshades crowned with smoke from dozens of cook fires. Men and women stood over them, their voices raised over the hiss of the oil and the snapping of the awnings.

And the place was even more crowded than the other packed boats. Fish and vegetables, caught fresh from the sea and grown on dirt-layered farm decks, sizzled and spat from grills and pans.

Of the many things Jane still didn't understand about Salvage, one was the food economy. She'd seen a dozen boats like this one all around the fleet, and whether they'd been intended as kitchens or just ended up that way, Jane couldn't say. But when she'd asked about food her first few days on Salvage, she'd been pointed to decks like these as if the rest should be self-explanatory. And when she'd picked a square of chewy flat bread topped with a fried gull's egg from a baking stone, no one had asked for her money.

As best she could tell, the people tending the cook fires worked on those boats the way she worked on the *Nossa Senhora*. It was simply another job that people were assigned and that they showed up to do, not because there was pay in it but simply because it kept the city running.

They dunked their hands in the saltwater basin near the gangplank. Even though their collars were still damp and their skin bright and sticky from the baths they'd just taken, they washed their hands because no Salvager would touch food otherwise.

Roman took a deep breath of the savory scents around them. He muscled through the crowd to the nearest stove and returned with a cross between a fish and a snake.

Two somethings.

"I found a message," Jane said, taking her portion.

With that, she explained her work on the *Nossa Senhora* and the message she'd found that morning.

"What did it say?" Roman asked.

Jane closed her eyes and pictured the scrap of paper in her hand and the then-live pigeon cradled in her arm. "Kennedy agitates. Refuses petition to interrogate the bounty. Demands privilege of salvage. Avise."

Roman raised his eyebrows. "Advise?"

"Probably." It was hard to know exactly what Salvagers' words meant, but it was easy to get close enough. "What do you think?"

"I think the eel is better hot," he said, pointing to the cooling twist of meat in her hand.

Jane considered the scorchmark-crusted flesh and took a bite. Salvagers seasoned their food as if eating it were a dare. She couldn't understand why, except that maybe their burning tongues distracted their heads and stomachs from the rocking and sloshing of the world around them.

"I'm worried this means someone's searching for you. Maybe both of us," Jane said quickly, as if spitting the words out might make them less likely to be true.

Roman looked at her, picking his teeth with a bone. "How so?"

"What else could it mean to 'interrogate the bounty'? We were picked up just a week ago. Whoever this Kennedy is, maybe he–"

"Kennedy's not a person," Roman said, selecting a long, fried tuber from a sun-warmed plate. "It's a ship."

"Are you sure?"

"How many Salvagers have you met with names like 'Kennedy'? They're all Leyal, Honor, Fey, Coraj, and what have you," he said.

"Well, maybe–"

"Also, *Kennedy* is one of the biggest ships on Salvage." He pointed to a deck, tiny at this distance but large enough to rise above its neighbors.

"You could have just said that."

Roman shrugged, smiling impishly as he sucked his fingers clean.

"But that still doesn't settle what they want and why they're agitating. Or agitated," Jane said. "What if someone is looking for us? Or you and the vault," she whispered.

He frowned. "It's possible. But if someone wanted to find me – or you – I've got to think they already would've. *Kennedy*'s not only one of the biggest, it's also one of the most influential. Its capitan has been stirring up trouble."

"Over what?"

He shook his head. "Engine room chatter only goes so far. But I'll keep my ear to the ground."

This all felt familiar. So did the dread clotting in her stomach. "If they're not after you, then what's this about?"

Roman shrugged, but Jane read in the lines in his brow that he was getting worried too.

"What else did they pick up? What else that could be this much trouble?" Jane asked.

"Oh, I'm trouble now?" Roman asked, grinning.

"The worst kind." Warmth briefly tickled her chest, and she didn't think it was just the food. "The kind that starts wars and–"

Suddenly, Roman's eyes flew wide with understanding.

Jane thought of it, too. "The Library," she said.

He nodded.

That sick feeling was congealing into something solid and substantial. And familiar.

Roman's furrowed brow cast long shadows where his bruises had been. "I've got to look," he said.

"You don't," she said, knowing he would anyway.

He met her gaze. "The last time someone went looking for something useful in the Library, Sato found an ancient formula for combustibles and used it to burn hundreds of young soldiers alive."

He didn't mention her unintentional role in that particular tragedy. He didn't have to.

"Nothing good comes from that place," he said. "And I helped Sato uncover it."

"So now you think whatever comes out of it is your responsibility," Jane said. She hated the idea, but she couldn't help but admire him for it. He had become a very different man from the one she'd met at Councilor Hollens's mansion.

"I'll be cautious," he said.

"No, you won't." Even he wasn't a skilled enough liar to make her believe that. And if he was going to rush into trouble, she couldn't let him go alone. "I'll go. If we're wrong and someone is onto you, then snooping around the *Kennedy* is the last place you should be."

"That's a risk I choose to take," he said. "I'm not letting anyone else endanger themselves on my behalf." He gave her a long, sober expression. His mind was made up.

But so was hers. "You can't stop me from coming with you," she whispered.

He erupted into a laugh loud enough that the people around them turned and looked. "I wouldn't dare try."

Jane felt heat rising in her face. She glanced away and saw some of the people around them still watching. A woman chewing a roasted potato. A man with a big straw hat shading his face. A couple sharing a basket of oysters.

They were looking and whispering.

Fear curdled in Jane's blood. "I think we're being watched."

"They probably don't see a sunburn like yours every day," Roman said, brushing his hand lightly across her arm. "You should find some ointment and stay in the shade."

Jane pulled back her sleeve. Next to the pale flesh of her upper arm, everything below the elbow appeared as though it had been left on one of the cook fires for a few hours.

But she might as well have been invisible. The others weren't paying her any mind. "They're staring at you," she said.

He grunted. "That's what you get for having too much fun around people named Purity and Innocente." It was a joke, but he wasn't laughing. And neither was she.

There was more she wanted to say, but she felt foolishly exposed out here. "We should go," she said, already leading him toward the gangway.

"You're right," he said, though he didn't sound happy about it.

"When should we meet? For the, um, errand we discussed. We'll want some sort of distraction."

He grinned. "The Crossing Day festival is in three days."

CHAPTER FIFTEEN
SAUVAGE

Malone made it her business to get to know every inch of the *Glasauge*.

At least, every inch she was permitted to visit.

The only deck she knew already – probably the only one she'd spent any amount of time on – was the one with crew quarters. An oval-shaped corridor wrapped around the deck and its tiny cabins with tinier windows. The two U-bends of the corridor connected to the lounge on one end and the mess on the other. At the center of the deck, inside the corridor, were washrooms and the ubiquitous storage compartments. It seemed that any wall panel, or any piece of furniture, could be opened up or pulled away to reveal another dimension filled with supplies.

The deck below was mostly storage. Crates were anchored to the floor and lashed to the walls. Malone had peeked through a sample of them, searching for anything of note – something she could use, perhaps, or something that might tell her more about the Continentals. So far, all she'd found were more sundries and foodstuffs. Tanks bulged at either end of the deck, filled – as she was told – with fuel, water, and waste. They all looked the same, but sniffing at the seals left little doubt as to which was which.

The deck was dark and cramped and, most importantly, the crew of the *Glasauge* rarely visited it.

The third and fourth decks, however, interested Malone the most.

Directly above crew quarters was the command deck. While Malone was politely ignored among the cabins and in the lounge, the crew paid her closer attention once she ascended the stairs. The forward end housed what Geist had called the "pilot house," where at any given time half a dozen crew members occupied themselves with the business of keeping the airship aloft and moving. There was more open space on this deck, and other rooms with navigational instruments, charts, and logbooks.

And on the back of the third deck was a room that was always locked. Malone had seen Geist and a handful of other crew enter and leave it, but she'd never been allowed inside. Any time she got close, the nearest crew member would shoo her away.

But she'd heard a strange sound coming from within. A soft, warbling murmur. It was almost drowned out by the humming of machinery from the next deck, but not quite.

The upper deck was nestled in the lower portion of the envelope – the big, rigid balloon – and the crew referred to it only as "engineering." As best Malone could tell, that section contained most of the equipment that propelled the airship and controlled its altitude. The brief glimpse she got of it was of compartments filled with humming, pumping machinery. Above that, Geist told her, were the gas bags that held the *Glasauge* aloft and the scaffolding that supported the envelope.

The more she saw of the ship, the more it seemed like a flying mystery, and its people even more so. Their hybrid language was still difficult to understand, though she'd gotten used to Geist's wording and cadence.

The others, though, had little to say to her. Malone got the feeling that most of them – Phelan excepted – wanted as little to do with her as possible. The stray bits of conversation she heard between them might have been backwards for all she understood.

After a couple of days, she was becoming stir-crazy. Geist

happily charged her with cleaning the decks. It was dull, unglamorous work, but it gave her an excuse to continue studying the ship without attracting too many eyes.

She monitored the timing of the shift rotations. They weren't as regimented or regular as she would have expected, but she got a sense for them nonetheless. She began to recognize individual crew members, and to learn who did what on the airship.

The best time for reconnaissance was the moonrise shift – from ten at night to six in the morning. The pace was slower. Quieter. It was easier to move around the decks without attracting the notice of the crew.

That was her favorite time.

They were four days out of Meyerston when she found the body.

She was sweeping the hall on the second deck. She wasn't supposed to enter the crew cabins, but as she'd learned the shift rotations, she'd gotten a sense for when each cabin was likeliest to be empty. She'd started combing them for clues – about Geist and his crew, what they wanted.

But she hadn't found much yet. She had to pick her moments carefully, waiting for the early and mid-shift lulls, when off-duty crew were occupied in their bunks or settled in the lounge or mess.

The cabin Malone really wanted into was Geist's, but that one was always locked.

So she explored as she could. She'd gone through the personal quarters of a navigator, a soldier, and three different people who always took their work shifts in the engine room. She'd found spare clothes, coins like the one Salazar had shown them, and a love letter with just enough familiar words to make her blush, but nothing that told her anything useful. Not without more context.

But that was fine. All she needed was more time, and she was sure to find something.

It was night. They had left land behind the day before

yesterday. Now, the moon gleamed over an endless expanse of dimpled water. It was enough to make Malone suddenly glad for the relative safety of the airship, so high above it.

It was also a stark reminder that she'd passed the point of no return.

She'd just finished her rounds on the cargo deck, and the crew deck was dark and quiet. The soft clink of dishes came from the mess, and a gentle murmur filtered in from the lounge. Poorly suppressed sighs and giggles came from some of the cabins – members of the crew paired off frequently and openly. It surprised Malone that this happened in a professional expeditionary force, but it was just one of many things that did.

In short, all was calm and quiet. Perfect for a few quick forays.

Malone passed the cook's cabin. He'd be sleeping. The next belonged to someone else she'd seen in the engine room. She paused and heard a gentle snoring coming from within.

At the next door, silence. The occupant was part of the control room crew, and Malone knew she'd seen him on the moonlight shift before.

She glanced down the hall. No movement from the galley, and none from the lounge. This was her chance.

Malone pushed the cabin door open and saw a body lying in the bunk. She froze.

Then, the metallic tang of blood assailed her senses.

It splashed the walls and soaked the pillow. Malone realized the body was a corpse.

She heard movement: the click of a door opening. Malone was already halfway into the cabin – she slid the rest of the way in and eased the door shut.

She waited by the door, listening as a torpid stride approached and then clopped past her position. A sleeper on the way to the washroom, most likely.

When the footsteps receded, she checked the body.

It was a young man in his mid-twenties. His throat had been cut, and a small, red-soaked towel lay over his neck and mouth.

There was no sign of struggle – no bruising on his arms, no skin or hair under his fingernails, and the bedsheets were still tucked under the mattress at his feet. Whoever had killed him had caught him asleep.

Or had been invited into his cabin.

Malone lifted the covers. The victim was dressed in a loose shirt and trousers. If he'd been out of them at the time of his death, she doubted very much his killer would have been able to get him back into them.

The body had barely cooled. Blood pooled where it pressed against the mattress, leaving long, dark bruises. He'd probably been dead a couple of hours.

Malone inspected the rest of his cabin. Leather boots tucked neatly under the bed, folded uniforms and underclothes in the shelf above it. The cabins were barely big enough to turn around in; there was little to search and even less to find. A glossy card identified the man as Michel Sharad. The leather case with its straight-bristled shaving brush, scuffed leather strop, and assortment of creams, oils, and powders established him as a man of meticulous habits.

The only thing missing from his case was the razor itself. A pair of looped leather straps gaped at the blade's absence.

By all appearances, then, someone had entered Sharad's room while he slept, slit his throat with his own razor, and disappeared, with the murder weapon still on hand.

Several concerns occurred to Malone almost at once.

The first was that a murderer was loose on the *Glasauge*, and as they were now floating over open water, they were all trapped together.

Barely behind that thought was another. She and Lachesse were the two people on board that Geist and his crew knew the least. And she was more physically capable than her older companion. Suspicion was likely to fall on her.

The last was that Michel Sharad had been part of the moonlight shift, which had started less than an hour ago. That meant someone was apt to come searching for him.

She needed to leave, and fast.

No sooner did Malone have this thought than she heard footsteps, swift and purposeful, approaching from the end of the hall. This was no midnight washroom trip. This was someone with a mission.

She held her breath and stood still, hoping the person in the hall would keep walking.

The footsteps stopped outside the cabin. Five quick raps rattled the door.

"Sharad," came a man's voice, "reveille und aufcome. You are en tard."

Malone considered the body in the bunk. The longer she stayed here, the guiltier she'd look if anyone opened the door.

Then again, she looked pretty guilty already.

The knocking came again, hard enough to shake the door on its hinges. "Sharad!" He said something too fast to follow, but in it she caught "watch officer."

Hope welled in Malone's chest. She willed him to go.

A heavy sigh hissed on the other side of the door. The crewman's footsteps, fast and heavy with irritation, receded down the hall.

She had one hand over the lever. When the footsteps faded, Malone counted a few extra seconds to give him time to head up the stair. Then, she opened the door.

Malone stepped into the hall and found herself staring at the *Glasauge*'s balding cook, Chernev, who was leaning out of his cabin with the same startled, confused look on his slack face she must have had right then.

Shit.

The cook's gaze sharpened as he recognized her. "Is not your cabine."

She needed to establish some meager control over the situation while she still could. "Did anyone else enter or leave the cabin?" Malone asked.

"Wass?" The cook licked his lips. He was uneasy.

"This is important."

His brow beetled with suspicion. "Attendey. We wait," he said. A Recolettan would have used the same mild tone to make a polite suggestion, but among the Continentals it was a command. He glanced between her and the stairs at the end of the hall, willing someone – someone with authority – to come and sort this mess out.

Presently, a man and a woman descended the tight spiral stairs. She led the way, and her stern and expressionless face remained just so when she saw Malone. Only the man's eyebrows moved in surprise.

The cook said something and pointed to Malone. His meaning was obvious enough.

The watch officer's face betrayed nothing, but Malone read plenty in the young cadet's expression. Confusion. Fear. Disgust, even. Under different circumstances, she might have been amused.

"There's a murderer on your ship," Malone said, as if she could get ahead of the suspicions by announcing it now. It was a long shot, but it was better than nothing.

"Wass ist this odeur?" the cadet asked, a quaver in his voice. The coppery musk of Sharad's blood was wafting into the hall.

"Stay beside," the watch officer said, motioning to Malone. She hadn't blinked once.

Malone eased into the hall, her hands up. "The killer appears to have used the man's razor. I expect he or she has hidden it elsewhere by now."

If anyone understood her, they gave no indication.

The watch officer shoved past Malone and into the doorway. Malone could only see her face in profile, but the woman's eyebrows shot up.

"Malabar. Bringen Geist," she said.

Malone saw the cook scuttle off. Then the young cadet slammed her into the wall, pressing his forearm into her neck and her cheek into the bulkhead.

"Perfid pestilander!" he roared in her ear. Gone was all of the careful civility of the Continentals. "Merde dreckt! Wass did you do?"

He had taken her by surprise, but his grip on her arm was weak and he was swaying with emotion. It would have been easy – and satisfying – to hook his ankle with hers, knock him from his feet, and see how he liked having his head rammed into hard surfaces.

But it would be a short-lived victory, and one that would only complicate her declaration of innocence.

So Malone swallowed her anger and her words. Anything she said now would only be distorted by the young cadet's wrath.

But the watch officer had a cooler head. "Valenti." She spoke with the chilly tone of command. He eased off her neck, but just barely.

It would be the bitterest of ironies to survive her hanging only to be hurled from the airship for a crime she didn't commit.

At least the fall would be faster.

One half of Malone's face was still pressed against the cold metal of the bulkhead, so she heard rather than saw Geist's approach, recognizing his swift, short stride.

"Wass has happened?" he said. His words were even more clipped than normal. Malone could imagine his expression, his lips thin and his jaw tight with tension.

The cadet, Valenti, cleared his throat into Malone's ear. "Sir, I was coming to cherch–"

"Not you," Geist said. "Her."

Malone was hauled away from the wall and spun to face Geist. He was dressed in loose crimson pajamas that shone and rippled like flowing water. They hung on his thin frame in a way that made him look both smaller and more authoritative than usual. His eyes were bright and alert, his mouth the same thin line she'd pictured. The only real sign he'd been sleeping was the crunched and crinkled mass of hair on one side of his head.

"I found Sharad dead in his cabin," she said. "His throat was cut. By his own straight razor, it seems. He's probably been dead for a couple of hours."

Geist's eyebrow quirked. "You found the razor?"

"No. It's missing from his kit."

He nodded over her shoulder. "Cherch her cabine." Cadet Valenti released Malone and hurried toward her quarters. "Wass were you doing in Sharad's cabine?" Geist asked.

"Investigating," she said. No point in hiding it.

Geist smirked, holding his chin with one hand. "Why?"

"It was supposed to be empty," Malone said.

"Here!" Valenti called down the hall. "Unter ze mattress!"

Malone spun. She would have thought it a tasteless joke, but Valenti was emerging from her cabin, holding a crusty razor aloft like a prize.

His face was flushed with victory, his eyes wide with conviction. She was guilty, and he was the avenging angel who had caught her.

Malone turned slowly, hoping she would not see the same look on Geist.

His expression was steady, and his eyes were on her. "I am hoping you will explain," he said.

"If I'd killed Sharad, I'd know better than to hide the evidence in my own room," she said. "And I wouldn't have returned to the scene after the job was done."

Geist inclined his head to one side. "Unless perhaps you planned on having this conversation now."

Malone wasn't sure if he was trying to goad her or if he was really that stupid. "You've got forty-two people under your command. How well do you know them?"

"Better than I know you."

"What do you think I'd want?"

Geist's face was motionless except for his lips. "I am hoping you tell me."

"I chose to stay to help you find Roman Arnault. If I didn't want that, I would have stayed on the farm." Once again, she wished she had.

"Then give me a better history. Why is the razor in your cabine?"

Malone opened her mouth to reply that she was the obvious scapegoat, and if he was going to torture her with questions this idiotic, he might as well toss her overboard now.

But another voice called from the hall behind her.

"Someone is sending you a message, you fools."

Malone turned. Lady Lachesse was sauntering toward them, her hair pulled into a madwoman's bun and her face a painted mask of irritation. Did the woman sleep in her cosmetics, or had she made herself up during their argument in the hall? Malone wasn't sure which possibility was more ridiculous.

Geist's mouth puckered into a prim little rosebud. "Is there something you will be telling us?"

"Isn't it obvious?" Lachesse said. "Whoever killed your young man left the weapon under Malone's mattress as a warning."

"Und this warning?" Geist asked.

Lachesse's eyes fluttered open in exasperation. "That they will kill Malone next, of course."

Geist was quiet, his eyes flitting from Malone to Lachesse to the watch officer next to him.

At last, he sighed. "We speak privately." He nodded to the watch officer. "Cherch the cabines und count off. If others are missing, I must know."

The woman made for the end of the corridor. Valenti fell into her orbit, casting a final rueful glare at Malone.

Only when that was settled did Geist pinch the bridge of his nose with something like real exhaustion. "Chernev," he said, his eyes closed, "I want caffee in the study."

The cook bowed and headed toward the galley.

Geist moved toward the stairs. "You will follow me."

Lachesse looked at Malone with heavy-lidded eyes. Without a word, she headed after Geist.

They both followed him up the spiral stairs to the command deck. The other crew on duty watched them over control panels and under furrowed brows. Curious, but not certain what was afoot.

He led them into the room in which he'd debriefed Malone on her first day.

Geist sat and gestured for them to do likewise. His back was to the windows, and the scant moonlight filtering into the room made it hard to see his face. The black cames crossing the windows resembled the bars of a prison cell.

A long silence stretched between them. Malone resisted the urge to speak up – when Geist was ready he would accuse or question them. Lachesse adjusted her gold bracelets with a loud jangling but held her tongue.

The door creaked open behind them. Phelan entered and set a tray on the table with a nervous rattle. Caffee and three small cups. She glanced at them with wide, anxious eyes, and quickly left. As soon as the door shut behind her, Geist poured himself a cup, drained it, and poured himself another.

"I would offer to you, but I am knowing you detest it. Still, you must spreck if you decide otherwise." He knocked back another glass of caffee. "Though you should do it rasch or I will be drinking yours en plus."

Lachesse frowned. "If that's all this is, then I'd just as soon return to bed."

"Setz," Geist said. "The others must esteem we are having a long chat." With that, he set his glass down and laced his hands in front of him. Another silence stretched out, but Geist appeared in no mood to break this one.

"You don't think we killed him," Malone said.

He scratched his chin. "No."

Some of the tension went out of her shoulders. "How did you know?"

He scoffed and shifted in his seat. "You are not an idiot. Und you have no reason." A tiny frown rippled across his drawn lips, gone as soon as it appeared.

"Who does?" Malone asked.

"It is not your concern."

Lachesse only raised an eyebrow. A shake of the head would have been too gauche for her.

"That's not how I work," Malone said. She crossed her arms.

"I am begging your pardon?" Geist asked.

"You brought me along to help you find Roman Arnault. I don't do half-jobs, Geist. I'm in or I'm out."

He raised his eyebrows and glanced toward the louvered window. "I am thinking this would be a stark mal time to be 'out.'"

"For both of us." She took a step toward him. "You have a traitor in your midst. I can help you find him."

The smile he gave her would have been polite on anyone else. "Speaking as a former detectif or as a former traitor?"

"Speaking as the one person on this ship with a bigger stake in finding Arnault than you."

He angled his head toward Lachesse. "I am seeing why you chose to hang her."

"I underestimated her," the whitenail said. "I would not advise you to do the same."

Despite herself, Malone felt pride welling up in her chest.

Geist rolled his eyes. It was the closest thing to agreement she was likely to get.

"Why would one of your crew kill another and frame me?" Malone asked.

"Politique is contentious. But you understand something of this, yes?" He drew his thumb along the side of his neck, mirroring her scar.

She waited.

He rubbed his goatee. "Some of my compatriots consider you... sauvage."

Lachesse harrumphed.

Geist spread his hands. "We have been out of contact for

hundreds of years. And where there is a lack of information, the imagination invents many details, does it not?"

Malone had seen plenty of evidence of that in how most of Geist's crew dodged and avoided her.

"Your own cities are isolated, no? And does not the fear of the unfamiliar color your impression?"

"Not in shades of boogeymen and nonsense. Besides, those are politicians' tall tales." Malone put an extra emphasis on that, just so Geist would have no doubt that he was included in that statement.

Lady Lachesse made an admirable show of studying her long, shimmering nails.

Geist's face lit up. "So you do comprend." He nodded as if that explained everything.

Malone looked to Lady Lachesse, who gave her a small shrug.

"Are you saying that your politicians want people to believe we're all savages?"

Geist's eyes were round with apology. "Only some."

"What do you want? Our land? Our goods? Our people?"

The Continental shook his head. "It is about power. There is great power in fear, no? Politics is theatre. Your Lady Lachesse knows this."

The whitenail breathed a long-suffering sigh. "I so dearly hope you have a point."

But Malone was thinking about Sundar and about how he would have relished this moment. His memory had snuck back up on her, and now it stung afresh like alcohol poured over a wound. To her surprise, the pain of his absence had not lessened. She only felt it less frequently.

Geist smiled blandly at Lady Lachesse. "My point is that your world is a pawn in ours. And there are very ambitious people on the Continent who tell very unpleasant stories to hold power."

"We'll tell others," Malone said, her voice suddenly thick in her throat. "Lachesse and I are proof."

Geist's smile puckered into a wince. "A woman who was

hanged and another with claws like a wild cat? You will forgive my indelicacy, but I fear you will not prove what you intend. Besides, people are stubborn creatures, no? Once they reach a conclusion, it becomes very hard to shake them from it. True investigators are rare."

The discussion of politics, angles, and narratives was making Malone's head spin. Or maybe it was just the smell of Lachesse's perfume.

Regardless, she needed facts.

"Getting us to the Continent ahead of Roman is your job," Malone said. "Mine is to find your murderer before something else happens. I need to know more about Sharad – who he was closest to on the *Glasauge*, who he might have quarreled with. Where the rest of the crew was in the hours before we found the body. What the schedule is, and any inconsistencies that might have arisen. How someone else could have gotten a key to this office."

Geist frowned. "I am thinking you should guard your back and keep your head down."

Malone looked at Lachesse, whose expression was carefully neutral. She'd never been much good at keeping her head down.

CHAPTER SIXTEEN
CROSSING DAY

Jane's burn had faded to a pale rose by the time of Crossing Day, three days after her initial meeting with Roman on the galley. They'd seen each other every day since, strolling across the decks to watch the locals and the distant behemoths that leapt and splashed. Their shift schedules made it difficult to find more than a few hours together, and the crowding on Salvage made it impossible to find any privacy, a fact that gnawed at her a little more with each meeting.

The mood began to change on Salvage, too – people grew eager and anxious with anticipatory energy.

Jane kept an eye on the pigeons of the *Nossa Senhora*. She didn't see any new red-tagged birds, and it would have been impossible to keep up with all of the regular traffic.

But she began seeing other people come to talk to Leyal. She couldn't figure what about – the conversations happened in low, tense voices behind closed doors.

Things were tense all around Salvage. People pulled longer shifts to get the boats ready for a day and night of revelry. The extended hours made them grumpy and unpredictable. But the worst was when the *Staten Island Ferry*, a moderately sized ship with several waterstills and a hundred beds, had to be scuttled. It sprang a leak and began sinking, and every Salvager in sight worked quickly to sever its moorings lest it pull other craft down with it.

Thanks to their swift cooperation, one of the *Ferry*'s waterstills and all of its inhabitants were evacuated. All except its capitan, who was condemned to go down with the ship he'd failed to maintain. To keep free of corruption.

The episode rattled Jane's neighbors, and it showed her just how seriously Salvagers took their mundane maintenance routines. Many of the people she talked to said the capitan had earned his death, and that his segundos were lucky the old laws weren't in force. A few confided that every ship went down eventually. All of them whispered it was an ill omen for Crossing Day, which marked Salvage's arrival at the midpoint of the ocean, ten days after their departure from the shores of Jane's homeland.

Which would mean they were halfway to the Continent and whatever it held for her, Roman, and the vault he meant to destroy. The thought unnerved and excited her all at once.

She awoke on Crossing Day to festival songs and the thick, rich smell of frying sweets. The festivities had already begun by the time she left her cabin and went to the salt boat to wash up; singers hooted and slurred, their voices already heavy with alcohol, and between the decks were hung colorful streamers and flags that had obviously seen too many years of rough use. The decks were busier and more crowded than she'd seen them yet, though the revelers didn't seem to mind.

Jane snagged a ginger cake and ate half on her way to meet Roman. She wrapped the rest for later.

He was waiting on the long deck of the *Horizon*, right where he'd promised. The railings and deckhouses were strung up like an enormous – and enormously colorful – spider's web.

His smile was that of a man with too many secrets.

And despite herself, Jane was happy to see it.

Two squarish packs rested at his feet. Roman adjusted one around her shoulders before slipping the other over his. "Our ticket to the party," he said, fastening the straps. He held out his arm. "The evening's festivities await."

She took it and smiled back. "They'll hardly begin before we arrive."

"Then we must be punctual. These Salvagers are a strict bunch."

Jane laughed but felt her nervousness creep into her voice. She didn't want to think of what that would mean if they were caught.

And yet she had the delicious feeling of being in on a secret together. Anticipation warmed her blood, and the festive mood buoyed her spirits.

Roman was giddy, too, walking with a spring in his step. He seized a cup of grog, the thin alcohol the Salvagers made. Jane had made a game of spotting the stills on the ships she visited. So far, she'd yet to find a ship without at least one.

"To christen the occasion," Roman said, holding the cup to her.

She took it, but something about the laundry chemical smell of the stuff or the excitement brewing in her blood turned her stomach. She forced it down anyway.

"So, which way is the *Kennedy*?" Jane asked.

"Just across that box ship – the *COSCO*."

There were at least four or five of the craft the locals called box ships – long ships that sat low in the water, their decks stacked with rows of rectangular boxes. She had always wondered what was inside them.

The nighttime chill was just creeping into the air when they climbed the gangway onto the ship with the letters "COSCO" painted onto its side.

The first time Jane had seen one of the box ships, she'd been at least a mile out, on the boat that had picked her and Roman up. From far away, the boxes looked like toy blocks, neatly stacked and still showing blushes of old color – blues, greens, reds, yellows.

Up close, there was nothing toylike about them. Stacked seven and eight high, they rose around her and Roman like canyon walls, climbing high enough that Jane had to crane her head back to see the tops. The sound of the festivities on the other ships faded away, warped and muffled by the ravine of metal.

Instead of shouts, songs, and cheers, Jane heard groaning metal, pattering footsteps, and high, whispering voices.

Roman pressed on like always, his head down and his gait accentuated by a slight limp. Jane couldn't help but look at the rows of boxes they passed between and at the trellises of rope ladders and metal rungs connecting them.

A boy and a girl ran across the aisle a dozen yards ahead, bare feet slapping the deck.

By the standards of Salvage, each box was large enough to house a family. In fact, some appeared to house several – bed nooks were slotted three high, like shelves against the walls, though Jane couldn't imagine climbing in or out of them without knocking her head. Clotheslines strung with tattered towels and trinkets marked off the space, suggesting privacy rather than creating it.

Jane was suddenly grateful to have her own berth, tiny though it was.

"There must be hundreds of homes like this," Jane said.

"Almost a thousand if you count the ones on the other box ships," Roman said.

A trio of children sat on the edge of one box, their swinging legs dangling over the top of the one below. They peered at Jane from behind a torn curtain.

"Are they safe?" Jane asked, marveling again at the height of the stacked boxes.

"As much as anything on Salvage." Roman said it with his usual dispassion, but Jane noted again how he kept his head down and straight ahead, as if to avoid looking at the crates. "Despite Salvagers' best efforts, everything here is falling apart." Jane thought of the *Staten Island Ferry*. "These ships, at least, are big enough to keep steady in rough water." His shrug was a little too stiff.

A pair of hammocks were strung inside the ground-level box on Jane's left, and the children in them passed a beaded string back and forth.

Jane looked around with dawning realization at the youngsters dozing in bunks in the next box, at the size of the clothes hung across the aisles, at the small, bare feet dangling from the top of the stacks.

"Roman," she said, "where are the adults?"

He sighed like he'd been hoping to avoid the subject. "Salvage has strict limits on childbearing. They've only so many ships, so there's only so much they can grow. Each resident is limited to two, but some have more." As if that explained it.

"So they live out here? By themselves?" What surprised Jane – besides the seeming cruelty – was the sheer number of children. She had yet to find a place where two people could be alone, let alone enough to produce so many offspring.

"Once they're five years of age," Roman said.

A girl with choppily cropped hair, no more than seven, watched Jane with eyes like backlit windows.

Jane remembered the ginger cake she'd left wrapped in her pocket. She took it out and gave it to the girl, regretting that she hadn't saved more of it.

"We should hurry," Roman said. Jane followed. She could think of nothing else to do.

They left the children and their box lofts and continued on.

The *Kennedy* loomed over even the crates, its dark bulk visible between the stacks. Jane had heard it was enormous; even so, she gasped when they reached the edge of the deck and the *Kennedy*'s full length was finally visible.

It must have been over a thousand feet long. The lip of the upper deck rose above them, and the tops of cobbled cabins and battlements peeked just over that.

The gangway to the *Kennedy* was longer than most; it had to be to make the steep climb to the deck.

"Just keep moving forward," Roman said. "Easy steps."

Jane hadn't realized she'd stopped, but then she looked down at the dark waters crashing beneath the gangway.

"You don't have to do this," he said behind her.

That was enough for her to take a deep breath and push onward. She fixed her sights on the square of light at the end of the swaying walkway.

Roman had explained that the *Kennedy* tended to be less open than most of the other ships on Salvage, but that its crew was likely to be more relaxed – and less numerous – during the festival.

And in any case, the special cargo he'd picked up would ease their passage.

A grouchy young man met them at the end of the walkway. He was just as cranky as Jane would expect for someone who'd gotten stuck with guard duty during the party.

"You passing aki?" he asked, barely making room for Jane and Roman to step off the gangway and into the relative comfort of the ship.

"With the good stuff," Roman said. "Better than sweet." He swung his pack from his shoulder and opened it up to show the young guard several jugs reeking of grog.

"The very good stuff," the guard said, his eyes fixed on Roman's bounty. "But you're pronto."

"Never too early for this," Roman said. "Why don't we leave one here?" He was already pulling a jug out. "Take the rest below."

"They're all in the hangar bay." The guard nodded, regarding Roman with new interest. "I conosse you somewhere?"

"Everyone conosses the man with the grog." Roman had already zipped up his pack and motioned to Jane with a jerk of his head.

"Some things are the same all over," Jane said once they were out of earshot.

Roman chuckled. "Never a truer word."

They kept their heads down and their voices low as they

moved through the *Kennedy*, hearing the sounds of distant revelry. As impressive as the ship looked from the outside, it was much the same as the others inside: worn, cramped, and dark, with only every third filament light burning.

The only difference was that it was much, much bigger.

"What are we looking for?" Jane asked. "Where would the *Kennedy* keep its bounty?"

"The engine room," Roman said. "Rumor is, there's a stash of pre-Catastrophe spoils there."

"So if they took something from the Library, that's where they'd keep it."

"We'll find out for sure."

Navigating the big ship wasn't as easy as she would have hoped. There were no signs or directions marked anywhere, just combinations of letters and numbers on the doors that meant little to her.

But even Jane's limited time on Salvage had taught her that engines and the like were usually located on lower decks, so down they went, maneuvering through steep, narrow stairwells.

Even the exterior view of the *Kennedy* didn't prepare her for the length of their descent. By the time they reached the bottom deck, Jane's knees were aching, and she was sweating beneath her pack.

"Where to now?" she asked.

Roman had his head angled back. "I smell the engine grease. We can't be far." They continued on until Jane spied a telltale smudge of black on a bulkhead. More than a week of cleaning and scrubbing had attuned her eye to minor blemishes. Whoever had been assigned to clean here had likely knocked off early to join the festivities above.

They were in the elbow of a narrow corridor. Bodiless footsteps echoed overhead and nearby like ghosts. The few crew folk who had stopped them above had been easily plied with a bottle of Roman's finest, but Jane didn't expect they'd have any such luck down here.

And from the grim, focused expression on Roman's face, she figured he was making the same calculation.

"Do you have a plan for getting in?"

She could tell from the firm set of his mouth and the thoughtful expression in his eyes that he did not.

"It's a big place," he finally said. "There's got to be more than one way."

She couldn't argue with that.

They eased along the corridor, moving naturally but carefully. Jane led the way, knowing that she had an easier chance of ducking out of sight than the six foot-plus Roman. They made good progress until they came to a junction where the corridor opened up to a room of piping, catwalks, and bulky, boxy machinery. The ambient hum droned out most of the other noise, but Jane noticed a shadow on the walkway above.

She pointed, and Roman nodded.

They edged around a bank of bulbous equipment. It was a tight squeeze, especially for Roman, but the piping overhead shielded them from view. Jane stopped at the end of the row, where she could just see the guard's shoes some forty feet away.

She was watching those shoes, waiting for them to move, when she felt Roman frantically tapping her shoulder. She turned.

He was pointing at the walkway behind him and gesturing for her to move forward. Then, she heard muffled footsteps and understood.

Someone was coming.

She crawled around the nearest machine and pressed herself against it, trying to stay far enough back that the guard above wouldn't see her. But Roman needed to hide too, and the machinery wasn't wide enough to cover them both. After a quick moment of silent negotiations and maneuvers, they settled with Roman squeezed against the equipment, his knees up, and Jane between them.

It was awkward, but the kind of awkward she wouldn't have

minded under other circumstances. She was thankful her back was to him so he couldn't see her blush.

The second guard sauntered over and called up to the first. "Todo clear?"

"All quiet," said the first.

The second scraped his shoe against the floor with a gritty crunch. "Been thinking about what Capitan said. Man's got a point."

"Ess," agreed the first, but cautiously.

"Too many people, not enough Salvage. You conosse it can't go forever."

"Ess blasphemy."

"Blasphemy to say what ess? It's just an aviso. God bendicted us with this motor. You don't think He destined us to use it?"

An uncomfortable silence followed, broken only by the sound of the second man's shoes grinding and squeaking against the deck.

"The problem," the first said, "ess that it's never gonna function. What's the plan then?"

"Who blasphemes now? It'll function. Just gotta find the right stuff."

The first guard snorted. "Ee an ocean with waves of sweet."

"You just think on whether you wanna sink or float." The second man retreated back the way he'd come, dragging his feet along the deck.

There was movement on the catwalk, too. Jane peered out just enough to see the first guard's heels as he watched the other go.

She scooted out of their hiding place and padded across the aisle toward the next bank of cover. There was a doorway just twenty feet away.

Roman followed close behind and gave her a nod once they were safely on the other side of the door. He looked uncharacteristically flustered, his throat bobbing and his neck red.

"What was that about?" Jane whispered. Not that she expected him to know, but she thought he might appreciate a neutral distraction.

He shrugged. "Hoping we'll figure that out whenever we find this stash."

"I guess we'll know it when we find it," Jane said.

"If we're right, it should include old books."

They made their way along. Even though the pipes, machines, and walkways were a jumble of crowded and incongruous shapes, they were almost all painted in fading shades of beige and gray, which made the occasional red pipe or yellow handle stand out all the more.

And when they reached the large red cylinder protruding from the wall, Jane was reasonably certain they'd found "it." Whatever *it* was.

It appeared to be built deeper into the ship, budding through in just this one spot. Makeshift scaffolding had been erected around it, and organized on the deck and the open workspaces nearby were all kinds of common and arcane tools and books.

Lots of books.

"Do you recognize this?" Jane asked.

Roman shook his head.

She began paging through the books. They had titles like *Neutron Physics* and *Nuclear Reactors*. The pages were no more intelligible than the titles, and they were filled with images just as complex and indecipherable as the equipment around her.

"This is a pre-Catastrophe engine," Roman said. "They're trying to study it. Or repair it." It was hard to tell what he thought of that.

Jane was still flipping through the books. Her hand stopped when she found one with very different imagery: a field of stars against the night sky. *ESA* was the title.

"Who passes aki?" called a voice from the other end of the room. One of the guards from before.

Jane spun and ducked behind a round metal tower. Roman

had taken cover across the aisle from her.

"Heard you aki," the man said. "Better if you come out now."

Roman held his finger to his lips. Jane nodded.

Then she understood what he was about to do and shook her head. Hard.

But it was too late. He was stepping out into the aisle, his hands up. "You got me," he said.

Jane stifled a curse.

"How'd you pass here? What are you doing?"

"Looking for the party. Someone told me I'd find a big one—" Roman grunted, and flesh hit flesh.

"You answer me in serio! Who sent?"

"No one," Roman said.

"Lie! You sound like a Continental."

Roman said nothing. Jane imagined there was little he could say.

"Shit. I conosse you. Your face."

Jane's mind buzzed with panic.

"We've never met," Roman said.

"No, you're him. The missing prince."

Jane remembered the way people had stared at him on the galley boat. The whispers. She'd thought it had been his laugh that had drawn their attention, but no, it must have been his recently healed face. And whatever that meant to them.

"I've got one of those faces," Roman said. It was a game attempt, but Jane could hear the strain in his voice, and besides, the other man already knew what he'd seen.

"Afavel!" the guard called. "Come quick!"

As footsteps clanged from the other room, Jane sought frantically for an escape. Or a place to hide. The only exit was back the way they'd come, and the equipment was wedged too tightly for her to hide. If the other man came searching, she could try to dodge around, but he'd flush her into view of the first guard if he made any real effort.

Besides, all she had at her disposal were tangled pipes,

cylinders plugged with old gauges...

And red. Against the wall was a small red square with a wheel attached. A hatch.

It read "DUCT KEEL."

The other guard trotted into the room and began a quick exchange with the first. Jane tucked her book under her arm and crawled to the hatch, keeping her head low. It came open with only the faintest squeak – she silently thanked Salvage's devout maintenance schedule for that – and left her just room enough to crawl inside with her pack. No sense in leaving evidence that someone else had been here.

She closed the hatch with a guilty throb in her heart. She was abandoning Roman again, but there was nothing she could do for him. Not now, anyway.

She would figure something out. But she had to get clear first.

The voices faded behind the hatch, and she climbed down a ladder. It was pitch black, so she took the rungs carefully. When she was sure she had solid ground beneath her, she tucked the book into her pack, beneath the grog bottles she still carried. As much as she wanted to leave them behind, they just might be her ticket out if her and Roman's descent into the *Kennedy* was any indication.

And if she managed to get out of this pit.

She crept forward, and the sound of her movements echoed down the narrow space. There was a distant light, and a thick pipe by her left hand. The good news and the bad news was that this crawlspace continued for a very long way. Long enough, she was sure, to get her beyond the engine room.

She tightened the straps of her pack and started crawling.

CHAPTER SEVENTEEN
NAVIGATION

Malone's initial investigation went as slowly as she would have expected. Few of the crew knew her, and none trusted her. Unfortunately, it all fit too well with what Geist had told her – to most of them, she was a savage, an untouchable.

Unfortunately, the (roughly) seven days remaining in their voyage were long when counted in hours sweeping corridors and wiping down bulkheads, but short for winning the trust of forty-two people.

Forty-one without Sharad.

She sorted through schedules and duty rotations, looking for anyone reporting absent for a shift (or anyone switching with someone else). She talked with Sharad's shift mates and acquaintances, with the crew who had shared meals with him and whose cabins were placed near his. She asked about unusual behavior, close friendships, special enmities.

Nothing.

The most obvious suspects were the crew who had been off duty at the time of the murder, but that only narrowed her list by twelve. She performed a more thorough search of Sharad's cabin, not expecting to find much.

The body had been removed, the bed stripped, and the walls cleaned of blood by the time Malone finally returned to the scene. There was no telling what else had been moved.

But as Malone poked around, she found something wedged under Sharad's bunk. It was a small, narrow tab of metal, something she probably would have missed if the dead man's belongings hadn't already been cleared away. She picked it up, flipped it over, and read "GINTNER" on the other side.

It sounded like a title. Or a name. Not one Malone had heard on board, but that didn't mean much.

Back in the corridor, Malone studied the door to Sharad's cabin. She had to press her nose nearly to the metal, but she found it – a patch of scuffing at eye level. She glanced in either direction. When she was certain she was alone, she pressed the little nameplate to the door. It fit neatly in the middle of the scuffing, with a few stray scratches extending beyond the corners, where someone would have dug in with a prying tool.

Malone continued down the hall. For the first time, she noticed similar markings on all the cabin doors – as if someone had meticulously removed all the nameplates.

The question was, why? And was the gintner the crew member who had originally had Sharad's cabin, or perhaps someone who had visited Sharad before the man's death?

Unfortunately, when she asked about the gintner, all she got were blank stares.

She learned little more about Sharad. He had been one of the younger, newer crew members. No one knew him as well as Malone would have hoped. Or no one wanted to talk to her about him. He had worked the night shift in the control compartment, he'd taken his meals alone, and he'd played cards with the others on his shift. Malone heard the same story from everyone she asked, almost word for word. It was a little too perfect.

And what was stranger still was that no one had reacted much to his death. Malone had come to expect a degree of stoicism from the Continentals, but this was extreme.

Lachesse noticed it, too.

They were standing on the observation gallery, three days after the murder, watching a sea like shattered glass and sipping diluted caffee. It wasn't the same as tea, but it was better than nothing.

The *Glasauge* was midway through its morning shift, so it was just the two of them in the lounge. Most of the off-duty crew were either sleeping or getting ready to sleep. Malone hadn't managed to do much of that since finding the body.

Lachesse was looking at her, an expression of patient forbearance on her painted face. Malone abruptly realized the woman had probably said something.

"Inspector, I can't figure out if you've got a whole world of private conversations going on in your head or nothing at all."

"Sorry." Malone took a sip of her diluted caffee. It was a notch better than awful.

Lachesse rotated her cup in her fingers. A red crescent from her lips marked the rim, and it spun in a slow circle.

The moment demanded conversation. "It's been too quiet," Malone said. "No one's talking about the murder. No one seems affected by it."

The door opened behind them. Chernev swept in, bearing a fresh pot of caffee. Lachesse held her cup out and allowed the man to refill it, which he did with shaking hands. The stream was a watery brown, already weakened to Lachesse's taste.

Then Malone noticed his balding head, reddening and beading with sweat, and the way he was gazing at Lachesse's nails. She'd seen dogs stare at meaty bones the same way.

Sauvage, indeed.

"I thought that was Phelan's job," Malone said.

He gave her a scowl. "Phelan is occupied."

"Mercy, Chernev," Lachesse said in her silkiest voice, growling the r's in the odd way of Geist and his crew.

His jowls melted into a smile. "Stark welcome." He left the pot and turned to go, ignoring Malone and her cup.

"Could I get some dried ham and cheese?" Malone called after him, trying to keep amusement out of her voice.

He didn't even look back. "In the mess!" He slammed the door.

Lachesse cleared her throat. "You were just noting that no one seems to be talking to you." She paused long enough to let the implication sink in. "What did you expect them to say?" she asked.

"Nothing. But I thought I'd hear them talking to each other. See them changing their routines. But it's like it didn't even happen."

"Hmm." Lachesse sipped her caffee again, aligning her lips with the red stain she'd already made. She was almost smiling.

"You know something?"

Now Lachesse did smile. "I thought it was obvious. Geist's problem is political, not personal. He's got someone on his crew who's trying to sabotage him, and he wants to resolve the problem with a minimum of fuss."

"That's your theory?"

"You flatter me. It's merely an observation."

Malone chewed on the idea. "Sharad was low level. His shift was easy enough to cover. How does murdering him sabotage Geist?"

"Perhaps it was about eliminating you. Or perhaps it was a distraction," Lachesse said.

"Murders usually work the other way around." But it was hard to imagine what would be more conspicuous than a murder. "I haven't seen any other signs of trouble."

"Then perhaps it's happening wherever we aren't."

If Lachesse weren't so matter-of-fact, Malone would have thought the woman was mocking her. Besides, there were places enough on the ship for someone to make trouble. In storage. In the engine room.

Behind that door Geist kept locked.

"The bigger question is how someone would intend to sabotage the *Glasauge*'s mission. And why," said Malone.

"I expect we'll find out soon enough." Lachesse was staring out at the sea. "But you were the one who went to the commune. What did Geist tell you?" *And how did he convince you to stay*, her eyes seemed to ask.

Malone remembered the dinner and the sense of belonging

with a physical ache. "He said Arnault's the key to some pre-Catastrophe cache. Something that his enemies could use to destroy us."

"That does sound dreadful."

"I'm not sure how much of it I believe," Malone admitted, to herself as much as to Lachesse.

"But when a man in a flying ship warns of death and destruction, best not to take any chances," said the whitenail.

Malone watched her out of the corner of her eye. "That why you came?"

"Somebody had to represent the city's interests, and you were certainly in no state to." Her fingernails formed a crisscrossing lattice where she held her cup. "Besides, at my age, you learn to take all the excitement you can find."

Malone almost laughed. "You said Ruthers came from the Continent."

"Indeed."

"What did he call... all of it?" Malone asked. "Recoletta. The communes. The place you and I come from." Geist had dodged that question at Meyerston.

Lachesse pondered the matter. "I don't recall him referring to it as anything in particular. Why do you ask?"

"Just wondering," Malone said.

Lachesse sighed. "I do wonder what he'd make of this."

"The airship? Or the hunt for Arnault?"

Lachesse turned to face Malone, both eyebrows arched in incredulity. "Skies above, woman, I was talking about the conspiracy."

Malone watched the whitenail's face, waiting for some sign that she was joking. "Explain."

"I thought you'd understood that much. That's why Geist doesn't want you investigating that boy's death. That's why his erstwhile crew mates won't talk to you. They've got something bigger to hide."

•••

The conversation with Lady Lachesse hadn't given her ideas so much as hunches. But with a little time and work, Malone figured she could poke and prod those hunches into something more substantial.

She made her rounds on the various decks. She paid special attention to the storage area, but she couldn't see that anything had changed down there. She played solitaire in the mess and noted who played cards together. She kept an eye on who paired off with whom in between shifts and kept an ear out for secrets whispered amidst words of passion.

Yet it was the sound of silence that caught her attention.

Geist's study – the one he always kept locked, the one from which she'd heard that peculiar purring noise – had gone quiet. Whatever equipment had kept up that warbling, musical drone was gone.

She needed to find a way inside.

Malone was cleaning the navigation room between shifts when she realized she was alone. She hadn't previously had this room to herself, but Halstrom, the navigator on duty, usually took her time with her pre-shift meal and talked with the officers in the pilot house for five to ten minutes before assuming her post.

The office was small, with one wide desk big enough to unroll various maps and charts upon, and drawers beneath for storing a variety of mysterious equipment.

Malone glanced into the curving corridor. She saw the closed doors of Geist's office at one end and the pilot house at the other, where a handful of crew members – Halstrom included – were chatting over cups of caffee. The unhurried melody of their conversation was just audible over the hum of the engine above.

She had time.

Malone checked the drawers. The topmost held equipment – pencils, protractors, a drawing compass, a navigational compass, and a dozen other enigmatic instruments of rounded, hash-marked edges and swinging arms. Nothing of use to her.

The next held four rolled paper tubes. Maps, she was sure. Yet when Malone unfurled them on the desk, all she saw were pinprick dots against a faint grid. Star charts, presumably.

The bottom drawer also held long rolls, and as Malone pressed them open against the desk she saw what she wanted. Maps, with the pale blue of water and the nibbled cheese contours of land.

The first three she checked didn't show her much. Or rather, they showed her too much from too close a range – fragments of coastline on the east, dotted with cities as varied and numerous as a farmer's freckles, many with mouth-clogging names like "Nantes-Neugeboren," "Salaam-de-Galicia," and "Luse Hai'an." She pored through them all, trying to wrap her mind around the scope of the vast land she was headed toward.

Then, she unrolled a map that was nearly blank, the line of coast nothing more than a shape opposite the sea. What had happened to the cities? Where was this blank stretch of nothingness?

She noticed the compass rose and realized she had the map upside down. She turned it and regarded the featureless expanse of land on the west. Malone realized that she was looking at her homeland – a broad, uncharted, and uncivilized place, little more than a border for the sea.

And across it, in thin, capital letters was the word, "PESTELAND." A vast list of names for the cities of the Continent, some closer together than Recoletta to its communes, and only one for the land that encompassed Recoletta, Madina, and dozens of other cities and communes.

Malone didn't know what the word meant, but the way it spanned the land, covering anything else that might have been there, bothered her.

A crescendo of noise from the corridor. The conversation from the pilot house rising and cutting off again as someone opened the door. Malone was out of time.

She rolled the maps up again and put them away. She was still bent over the closed drawer when Halstrom's heavy steps sounded behind her.

"Keska say?" the woman asked.

For the first time, Malone was faintly grateful for the language barrier. She waved her cleaning rag about. "Cleaning. Filthy. See?" She showed Halstrom one dirt-black side.

Halstrom squinted at her. The words she spoke were unintelligible, but her gesture – one outstretched arm pointed at the door – was clear enough.

Lachesse was in the lounge, sipping watered-down caffee when Malone returned.

"I don't know how you manage so much of that stuff," Malone said. Even diluted, the odor from the cup was strong enough to hit the back of her tongue with the memory of the stale, bitter flavor.

"One must learn to adapt, Inspector." Lachesse sipped her beverage daintily. "How goes your investigation?"

"Barely," Malone said. "Hard to investigate people you know nothing about. I thought you whitenails were buttoned up, but these people – I only understand a few of them."

Lachesse's chuckle was a warm, purring sound. "It takes practice. And patience."

Malone paused. "What?"

The woman looked into her cup as she swirled its contents around. "I think we're past coyness. Patience has never been your strong suit."

"No, I mean – you understand them?" Even the progress Malone had made only meant she could understand a few of the slowest, clearest speakers.

Lachesse blinked at her over the rim of her cup. "Only some of it. As best I can tell, their parlance is a mix of languages, including our own and others that share a common root. Skies above, what did you think I was doing in here all day?"

Malone glanced at the big, wide window before Lachesse. "Exasperating me."

"That has been a pleasant side effect."

Something else occurred to Malone. "You think you've learned enough to translate something?" Asking Lachesse for help made her feel a little dirty, but it wasn't like she had options.

"I could try."

Malone told her about her sortie into the navigation room and about the maps she'd found there. "The Continent's big. Bigger than I thought possible." She paused. "Ruthers ever say anything about that to you?"

The whitenail shrugged. "In his way."

"If those maps are to be believed, there are cities everywhere. My head hurt just looking at them. But then I found another – a map of the land where we came from."

"Oh?" Lachesse said. "And what was on it?"

"A big, empty space with the word 'PESTELAND' written across it."

Lachesse cocked her head. "Come again?"

"Um. 'Peest-land'? 'Pesty-land'?" Malone had no idea how the words were pronounced and a sneaking suspicion that Lachesse was enjoying her fumbling a little too much.

"'Pestiland'?" the woman finally offered, glossing over the middle syllable much like Geist and his crew did.

"Probably. What's it mean?"

The whitenail hesitated, her brows drawn together in concern. "'Place of disease.' 'Land of plagues.' Something of the sort," she said. Etched in the lines of Lachesse's face, Malone saw the same question that rose in her own mind: what did it mean?

She remembered, then, Geist's strange abstention from the food at Meyerston. Valenti's outburst. The crew's habit of giving her a wide berth, of avoiding contact with the things she touched.

Geist's ready suggestion that she scrub the airship down, deck by deck, every day.

"I do suppose you have a new lead, Inspector."

Suddenly, the task of getting into Geist's office didn't seem as impossible. "Maybe you can help," she said to Lachesse, explaining her interest in Geist's office.

"How do you plan to get inside?"

"I hadn't gotten that far," Malone said, feeling like she was admitting a shameful secret. "I was wondering if you had an angle."

Lachesse smirked. "I daresay you won't like it." The whitenail made it sound like a challenge. Malone suspected she was right, but any idea was better than none.

"Sabotage the airship," Lachesse said.

She had no words for Lachesse's proposal, but the look on her face must have been answer enough.

The whitenail shrugged, gazing back through bored, heavy-lidded eyes. "You need Geist worried enough to make a mistake. And you need his crew distracted enough to ignore you."

"Sneaking into Geist's cabin won't matter if we're all dead."

Lachesse's face puckered into a frown. "Oh, do relax. This is a large and complex conveyance. I highly doubt that any one thing you could do will irrevocably commit us to destruction. Besides, I'm certain one of the forty people on this airship can figure out what to do."

It made sense, but doubt still gnawed at the corners of her mind. "That's a lot of 'ifs' from someone who knows nothing about airships."

The old whitenail's grin was sly. "No, but I know a thing or two about money. Enough to know you don't invest in something like this and then give it a 'destroy' button. You'll recall that I oversaw a considerable fortune in the railroad industry." Lachesse's modesty was as false as her rouged cheeks.

"Sato crashed that pretty handily for you," Malone said.

Malone would have replayed the entire conversation just for the chagrin on Lachesse's face. "Sato was an unexpected variable."

Malone nodded, pleased at hearing the whitenail make her point for her.

Lachesse set her cup down on the table with a sigh of exasperation. "I thought we were both in agreement to do what's necessary to see this misadventure through."

"I didn't think that included suicide."

"Considering the circumstances under which we came to be here, perhaps you should be grateful for the opportunity." Lachesse focused her gaze on Malone's neck.

Malone knew she was right, which only annoyed her further. "I don't even know where to begin."

"Fouling complex machinery, creating general violence and mayhem?" Lachesse smiled. "I'm certain you'll figure something out."

Malone knew she was right again, even as her thoughts drifted to the engine room. "Just... be ready," she said.

"I always am."

Malone made for the corridor and stopped. "One more thing. Do you know who the gintner is?"

Lachesse paused. "You're speaking of the crew, I assume? No. I rarely hear them address each other by title. What is a gintner?"

Malone shrugged. "For now? Just a title."

Now that Malone actually had a mind to visit the engine room, it seemed absurd to her how poorly -guarded it was. Like locking the front door only to leave the back wide open. The thought made her neck itch.

Then again, Geist and his crew probably hadn't bargained on anyone trying anything as reckless as what she was about to attempt.

And with just a few days remaining before they reached the Continent, she didn't have time to be careful.

Malone waited for the moonrise shift, when only two engineers would be on duty. When everyone off shift – including Geist – would be lulled into a false calm by the ghost light of the moon on the water.

The corridors were dim and quiet when Malone set about her work. Only the chime of silverware on dishes rose above the gentle buzz of snores, whispers, and moans behind cabin doors. The night belonged to her.

That realization did nothing to still her trembling hands or dry the sheen of sweat that coated them as she made her way to the engine room.

But if she was going to go down, perhaps it was better to have it happen by her own hand than by someone else's.

No one stopped her as she climbed to the upper deck. No one seemed to notice.

The engine room was hot and muggy, a forest of tangled metal and twisting pipes. It was a big room made small by the clutter of equipment, valves, and gauges, but under the circumstances Malone expected that would work to her advantage.

The somnolent chuff of steam vents, the groan of pipes, and the underfoot hum of motors masked her careful movements, but the two engineers were less cautious. Malone heard their voices and felt their plodding footsteps rattle the metal grating beneath her.

If only she could make out what they were saying.

The voices altered their tempo, and footsteps plodded closer. Someone was coming.

Malone glanced around. The bundles of piping and banks of equipment formed rough aisles, but what she really needed was...

A ladder. There, in the corner, was a yellow ladder rising to the envelope. Malone scurried to it and climbed with swift, silent movements. She pulled herself into the envelope just as a man crossed into view below.

The space Malone found herself in was long and wide, but with a low ceiling. The only light filtered in from the engine room below, visible through the slats of the metal grating beneath her. It cast stripes of light on dark, bulging surfaces overhead.

Gas bags. Whatever held the *Glasauge* aloft, it was inside the balloons above her head. The realization that they were almost close enough to touch made her shiver with dread.

The sliver of walkable space was almost as cluttered as the engine room below. Knee-high ribs of scaffolding curved along the floor every twenty feet, rising along the envelope and disappearing behind the gas bags. Cables, as faint in the darkness as spiders' webs, were strung along the narrow space.

At least Malone had a better – and safer – view of the engine room. It was probably fifty feet long and half as wide. Not as big as the other decks, but just as densely packed. One engineer – the one whose path had almost crossed hers – was making the rounds, checking gauges and dials. He walked with a loose, ambling gait, his hands shoved in his pockets, in a way that suggested he didn't expect to find anything requiring his attention.

That only made her regret Lachesse's plan more.

The other engineer sat at the forward end of the deck, swinging her legs over the edge of her chair like a bored child. A bell rang on the control panel next to her, and she picked up two black objects about the size and shape of teacups. She held one to her ear and the other in front of her mouth.

"Yah?" After a pause, the woman nodded to herself and muttered something with the general cadence of confirmation. "Gonzalo," she called across the deck. Malone couldn't keep track of what the woman said after that, but it was enough to send the other engineer – Gonzalo – ambling toward her.

Malone followed, crouching low and extending her arms before her.

Something banged against her shin. Malone stifled her grunt of pain, but there wasn't anything she could do about the warbling note that carried through the scaffolding.

Gonzalo looked up, but his companion urged him on with a few clipped syllables.

Malone picked her way forward, more carefully now. By the time she had stepped over another ridge of scaffolding and pulled herself through the web of cables, Gonzalo and the female engineer were in the middle of a discussion. She couldn't understand the words, but the sharp tone and waving arms suggested a disagreement. The female engineer pointed between the device she'd spoken into and a round gauge next to it.

Gonzalo threw up his hands and shook his head. After a few more words from his counterpart, he raised his palms in a placating gesture and went back to the rows of machinery.

Malone followed Gonzalo back into the wilderness of machinery. She was close enough to see the redness on the back of his neck.

He studied the instruments before him. He twisted one knob with a furtive glance at the accompanying gauge. Emboldened, he twisted a little more.

The words he called to the front were a hopeful question. The response that came back was an irritated negative.

Gonzalo's anxious sigh was loud enough that Malone could picture his puffed cheeks and puckered lips. He worked his fingers through his hair like a junior inspector puzzling through his exams.

She didn't know Gonzalo, but she'd seen that same look on a hundred callow trainees before him. He had no idea what he was doing.

He tried a few more levers and wheels. Something in the gas bags groaned above Malone, and she tensed. But the other engineer made noises of approval, and Malone felt her body unclench, saw Gonzalo's do the same. He marched back to the other end of the deck. She followed.

Malone picked her way between the cables and through the scaffolding, careful to avoid another noisy – and painful – stumble. Yet as she stepped between two curving crossbars, her foot hit something, and that something skidded across the grating.

Malone froze, holding her weight on one foot and holding the cables for balance. It was awkward, but she didn't dare move.

She slowly pointed her gaze downward and saw Gonzalo and the other engineer also frozen, staring up toward her feet.

After what seemed like an interminable pause, the female engineer shrugged and resumed her end of the conversation.

But Gonzalo still gazed up.

He started toward the other end of the deck.

Malone wanted to believe he was only going to check on equipment, but she had the sinking feeling he was heading toward the ladder.

She needed to hide.

As Gonzalo navigated the equipment, Malone considered her options. The walkway in the envelope was small and dark. If Gonzalo didn't search too hard, she might be able to hide behind some of the scaffolding, or what little curved beneath the gas bags...

Of course. The scaffolding curved along the side of the envelope, where most of it was hidden by the gas bags. If she could squeeze herself in the middle of it, she might be able to crawl out of view.

The other engineer called out to Gonzalo, and he answered in defiance. He had almost reached the ladder. She was almost out of time.

Malone followed the nearest rib of scaffolding and began pulling herself up the curved wall of the envelope, using the crossbars as rungs. Like most ideas, it was a lot sounder in theory than in practice. The space between the gas bags and the envelope was a lot smaller than she'd expected. She pulled herself into the center of the scaffolding and squeezed and writhed her way up, the cold metal of the envelope scraping her back and the thick canvas of the balloon pressing against her face. She tried not to think too much about how easy it might be to put her foot through one or the other.

Or how she'd manage to get down.

She stopped when she'd climbed high enough that Gonzalo wouldn't see her unless he came looking with her hiding place in mind. And from what little she'd seen, she was reasonably confident he didn't possess that kind of gumption.

But she heard him searching below. His tread was heavy and clumsy, and he grunted as he pushed his way through the cables and scaffolding. His voice rose in a lilting question.

He worked his way to the last spot she had stumbled. He was moving slowly – too slowly. Her arms and legs were starting to cramp from holding her position for too long, and her head was starting to ache.

Quite badly, in fact.

Gonzalo was still fumbling around somewhere below when Malone realized what an odd thing her sudden headache was. And she noticed something else, too – a sweet, heavy smell. Like overripe fruit.

Malone had smelled something similar only three times during her tenure as inspector of the Municipal Police, but she recognized it well enough. It was the smell of high-grade explosives.

She looked into the darkness above her. As her eyes adjusted, she saw two dark bundles like spiders' nests, bound to the poles. They were barely five feet over her head – someone had crawled into this position and fastened them in place.

And there was no telling how many others there were – in the envelope and elsewhere on the ship.

Down below, Gonzalo had started whistling to himself as he searched. Malone seriously considered showing herself to the little twit just so they could both march down and alert Geist, but assuming the culprit was keeping an ear to the ground, that could turn out very badly indeed.

So she waited, breathing as little as she dared and listening for Gonzalo's retreat.

At last, he tramped and grunted his way back toward the ladder, and Malone let out a shaky breath. When she climbed down, her muscles felt like they'd been sown with stones. Her back felt like she'd slept on a bed of them.

And her head felt like she'd been pummeled with one.

Suddenly, the idea of sabotaging the *Glasauge* seemed like an incredibly poor one.

CHAPTER EIGHTEEN
THE PERFECT STORM

Jane was waiting in line for water when she heard a sound she hadn't heard in two weeks: the warbling cry of a gull.

The bird was perched on the railing of the stillship, preening its gray feathers against a grayer sky. The horizon had been dimmed with thick clouds all afternoon, and the seas stirred with more than the usual chop. The result on Salvage seemed to be a darkening of everyone's moods and an agitation of their tempers.

"Fresh bird afinal," said the man behind Jane. "Only good thing about nearing the terrens."

The woman next to him grunted. "In a week's time, ye'll be lamenting the plumes in your teeth."

"Why no? Ess weeks of fish ee a week of bird. Only natural to desire variety."

"Don't tell me of variety!" The woman's voice took on an edge that sounded like it had been sharpened over many previous arguments. "Give you yellowfin, you desire sea bass. Give you sea bass, you desire skipjack. Give you a good, honest woman, you–"

"Calm now," the man said. The ends of Jane's ears were burning, and she fought the urge to turn around to look at the bickering couple. Not everyone in line ahead of her was resisting that temptation.

But the woman was still building up steam. "You could live on the Continent ee eat–"

A collective gasp shuddered through the line. The man in front of Jane spun around and glared at the couple.

"Stow it or you'll discuss with segundos," he said. The line lapsed into an embarrassed silence, and for a while the only noises were the crying of the gull and the weird music the wind played on the cables.

Jane considered – for maybe the hundredth time – going to the segundos herself about Roman's disappearance on the *Kennedy*. But what would she say? That she'd lied about who Roman was and why he wanted passage? That they'd both been sneaking where they weren't allowed when he'd been caught?

She'd spent sleepless nights running through the scenario, and it always ended one of two ways. At best, the almirante and the other capitans stormed the *Kennedy*, seized Roman themselves, and locked him up even more carefully. At worst, they killed Roman and threw her overboard as a "perturber." She'd seen enough power struggles play out back in Recoletta to know this one wouldn't end any better.

Her best chance, slim as it was, was to wait for an opportunity to get close to Roman herself. The *Kennedy* was just one ship, and from what she'd observed it was at odds with the rest of Salvage. And from the way its crew had talked about Roman, she knew they valued him enough to keep him safe and healthy, at least for the time being.

She had carted the water halfway back to the *Nossa Senhora* when three long buzzes rang across the decks. After a pause of several seconds, the cycle repeated, and soon other ships were picking up the echo, spreading the signal across Salvage. Less than a minute later, flags were rising from half of the decks Jane could see, all bearing the same image: a black square on an orange field.

The wind had started to pick up, and everyone else Jane could see on deck was speeding up too. She'd internalized enough of the native ethos by now that she couldn't bear the thought of leaving a full cart of water to the elements and to chance, so she hurried back to the *Nossa Senhora* and, she hoped, to safety.

Leyal was scuttling around with more speed and energy than she'd thought possible. His faded denim eyes widened as he saw her.

"Go, companyera. Harbor yourself."

Jane secured the water cart in a way that had now become routine. "What's going on?"

"A churn," he said, breathless as he cinched and double-latched the coops. "Big one. Got to segure everything ee prepare for cast-off."

A heavy feeling crept into Jane's belly. "Cast-off?"

"Separate the flotilla. Keep the boats from hitting one another too much. Prevent one sink from taking all."

Leyal's explanation sent a charge of adrenaline through Jane. "Something's going to sink?"

He tied off the last of the cages and put his hand over his heart. "Let us hope not."

Jane followed him out to the deck and saw the mixture of shame and fear that crossed his face as he closed the door on all of his beloved pigeons. Outside, the warning klaxons were still sounding, and the orange and black flags snapped in the whipping wind. More people were out on the decks, all moving in the same direction.

Leyal tugged at her elbow. "We harbor on the *Oasis*. Ess safer on the big ship – more weight, steadier in the salt. Come, pressa."

On the other side of the gangway, a steady stream of people was surging onto the big liner.

But the *Kennedy* lay in the opposite direction. She would never get another distraction like this.

"Don't wait for me," Jane said. She took off before Leyal could stop her.

The shrieking wind and slapping waves soon drowned out his cries. Twelve decks bobbed between her and the *Kennedy*, and those she could see were clear – almost everyone was clustered around the *Oasis*. The only people in her path were too busy with the mooring lines to pay any attention to her.

The decks rose and fell, and the gangways rippled like ribbons in the wind. Some dipped perilously low to the water, free now of the tension from neighboring boats that had held them taut. Jane tore across the heaving deck of a big schooner, loping and weaving in time with the motion beneath her. The hull of the *Kennedy* was finally visible, rising just a few decks away.

She had almost reached the next gangway when a hand grabbed her arm and almost sent her crashing onto the deck.

"Wrong direction!" he yelled, pointing back toward the *Oasis*. "Get to harbor!" The tendons on his neck stood out from the effort of his shouting, but even so his voice was a thin whine above the noise of the storm.

"Let me go!" Jane said, trying to pull out of his grip.

He shook his head. "There's nothing – we've cast off!"

Jane looked past him. Sure enough, the gangway – the one she'd planned to cross – was hanging limply from the deck of the next boat, which was already rising and falling with its own motion. They were drifting apart, but they didn't seem to have drifted far yet.

The man gripping Jane's arm looked away and hollered something to his crew mates, who were now converging.

Which meant he was distracted.

Jane kneed him in the groin.

He doubled over, his cry of pain muffled by the wind and waves. The other four men were running toward her now.

Jane dashed toward the hanging gangway. It was drifting farther away by the second, but she didn't dare slow down. The crewmen couldn't be more than a few steps behind her. Her feet skidded and slid on the wet, rolling deck, and she prayed she wouldn't slip.

The edge of the deck was a few long strides away now; the gap in the railing still pointed toward the hanging gangway. It was farther away than she'd thought... five feet? Maybe six? She might make it.

She had to try.

Jane pushed herself off the edge and launched over the water, trying not to wonder whether, if she missed, the crewmen behind would pull her out.

Jane flew through the air, her arms stretched out and her legs extended behind her. The lip of the next deck was getting closer, fast.

But she was falling faster.

She was halfway through her arc when she realized she wasn't going to make the deck. Nevertheless, she reached with everything – arms, fingers, body – and hoped for something to grab onto.

Sure enough, her fingers found the slats of the hanging gangway just as her body found the unforgiving hull of the ship. She grabbed tightly to the former while her body slammed into the latter, a wave of pain rolling through her chest, stomach, knees, and shins.

But she was still holding on. Jane climbed, pulling with every ounce of strength until her dangling feet found purchase in the gangway. The slats were wide and tightly spaced, but under the circumstances, they'd have to do for rungs.

A wave doused Jane, and she clung to the gangway as the water threatened to sweep her off it. With the *Kennedy* just a few decks away and the swells growing rougher still, Jane moved more slowly than she would have liked. It would be a shame to have made the jump just to fall into the sea.

But as the crewmen shouted their consternation behind her, Jane allowed herself a small smile.

She finally pulled herself onto the deck and held to the railing as she took stock.

Her knees were numb with pain, and one of her hands was bleeding – she'd managed to pop off a fingernail somewhere during her climb.

And something was pressing into her ribs.

She swallowed her horror and felt her abdomen, relieved to find the familiar shape of her book. She'd kept it close since escaping the *Kennedy* the first time. Which was a good thing, because she didn't think she'd be going back to her berth on the *Lazy May* any time soon.

But the way ahead was clear, with ever-larger ships rising like stairs toward the *Kennedy*. Waves were washing over the decks now, tossing the boats against each other with bone-thudding crashes. The bigger craft would be steadier – she just had to make it to the *Kennedy*. And Roman. They could figure out the next part together.

They wouldn't get another opportunity like this, anyway.

When she was sure her legs were steady enough to carry her, she hurried onward, bracing herself against railings and bulwarks as she climbed the decks to her destination.

The ships heaved from side to side, and Jane felt as though she were outrunning the ever-rising waves. The final gangway to the *Kennedy* billowed and snapped beneath her, but she kept both hands on the ropes and her eyes on the deck above and ahead of her. When she finally set foot on the enormous ship, she allowed herself a moment to get her bearings.

The broad deck was empty as far as she could see, which was a good sign.

Her problem now was where to go next. After all, a small city hummed and ran beneath her feet.

A small city that was, like all the other ships of Salvage, currently in lockdown.

And if the *Kennedy* was anything like the other ships, that would mean most of its crew were harboring someplace safe rather than manning their usual posts. After all, who would be running around in a storm like this?

The deckhouse port was unlocked. She found the hatch leading to the lower levels and followed it the only way she could – down.

The passageways were emptier and quieter than they'd been when she and Roman had passed through, and Jane found herself careening from one side to the other with the motion of the ship. The one she presently traveled seemed to run the length of the *Kennedy*. It was silent save for her footsteps and the muffled pounding of the storm outside, and room after room she passed was deserted.

At the next stairwell, Jane descended another couple of levels, trying to remember the route she and Roman had taken before. The *Kennedy* was large enough to have a brig, which was the likeliest place for the crew to keep Roman. She just had to find it. And a good excuse to visit it.

She estimated that she was headed toward the middle of the ship. Which might give her a better reference point for finding Roman.

Or it might get her caught.

Either way, the swaying deck beneath her reminded her that the storm was picking up outside.

Presently, she heard the drone of voices – many people gathered together, murmuring and shuffling somewhere below –

Jane gasped as she cannoned into a woman coming around the corner at a fast clip.

"What're you doing aki?" the woman asked, glaring at Jane as if the collision were entirely her fault. In her loose, ragged shirt and trousers, she could have been anyone, but the pin on her collar marked her as a segundo – an officer of the ship.

"Final checks," Jane mumbled, trying to keep her answer – and her accent – as ambiguous as possible. She ducked her head a little lower.

"Shoulda finished twenty minutes antes," the woman said, suspicious.

Jane remembered that on Salvage, people didn't grovel and scrape. They talked back, even to authority.

"Ee so? Nobody tells me," Jane said, mimicking the rhythmic accent and surly demeanor of the Salvagers.

The woman grunted. She seemed to buy it. "Pass to the hangar. The aviso's in progress."

Jane was evidently supposed to know where the hangar was, so she nodded and turned toward the hallway the woman had just vacated, figuring it was her safest bet.

The commotion coming from belowdecks sounded louder. Jane found herself both wondering and dreading what she might find there.

She took another stairway down and after that, the noise of the crowd was guide enough. She followed it to an immense, high-ceilinged room, almost as high as the ballroom in Brummell Hall and more than twice as long. Jane had to pinch herself when she remembered that this room was only one part (albeit an enormous one) of the great ship *Kennedy*.

And it was full of people.

Most of them were gathered at the other end of the hangar, where the speaker, little more than a smudge of color from here, stood on a catwalk overlooking them all. As the cheers and applause of the crowd died down he raised his voice, which was little more than a forceful mumble at this distance.

She noticed a sign for the galley. It pointed to the other side of the ship, across the hangar and its massive crowd. Perhaps she could find some food there to take to Roman – that would provide a likely enough story for asking directions to the brig.

For a moment, she considered going up another couple of decks and cutting across that way, but that carried the risk of running into another prowling segundo. Easier to blend in among the crowd.

Jane pressed forward, keeping her head down and her pace even. The rocking deck helped. Everyone was swaying and jostling to keep their balance, and she used the collective motion to slip ahead. Under other circumstances, the sight of a room full of serious, stern people tripping over themselves as they slid around the room together would have been funny, but as it was Jane felt her heart in her mouth every time she bumped into someone.

She also found herself wondering what the speaker was saying to leave everyone else so serious and stern.

She was halfway across the hangar before she could make anything out.

"– tyranny of… Continent–"

At least, that was what it sounded like. But Salvagers were always going on about the twin evils of the Continent on one coast and the buried cities on the other. She kept weaving forward.

"– the almirante's idiocy–"

Something unpleasant tingled through Jane's blood. However brusque Salvagers were with one another, and even with the segundos, they never criticized the almirante. At best, denunciatory speech was punished with a few hard shifts cleaning the latrines. At worst, it was mutiny, which was punishable by death – casting out.

Jane had internalized that thoroughly enough that even hearing this kind of talk made her feel nervous and exposed.

"– this churn… a bendiction from God–"

The hairs rose along the back of Jane's neck. The wind and waves were playing the hull like a great drum, and the hangar echoed horribly, and half of the speaker's words sounded like mush, but there was no mistaking the other half.

This reminded her of the exchange she and Roman had overheard in the engine room – about the future of Salvage, the destiny of the *Kennedy*, and strange "bendictions" from God.

She hazarded a glance at the faces of the men and women around her. She'd taken their rigid expressions for fear at the storm and their somberness for concentration with fundamental problems of gravity, but she realized now that she'd misread them completely.

These were the deadly earnest faces of men and women committing themselves to a desperate act of high treason. And Jane had seen more than enough of that for one lifetime.

"– so long we tell… do not hear–"

She wanted to get away as soon as possible, but she still had to find Roman. She'd made it more than halfway through the hangar. Just past the catwalk where the speaker roosted were more doors. All she had to do to reach them was muscle and squirm through a few hundred packed, angry people.

At least she'd had practice.

Jane continued to move with the rocking of the ship, disguising her maneuvering as counterbalancing. And, as short as she was, no one seemed to notice her elbowing ahead. Or no one cared.

She was able to catch more of the speaker's tirade as she got closer, too.

"– afinal, we have the opportunity ee the recourses to escape."

A raucous cheer went up from the crowd. Jane joined in, shouting and clapping her sweat-slick hands.

"As the churn gives us passage through the flotilla, God gives us a ticket to liberty! A motor that does not fatigue o succumb to corruption!"

Another cheer went up. Jane couldn't have said what it was, but something in the speech was turning her belly to ice.

"Companyeros! With us is the Continental fugitive! The disappeared prince whose blood remedies disease ee waters terrens."

Jane didn't understand what the speaker meant, but he was talking about Roman. He had to be.

"With his blood, we buy our future!"

Jane followed the next chorus of whooping and applause to the speaker and his escort, who were now standing almost directly over her. She couldn't make out the details of their faces, but their clothes were stained and spattered with dark red patches.

Blood.

Surely they wouldn't have killed Roman – they needed him alive. She told herself as much again and again, but it didn't stem the dread rising in her chest.

She needed to find him. Fast.

The doors leading out of the hangar were just a stone's throw away. Jane mimicked the zealous expression she saw on the faces around her and wove her way toward the exit.

She had just reached it when a humorless young man stepped in front of her.

"Discourteous to abandon the capitan's talk, no?"

Before Jane could pick an excuse, the lady next to him stepped forward.

"Companyera," she said, "what's this with your hand?"

Jane looked at her left hand. The finger that had lost a nail was still bleeding impressively.

"Accident," Jane said. "Just want to clean it up." She held it out toward the young man.

He stepped back. "Use the second head. First ess still a disaster." He blanched, though Jane didn't have time to consider whether it was at her bleeding finger or the state of the bathroom. She hurried on. Signs for the galley pointed ahead, beyond the bathrooms.

She wondered if all of the *Kennedy*'s crew was as eager to break away as the people in the hangar. Salvagers were loyal to their capitans, but mustering a rebellion of hundreds seemed like an iffy endeavor.

Unless, of course, the ringleader and his collaborators were counting on the bulk of the crew to be too disorganized – or too afraid – to stop them. Maybe some of the others in the crowd had been doing the same thing she had – putting on an act while they navigated their way to an exit.

Maybe she could find someone who'd be sympathetic.

She continued along the corridor where it seemed widest, following the thick red stripe along the bulkhead. At the first major junction, the stripe blurred and dripped, as if it had been smeared.

Except it hadn't, of course. No, Jane was looking at bloodstains. And they weren't just on the bulkhead. They streaked the deck and the pipes snaking across the ceiling in long, distorted handprints.

And they seemed to lead toward the door on her left.

She pressed her ear to the cool metal, careful to avoid touching the blood. Silence.

She didn't really want to see what was on the other side, but she felt she should. If only to reassure herself that it wasn't Roman.

Jane took a deep breath and pushed the door open with a trembling hand. She fixed her eyes on her toes and raised them slowly, degree by degree.

She saw a broken tile floor stamped with red bootprints.

A pool of blood sloshing with the waves and oozing down the drain.

Hands. Legs. Bodies, sprawled and heaped on the floor.

And for one awful moment, they all had cotton-white hair, aquiline noses, and blue eyes that stared back at her.

But the moment passed, and Jane saw that none of them were Ruthers, and they didn't appear to be Roman, either. Jane felt relief, and almost as quickly, shame.

"Ah."

Jane's heart thudded. She turned. A man sat slumped against the wall, his head resting against the first in a row of metal basins.

He was looking back at her.

"Y-yes?" Jane said. Words felt as slippery as oil on her tongue.

He opened his mouth for a long time before he managed another sound. "Be," he finally said.

Jane waited for the rest, but he only stared back, his mouth opening and closing silently.

"Be?" Jane said. "You want to be something?" She felt silly and helpless asking a dying man for clarification on what could be the ramblings of a delirious brain, but it seemed right to acknowledge him. And as much as she hated being in this room filled with death, it seemed wrong to leave.

So she knelt, braced herself against the wall, and took one of his hands in hers.

"What can I do?"

His eyes found hers and sparked.

"Trade," he groaned.

"Trade?" Jane asked. "You want to – oh." She swallowed. "You were betrayed."

The dying man moaned one long syllable, his eyes rolling back in his head. The ship rocked, unbalancing her for one perilous second.

"I'm sorry," she whispered. Then she realized she could offer him more than sympathy. "You can help me get back at them."

The man's eyes circled back to her and widened with interest.

"There's a prisoner here. Roman Arnault." Saying his name still felt like a breach of trust, though she couldn't imagine it would matter under the circumstances. "Help me find him, and I'll take him from the ones who betrayed you."

The man's paper-dry tongue darted between his lips. "Kill."

Dread shivered down Jane's spine. "What?"

"Kill him."

The words left her cold. Still, she knew what she had to say. "Of course. Tell me where he is."

The dying man closed his eyes long enough that Jane thought she'd lost him. But then his throat bobbed in one slow, smooth motion.

"One. Thirty-two. Two. L."

It sounded like gibberish, but the man spoke slowly and carefully, and when Jane repeated the same sequence back, he groaned softly.

She'd seen codes like that written around the ship. She hadn't given much thought to what they might mean, but now she suspected they were directions, albeit strange ones.

"Thank you," Jane said. "Which way?"

He gazed toward the left, down the corridor she had just crossed.

It wasn't much, but it would have to be enough.

Jane gave his hand a final squeeze and tried to ignore the cold feeling seeping into her bones.

The racket from the hangar was still dimly audible. She watched the bulkheads, using the numbers to guide her. She found 1-32-4-A. Roman had to be near.

She turned a corner and saw what she'd hoped and dreaded: a cluster of guards leaning against the bulkhead.

They were guarding Roman. They had to be. She just needed to get rid of them.

Jane ducked back around the corridor. She guessed there were three or four, but it was hard to tell from the way they stood together in the narrow space.

The ship rocked, and Jane grabbed the handrail to steady herself. She didn't imagine she'd be able to talk her way past the guards, and her original idea of bringing something from the galley wouldn't be enough, so she'd need to get them away from their post.

She needed a distraction.

Jane went back the way she'd come. If she'd learned one thing from her adventures with Roman, it was that there was always something within reach that you could use if you looked hard enough.

She checked the first compartment. It was a stateroom with two stacked beds, a tiny closet filled with clothes, and a cracked mirror. The next compartment wasn't much different. The next was storage for folded canvas sheets and machine parts.

The hangar bay wasn't far off. That might be the best place to cause a stir, though what she'd do and how she'd get away –

The boat leaned dangerously, and Jane clung to the railing with both hands. As she did, she saw something strange fixed to the bulkhead.

It was a box about the size of her open hand. It was painted red and placed at eye level.

It said: FIRE. And below that was a black tab that read "PUSH IN PULL DOWN."

The meaning was ambiguous – was it supposed to create a fire? How could a little red box accomplish that, and what would be the purpose?

Jane didn't know any of that, but she was reasonably sure that, whatever else it did, it would cause a suitable distraction.

So she pushed the black tab and pulled down. Then she waited.

For two long seconds, nothing happened. Then a shrill alarm bleated and echoed down the passageway.

Jane had never heard anything like it and would be happy if she never did again. It sounded as if the whole ship were screaming at her in its rusty, disused voice. Lights strobed to life, brighter by far than the ones that lit the rest of the ship.

The burst of sound and light disoriented her, but soon she heard commotion coming from the direction of the guards. She ducked into the storage compartment and pressed an ear to the bulkhead, listening for the sound of running men over the warbling, shrieking alarm.

Their voices and footsteps blended into a cacophonous drone, moving back toward the hangar bay. She gave them half a minute before poking her head back into the passageway.

It was empty. Though it was only a matter of time before the crowd of hundreds boiled out of the hangar bay to hunt down the source of the commotion.

Jane hurried toward Roman's compartment. The strobe was dizzying, and she kept her gaze low to avoid the worst of it. She couldn't believe how well this was working – if they fled in the opposite direction of the hangar bay, they could probably avoid running into any –

A hand snagged her arm, and two hard eyes met hers.

"What're you doing?" The guard had been standing behind the bulkhead, and Jane hadn't seen him.

"The alarm!" Jane said through the sudden dryness in her mouth. "There's a fire near the hangar bay – you've got to hurry!"

It was an admirable effort, but the guard wasn't buying it.

In fact, he was raising his baton.

And the compartment door was opening at his back.

The hinges shrieked, and the guard began to turn. Roman appeared behind him, a series of slow-motion images in the flashing light.

"Move!" he shouted.

Jane dodged to the side, and Roman drove his shoulder into the guard's back. He flew across the narrow passageway, and his head slammed into the bulkhead with a crack that made Jane wince. He crumpled to the floor with a cry of pain that cut through the siren.

Roman stood in the doorway, looking both surprised and pleased despite the danger. The door that swung open and closed behind him revealed a plain stateroom with a thin cot.

Jane blinked, trying to piece together what had just transpired around the chaos of light, noise, and her own thudding heart.

Roman raised his cuffed hands and held up a pin and a crooked length of wire. "Very carefully."

She felt warm all over. "Were you waiting for–"

"An opportunity." He grinned. And reached his shackled hands toward her, drawing her close and –

The ship rolled again, flinging Jane to the deck and Roman back toward the compartment. He grabbed at the edge of the bulkhead.

"The key! Quick!" he said.

Jane scrambled to get her bearings. The guard was still on the floor, curled up like a dying insect and blinking through his pain. Jane took advantage of his disorientation and dove for his pockets.

He grabbed at her wrists with one hand. "Whub ye hink ye doon?"

She twisted out of his grasp easily enough, but his thrashing was making her task more difficult than it should have been.

He let out a gurgling laugh and spat a bloody mass – maybe a chunk of tongue, maybe not – onto his chest. "Where ye gung go? Yer onna hip."

She tore one hand away again, plunging the other behind his

belt. Her fingers found metal.

The deck swayed, and Jane fought to keep her grip. The warbling siren and the flaring lights were giving her a headache. Then the man laughed again, and Jane saw the baton in his other hand, already rising over his head to come down on hers.

Just then, Roman's boot swung into the guard's neck. With a strangled cry, the guard released both Jane and the baton. She pulled the key out from under him and scooted away.

"They'll be back any minute now," Roman said, holding out his hands again. Jane fumbled with the key, fighting the swaying motion of the ship and the disorientation of the strobing lights.

Finally, the key clicked into place and the cuffs sprang open.

"This way," Roman said, heading down the passageway. Toward the hangar.

"Not that way!" Jane said.

"You know another way outside?" Roman asked, following.

"Let's get up a few decks first."

They found a ladder and climbed as quickly as they could. Jane's body had already taken a beating, but she couldn't afford to slow down now. The ladder ended at deck 03.

"We're just under the surface," said Roman. "Nearly there."

The tossing of the storm flung her across the passageway as she made her careening progress forward. Roman stumbled along behind her, thudding into the bulkheads on either side as the ship pitched.

And beneath the roar of the storm and the wail of the siren, Jane heard the distant rumbling that could only be crewmen running through the ship, looking for them.

And shouts, loud enough that they had to be on the same deck. Jane slipped and fell flat, cursing and scrambling to get up. Her arms, her legs, even her stomach was wet, and –

"Water," Roman said, pulling her up. "Look." He pointed to a puddle oozing into the passageway from the next intersection.

"An exit," Jane said.

They followed it to a metal door with a wheel. The storm was louder than ever on the other side – Jane never would have thought she'd be so relieved to hear it. It took their combined strength to rotate the wheel and push the door open.

They stumbled onto a balcony, and Jane went from being blinded and deafened by the strobe and sirens to being blinded and deafened by the waves and wind.

Yet through the rain and sea spray, Jane saw a gangway swinging from the edge of the balcony.

"You first. They won't shoot me," Roman said before she could argue.

Jane clambered onto the gangway, Roman following close behind.

The shape of the next ship was hazy in the dark and rain, but it was a big one. Stacked with neat, massive rows of crates.

The box ship *COSCO*.

"Faster!" Roman shouted behind her. The storm almost drowned out his voice. But the gangway was bouncing and swinging, and Jane was already moving faster than seemed safe.

"They've found us!" he said. Two big impacts ripped through the gangway – Jane suspected those were their pursuers, but she didn't dare look back to confirm.

Nor did she have to. Lights and shadows ran along a parallel gangway a couple of hundred feet away. The *Kennedy*'s crew were trying to cut them off.

And they were making headway.

Jane pushed herself to go faster, ignoring the pain in her abused joints and the fury of the water thrashing below.

She hit the deck of the box ship barely a second before Roman. He was already heading into the canyon of crates, tugging her along.

She found her footing and ran along beside him. "What's your plan?" she asked.

The deck swayed. He caromed into a metal crate, then pushed off again. "Get out of sight. Fast as possible." It wasn't what she'd meant, but it would have to do for now. He swerved down a passage between the stacks, and she followed.

In that sense, anyway, the storm and dark were on their side.

They kept up their winding path, running fast enough that they were slipping along the deck and crashing into the boxes. Nearly all had been drawn shut. Yet Jane caught glimpses from the narrow gaps between them: eyes, wide and pale, watching her. But she couldn't stop to look back. She and Roman were moving toward the superstructure, which loomed above the stacks like the peak of a mountain.

Roman slowed near a ladder. "Up," he panted.

They climbed. Jane felt movement through the boxes on the other side of the ladder, like the arrhythmic heartbeat of a behemoth. The rungs were perilously slick, and the ship heaved and rocked as though it were trying to throw them from its back. When they reached the top of the stack, they hunkered down to keep from sliding off and looked.

To their left, the deck of the *Kennedy* glowed with their pursuers' lanterns and searchlights. To their right was a wide, turbulent stretch of open water between the *COSCO* and the cabin ship beyond it.

There was nowhere else to run.

"We'll open one of these containers," Roman said. "Hide inside. There's no way they can search them all before we reach the Continent. When we make landfall, we slip away."

In his strained voice were the many unspoken ifs – if they found food and water to sustain them, if their captors stuck to their course, if they were able to sneak and swim away before the crew or the currents took them.

If the children inside didn't give them up.

"I've got another idea," Jane said.

He looked to her, hopeful.

She pointed. "That."

It looked like a big, orange shoe, but it had the general shape of things that were meant to go in the water, according to her time on Salvage. It also looked reassuringly watertight.

A shout rang across the ship. A pair of figures stood on the stacks about a hundred feet away. They'd been spotted.

"Hurry," Jane said, scrambling back to the ladder.

Climbing down was harder than climbing up. She took the rungs two at a time until one unexpected toss of the waves tore her feet from the ladder and left her clinging to safety with only her slick, much-abused hands.

"Slide!" Roman called down.

She didn't know what he meant, but when she looked up she saw his boots a foot from her head, squeezing the sides of the ladder. She copied his posture, uttering a brief prayer to no one in particular as she released the rungs and grabbed the sides of the ladder.

She slid down, faster than she'd hoped but slower than Roman's urging suggested. The poles squealed through her grip, but it was all over in a few hair-raising seconds. She hit the ground with a thump that shook her whole body, and as she staggered back from the ladder Roman grabbed her elbow and yanked her toward the summit of the superstructure.

He yelled something as he pulled her forward, but "too close" was all she caught.

She risked a glance over her shoulder, long enough to see lantern light bouncing along not fifteen feet behind them.

Jane threw all of her strength into a burst of speed. Too late, she realized it was too much.

The deck rose to meet her. Roman was a smudge in the darkness, and he stopped and turned even as she shouted him onward.

He was looking beyond her, his mouth slack and open.

Something slammed into the deck behind her. Jane looked back and saw a man splayed on the deck, surrounded by four or five short-statured people.

Children. The children from the stacks.

Roman bellowed something, and she sprang to her feet. They ran ahead together.

When they reached the superstructure and saw the lifeboat perched a mere three flights up, Jane wanted to cry with relief.

Then she saw the dark silhouettes and swinging lanterns of their pursuers converging behind them and on the other side of the deck, trying to cut them off.

Jane pulled herself up the stairs two and three steps at a time, not daring to slow until the bright orange stern of the craft appeared in front of her.

It was even smaller than it had looked from the top of the stacks, and the whole thing was angled down toward the water. Jane opened the door and saw one seat nestled amidst a panel of button, knobs, and levers, and an aisle descending toward the bow. Roman swung inside and Jane followed suit, pulling the door closed behind her.

"Okay, how do we lower this into the water?" Jane asked.

"We're lashed to the scaffolding," Roman said, already tearing through a compartment set under the helmsman's seat. "I've got to cut us free before we can go anywhere." He found a knife and tucked it into his belt. "Lock the door and keep them out until we're loose."

Before she could ask how he expected her to deter a bunch of desperate, armed mutineers, he was clambering down the seats like a ladder and heading toward a door set in the side of the craft.

Hers was the easy job, she told herself. All she had to do was lock up.

Unfortunately, there was nothing that looked like the latch. If this was an escape vessel, it had been built to let people in, not keep them out.

Shouts rose over the roar of the storm. The mutineers were coming.

Jane searched the compartment as Roman had. She found several orange sticks, a white box with a red cross, a wrench, a length of rope, and a black box with a faded decal on the front.

She opened the box, and inside she found an orange gun and

six red cylinders.

They were coming up the stairs, their feet pounding hard enough that she could feel their frantic rhythm in the deck.

Jane had never seen a gun like this, but the mechanism seemed straightforward enough. She chased Ruthers's memory away as she pulled the barrel down, saw it was empty. She loaded one of the red cylinders into it and snapped it closed.

She thumbed the hammer back and raised the gun just as the door flew open.

The man who'd opened it jumped back just as quickly, staring at the orange pistol in her hands. There were five others with him, all with the same adrenaline-addled expressions.

Three of them held guns, all pointed at the deck. They were watching her, trying to decide whether she had the nerve to use hers.

And so was she. Because pointing a gun at these men and women standing between her and freedom felt too much like being in Ruthers's chambers more than three weeks ago, weighing the value of his life and her and Roman's liberty.

Except with Ruthers, she'd known without a doubt what she was prepared to do. Now, faced with the prospect of inviting six more phantoms into her psyche, she wasn't so sure.

But she couldn't let them know it.

"Back," she said. "And drop your guns."

They took a couple perfunctory steps back, but they held onto their weapons. Not an encouraging sign.

The man who had opened the door raised his hands and gave her a wolfish smile through the hair whipping around his face. "Listen," he said, "ess six of us ee two of you." He slid one foot along the deck, edging forward again.

"About to be five," she said, aiming the gun at him. She locked her arms to keep them from trembling. She couldn't afford to let them see how badly she wanted to avoid this.

He froze. Then he laughed. "You won't shoot. If you do, my companyeros'll fill ye with holes right pronto." He took another sliding step. "So let's–"

"Shoot her, and I jump!" Roman roared from his perch outside the lifeboat. "I'm no good to you dead!"

Their faces went rigid. Only their eyes moved as they looked between her and Roman, trying to weigh how much their quarry valued survival over freedom and whether they'd be in bigger trouble for killing him or letting him escape.

And even though she hated that they'd instantly found Roman's threat more credible than hers, she was mostly relieved.

Then the man standing next to the door lunged. Jane instinctively turned her gun away from him and fired.

The projectile exploded on the platform only a few yards away. Even as she shut her eyes against the blast, bright red light flared in her vision. The mutineers were screaming over a hissing that sounded like frying oil. She tried not to think about it as she opened her eyes to grab at the door.

Unfortunately, she could hardly see through the thick, acrid smoke. But she fumbled for the handle and pulled it shut, sliding the wrench through it for good measure. It might buy her a little time.

Maybe even enough, if Roman finished whatever he was doing soon.

Seconds later, she heard the thump of the aft door slamming shut, then Roman's voice rising above the din.

"Get us out of here!"

"I thought you–"

"I cut the safeties. The controls are up there with you."

Of course they were. But smoke choked the air in the cabin, and between that and the darkness, Jane couldn't see more than vague shapes on the control panel.

And the shouts from outside were growing less frantic and more purposeful. Their pursuers were regrouping.

Jane found a button and pressed it. Nothing.

Thumps came from outside the lifeboat. They were trying to get in.

She grabbed a handle, pushed it and pulled it. Some mechanism in the craft grumbled loudly enough to startle their pursuers into inaction, but Jane knew it wouldn't last.

"Jane..." Roman's voice rose with a singsong note of worry.

"Working on it!"

"Fasten yourself in!" A metallic click pierced the racket.

She was tempted to ask why, but suspended a hundred feet over the water the answer was obvious enough. It had probably been too much to hope for a slow, gentle descent.

She groped for the straps around her seat and for the metal clasps at the ends. She'd just fitted them together and heard the confirming click when the door behind her started to rattle.

A few seconds of that, and they'd dislodge the wrench and have the door open. She was out of time.

As she braced herself, her knee brushed up against something. A handle, bright red and just visible through the haze.

Jane pulled it.

The rattling stopped, and the ground fell out from under her.

Between the smoke and the old, fogged portholes, she couldn't see anything, but her body told her she was falling – and fast. As they shot toward the sea, Jane only had time to be grateful that she wouldn't have long to wonder whether or not this had been a good idea.

They crashed into the water. The impact hurled her against the restraints. And then she was still tumbling, and for a moment there was only the smoke, the lurching of the craft, and the crash of waves outside.

Then Roman's face appeared in front of hers, and he was saying something.

She just laughed. For a moment, she allowed herself to feel joy and relief – they were free and alive. For the moment.

Roman frowned, and his mouth formed familiar shapes.

"Are you okay?"

Jane nodded, still smiling, but the euphoria began to slip away.

"Good, because we've got to go." He pointed up and behind

her, at one of the fogged and scuffed windows in the "ankle" of the shoe.

The lights of the *Kennedy* hovered above and behind them, and they were bearing down. Fast.

And Roman was looking at her like he expected she'd figured this out from her two minutes at the control panel.

She reached over and tried the handle that had startled the mutineers. Sure enough, gentle force pressed her back into her seat, and the waves outside the window began to pass by more quickly.

Roman looked at her, then back at the aft window.

"Can you make it go faster?" he asked.

She checked the handle. It was already pushed as far forward as it would go. "I think–"

The lifeboat rolled. Jane was still strapped in, but Roman tumbled and flailed.

"Head into the waves," Roman said, bracing himself in the small space.

Jane spun the wheel, but controlling the craft was easier said than done. Before she knew it, they'd whirled all the way around to face the *Kennedy*. Its bow wave was a gleaming crest ahead of them.

"Turn back! Quick!" Roman cried.

But Jane had a different idea. She kept her nose forward, aiming for the long side of the *COSCO*. There was still a wide lane between it and the smaller boats tethered to the next group of ships.

"Good thinking." Roman coughed and squeezed her shoulder as they passed into the box ship's shadow. The smoke was clearing slowly, but they didn't dare open either of the doors with the sea churning so violently. "We should–"

A thundering splash from behind them cut him off, and the wave shoved them forward. Jane's gut went to ice.

"What was that?" she asked.

He was staring out the aft window again. "Go. Fast as you can."

A massive, dark rectangle plunged into the water several dozen yards ahead. As the outbound wave pushed their nose up, Jane got a look at the stacks of the box ship, listing toward them.

She felt sick, thinking of the children she'd seen in those same crates. All she could do was swerve away and hope they'd gotten out. "Is the *Kennedy* doing that?"

"No idea," Roman called, still watching the big craft from the aft window. "I think we're clear," he said. "Turn us back so we can find a way through."

"That'll put us in view of the *Kennedy* again," Jane said.

"I know, but there's no way through here," he said, pointing to the smaller boats bobbing on the waves. "Besides, what can they do?"

Jane didn't want to find out, but she didn't see another route.

And as they passed the bow of the box ship, they discovered what the *Kennedy* could do.

They had a wide, clear lane alongside the next tethered cluster, leading to the blended horizon of gray waves and sea beyond. Jane was heading for it when a sound like an immense raspberry rattled through the air. There was a pause, and then another.

Jane kept her eyes forward. They couldn't risk getting flipped by another wave. "What are they doing?" she asked.

Roman pressed his face closer to the aft window.

"They're... shooting at us."

A ridge of white water rose fore and port. Jane risked a glance back and saw an orange glow spitting from somewhere just under the surface deck of the *Kennedy*.

"We can't outrun that gun," Roman said.

"I know."

She turned again, angling to put the waves at their back. "There," she said, pointing.

Roman looked out the fore window. "You think we can fit?"

"Probably." Jane said it with more conviction than she felt. "But you should fasten yourself in again."

Roman hustled below and into one of the harnesses. There

was a gap between two mid-sized boats ahead, but it was closing faster than she'd thought.

And behind, the *Kennedy* fired another volley into the water. This one was close enough that Jane could feel the wave.

The gap narrowed ahead. They were just a dozen yards away.

"I thought they wanted you alive," Jane called down to Roman.

Two looming bows filled the view.

"I thought you did, too," he said. She glanced down long enough to see him smile.

They sped through the gap but clipped their aft end on one of the ships. Jane tossed this way and that, thankful again for the restraints.

"Made it?" Roman called up.

"Almost." A maze of ships rose ahead of them, but they were clear of the *Kennedy* and its guns.

Another wave threw them against the side of a passenger boat. "I'll try to get us out of here," Jane said, feeling a return of the old nausea.

"Do," said Roman. He sounded as queasy as she felt.

But she kept her gorge down until they were clear of Salvage's flotilla and had ridden past the worst of the storm. When at last the floating city was a dim blur on the horizon and the waves had calmed to a gentle rocking, Jane pulled off her restraints, opened the aft door, and vomited into the ocean.

Fresh air had never tasted so sweet. She swallowed it in deep, slow breaths and splashed water on her face and neck. When she ducked back inside, Roman had opened cabinets and compartments all around the interior and was consolidating their contents in a pile.

It was disconcertingly small.

"Looks like they kept this stocked, but not for long journeys," he said. "I'd estimate several days' water if we're careful, about as much food if none of it's spoiled." He looked up at her. "It's not too late to turn around. Ride out the storm, then surrender ourselves to the almirante. I imagine they'd be sympathetic, especially if you tell them about the mutiny."

All this trouble, and he'd consider going back? "But then they'd know why the mutineers seized you. Who you are, and what you mean to the Continent."

He smiled sadly. "Better than dying out here, isn't it?"

And then she got it. It wouldn't be better – not to him, of course. Left to his own devices, he'd just as soon make this lifeboat his coffin as return to captivity.

But he wouldn't bring that death on her.

Fortunately, Jane remembered seeing the gull earlier in the day. She laughed with delight. Roman's brow furrowed.

"As long as we keep this thing pointing east," she said, flicking the dome of the console compass, "we'll make it. We've just got to last another day or two on our own." She stretched her arms and legs until she felt a satisfying twinge in her limbs.

Roman settled into one of the seats, suddenly absorbed in the mechanism of the straps and clasp. His face was a mask of false concentration.

She pulled him into a deep, long kiss. She hadn't known she was going to do it, but as she ran her fingers through his hair and her tongue over his, she realized she'd been thinking about it since they got clear of Salvage. He tasted terrible, salty and sour and in need of a good scrubbing, but she didn't care.

At that moment, all she wanted was more.

She was reaching for the buttons on his shirt when he pulled away.

"What?" It was the only word she could think of over the throbbing ache.

"I don't think this is a good idea," he said.

She wasn't certain it was, either, but she'd have been perfectly happy to figure that out once she'd calmed the molten honey in her belly. This was the first time they'd truly had a moment of solitude and safety. It seemed right to enjoy it.

"I don't know what's going to happen when we reach the

Continent," she said. "I–"

"That's why we should keep our wits about us." Roman kissed her forehead. "Believe me, there's nothing I'd like more, but..."

But he couldn't meet her eyes.

"I understand," Jane said. It was the kind of thing one was supposed to say in situations like this.

He winced. "We should try to rest. Save our strength." He was already reclining on the row of seats, turning his back to her.

Jane settled into a corner by the helm. Unfortunately, sleep was the furthest thing from her mind.

She shifted and stretched, trying to get comfortable. But something was pressing against her chest, something hard with sharp edges.

Jane remembered the book and pulled it out of her chemise. Now that they were clear of the storm clouds, the moon was just bright enough to illuminate the cover with its field of stars.

She flipped to the first page.

CHAPTER NINETEEN
A LITTLE DEATH

Lachesse was alone in the lounge when Malone found her, a half-empty caffee cup on the table next to her. She took in Malone's story with preternatural stoicism, but Malone detected a nervous tightening of the muscles beneath her layers of cosmetics.

"You saw only two?" the whitenail asked.

"In the dark," Malone said. "No telling how many others are tucked away up there. Or elsewhere on the ship."

"Have you told anyone else about this?" Lachesse asked.

"You're the first."

"Good. Tell no one else."

Confusion tickled at the back of Malone's neck. "But Geist—"

"Will do what, exactly?" Lachesse blinked her painted eyes at Malone. "If he starts looking for them, then whoever planted them may get desperate."

"So we move fast. Confine everyone to quarters, have Geist and his most trusted people search the ship."

Lachesse dismissed the idea with a flick of her wrist. "As you said, we've no way of knowing where they all are. And it only takes one to bring down the entire ship."

A current of frustration surged through Malone. She had to fight to keep her voice down, to force it through a jaw rigid with annoyance. "We can't just stand around and do nothing. Geist knows his people, he could tell us—"

Lachesse's laugh struck a sharp, discordant note. "Inspector, the man has a murderer among his crew, and he told you almost nothing about it. I wouldn't be so quick to trust him, much less his handling of the situation." She raised an eyebrow. "I would have thought the last year in Recoletta would have instilled in you a healthier sense of suspicion."

"I've got enough suspicion to go around. It's this waiting and hoping the bombs don't go off that bothers me." She shook her head. "I've got to start taking them down. As many as I can find. There's a window that opens in the mess, and another–"

"You'll do no such thing," Lachesse said in a tone that raised Malone's temperature. "Setting aside for a moment that you'll end us all if you drop one–"

The hairs along the back of Malone's neck bristled. "I'm sure I can manage."

"– you're forgetting that you don't even know how many there are," Lachesse said. "And if our culprit is circumspect – as, indeed, one would have to be to execute a plot of this nature – he'll notice if a few of his bombs suddenly go missing."

"It's better than doing nothing," Malone said.

"Nothing is what's happened so far, and we're all still alive," Lachesse said, her voice as smooth and firm as polished steel. "Besides, I'm hardly suggesting we do nothing. But instead of tipping our hand, we should seize the advantage you so fortuitously found and learn just who we're up against. And why he's biding his time." Lachesse paused, waiting.

Clouds were gathering outside. Malone couldn't see them except for the way they blotted out the stars. "Biding his time," she said. She had the sneaking suspicion the old whitenail was onto something.

"Indeed," Lachesse said, placing a long-nailed finger against her cheek. "It's why these bombs haven't gone off yet that interests me."

"Let's hear it," Malone said. She was starting to respect Lachesse's cleverness, but the woman had an unfortunate taste for theatrics. Almost like Sundar had.

· "Someone placed those bombs and, I take it, engaged in a fair bit of planning and subterfuge to accomplish that. Yet if they'd only wanted to frustrate Geist's mission, they would have triggered them already."

"They're waiting for something specific," Malone said.

"Something that hasn't happened yet," said Lachesse.

"Retrieving Arnault," Malone said, understanding quickening her pulse. "Someone didn't want him brought back to the Continent."

"Or someone wanted him dead," Lachesse said.

"But that still doesn't answer it," Malone said. "Not completely. If someone wanted to sabotage Geist's mission, they could have destroyed the *Glasauge* at any point on the journey over."

"Perhaps they wanted to make it back to the Continent first," said Lachesse.

"And if they wanted to kill Arnault, a bomb is a lot of trouble where a bullet or knife would do."

"But far more anonymous. And that's assuming our culprit could get close enough to Arnault to use the other methods you mention."

Lachesse had a point. If Arnault possessed the kind of "key" Lachesse had described, Malone couldn't imagine Geist would take any chances with him.

"And somehow Sharad fits into all of this," Malone said.

Lachesse leveled her gaze at Malone. "Perhaps he found the bombs first. And told the wrong person."

Malone missed the days when people simply murdered each other over money and sex. She held up her hands in surrender. "I won't tell Geist, and I won't tamper with the bombs. Not until we know better what's going on."

The whitenail nodded her satisfaction. "Now, I think we'd better redouble our efforts to get into Geist's office." Lachesse plucked her caffee cup from the table and peered into it with a dispassionate eye. "He'll have records. Files on his staff, something that would tell us who everyone is, and maybe who stands out from the crowd." She set her cup down and began fidgeting with one of her rings.

"Let's just hope it's something we can read," Malone said.

"Leave that to me," Lachesse said.

"We still haven't solved the biggest problem – how to get into Geist's office. And now, without drawing extra attention to the engine room," Malone said. But Lachesse said nothing, and when Malone glanced over, the whitenail had twisted a large opal off one of her rings, revealing a small compartment within. "What are you doing?" Malone asked.

Lachesse tapped some kind of white powder from the ring into her caffee cup and secured the opal once more.

Dread prickled up Malone's neck. "Is that–"

The whitenail raised her cup and tossed the concoction back before Malone could finish. She grimaced as she swallowed. "Skies above, that tastes worse than I'd feared." She coughed. "Though, I hardly expected to use it on myself."

A chill zipped through Malone's spine. "What have you done?"

The old woman shuddered. "I've done what's necessary. Dear me, but you look aghast. Upset, even." Wrapped up in her heavy fabric and jewelry, Lachesse suddenly seemed smothered by it. She coughed again, and the back of her hand came away speckled with blood. Lachesse regarded it impassively. "That should be most convincing."

Malone caught her by the shoulders just as she began to sink to the ground. Her own palms were cold and clammy, but Lachesse felt like a hot coal wrapped in silk. Malone eased her into a chair. "You're dying, you old fool." The idea upset her more than she wanted to admit.

Lachesse's eyes rolled wildly and refocused on Malone. "I should hope not." Her voice was fading, but the verve was still there. "Not if you move quickly."

Malone felt her own pulse speed. Her blood warmed with urgency and something like affection for this crafty, brave old woman. "Tell me," she said, her mouth dry.

"Chernev has medicines." Lachesse winced and clenched her blood-speckled hand over her chest. "But you wouldn't know. You would go to Geist."

A distraction, and as urgent a one as anybody could devise. Malone squeezed Lachesse's hand. "Just hold on."

Lachesse murmured something, but it was too faint to make out. Her cup fell with a heavy thud.

Malone was already sprinting down the corridor, calling for Geist. She found his cabin and hammered on the door. "This is an emergency!"

Other doors opened, and heads poked out in various states of concern, confusion, and consternation. Malone pounded the door again. "She's dying, Geist!"

The door opened, and Geist himself stood before her in an oversized dressing gown, blinking the sleep from his eyes. "Who–"

"Lachesse, she had some kind of fit. Coughing blood, elevated temperature, fainting. She's in the lounge – you've got to hurry." Malone didn't even have to try to get the panic into her voice.

Geist tightened the sash around his waist. "Fetch Chernev at once and tell him to bring his bag. I shall meet you there." Geist rushed toward the lounge. Leaving his door unlocked.

Malone tried not to pay too much attention to it and hoped the bystanders wouldn't give it much thought, either. She hurried around the bend toward the cook's cabin.

He was already standing in the hall, looking for the cause of the commotion. Unease creased his brow as he met Malone's eye.

"Get your bag and go to the lounge immediately," Malone said. "Something's happened to Lachesse."

At the sound of the whitenail's name, the cook's doubt evaporated into alarm. He muttered something to himself and reached back into his cabin for a scuffed leather satchel. When he emerged, he was all business.

He rushed toward the lounge, forgetting about her in an instant.

But the other crew members – those who had been asleep –

were still watching bemusedly and had zeroed in on her as the likeliest source of answers.

Not that she had any to give.

She made her way down the hall and into the washroom, hoping her dishevelment would make that a believable-enough destination.

The door on the other end opened into the opposite corridor – the one with Geist's cabin. And, hopefully, the key to Geist's office.

No one was standing in the corridor, but a handful of people were still peering out from their cabins, waiting for the chaos to transform into something more actionable.

So she'd give them something actionable.

"You," she said, pointing to the nearest crew member. "Get fresh towels to the lounge." It seemed like a reasonable enough request, and it would at least draw their focus away from her. "The rest of you, clear the corridor. Lachesse is... unwell."

A collective gasp ripped down the corridor. The unlucky woman Malone had singled out bit her lip and frowned, and everyone else disappeared back into their cabins, as quickly as if Malone had announced she had the pox.

Of course, if these people really did believe she and Lachesse came from a land of disease, then she had done just that for all intents and purposes.

The remaining crew member cleared her throat. "I-I am a pilot. I know nothing of medicine." Her face was ashen with dread.

"Then clear out of the way," Malone said.

The woman disappeared into her cabin without another word. Malone only hoped the crew didn't take Lachesse's sudden malady as a reason to purge them both from their ship.

But the corridor was clear, so she pushed those worries aside for the time being and slipped into Geist's cabin.

It was as small as all the others, and Geist had little to store in it besides clothes – all two sizes too big – and a few grooming implements. She rifled through shelves and under the bed, but could only find Geist's personal belongings. If he were going to keep something important –something he used frequently – where would it be?

Somewhere easily accessible but not too obvious. Malone checked the pockets of his folded shirts, inside his shoes, under his pillow, hoping all the while he didn't have the damn thing tucked under the dressing gown he was wearing.

Her gaze fell on his shaving kit. Of course – something he used every morning.

She peeled it open and sure enough, between the comb and the razor, was a polished key. She pocketed it and left, closing the cabin door behind her.

The corridor was empty, and the voices of Geist and the cook, low and urgent, carried from the lounge. Malone desperately wanted to know how Lachesse was faring, but if she missed the chance to get into Geist's office then the whitenail's sacrifice would be for naught.

Something rumbled in the distance – thunder. Malone hadn't heard that sound since leaving Recoletta.

She continued up the stairs and to the command deck. The officers in the pilot house were talking animatedly with one another. They hadn't noticed her.

She hoped they'd stay busy long enough for her to get into the office. She headed toward the door, not looking back at the pilot house and not breaking her stride. Experience had taught Malone that the best way to go unnoticed was to act as though she belonged.

She reached the door without incident and tried the key in the lock, praying for a fit. She twisted it one way and the other and heard a click like the music of angels.

As Malone slipped inside she saw one of the officers in the pilot house just beginning to turn. It wasn't clear if he'd seen her or not, but she'd find out soon enough.

She locked it behind her, just to be safe. For now, there was work to be done.

Like everything on the *Glasauge* – everything but the envelope and its massive gas bags – Geist's office was smaller than she would have guessed from the outside. Yet as with the rest of the airship, every space was put to use. There were latched shelves set into the walls and hinged compartments in the floor.

And somehow Malone had to find a lead as to who on Geist's crew might plant bombs and murder his compatriots.

She checked the shelves first. She found books, most of them unintelligible. A thin logbook that looked like a list of ciphers. She tried the next shelf. More books.

Yet as she worked her way through the office, she smelled something odd. Her blood ran cold at the memory of the explosives she'd found the last time she went sneaking around, but this odor was different. Muskier.

In the corner she found a narrow hutch fronted with wire mesh. The inside was lined with straw, feathers, and an unmistakable spackling of bird droppings.

Otherwise, it was empty.

Before she could ponder this further, someone hammered on the door. She jumped.

"Malone, I know you are there. Please to come out now," Geist called from the other side, his voice a calm counterpoint to the heavy blows against the door.

If he knew she was here, she might as well get what she came for. She moved to the desk as the pounding continued, louder and heavier by the moment. She checked the drawers. Pens, wax stamps, a box of matches.

"I comprend your curiosity, but I am becoming malhumored," Geist called out. "Come out now, pleece." His tone was still measured and calm, but there was an edge to his voice that she hadn't heard before.

She tried the next drawer. A sheaf of papers. This was more promising.

More pounding. "Lachesse is recovering. She is safe. As are we all, but that may not be so unless you open this door."

Malone had heard her share of threats, but with Geist it was difficult to tell if this was a threat or a simple observation of fact.

Regardless, whether or not he killed her would have very little to do with whether she opened the door now. But if she could figure out who was planting bombs and slaying his crew, she might – just maybe – have a chance.

So she focused her attention on puzzling through the papers in the desk. She had become so accustomed to hearing and seeing foreign words that it took a moment for her eyes to pick out the word "crew" amidst the unreadable terms on the first page.

Her pulse raced, and she flipped to the next page. The pounding on the door resumed with a heavy, rhythmic quality. Geist and his people were trying to break it down.

She quickly scanned what appeared to be a list of terms. None she recognized, unfortunately, until she hit "GINTNER, ZOYA MARIA."

The placard she'd found wasn't a title, she realized. It was a name.

She flipped ahead to another page bearing the same name. Clipped to it was an image – not a painting, but a black and white apparition of reality, just like the image of Roman that Geist had shown her – of a woman with wide, dark eyes and dark hair, her expression as still and serious as a corpse's.

Malone had never seen her before. And she was pretty certain she'd seen everyone on the ship, even if she didn't know their names.

The pounding outside continued. The hinges jingled like pocket change, and a dent rose from the center of the door.

She flipped back to the crew list and scanned the names. There were nearly a hundred of them, and she didn't see one she recognized. She checked twice, but she couldn't find Sharad, Chernev, or Valenti.

And she couldn't find Geist.

The door groaned and rattled as Geist and his followers – whoever they were – smashed it from its hinges.

Malone turned quickly through the rest of the pages and their accompanying images. They depicted men and women of all ages and physiognomies, but none she recognized. The capitan – what she presumed to be the captain – was a woman with a hooked nose and a matronly build.

The door flew open in a crash. Geist burst in, six crew members crowding behind him in the tight space.

His face was as impassive as ever, but his eyes burned with rage. He tugged back the sleeves of his dressing gown – one, Malone realized, that had never been made for him – and smoothed back a stray lock of hair.

"If I had known you would be such trouble, I would have left you in Recoletta," he said, as evenly as though she had made him late for his train.

"If I'd known you'd stolen this airship, I might have stayed," Malone said.

"Regrettable for us both," he said. He made a chopping motion with his hand, and four of the crew next to him rushed to Malone's side. Two held her arms while the other two patted her down. "Tell us about your plans here," he said.

"I should ask you the same."

A fist came from her left and struck her jaw. Not the worst she'd had, but enough for her to know that Geist meant business.

"I shall rephrase," said Geist. "Why did you break into this office?"

"You left it locked." This time, the punch came from her right and landed hard enough for her to taste blood. She spat a red gob onto the floorboards. "You'll ruin your woodwork."

Geist smirked. "I respect your kraft, but you are alone here."

At least he didn't seem to know Lachesse had been in on it. That, or he was waiting for her to slip and give the old woman up. Either way, if she was going down, she wasn't taking anyone with her. Not even Lachesse.

The newfound loyalty surprised her.

He pinched the bridge of his nose. "You comprend that I must have trust in the people on my ship. I can show you mercy, but you must tell me all."

Malone had heard lines like that before. "You lied about who you are. How can I believe anything you say?" she asked.

He rubbed his goatee. "You might as well take the chance."

She knew the tactics well enough to know that Geist would kill or spare her based on whatever internal calculation of risk he'd already made, regardless of what she said.

"Go to hell," Malone said.

He lowered his head and made a circling motion with one finger. Three pairs of hands seized her from behind and marched her out of the office. Malone didn't fight them – she didn't have anywhere to run. Geist led the way down the corridor and toward the stairs. The on-duty crew watched with the darting, surreptitious glances of schoolchildren seeing another being led away for punishment.

And from the quick, embarrassed way they averted their gazes from hers, Malone knew punishment was forthcoming.

They wound down the stairs. Malone couldn't see anything past the first curve of the corridors on the stateroom level, much less the lounge on the other end. But all was quiet.

They continued down to the storage deck. It was empty except for the crates and pallets, and by Malone's guess it would be lighter by one person by the time this business was finished.

Malone's escort marched her to the middle of the deck. Geist waved them – and the two with him – away, and the floor shuddered as they trooped a dozen feet behind her.

Geist turned to her. "I give you another opportunity to declare yourself. Anything you spreck, only I shall hear."

She'd already told him to go to hell. She thought of all the things she could say. Why did he care whether a Recolettan knew he and his people were not the assigned crew of the *Glasauge*? Why had he interrupted her first execution if he was just going to put her through another now?

"You brought me to find Arnault. Now, you're going to kill me over this?"

Geist's expression was pained. "I bear you no malintent. But I cannot have treachery on my ship."

It was hardly fair that this should all fall on her shoulders. With a word, she could have Lachesse brought down to share her misery. After all the old woman had put her through, it would have been easy enough.

Yet she had no desire to inform on Lachesse, and she couldn't figure out if it was because of what the old whitenail had said about doing what was necessary to protect the city, or because of the tightness she'd felt in her chest when she saw her begin to slip.

Perhaps she could have figured it out if she'd had more time.

Geist shook his head. "I can at the very least offer you an end that will be much quicker than the slow strangulation your compatriots inflicted on you." He snapped his fingers, and four rough hands gripped her again and shoved her toward the aft end of the deck. One of the crew jogged ahead and began spinning a wheel on the bulkhead. He pulled it, and a widening rectangle of gray sky appeared.

"I apologize if this seems overly elaborate, but the firing of weapons in a space such as this is not recommended," Geist said. "And I have no inclination to execute you in the manner that your collaborator executed poor Sharad."

Alarm bells went off in her head.

"My collaborator?" she asked.

"Do not play the imbecile. You did not kill him." But he seemed certain that she knew who had. And if he believed that person was Lachesse, then he'd already have her out here.

She wondered exactly what she was being accused of. "I don't know who killed him," Malone said.

But Geist only shook his head sadly. One of the others shoved her onto her knees.

The sky was an iron gray blurred with clouds. The sea below was an oily black, shining with reflected moonlight. The vista was more magnificent and terrifying than the one she'd seen hemmed in by the lounge's windows. A cold, moaning wind pulled tears from her eyes. It smelled like a storm was approaching.

Geist stood close enough that the wind was cracking apart the careful shell of his hair and just far enough to be prudent. "I do not know the customs of your land, but if there are any final words you wish to spreck, or any words you wish sprecken over you, I will oblige you as I can."

Malone had one card left to play. It would either earn her Geist's gratitude or cement his notion of her treachery. Then again, he was already convinced of that.

"You do have a saboteur on your ship," she said. "I don't know who it is, but they've rigged the envelope with explosives."

He stared at her, unblinking despite the wind.

A surge of annoyance warmed her face. "Go check if you don't believe me. But please do it before you throw me out."

Geist's eyes were riveted to her face as though it held a pattern he was afraid he might miss. "Und who are you thinking planted them?"

"That's what I was searching your office for." That, and a clue as to what might have set Sharad and his murderer apart. But that seemed like the lesser problem at the moment.

And he was looking above her at the other crew, saying something in that mongrel language that Lachesse had managed to decipher. As clever as the old whitenail was, maybe she would live to see the Continent. Malone found she didn't begrudge her that.

But Geist wasn't nearly as grateful as he should have been. So Malone turned to regard the sea that would swallow her. She would die with both eyes open.

And, as her vision adjusted to the inky blackness, she saw something almost directly below her, a dull shadow breaking up the shimmering surface of the water. It was large and ovoid, almost like the envelope of the *Glasauge*.

No, exactly like it.

"Are they with you?" she asked.

Geist, who had been engaged in a rapid-fire back-and-forth with the others, raised a hand for silence. He leaned forward, one hand on a crossbar.

"Directly below us. That's another airship," Malone said.

Several tense seconds passed. Geist swore. He said something with the quick, decisive cadence of an order. Malone felt herself hauled back from the door. One crewman slammed it shut and spun the wheel.

The others were moving with quiet, efficient urgency. Geist knelt in front of Malone and gripped her shoulder. "You broke into my office. Why?" He was watching her intently. Malone had the sense that he would decide much based on her answer.

"To learn who your people are. I thought there might be something that would distinguish Sharad's killer. And whoever planted those bombs."

Geist's face betrayed nothing. His scar was a slash of darkness across his face. "Your collaborator in this – it was Lachesse."

There was no point in denying it now. "Obviously."

He cursed under his breath. "Then it seems we have a most dire misunderstanding. I will explique when there is time, but for now I hope you will accept my sincerest apologies."

He rose and offered a hand, but Malone stood on her own. The others had already left the cargo bay, and from the decks above, Malone heard stamping feet and shouted orders. Geist hastened toward the stairs.

"What's going on?" Malone asked.

"We are under attack."

Malone followed Geist to the pilot house, and no one moved to stop her. In fact, no one seemed to notice – the crew was too busy issuing orders and making quick adjustments to the ship's machinery with shaking hands.

"Who's attacking us?" she asked.

"I must explique at another, calmer time. But let us say for now that there are others from the Continent who want Roman

Arnault, as well."

A bell rang, and the airship angled nose down. Malone grabbed a metal crossbeam for support. "But you don't have Roman Arnault."

"Ya, und I am afraid they are knowing this," Geist said. He barked an order, and one of the crew pulled a metal horn from the wall and repeated Geist's words into it. The *Glasauge* leveled out.

Malone worked through the implications. "They're going to shoot us down."

"They will try." He exchanged a few quick words with the man standing by the horn. He turned to the woman standing next to a panel of levers and knobs – almost all of which were painted red – and said, "fewer!" Or something that sounded like that.

The woman twisted a key and pulled a lever. Something distant rumbled beneath their feet, and everyone in the pilot house held their breath.

The man with the speaking horn listened to chatter coming out of the other end and shook his head. Whatever they'd been waiting for, it hadn't happened.

"This one snuck beneath us under the cover of night. A risky move, but now they are close. There will be more ships waiting at a distance. We must destroy this one before it signals the others," Geist said to Malone.

Malone thought of the explosives she'd found in the envelope. She didn't want to announce their presence in front of so many of the crew, but entering a battle with them aboard could be a disaster.

"Geist," she said, leaning close and lowering her voice as much as she could amidst the din. "Those explosives. We should–"

He cut her off with a chopping motion. "Ya, I placed them there."

Malone looked around. The younger crew members – the man by the speaking horn and the other at the elevator panel –

flinched, but the helmsman and the woman at the weapons panel didn't react. Either they hadn't heard, or they already knew. "But why–"

"I have no time for your questions, Malone. I have a battle to fight." Geist issued another rapid stream of orders to the woman at the weapon controls. The floor shuddered again, followed by a tense silence and another exchange on the horn.

It was another miss.

The chatter grew more urgent. Malone only caught a few familiar-sounding words, but the pale knuckles and sweat-beaded brows spoke clearly enough.

Suddenly, the sky flared with light. Malone squeezed her eyes shut against it as the sky, the sea, and the inside of the pilot house were momentarily bathed in a blinding, white glow. Within seconds, it faded to a pale ember floating some distance to the right of the *Glasauge*.

"This is the signal," Geist groaned. A flurry of curses erupted from the other crew. Geist cut through them with a bark to the weapons master. She unloaded another bombardment. It was another miss.

A trail of light shot past the windows. It was distant, but close enough to raise the hairs on Malone's neck.

"The cannons," Geist said, his voice tight. "They are puissant, but inexact."

"Good, then," Malone said.

"Except they need only hit one of us, but we must hit many of them. See, they converge already." He pointed out the window at a small, dark shape just starting to blur the horizon. Another missile burned below them, disappearing into the distance beyond.

"At least one more is behind us. This one is closer, I think." Geist snapped an order to the weapons master. She peered into a scope at her console and rotated a handle around a set of bold hash marks. Malone felt something grind into place through the decking.

The weapons master shouted down the corridor, and another shout echoed back.

Geist raised his hand. "Fewer!"

The woman pulled another lever down, and the *Glasauge* bucked. The airship was still heaving when a cry rose from the aft end of the command deck. Without understanding the words, Malone knew it was a miss.

Another missile streaked by. This one was close enough to draw a startled curse from Geist. Malone's heart leapt at the thought of the explosives swinging and bouncing along with the rest of the craft, but it gave her an idea.

"Is the first airship still below us?" Malone asked.

"Ya, und dodging everything we drop!"

"Can we descend to a point just above it?"

Geist shook his head. "Then bombardment becomes impossible. If we destroy them from so close, we will only be saving these others the trouble." His gaze flickered upwards, toward the envelope and the explosives nestled there.

"But if we get close, then maybe the others will stop shooting at us," said Malone.

Geist's lips moved as he thought it over. "It is perilous. We must maintain a position above them to avoid their light guns." Another projectile slashed a bright line across the sky. "But at this moment, perhaps it is the lesser risk." He called out an order to the bustling pilot house. To the crew's credit they didn't hesitate, but set about their adjustments with their eyes a few degrees wider and their mouths frozen into rigid lines.

The *Glasauge* angled down, and Malone held to the bulkhead for stability. As the sea rose into view, her stomach climbed into her chest. Yet despite feeling as if she were about to fall into the forward windows, the gradual slide of scenery betrayed nothing more than a slow, steady descent. The enemy airship ahead was slowly rising above them, but it wasn't firing again. Not yet.

There was something surreal about the battle unfolding around them. The floating behemoths weren't built for speed or agility, so they maneuvered around one another with slow, dignified grace. And yet each change in altitude or course came from a flurry of orders, confirmations, and adjustments. The missiles that streaked past them punctuated the long, tense moments of waiting, pulled them back into real time.

At last they leveled out, and the room let up a collective sigh of relief.

A man jogged and stumbled from the aft end of the deck to jabber something at Geist, who smiled.

"We have successfully established a position over the airship *Chasseur*," Geist announced. The others cheered – the weapons master hugged the helmsman, and the pair stationed by the elevator panel shared a quick handshake. "Be on the alert, for they will cherch for a way around or above us, und we cannot risk their mid-range guns. Martens," he said to the weapons master, "focus the cannon on the target behind us. If we must escape, I do not want to have to dodge their attack."

The woman nodded and busied herself with the knobs and scopes of the weapons panel. For several tense moments, the battle played out in the turning of wheels, the flipping of levers, and the spinning of dials as the crew of the *Glasauge* sought to maintain their spot directly over the *Chasseur*.

Martens, meanwhile, fired one missile after the next until a bright, violent glow of orange briefly lit the windows. A triumphant cry came from down the hall. The pilot house erupted in cheers and embraces once more.

"Bravo!" Geist said, clapping the weapons master on the shoulder. "Goot, Martens."

Malone released a breath she didn't know she'd been holding. She didn't much feel like celebrating the fiery death of a few dozen strangers, especially when the battle was far from over.

"Four plus," said the man by the speaking horn nodding to Geist and then Malone.

"Maintain our position relative to the *Chasseur*," he said. "We can pick each of them off so long as–"

Something screamed past the windows and made a glowing splash in the sea just past them.

The man with the speaking horn yelled something in the Continent's motley tongue. But Malone read "behind and above" in his panicked hand gestures.

Some of their pursuers, at least, were willing to sacrifice the *Chasseur*.

Geist was translating these directions into orders for Martens when the floor shuddered and began tilting upwards.

A massive gray shape loomed in the windows and blotted out the sea below. The sight alone would have been bad enough, but then Malone saw the horror and panic on the faces of the crew.

Malone gulped a breath. "Are they–"

"They will knock us out of the sky!" Geist said. Metal shrieked as the *Chasseur*'s envelope scraped the *Glasauge*'s hull. "And they will destroy their own ship, the idiots!"

Another projectile splashed into the ocean. This one was closer.

"At this rate, they don't have much to lose," Malone said.

Another crewman rushed into the pilot house and grabbed Geist's arm, pointing at the ceiling. Malone didn't catch much, but she heard, "Uber, uber!"

"They're going to box us in," Malone said, holding on for balance. "Box us in and bombard us."

Geist said nothing, but his sudden pallor was confirmation enough. He issued another string of commands to the crew, most of whom were holding onto the panels and bulkheads around them. They dialed back throttles and spun wheels. They were slowing.

"You can't fight them," Malone said. "There are too many to–"

"I know when to flee," Geist said. Sure enough, they weren't slowing, they were turning and rising. And the *Chasseur* was sliding past beneath them. The other airships would be mostly behind them now, so they'd only have to worry about enemy fire from one direction.

So long as they could outrun their pursuers.

"How fast can the *Glasauge* go?" Malone asked.

"Not fast enough. But we will have cover."

Before Malone could ask anything else, a luminous mass of storm clouds swung into view. They rose almost from the sea to the upper reaches of the sky, flashing with lightning.

"It is probable they sink us," Geist said. "But it is also probable they dissuade our pursuers, no? Onward."

The helmsman tipped the throttle forward, and the airship sped on.

"You may want to find someplace secure," he said to Malone. "If we make it into the storm then the next moments may be violent." If it weren't for their peril, Geist's understatement would have been laughable.

She would just as soon have stayed to see how it all played out, but it occurred to her that she ought to check on Lachesse.

The airship tilted steeply upward just as she reached the stairs. She held on to the railing, squeezing past rushing crew members and making her way down in a careful sidestep.

The cabin deck was in as much chaos as the command deck above. Already the airship began to rattle and jump with the winds outside. People rushed to and fro, hastily dressing themselves, grabbing supplies, and shouting hurried exchanges. The lounge was empty, but Lachesse was in her cabin, Chernev busying himself at her side.

Lachesse's face was pale, but her eyes were open. They widened at Malone.

"You survived," Malone said.

The whitenail's eyelids fluttered with exasperation. "Skies above, I should hope so. I only took one."

Heat rose in Malone's throat. She felt embarrassed and angry all at once. "You should have told me what you were doing. You're lucky I didn't abandon my search to come back for you."

Lachesse smiled. "You're not the fretting type, Malone. I knew you'd do what was necessary. Besides, it all worked out in the end." Another sharp ascent rolled Lachesse to the edge of her bunk and against the bulkhead.

"Maybe not for long," Malone said. "We're under attack."

Chernev glanced discreetly around and nodded, his eyes sober and round. "They come from the Continent," he said. They dropped several feet at once, and Malone's stomach lurched.

"Except they didn't steal their ships, did they?" Malone asked.

Chernev grimaced and occupied himself with the contents of his bag. "This is a question for Geist."

Lachesse coughed. "What did you learn?"

Malone summarized the events since their last meeting as briefly as she could, raising her voice around the shouting of the crew and the groan of metal. The *Glasauge* was bustling and rattling along, but Malone doubted it was intended to maneuver like this for extended periods of time.

Lachesse raised her eyebrows. "So, Geist released you when he realized he'd given you too much credit."

"When he realized I was working with you and not with whoever killed Sharad."

"Who is, I presume, still at large," Lachesse said. Malone was dimly aware of the whitenail staring at her through heavy-lidded eyes. "You have that air about you."

"What?"

"The one you have just before you say something dreadful and disastrous," said Lachesse.

Even Chernev was looking on with a sense of foreboding.

"Something Geist said – our pursuers, they know the *Glasauge* doesn't have Roman Arnault. Which means someone on board got a message out."

"Or these pursuers made it to Recoletta and caught up," Lachesse said.

"Did you see any other airships in pursuit? Before today?" Malone asked Chernev.

The cook glanced between the two women, seemingly considering whether there was a reason not to answer. "No other ships," he said, making an effort to speak slowly. "Not since leaving the Continent." The airship rumbled again. Light streaked by in the distance. The drone of the storm built outside.

Malone remembered the wide stretches of blank space on the maps in the navigation room. She shook her head. "They couldn't have followed the *Glasauge* to Recoletta, found out that Arnault had already left, and caught up to us here, all without getting spotted somewhere in between."

"Too great a coincidence," Lachesse said.

"And too big a space. What's likelier is that someone sent a message providing the *Glasauge*'s location. And revealing that Arnault wasn't on the ship."

"What kind of message?" the whitenail asked.

"I don't know." Malone nodded at Chernev. "But he does."

The cook had been fidgeting with the same strip of bandage, winding and unwinding it into a loose curl of cloth. He bit his lip but said nothing.

"Chernev," Malone said, "if you know something, you need to tell us. Now."

He cleared his throat. "Geist–"

"Is busy trying to keep the *Glasauge* in the air. And if you want to help me do the same, you'll tell me how someone could have gotten a message to the Continent."

He frowned, bit his lip again, and finally let out a big puff of air, like a man surfacing after holding his breath a long while. "It must be the pigeons."

Malone wasn't sure she'd heard him correctly. "Pigeons?"

"Naturalleesh. They transport messages. Geist guards – guarded them in his office. For crucial matters only."

It was starting to come together. "But someone let them out. The night Sharad was killed."

Chernev only hesitated a moment before nodding.

"Then we must be close to land. To the Continent," Lachesse said.

"Ya," Chernev said. "Stark." That also explained how the fleet of airships had converged so perfectly.

The airship shuddered again. This time, Malone felt the rattle in the walls.

The view outside the window was a boiling gray soup. The *Glasauge* shook and jounced like a carriage rolling through pocked and uneven streets.

"Is there a way off this ship? I mean, a way to escape and leave it behind?" Malone asked. It sounded like a foolish question, but Chernev's eyes lit with recognition.

"The rafts. But you must be near the ocean to use them," he said.

Malone's mind quickened with a suspicion. "The rafts – where are they?"

The cook pursed his lips. Lying in bed, Lachesse somehow mustered all of her whitenail authority to glare at him. "Tell her," she said.

"The lower deck," he said. "The orange box by the gran cargo port."

Malone sprang from the room and hurried down the narrow corridor. The deck rocked and bobbed underfoot, flinging her into the walls and the panicked crew squeezed between them. The press of bodies clogged the way, but Malone squeezed and elbowed her way to the stairs, ignoring cries of protest.

More of the crew had crowded onto the cargo deck, but there was room enough for everyone to spread out. They stood around at nervous attention, as though they were all waiting for something to happen. Malone climbed onto a stack of pallets to scan the deck.

A bright orange crate nestled at the other side of the deck like a beacon in the darkness.

Malone fought her way to it. It was still shut, and as she laid her hand on the lid someone else grabbed her arm.

"We wait," said a man with a crooked nose.

At least she could be sure no one would tamper with the rafts. "Fine," she said, "where–"

A sudden ascent pulled Malone's guts into her knees and

knocked her off her feet. She fell into the person behind her and tried to steady herself against a tangle of flailing limbs. When she righted herself, the man with the crooked nose was holding to the orange crate with a white-knuckled grip.

They were still rising – Malone felt it in the steady pull of the deck.

"What's happening?" she asked the man.

"Abrupt ascent," he said. "The winds push us, we rise, and the gas bags must decharge. Or explose." His eyes were white with animal terror.

Malone pushed her way back to the stairs. She had to get back to the control deck.

She pushed her way through the throng as the deck swooped and bounced. Once she got past the stairs, the way was clearer. Probably because most of the off-duty crew had already crowded into the cargo bay. Either way, she heard Geist yelling before she even reached the command deck.

The pilot house was chaos. The man with the speaking horn was shouting into it, plugging an ear with one finger. One crewman was leaning against a bulkhead, feeling at a bloody spot on the side of her head. Three others were staring at the elevator panel, and it wasn't clear which of them Geist was yelling at.

What was clear was that the *Glasauge* was out of control, and they didn't know how to stop it. But Malone had a suspicion.

Something wet drizzled onto the back of her neck. She touched the spot, and her fingers came away red with blood. She looked up. More was trickling through the seam in the plating.

She climbed the ladder to the engine room. This time, she didn't care who saw her.

The engineering deck was strangely calm, the shouts from below muffled and distorted by layers of metal and by coughing, grumbling machinery. The air was thick with leaking steam and engine grease.

And blood.

A boot lay still against a backdrop pumping pistons. Malone

rounded the corner and recognized Gonzalo, the hapless engineer she'd spied nights ago. His body was still warm, but his pulse had already died, and blood trickled through the grating around his head. An oil-smeared print led deeper into the deck.

Malone crept ahead. Something buzzed near the other end of the deck. She dimly recognized it as the speaking horn.

Gonzalo's more competent counterpart was lying next to a burst pipe. She was breathing, but just barely. Her knuckles were worn red, and a seam had torn at the shoulder of her uniform. There had been a fight, and the victor had moved onward, where drops of blood now flecked the grating.

The horn buzzed again. Malone pressed forward, following the noise and the trail of blood.

She moved as quietly as she could, but she needn't have worried. When she was almost in sight of the speaking horn, a rhythmic clanking began.

The culprit was kneeling by a boxy apparatus, a wrench in one hand and a hammer in the other. A toolbox lay several feet away, its contents scattered and sliding around on the rocking deck. The woman was hammering one end of the wrench, heedless of the blood on her tools and frantically trying to loosen one of the bolts on the front of the device. Just beyond her was a lever with a bright yellow handle with the words "GAS LEVAGE" written above it. It was toggled all the way to the left, the indicator below it at the end of a vivid band of red.

The woman looked up at Malone, her brow shining and eyes bright. It was Phelan.

Malone held her ground and eyed the overturned toolbox. It was slightly farther from Phelan, but not far enough that Phelan wouldn't get a good crack at her skull before she could grab anything.

But Phelan was smiling at her with relief. "So many times I wanted to spreck with you. So many times I considered it," she said. Her words sounded all the more mad for her precise, Continental speech.

The deck swooped beneath them.

Malone wasn't sure where this was going. "I'm here now," she said, hoping to soothe Phelan and draw her out further.

She took a careful step toward the fallen tools.

"Yah," Phelan said, her eyes fever-bright. "I always desired to ask of him. Now there is so little time."

A downdraft pummeled the *Glasauge*. Malone's stomach fluttered as the invisible hand of gravity lifted her up half a foot and dropped her back down.

"You're talking about Arnault," she said. "Roman Arnault."

"You knew him well, ya?" Phelan said "him" with the kind of throaty reverence that Sato had adopted when speaking about the Library.

Now was not the time to point out that she had almost killed him on a couple of occasions and had wanted to on many more. "Let's get to the rafts," she said. "Then you can ask me anything you want. We'll have all the time in the world."

That seemed to remind Phelan of something, and she renewed her assault on the panel. "No. Time." She punctuated her words with hammer blows, saying more Malone didn't understand.

The airship groaned, and the steady ascent pressed Malone gently into the deck. She eyed the lever, stuck where it was in the red. "Phelan, let me move that lever over. We can—"

"No!" Phelan looked up at Malone, and for an instant Malone thought the woman was about to rush at her. "Do you not comprend? We must alles elevate. Alles go down." She shook her head and relaxed. "There is no other way."

The slanting, skewing gravity pressed Malone against the bulkhead and slid a fallen hammer a few inches closer to her.

Phelan grabbed at the panel for balance, and Malone took a small step forward while the woman was distracted. She just needed a few more diversions.

"What's the one thing you've always wanted to know about him?" Malone asked.

Phelan sighed loudly, throwing all her weight onto the wrench.

"There must be something," Malone said, sliding one foot forward.

Phelan eased off the wrench. "There is a history that he can recount the complete life of a person from the touch of a hand. Is it vert?"

Malone was stunned. "You're talking about miracles," she said.

Phelan laid the wrench across her lap and wiped her brow with her other hand. If she would just move it a little farther away, Malone might have a chance.

"He has a talent to comprend the past," Phelan said.

Malone swallowed. "When we find him together, you can ask him yourself."

Phelan laughed and shook her head sadly. "The honor–"

Something distant buckled overhead. Malone winced at the sound, half-expecting an explosion to follow. Slowly, as the *Glasauge*'s nose began to dip, Malone's world tilted to the right.

The hammer slid out of view between a bank of pipes.

"Phelan, take us down. We'll die up here." Malone braced herself against a humming panel.

"I cannot let them find him!" Phelan said, throwing all her weight onto the wrench again. The bolt came loose with a snap. She laughed with delirious joy and worked faster, unscrewing it.

"Arnault is just a man," Malone said, easing forward again. "A very clever, complicated man."

Phelan set the wrench at her side and set to work on the bolt with her fingers. She was unarmed. If Malone could take her by surprise, then maybe –

"He is our sauveur," Phelan said. "And they desire to assassinate him."

Malone stopped. "Who wants to kill Roman?"

"Geist und the rest, they–"

A gunshot rang out in the cramped space, and Phelan's head

snapped forward with a burst of blood, bone, and tissue. Malone instinctively crouched, pressing her back to the bulkhead and looking for the attacker.

"Alles clear," called a voice behind the boilers, just on the other side of Phelan's corpse. Martens emerged and made for the lever, tugging it out of the red.

Geist stepped forth from the same spot, a gun still in his hand. "Thank you for the excellent distraction, Malone. I only wish we could have stopped her sooner."

"You've got some explaining to do," Malone said.

"Ya, but now is a bad time. Will you come with us calmly, without causing trouble?" He still held his gun, albeit lightly.

The deck rumbled and bucked. "I want to get off this thing alive just as much as you do," Malone said.

"That is very good, because it is most unwise to fire a gun on an airship." He holstered his pistol and said something to Martens.

She was fiddling with an instrument panel near the lever, and as she responded she shook her head.

"We are caught in an updraft," Geist said to Malone. "The higher we rise, the more the gas expands, until the bags pop."

"And your explosives detonate," Malone said.

"Naturellment. Only, I do not plan for us to be on the ship when it happens."

"Add that to the list of things you're explaining later," Malone said.

"Ya. For now, we decharge the bags and hope in the skills of my pilots." Malone followed Geist and Martens out of engineering and toward the cargo deck.

The airship swayed and shook more with each passing minute, and Malone's joints were already taking a battering. And any minute, she feared, the bombs would go off.

But once they reached the hold and Malone found Lachesse resting – somehow – by the cargo door in the back, there was nothing to do but wait. So Malone breathed the nervous stink of forty other bodies, watched the swirling grays outside the window, and listened to the sounds of wind and rain and voices.

The *Glasauge* creaked. Rain drummed against the hull.

Not rain – spray.

Geist and two others opened the wide cargo doors at the stern. Waves whipped at the airship about a hundred feet below.

The crew tore the orange crate open and pulled out floppy orange cushions that began inflating. People were congealing around them, forming up.

Malone found Lachesse. "I think we're going to have to jump," she said.

The whitenail nodded.

"Keep your body straight. And get rid of anything you think you can leave behind."

The others were already jumping into the water, moving as quickly as possible to land close to each other and the life rafts. Lachesse looked raw and diminished, like a colorful beetle that had just molted. When their turn came, Malone pointed her toes, shut her eyes, and held a deep breath.

She fell for a long time before she hit the water. And when she did, it felt like an even longer time before she breached the surface again. But she pulled and kicked and promised herself that she hadn't been pulled back from the edge just to die in the cold water now.

An orange raft bobbed in the waves. Members of Geist's crew leaned out from its sheltered dome, calling to their fellows and pulling them aboard. Malone swam, fighting exhaustion and cold and the heavy pull of the water.

At last she made it and caught her breath. She looked up for the *Glasauge*, but it was nowhere to be seen. She searched the sky and saw nothing until a brilliant fireball exploded hundreds of feet above and in the distance.

The man next to her muttered something that sounded like a prayer.

CHAPTER TWENTY
BABEL

The first thing Jane Lin saw of the Continent was a wall.

It was big and wide enough that at first she thought it was just a cliff stretching across the coastline. But as they sailed closer, she saw that it was smooth and even topped with lights.

She looked to Roman for answers, but he lay asleep on the seats.

After their daring escape from Salvage, the rest of their journey had been uneventful. By the time the storm had cleared and the sun had risen the next morning, Salvage had become merely a smudge on the horizon, and they themselves were no doubt too small for the floating city to follow, assuming the crew of the *Kennedy* would even tell the rest of the fleet of their escape. Jane and Roman had followed the compass east and rationed the boat's supply of water and stale crackers. Roman had mostly slept – Jane hadn't realized it was possible for a person to sleep so long, but he never ceased to astonish her.

At least she'd brought something to read.

The book was filled with fantastical stories of extraordinary machines and incredible journeys. She was just happy to have something to take her mind away from visions of Ruthers and Malone, especially since all she could do was wait.

Roman awoke long enough to share a meal of crackers and protein paste. As they ate, he explained some of what had transpired on Salvage – that the captain of the *Kennedy* had planned to trade him to the Continent in exchange for materials to repair their pre-Catastrophe engine.

Jane had surmised as much. What unsettled her more was what that said about their destination. And about Roman. "Does the Continent really have the resources to fix something like that?"

Roman hesitated long enough to scoop a chunk of paste onto his cracker. "Salvage thinks they do, which is what matters."

"I'm asking what you think."

He glanced at her quickly before returning his attention to his food. "Probably. Somewhere. It might take some digging to find it." He took a bite and chewed half-heartedly.

"But they'd find it to get you back," she said.

He nodded, swallowing with some difficulty.

But the questions were bubbling up inside her now – all the things she'd been wondering over after his capture. "They recognized you. They called you a missing prince! What does that even mean?"

Roman grimaced and set the rest of his cracker aside. "It means we'll have to be even more careful on the Continent, because it's only going to get worse. My family is well known for things I'm not proud of." He shifted and tugged at his shirt as though he were suddenly warm.

"But that's not on you," she said.

He paused, studying his knuckles. "When we left Recoletta, do you remember what you told me? About needing time to sort things out?"

Jane heard the fragility in his voice. She nodded, reminding herself that he wasn't used to confiding in anyone.

"Thank you," he said.

Whatever was on his mind, she supposed it had something to do with the vault. After all, that was what had driven his family from the Continent as well as what had brought him back. Unspoken between them was the question of how they would destroy it and whether such a thing was even possible. She only hoped he'd be ready to open up before they reached it.

Roman retreated to sleep again, and Jane returned to her book.

They reached the coast just as dark was falling. A beach some fifty yards wide spread out beneath the wall, room enough for them to ground their lifeboat. The little craft, sun-bleached as it was, made a target they were eager to abandon.

They divided their meager supplies – some blankets, more stale crackers, and a few canteens of water – between them and set off along the beach. The dark made it hard to see far, but Jane couldn't discern any breaks or gates in the wall.

"Was this here when you left?" she asked Roman.

Roman nodded. "It's been here for generations. One of the first Gran Meisterworks of the Continent, as they call them."

Jane marveled at it, wondering how many people and how many years it had taken to build such a thing. "Are there more walls like this, then?"

"No. The Gran Meisterworks are all different, but they're all ambitious feats with a specific purpose in mind. The airships were the Gran Meisterwork when I was young."

"Airships?"

He screwed up his face in thought and made a vague gesture as though he were holding a large ball. "Big, flying contraptions. They were only ideas when I left, and that was more than twenty-five years ago."

The idea seemed both exotic and perilous in a way that excited her. "Why would they build something like that?" Jane said.

Roman hesitated. Jane caught it but said nothing. "Transportation, of course. You wouldn't need train tracks to move around," Roman finally said.

It was an interesting notion, a land with the ability and the need to move people so freely. Not like the buried cities, where most people spent their whole lives siloed in one place. And yet the wall stood in silent protest of that principle. "Is this for keeping Continentals in? Or keeping others out?" Jane asked.

He didn't answer immediately. "It was built to keep out Salvagers," he eventually said, "and also people like us." And there was the thought he'd been gnawing on and talking around.

"From the buried cities, you mean. People like me."

Roman angled further up the beach. "There's firmer ground here. Easier walking." They continued in silence for a few minutes. "There's a port up ahead – see the light on the horizon? We can pass through there if we must. There shouldn't be anything unusual about two people walking up from the beach."

Jane heard the hesitation in his voice. "You don't sound so sure of that," she said.

"I don't know what's changed since I left. But it's better if we can get in through one of the fisher's gates. There should be small doors every few miles where people can pass through to get to the beach. They're supposed to be locked and guarded, but they rarely are – or were when I was here. Not away from the big cities, anyway."

It wasn't long before they came to one such doorway set into the wall. The wooden door was propped open, and tracks gouged the sand around it.

"Someone must have gone through recently," Jane said. "And headed the other way."

"Then we'll keep our heads down," Roman said.

The land on the other side of the wall was gray in the moonlight, with rolling hills and low trees. Buildings rose in the distance, bigger than the houses and shops of the communes, and certainly more numerous.

"That's the port," Roman said. "Our best chance of getting further inland will be there."

Jane supposed she should have been exhausted, but after the long, quiet ride to the coast and the weeks of anticipation about what the Continent would hold, she felt as if she were just waking up. The cool air was brisk and enlivening, and it felt good to stretch her legs.

"We really made it," she said. After so much running, so many close escapes, she could hardly believe it.

"We've still got hundreds of miles to go," Roman said.

"And now we've got solid ground under us." Her stomach

rumbled, but she couldn't bring herself to eat another cracker or dollop of protein paste. "And soon we'll have food that doesn't taste like it's been around since the Catastrophe." She glanced up at Roman, but his face was set in a stern frown and focused on the road ahead. "So, what now?"

"We get to Nouvelle Paris. It's a big city, so finding transport to Cologne-de-le-Kur and the vault shouldn't be too difficult."

Jane caught a hint of tightness in his voice. "If the vault's in Cologne-de-le-Kur, what else is in Nouvelle Paris?" she asked.

"My family's estate. We should be able to find help. Resources." The tension in his voice suggested that he was not looking forward to the visit.

It seemed a poor time to joke about meeting his relatives, so Jane kept the thought to herself and turned her attention back to their destination.

There was something unusual about the port town growing on the horizon, and it took Jane a few moments of watching the shape rise like a lumpy cake before she could put a finger on it.

The buildings were big – taller than the shops at the farming communes and sprawling almost as widely as the verandas of Recoletta. But it wasn't just their size that stood out. It was their shape. Or shapes, to be more accurate. Boxy edifices sprouted long, arching arms that reached over other buildings, or in some cases melted into them. Runty little hovels huddled beneath them like plants starved for light.

"Is… is that normal?" Jane asked. The question felt strangely rude, but she didn't quite know how to express the bizarreness of the scene.

"It's the Continent," Roman said.

By the time they were close enough for the streetlights to cast color on the buildings, Jane saw their materials were just as varied and mismatched. Brick attachments connected wood and plaster to polished glass. Bright, new tile glistened upon grizzled stone facades.

Something about the place made Jane dizzy. It reminded her of Salvage, except in Salvage everything had been old and only patched up or patched together. This place was a mix of old and new: ancient buildings hollowed out, cleaned up, and refurbished, colonized by modern developments like termite-eaten trunks overgrown with creeper vines.

As Jane looked on, she decided that it wasn't just that the newer buildings seemed out of sync with the old. They also seemed out of sync with each other. Built in a dozen different styles, it was as if their architects had never bothered to speak with each other, as if their construction crews had worked around and on top of one another. Tall, wide windows peered into dark alleyways, and shaded colonnades zigzagged around asymmetrical plazas.

She almost gasped when she saw the people.

It wasn't them so much as what they were wearing. She'd expected the Continentals to wear unusual styles. In Madina and then again on Salvage, she'd gotten used to wearing them herself.

But the Continentals' clothes, like their buildings, were a mismatched assortment of disparate pieces.

Some wore flowing cotton blouses that hung to their knees, draped over rough denim slacks. Others wore leather overcoats over silk pajamas or crisp linen dresses belted at the waist.

It was impossible to tell who was who simply by the fabric and cut of their clothing. The lack of distinction was both disorienting and thrilling.

She was so busy watching the crowds that she didn't see the man and woman in front of her until she'd run into them.

"I'm so sorry," Jane said, "please—"

But the man glared down his nose, taking in her and Roman's attire, and sniffed. "This is a loyalist town. Watch where you go und do not cause difficulties."

Jane muttered another apology as the haughty couple continued on their way. When they were out of earshot, she leaned in to Roman.

"A 'loyalist town'? What's that mean?"

He shook his head. "Like I said, a lot's changed."

But she realized that the two of them stood out.

She caught a few wayward glances from passers-by. They'd worn the same ratty clothes since escaping the floating city, so they must have looked and smelled like something that had been dragged from the sea and left to ferment in the sun. They'd need to find fresh clothes if they wanted to blend in.

They passed under hanging lights that buzzed with electricity. She'd seen a few in Madina and on Salvage, but never this many. The chatter that drifted through the air and the words adorning the buildings had the just-familiar sound of a language that was not quite her own but that was close enough to be mostly intelligible. Thankfully, after two and a half weeks on Salvage, she'd become used to interpreting.

Roman's shoulders were hunched and his chin was down. He scanned the crowd without moving his head. It was an expression she'd seen on him before – he was keeping watch and trying to avoid notice.

"We should find a residential neighborhood," Jane said.

He turned just enough for her to see his raised eyebrow. "Coastal real estate's always overpriced."

"Then I'm sure the clothes are nice. And someone's bound to have hung them out on a night like this."

Roman smiled and for a moment Jane felt only warmth through the cool air.

For all that was new and strange about the town, the clotheslines strung between windows made a familiar sight. Roman was just tall enough to pull a few garments from the lowest of them. They retreated to a quiet alley to change, Jane into dark wool trousers and a pale silk blouse, and Roman into plain, loose slacks and a richly embroidered shirt. They fit well enough and were only a little damp. Jane had no idea if they were even wearing the clothes properly, but it seemed like an improvement over their salt- and grease-stained rags. Even if she did cringe at putting clean clothes on over unwashed skin.

"On to the train station," she said.

"Or something like that," said Roman.

They continued down quiet side streets, paved in patchwork with cobblestones, flagstones, and cracked slabs so that it was impossible to tell what was old and what merely imitated it. When they reached a bank of signs they found one labeled "Station" and followed it.

They were headed toward a plaza – or so Jane thought. It was difficult to tell with the way the streets widened, narrowed, and twisted around buildings that peaked and shrank. But she heard noise ahead – the low roar of chattering people gathered together.

Roman was a few steps ahead, his shoulders rigid and his gait stiff. The street opened into a broad square – or more like a lopsided heptagon, maybe – and Jane saw people gathered on terraces, calling down from balconies, looking up at the statue...

"We should find another way around," Roman said, but it was too late. She'd seen it.

There, looming in the middle of the plaza, was a twenty-foot statue of a man who looked strikingly like Roman.

Jane dodged around him to get a better view.

The figure stood with one foot forward, his shoulders thrown back and his short hair ruffled by an imaginary breeze. He wore well-tailored trousers and a loose shirt with long, squared-off tails, similar to styles she'd seen around town. One hand clutched a long-necked flask, the other, a syringe. His expression was beatific, the empty eyes gazing into some distant vista.

Jane felt a hand on her shoulder and heard Roman's voice in her ear. "Jane, we should go."

But she was transfixed by the words on the plinth of the statue: "FARAJ ARNAULT, SAUVEUR OF THE CONTINENT."

"Please," he said, "before someone sees us." His breath was a warm patter on the back of her neck, as faint and rapid as a bird's heartbeat.

The sensation brought her back to the present, and she allowed Roman to lead her into the alleys. His hands were slick with sweat, and his gaze darted from side to side as he checked to see whether anyone was watching them.

They didn't slow down until they were two streets away and beyond most of the evening traffic.

"We need to be careful," he said. He was still peering around, not meeting her eye.

But they were going onward. To a larger city, he'd said. Where his family estate sat.

"Roman, are there more," she said, nodding back toward the plaza with the statue, "where we're going? In Nouvelle Paris?"

He barked with bitter laughter. "There are streets named after him. Paintings of my entire family in the National Gallery. Yes, there's much more."

No wonder they had recognized him on Salvage.

He still wouldn't meet her gaze, but in his wide, flickering eyes, Jane saw the look of a haunted animal. A few things were clicking into place for her – his suspicion of authority, his distaste for the spotlight – but what she still didn't know was why these things bothered him so much.

Yet it was clear that for a man who guarded his privacy as much as Roman did, few things could be worse than having his family name and image held up around the Continent.

"I'm sorry, Roman," she said, without really understanding why.

"For the honor of descending from such a noble man?" he said hollowly.

"What did he do?" Jane asked.

He pressed onward. "The sign for the station was pointing this way," he said. "I'm sure we'll find another route."

But as it turned out, they didn't need to. After they'd passed a few more streets, a tall spire pierced the lumpy canopy of buildings. Three enormous, egg-shaped balloons hovered next to it, and suspended below each was a long compartment like a train car.

"Are there people in that thing?" Jane asked.

Roman only shrugged. He appeared too exhausted for wonder.

"Maybe one of those is going our way," she said.

As they drew closer, Jane was so distracted by the height of the tower and the impossible size of the airships that she didn't notice anything else until she felt Roman tense beside her.

Then she saw the crowd of people gathered around the base of the tower.

"It's fine," she whispered. "Most of them don't even look like they're going up. See? They're all focused on something else."

When she got close enough, she saw what it was.

The low wall around the base of the tower was plastered with posters, much like the bulletin boards of Recoletta. The posters showed a man with dark hair, delicate features, and a long scar across his left cheek.

Even without reading the text underneath, Jane recognized the bold lettering and stark lines of a wanted poster.

The crowd in front of it sounded like they were arguing. "What are they saying?" Jane asked.

Roman seemed relieved, at least, that the crowd's attention was focused elsewhere. "It's about the man in the poster. Geist." Roman listened for a moment. "They're saying he stole one of these." He jerked his head up at the moored behemoths.

Jane listened, too, trying to hear in the agglomerated babble the words and meaning that Roman had found. It was there, faint but growing clearer as she got a sense for the shapes and sounds of syllables. Ballon, stehl, pirat.

"They're arguing over whether he's alive or dead. Something about a crash at sea," Roman said.

Jane could hear much of that, too. Crash, sturm, viv. But there seemed to be something else that he wasn't translating. Assassinat, fameel, escahp.

She wasn't sure whether he was leaving something out on purpose or whether he was just distracted. He jerked his head toward a gate. "This way."

No sooner had they passed through it than two guards stepped out of the shadows at the base of the tower, dressed in black and crimson silk. They were probably the only two matching outfits Jane had seen since reaching the Continent.

"Un minoot," the male guard said, holding up a hand. "Identification, pleece."

"I was forgetting it there," Roman said. The local patois was starting to make an intuitive kind of sense to Jane. Most of the words were similar to those she already knew, with some syllables drawn out and others clipped short. "En the one arriving from Nouvelle Paris." Roman pointed to the airships.

The guard gave him a doubtful frown that Jane supposed was common to guards around the world. "You are choosing a goot time to leave that place."

Jane hazarded a quick glance at Roman, wondering what the guard meant by that.

The first guard turned to the female guard next to him. "Go und cherch for the gentleman's documents."

The woman nodded and called a lift from the bottom of the tower. Jane was content to be politely ignored, but the first guard's attention was on her already.

"Und you?" he said. "Wass of your documents?"

Jane nodded to Roman. "He also was having mine," she said, trying to put the same unusual accent on her words. It came naturally enough, and anyway, it was merely a stronger version of the slight accent she'd heard from Roman since their meeting.

The guard's eyes narrowed. "Where are you from?"

She thought she'd been doing well, anyway.

"Second Lichtenstein," Roman said.

Something about the name delighted Jane, and anyway, it seemed to satisfy the guard who now focused his full attention on Roman.

"Sir, you are sembling familiar," he said. From anyone else it would have been an innocuous comment, casually offered and easily brushed off, but to a guard whose suspicions were already aroused, it was nearly an accusation. "Have I seen you before?"

Roman bristled admirably. "Most likely when I was passing through here earlier."

The guard frowned. "I only just arrived at my post."

"Then how am I knowing?" Roman asked.

Shouts erupted behind them. Jane peeked around the wall and saw that some kind of argument had broken out between members of the crowd. Voices climbed in pitch and pointed index fingers soared.

A woman stood in the middle of the action, her clothes almost as worn and dirtied as those she and Roman had abandoned. Her dark hair was wild and her eyes flashed as she spun her head this way and that. She looked – and sounded – like she was in a panic, so it took Jane a few seconds to make out what the woman was saying.

"He is here! I have seen him!"

Jane's heart leapt into her throat.

But she channeled her alarm and whirled back to grab Roman's sleeve. "They're fighting! We can come back tomorrow."

The guard cursed and squeezed past them. "Pardon."

He'd only be out of sight for a moment, but that was all they needed. Jane and Roman rushed past the now-empty post and around the corner to one of the waiting lifts. When the doors closed on them, Jane laughed, all the pent-up tension of the last few hours rolling out of her at once.

She'd just contained it when they reached the top.

The lift released them onto a wide balcony that ran all the way around the tower. A shrieking chorus of wind whipped across it. Jane had never been this high off the ground, but the view of the motley city through the opening doors was strangely beautiful. The mismatched buildings tumbled over one another below her, their bent backs and jutting angles reminding her of children at play.

"All aboard for Nouvelle Paris!" cried a voice from one corner of the tower. There, tethered to a mooring, was one of the great airships. Several uniformed men and women were already bustling about, casting off lines to prepare for departure.

Jane and Roman hurried over. The breeze snapped at her clothes and tugged her hair. A walkway extended from the main balcony to the open door of the craft. The man guarding it eyed them officiously. "You have tickets?"

"We're running late," Roman said. "But this should suffice." He withdrew one of the coins Jane had taken back in Recoletta and dropped it into the attendant's hand.

The man's eyebrows climbed an inch.

"You must be careful about showing such wealth when you reach the city. Things are getting especially bad in Nouvelle Paris of late – many demonstrations, many agitations. Not like here." He gave them a conspiratorial look. "But you will be setzing in premier class," he said. "Pleece follow." He led the way across the catwalk.

He was several feet ahead before Roman leaned close to Jane. "Better than crackers and protein paste," he whispered.

Jane heard him, but any pleasure at their victory had disappeared into the yawning void below the walkway.

So had her ability to move.

It felt as though the wind might carry her away. But then Roman's steadying hands found her shoulder and the small of her back. "You can do this," he said. "One step after the other."

Jane slid one foot forward.

"That's it," Roman said. "Just like the gangplanks."

She stopped again, remembering the crashing waves around the *Kennedy*, the long crates falling into the sea. "That's not helping."

"Then remember there's hot food, a soft chair, and probably a bottle of wine waiting inside," he said.

Jane sucked in a deep breath and hurried the rest of the way across. She tried not to think about the way the catwalk rattled and swayed underfoot.

The interior of the airship was warm and inviting, paneled with russet-hued wood. The scent of mingled perfumes – honeysuckle and rose mixed with lavender and jasmine – hung in the air. Their usher was politely waiting, ignoring their delay. "This way, pleece."

He led them past double doors, where the rippled glass

framed a distorted picture of a crowded lounge. The people in it undulated like fish beneath the waves.

They followed the usher up a spiraling, wrought iron staircase to a third deck. There, the man opened the glass doors and bowed.

The deck reminded Jane of fancy salons in Recoletta where whitenails had listened to the music of strings. A wide aisle ran between two rows of cushioned, cordoned seats. The deck must have been twenty deep, but the soft, low light and the way the carpets and curtains swallowed all sound made it easy to pretend she and Roman were the only two people around.

"Your setz," the usher said.

What he pointed to wasn't so much a pair of seats as a small cabin. A velvet curtain as thick as a tenement wall hung open before a linen-draped table and a pair of wide, cushioned seats.

"I should have told you how valuable those coins are," Roman said.

They took their seats. Jane groaned with pleasure as she sank into hers. "I could sleep in this," she said. It was softer than her bed back in Recoletta, to say nothing of the bunk she'd spent the last few weeks in.

"You should," said Roman. "The trip will take all night."

Another liveried attendant appeared at the table. "Dinner will be served shortly," he said. "Curried chickpea salad und filet mignon."

"Very goot," said Roman.

Jane didn't know what most of those things were, but they sounded good to her too.

The airship shifted, and the scenery outside the window began to move. A murmur of exhilaration rippled through the deck. They were off.

Jane watched out the window. She didn't realize she'd been clutching the seat until Roman gently pried her fingers away.

"Think of it this way," he said, giving her hand a gentle squeeze. "You wanted to see the Continent. Tonight, you'll see miles of it."

Jane smiled, but she noticed that his palm was cold and slick.

Dinner arrived when the port town was just a glimmering in the distance. Jane felt she'd never tasted anything so good. The chickpeas were large and pale, with a rich, meaty flavor that sat heavily on her tongue. She was still savoring them when the main course arrived.

The filet was a thick round of meat that sliced as easily as butter to reveal a deep pink center. She'd never seen anything quite like it, not even in the homes of her wealthy Vineyard clientele. She carved off a bite and popped it into her mouth.

She'd never tasted anything quite like it, either.

"Roman, what is this?"

His attention was focused on his own plate, where he was picking through his chickpeas. "It's called a 'filet.' Tender, isn't it?"

It really was. "I've never had this."

He shrugged over his plate. "It's an expensive cut of meat." He didn't look up. Anyone else might have been fooled, but Jane knew him too well by now.

"No, I've never had this animal before. What is it?"

He wiped his mouth with a pristine linen napkin. Jane caught a grimace at the corners of his mouth. "Would you enjoy it as much if I told you?" he asked with faux jocularity.

A horrible thought occurred to her, and she realized that Roman hadn't even touched his filet. She pushed the plate away. "Skies above, is this…"

He held up a placating hand. "It's just beef." He sliced off a bite and ate it.

But this was still different. "I've had beef before. It didn't taste like this."

"You've had bison. This is from a cow." He made a sound like a rusty hinge. "It's similar. But smaller."

Jane had eagerly anticipated a break from fish, but she hadn't much considered what people ate on the Continent. "Are the animals here that different?" She thought of the strange clothing and stranger architecture.

"Some," Roman said. He seemed to be waiting for her to ask something else. Dreading it.

"So if we have bison and the Continent has cows–"

"Cattle."

"Whatever. Why do we both call it beef?" Jane asked.

Roman sighed. "You used to have cattle."

"Before the Catastrophe, you mean?"

Roman nodded.

"So what happened? Did we eat them all? Did they all move away? Get sick and die?" She'd meant it as a joke, but the unease that shivered across Roman's face told her she'd hit on something. "What happened, Roman?"

He winced. "There was a plague. Stories say that it developed because the farmers there used the wrong medicine on the cattle. It was supposed to keep them from getting sick, but instead it turned their own bodies against them. It killed them all – an entire nation's worth of cattle – in less than a year." Roman stopped, but that wasn't the end.

The deck was quiet. She hoped it was just the insulation of the curtains, but she lowered her voice anyway.

"In these stories – what happened next?"

Roman was quiet for a long time, massaging his knuckles and gazing blankly at Jane's half-eaten dinner. "The disease spread to people."

Jane took it in with a deep breath. Then she pulled the golden cord in the corner of their nook. The thick, velvety drapes came loose and fell closed, blocking out the activity in the corridor.

He sighed. "This is the disease my forefather cured. As it was ravaging your homeland – the Pesteland – the Continent did everything in its power to prevent your people from coming to us. They put up barriers and checkpoints. Eventually, they began attacking the boats and airships that tried to reach us." He hesitated. "Eventually, they didn't have to. Those the disease didn't kill fell to rioting and violence. The few who survived sealed themselves in massive underground bunkers."

"The buried cities," Jane said. It was like hearing a familiar story told out of order. She didn't want to hear it, but she knew she had to. "That was the Catastrophe."

"None of the Continent's precautions mattered," Roman said. "The disease reached us too. Only we had a head start in developing the cure."

It should have been good news, but Roman's somber tone suggested otherwise.

"That's how the Continent survived like this," Jane said, willing a happy ending for the shining cities beneath her.

But Roman uttered his dry, humorless chuckle. "The only workable cure saved some of the sick at the expense of nearly all of the healthy. Do you understand? My ancestor killed more people than any man or woman in history."

Jane spoke carefully, searching for the words that would pry him from his dark reverie. "It doesn't seem like he had much choice," she said.

He reached across the table and took her hands. His own were cold. "And I never want to be in that position. Do you understand?"

Suddenly, she did. In Recoletta, the night he'd helped her escape Sato, he'd said things she hadn't understood at the time – about the corrupt and violent cycles in which people lived.

Now, she understood his dark fatalism, his fear of power and his skepticism towards those who sought it. She understood a life of waiting in the shadows, hiding from the terrible burden of authority and the moral blot he saw in himself. She understood self-loathing disguised as humor.

"The Continent reveres Faraj Arnault." He shook his head. "My family – my direct bloodline – is the only one that has access to the vault. Any descendants I have would bear the same burden." He gave her a careful, quiet look.

Jane waited.

"My forebears have been tyrants, sybarites, and political hostages. I don't want to be any of those things. I don't want to be him."

"You're not," she said. "You chose to come here to destroy it. That's proof enough."

He drew his hands back and considered the expanse of tablecloth between them. "I should have told you sooner, but I didn't know what you'd think of me if you knew who I am."

Jane took his face in her hands and kissed him. After a moment's hesitation, he yielded.

"You are a brave and maddening man, and I love you," she said.

He kissed her again, this time matching her ardor with his own.

The curtain drew back. Light and sound wafted into the compartment. Jane and Roman pulled away, staring at the table and biting back mischievous grins as the steward stammered apologies and cleared the table.

So much for any hope of privacy.

The curtain slid shut again. Jane looked back at Roman and for a moment saw only the whites of his eyes and his gleaming teeth in the semidarkness.

"If that's the story behind your ancestor," she said, "then what does anyone want with the vault now?"

His smile faded. "Over time, people began telling a happier story of what Faraj Arnault did. Unfortunately, that means they've forgotten that whatever remedy he left behind is a danger."

Gooseflesh prickled her skin. "You think what's in there could still kill?"

"I think he sealed his laboratory for a reason. And I've never been an optimist."

And yet the talk of old, mysterious technologies reminded her of another.

She found the book and showed it to him.

"With so many old stories about stories, I was wondering how you tell which ones are real," she said.

CHAPTER TWENTY-ONE

COLLISION COURSE

The ride on the storm-tossed sea was a blur of heaving waves, cold spray, and vomit. Malone hunkered down in the life raft with a dozen or so other shivering bodies, helpless to do anything but wait.

Hours passed. Gray morning blurred the sky, and a whistle split the air – two short blasts and one long. One of Malone's fellow passengers answered back in kind, with one long and two short. Somewhere in the distance, an identical call shrieked over the dying storm.

A light crested the waves. Then a prow. The other survivors let forth a ragged cheer, and soon they were being pulled aboard, wrapped in blankets, and plied with mugs of warm water and hot caffee, which Malone discovered she liked only marginally more than the room-temperature variety. Still, the heat felt good.

Then they were headed off toward another orange fleck bobbing in the distance.

Malone took stock of the crowd with her. Her fellow survivors seemed to be doing the same, questioning one another in low, concerned voices, answering with the shaking of heads and squeezing of shoulders.

She'd lost track of Lachesse somewhere in the fall, the crashing waves, and the scramble to the rafts. She'd told herself that the whitenail must have been pulled into one of the others, but she wasn't among the shivering, huddled shapes now.

Malone went to the front of the boat to wait.

Eventually, they drew close to the next life raft and hauled its bedraggled passengers aboard – men and women in the poorly sized airship uniforms, shrugging into blankets and embracing waiting comrades and cups of caffee.

The last person to climb aboard was Geist. He met Malone's gaze and shook his head.

Malone went to the back of the boat to watch the sea. Just in case.

Her third cup of caffee was cold by the time Geist approached her.

"I am sorry," he said. "The jump was risky for us all. We lost eleven persons. But none would be here now without your rasch action."

"And hers." But she hadn't been fast enough. It was a familiar and painful feeling. And it was impossible not to think about Sundar at the library and the inspectors at the train station, all of whom would have been alive if she had figured out what was happening just a little faster.

Geist only nodded. For a few minutes, they stood in blessed silence. Malone was glad, at least, that he didn't offer any soothing platitudes about Lachesse or her death or what it meant. She was pretty certain the whitenail would have considered it empty nonsense.

Malone thought back to the explosives. "You always intended to destroy the *Glasauge*, didn't you?"

"It is a most practical way to feign death. Though I was hoping to do it in a more controlled manner."

"But you stole it. And dressed your band of thieves in other people's uniforms." She should have felt more satisfaction than she did at piecing things together.

"You make it sound easy."

It was remarkable, really. But something was still missing. The purpose of Geist's journey – his motive for crossing the sea, the reason she was still alive and Lachesse now dead. She thought back to her final, brief conversation with Phelan. "You always meant to kill Roman Arnault. Not to save him."

Geist hesitated before he answered. "That is also vert."

"Why did you lie?" She wasn't angry yet. Just curious.

He blinked at her, owlish in his bemusement. "You told me you tried to save him. You went to the gibbet for his sake."

"So you told me what you thought I wanted to hear."

"Naturalleesh." He shrugged.

A shrill, quivering melody sang through her blood. It was more than just the caffee. "Why do you want to kill Arnault?"

Geist stared into the depths of his own cup. "One wishes for something starker to drink, no?" He drained it and set it at his feet. "This will have to suffice." He reached into his jacket – the dry one he'd been given after coming aboard – and produced a long cigarette and a metal box as long as Malone's thumb and twice as wide. He turned his back to the wind and struck a flame from the box, lighting the end of his cigarette.

He took a deep drag, closing his eyes and sighing in a way that was almost obscene.

"We could not risk the flamme on the *Glasauge*. Forgive me, this is a long-delayed plaisure." He blew a stream of smoke from his nostrils. His eyes were still closed when he resumed talking. "I told you that Roman Arnault possesses something belonging to the Continent. Perhaps it is more vert to say that he himself belongs to the Continent. Und his ancestors, und whatever children he may sire, all are our heritage."

"You're talking about the vault," Malone said. Arnault had explained that it – whatever it was – wouldn't open without him.

Geist's eyes snapped open. He blinked through the smoke. "You know of this?"

"Now would be the time to tell me more."

He took another puff. "Roman is very special to the Continent. His ancestor developed a cure that saved us from a devastating disease."

Something clicked in Malone's brain. "The 'Pesteland.' This

disease afflicted us too."

Geist hesitated again, but nodded. "Ya. Und more gravely."

"Then why would you want to kill Roman?"

"Because the people venerate him."

Malone had seen that much in Phelan's strange devotion to a man she would never meet. And yet there had to be more to it.

Geist leaned on the railing in a gesture that seemed unnaturally informal for him. "His family has been in power for centuries, guarded in their manor outside Nouvelle Paris. When he and his parents disappeared years ago, there were those of us who rejoiced. Perhaps, at last, we could resolve our own problems instead of depending on these inbred aristocrats."

"But nothing changed," Malone said. This much, at least, was familiar.

"No. For one, he had several cousins of the same line." He tapped ash onto the railing, watching the grains blow away.

"So why not leave Roman in Recoletta?"

"I gladly would have. But things worsen here – there are new tensions with Salvage and new questions of how to deal with the buried cities, especially after your conflicts." His lips puckered around his cigarette, as if the very topic were distasteful.

Warning bells rang in Malone's head. "What do you know about our conflicts?"

"Mostly what the man Sato told us. That the buried cities are in a state of disaster, led by corrupt and dangerous politiques." He flicked another speck of ash over the railing.

That sounded like Sato, all right. "You never told me you knew him."

He shrugged. "I did not know him personally. Und you did not ask."

"Let me guess. He also told you Roman was back in Recoletta."

He squinted at her through the smoke. "Your tone – I cannot comprend if you are joking. But ya, of course he told. No one esteemed him at first – for a time, everyone was telling histories that the missing Arnault was a beggar, a highwayman, or some other romantic nonsense." He waved the smoke away with his free hand. "But Sato's story eventually won him much influence."

This was sounding all too familiar. "Did he start trouble here, too? Is that how you came to oppose the Arnaults?"

Geist was quiet for a moment. "It was a longer process. But as I said, he was influential for a time."

"I'll bet he enjoyed that," Malone said. For all Sato's railing against Recoletta's rulers and elites, she'd seen few people relish the theatrics as much as he had.

"Ach, I am thinking so." Geist's eyes flared at some private memory.

But that still didn't explain Geist's excursion to Recoletta. "What changed? Why come for Roman now?"

"He became the last of his bloodline. The last Arnault, the last one capable of opening the vault." Geist took a deep drag on his cigarette and stared out at the horizon. "The Continent is too tied to the past. Sometimes I envy your people. Your buried cities. You at least had the ability to start fresh."

Malone had never thought of things that way and wasn't sure that anyone else in Recoletta would, either. "Sometimes an imagined history is a greater burden than the real thing."

He laughed. "How true. Whatever we do not have, we invent."

"So," Malone said, "what now?"

"Now, we go to the Continent. Und we try to intercept Arnault before he reaches Nouvelle Paris. For I am not thinking Arnault traveled so far to live on the boats."

Malone couldn't imagine that Jane would have, either. But she remembered the maps she'd seen of the Continent, broad and dense with cities. There was no telling where on it Roman and Jane might be. Assuming they'd even reached the Continent yet.

Geist seemed to read the question in her eyes. "My people say Salvage passed just south of us. Into the same sturm. The closest cities would be Nantes-Neugeboren und Renaissance du

Rochelle." He traced a line in the air with his cigarette.

Malone tried to make sense of this new tangle of syllables. "How far are these... places from each other?"

Geist shrugged. "A hundred und twenty kilometers. Perhaps more."

The distance meant no more to her than the names. "A hundred what? More than two hours' walk?"

He laughed. "Assuredly."

"Fine. It's a lot of ground to cover."

"I hoped to be better prepared. I would have notified my colleagues here if not for the loss of my messenger pigeons." Geist sniffed.

Malone waved the concern away. No point in dwelling on how things might have gone more smoothly. "The question is, what would they do next?"

"They would undoubtedly surrender themselves to the nearest constables," Geist said. "Such constables would then escort them to Nouvelle Paris under heavy guard." He frowned, picking a speck of tobacco from his lip.

But something about the idea didn't feel right. Jane was too cautious. Too distrustful of authority. Not that she could blame the young woman. "Jane will want to move carefully. Quietly. She'll get the lay of the land before she lets Roman reveal himself to anyone."

Geist laughed. "Are all laundresses such masterminds in the buried cities? Besides, Roman will hardly have to reveal himself. If the family resemblance is as strong as I am told, then people will recognize him."

Malone chewed on the question. "How would someone keeping a low profile get to Nouvelle Paris?"

He rubbed his goatee. "There are many methods. Overland, one can go by foot or by carriage. But there will be boocoo stops und boocoo villages. Faster and easier is by airship."

"Like the one we were on?" Malone asked.

He held one hand out and made a balancing motion. "A little

different. Made to carry passengers, not soldiers. Und made for shorter distances."

Malone thought it over. There were still a million places Jane and Roman could be, including a watery grave somewhere in the middle of the sea.

But if they'd wanted to flee, there were other refuges beyond the buried cities they could have sought. Yet Salazar's account had them headed toward the floating city.

And as much as Malone wanted to believe otherwise, she couldn't imagine Jane – the one who had shot Augustus Ruthers, stirred up the masses, and destroyed Recoletta's fragile peace – being content on a rusting flotilla or in some foreign wilderness. No, if she'd come this far with Arnault, she wouldn't stop until she'd reached the Continent's seat of power.

"They're on one of the airships," Malone said. "Or they will be." Depending on when, exactly, they'd arrived.

Geist frowned. "Are you so certain?"

"Of course not. But we've got to bet on something if we're to have any chance of intercepting them."

He examined the dwindling nub of his cigarette. "I will beg your pardon, but that is still the problem. Four airships leave daily from Renaissance du Rochelle to Nouvelle Paris. Five more from Nantes-Neugeboren. The journey is nearly fifteen hours. Once they are airborne, we cannot identify Arnault or his associate, let alone intercept them."

"There must be ways to contact the airships if they're going to be airborne that long," Malone said.

"Messages coded in lights," Geist said. "But these means are not available to us."

The plan was still forming in her mind, but only Geist and the other Continentals would know if it would actually work.

"You said you're a wanted man here – that you stole an airship."

"Indeed." Geist's tone was measured and careful.

"If someone spread the rumor that you had been spotted at the stations – whatever you call them – at Nance and Rennysense..."

"Renaissance du Rochelle."

"If someone spotted you there, any airship en route from either city would be searched. Maybe grounded, right?"

"Maybe possible. Certainment, the passengers would be interrogated. Identified," Geist said, realization dawning on his face.

"You said Arnault would be recognizable here," said Malone.

"Ya." Geist smiled, sucking at the end of his cigarette again. "Und the gendarmerie will show up in force to await his arrival. This means they will reach Nouvelle Paris, but we can do little to prevent that much. This, at least, will be easier than searching every arriving airship."

"You said you have supporters," Malone said, catching some of his confidence in the plan. "Once you know when and where he's arriving, you can create a distraction and nab him in the confusion."

Already Geist was planning – Malone saw it in his eyes.

"I want one promise," she said.

"Ya?" It wasn't an agreement.

"Arnault's yours," Malone said. She wasn't happy about handing him over, but as there was little she could do to stop Geist, she might as well trade him. "But I'm taking Jane back to Recoletta." At least someone might still face justice.

"This is fair," Geist said. He didn't mention that Arnault was not hers to give, and he didn't have to. "It is a worthy trade." He tossed the butt of his cigarette into the water. "It will be a shame to return from the dead so soon," he said. "I was looking forward to a little anonymity."

She was asleep when they reached the Continent. As so often happened, she hadn't realized how tired she was until she lay down. Once she did, it was as though only seconds passed before the jostling of the boat and low, urgent voices jolted her awake.

They were moored in a sheltered cove. The others were unloading themselves and a few basic supplies. Geist was overseeing the action, a cigarette in one hand and caffee in the other, in much the same state as she'd left him.

A wall towered over them and stretched along the coast. The sun was veiled in gray clouds, but Malone had the sense that it was early afternoon.

She ran her fingers through her hair – which was stiff with salt and greasy with oil – and straightened her borrowed clothes. They were a rumpled, stained mess, but at least they were dry.

Geist approached. "Come. Martens rides already for Renaissance du Rochelle und Valenti for Nantes-Neugeboren. We have many kilometers to Nouvelle Paris."

Malone followed him onto an old, barnacle-encrusted dock and then land. It felt good to have solid ground under her feet once more. "What's our plan for getting around?" she asked Geist.

"We must be prudent. The Continent knows my face. Und those of my associates." He gave her a businesslike smile.

"I can't buy train tickets for everyone."

He seemed to miss the joke. "This is not necessary. We will take the cycles."

Before Malone could ask what those were, they'd passed through a door in the wall and into a wide, rolling meadow. There were no immediate signs of habitation – no buildings, no rising tendrils of smoke, not even a footpath – but tree-topped hills blocked the horizon in the near distance. And propped against the wall was a row of waist-high contraptions with two thin wheels and a mechanism of gears and chains.

No sooner had they reached the other side than Geist and his crew turned to one another again with resigned, doleful expressions. They embraced, exchanged kisses on the cheek, and muttered low, fervent words of farewell.

Malone was still examining the wheeled contraptions, discerning with rising apprehension where a person might sit on such a device, and just how far forward the handlebars would pull them, when a man with straw-blond hair approached, wrapped her up in a quick hug, and planted a kiss on her cheek.

"Mercy," he said. Before Malone could say anything, he had melted back into the crowd, only to be replaced by another man, another embrace, another expression of awkwardly sincere gratitude.

At some point, she felt her neck moist with tears.

She must have endured this ritual a dozen or so times before Geist tugged at her elbow.

"We must go," he said. The others split up and took off, perched upon the cycles from the wall.

Malone brushed at the dampness on her neck. Geist saw her examining her wet fingertips. "You do a great thing with us," he said. "They honor you."

But she was too embarrassed to ask why. Besides, it felt wrong to celebrate, with Lachesse and the others dead and with Jane and Arnault still so far away.

She followed Geist to the row of cycles. "What happens if Arnault does reach this vault?"

"The greater problem is what happens after. I told you the vault is the place of an ancient cure, yes? Some believe it holds much more. Weapons. Knowledge. Ancient means of considerable potency."

"Some believe," Malone echoed. "But you don't."

He pulled a cycle from the wall and swung a leg over the frame. "I do not know, and I do not wish to take the chance. Besides, if others believe, then what does it matter if these things are not there? The gouverneurs will tell the people what they want to hear, und the people will believe. They will spend boocoo blood, time, and money on the campaign und on the appearance of progress."

There was something Malone was missing – she felt its absence like a hole in her pockets. "What campaign?"

An uncomfortable silence followed. Geist balanced on the cycle with only his toes touching the ground. "The campaign to destroy Salvage und the Pest – the buried cities," he said.

Malone blinked. "What? Why would–"

He scowled at his handlebars. "This disease I explained to you? The one that destroyed your civilization und nearly destroyed ours? You created it, with unnatural medicine und grotesque experiments. You–" He broke off. "Forgive me. I know this was not your doing, but that of your ancestors." He sighed. "You see how contagious this manner of thinking becomes."

Malone thought back to the early discomfort Geist's crew had displayed around her. "But why destroy us now? That was, what, hundreds of years ago?"

Geist's laugh had a vicious edge to it. "Only hundreds, I should say. Such time feels long, perhaps, when you have no history. But we have held on to the things we remember. I told you things have not been so good here, ya? Difficult problems with more difficult solutions. They divide us. But uniting people against a common enemy? That is easy."

Malone took a deep breath. She smelled a familiar scent of musk and amber. For a moment, she wondered if some of Lady Lachesse's perfume had rubbed off on her, but there was no way it could have survived her dive into the sea.

"Why tell me now?" she asked. "If you wanted my help against a threat to the buried cities, why not tell me what was at stake when you picked me up?"

He laughed again, and this time he actually sounded amused. "We liberated you from a gibbet, Malone. I was knowing little of your circumstances or temperament. Maybe you would have been happy to see the ruin of the ones who hanged you! Und even if not, would it not have sounded as though I was telling you wass you wanted to hear? Would you have esteemed me?"

She probably wouldn't have, and she might not even now, except for the rigid horror she saw on Chernev's face as he pulled a cycle free, the red shame creeping up his neck as he pretended not to eavesdrop.

And then there was the coastal wall and the arsenal of airships. She could easily believe that a people who built those things had both the will and the means to lay waste to Recoletta and the other buried cities.

Her pulse beat faster. "Then why are we chasing Arnault? We should go straight to the vault. Demolish it."

Geist's eyebrows rose in amusement. "The vault is impermeable. It cannot be destroyed."

"Anything can be destroyed." Malone thought back to Sato, threatening the Library with his strange, unquenchable fire.

"Not by means at our disposal," Geist said. "Besides, a person such as Roman is much easier to destroy."

Unease festered inside her. She considered the cycles and the leather-wrapped wedges that passed for seats. They looked like a fast ticket to a hemorrhoid. "We're not going all the way on those," she said. It was a prayer more than anything.

Geist laughed. "I am afraid not. We must make the journey to Nantes-Neugeboren, but after that we will take the rail to Nouvelle Paris. We must sneak aboard – I must confess that it will not be a comfortable journey."

CHAPTER TWENTY-TWO

HEIR TO THE THRONE

Jane awoke to frantically whispering voices. She wasn't sure how much time had passed since dinner, but it was still dark outside. After the meal, the stewards had folded the table away and expanded the seats into a pair of narrow but comfortable beds. Roman had still been paging through her book and its descriptions of marvelous machines and their fantastical journeys.

Many of which, if the stories were true, had been built and planned by the hands and minds of the pre-Catastrophe Continent. The same ones that had raised defenses against the buried cities – or whatever they'd been at the time – and perished or survived in the aftermath.

He'd been describing one of the sites where these contraptions had supposedly been constructed – a half-flooded land with names of long, loping syllables – when Jane drifted off.

Now, as she twitched aside the velvet curtain, the stewards were whispering amongst themselves and rousing passengers from their compartments, apologizing with their hands tented before them.

No, they weren't apologizing. They were receiving something. Small, leatherbound booklets.

"Hey." Jane nudged Roman. "Wake up."

His eyes opened and focused on her, instantly alert.

But before she could say anything further, a soft rapping came from just outside the curtain. "Excusee, mister, madame. I must now see your identification, pleece."

"Un minoot," Roman said. He mussed his hair and rubbed some color into his eyes. When he pulled back the curtain, he looked raw from interrupted sleep.

"I am needing to see your identification," the steward said, writhing under Roman's cranky glare. The young man mustered a weak smile of insistence.

With a guttural sigh, Roman began fumbling around the compartment, muttering to himself.

Jane picked through the blankets and pillows, too, pretending to fish for the identification she did not have and praying the young steward would ignore her.

Just then, Roman's muttering rose to a grumble. "Where are the bags? I left them right here. If you lost–"

"Ya, it was those two!" called a familiar voice. Jane glanced up from her search and recognized the gray-haired man who had accepted their bribe earlier. "They had no ticket, no documents. I merely assumed–"

"Wass you assumed is clar enough," said another voice. A woman stood between the steward and the usher, her back ramrod straight and her shoulders forming crisp right angles beneath her uniform. "You," she said, turning her probing stare on Roman and Jane, "must produce your documents at once. Or explique their absence." Her voice carried none of the discomfort and apology of the steward's.

Roman's face split in a guilty, sleepy smile. "Pardon. It is our anniversary, und I only wished to take my–"

Jane's fluttering heart nearly stopped when the woman grabbed Roman by his shirtfront and hauled him from the bed.

"It is he," the gray-haired usher said, licking a sudden glistening of sweat from his upper lip.

"That is not possible," said the young steward. "He is much too tall. Und where is the scar?"

But whatever doubt flickered between the two men didn't reach the woman. "He will spreck," she said. "Bring the woman."

The steward and the usher each grabbed one of her arms and

hauled her out of her refuge and toward the door. Startled, curious faces peered at them and whispered from behind curtains.

For now, Jane allowed herself to be pushed along and tried to calm her racing heart with deep, steady breaths.

They went up the stairs to a plain, cramped deck that looked like the equivalent of the servants' passage. Jane ignored the bickering of the two men escorting her and listened instead to the questions the woman was hurling at Roman: What are you doing on this ship? Who are your associates? Where is he?

She racked her sleep-fogged brain for answers, but all of this was making less and less sense.

They kept pressing forward, past stewards and crew members whose visible anxiety mirrored Jane's own, until they reached a cramped storage room insulated by the rumbling and chuffing of machinery overhead. It reminded her of the tiny cabin in which she'd first been questioned on Salvage, only this woman did not appear to have any of the patience of her interrogator.

Her heart sank.

The two men shoved her against the wall next to Roman and backed away with downcast eyes. Eager to disengage themselves from whatever happened next.

The woman was still looking between her and Roman with a stare like a hot poker.

"You were courageous und foolish to attempt this again. Especially after killing so many of our comrades." She rolled up one sleeve.

Jane didn't know what the woman was talking about. She seemed to recognize Roman, but this wasn't the welcome Jane had expected for an absent prince. Either Roman was just as confused, or he simply thought silence the wisest course.

Meanwhile, the usher was still staring at Roman with puzzled absorption – like he recognized him, but he couldn't figure out how.

"You must know it is not you we cherch," the woman said, adjusting her other sleeve. "Tell us where he is, und you will be handled well." The alternative was as clear as the scars on the woman's now-bare arms.

There had to be a misunderstanding. And yet Roman said nothing to correct it.

"You."

Jane felt rough fingers on her chin as the woman turned her face up.

"Tell me. Where is he?" The woman's grip was slick with sweat – however angry she was, she was nervous, too.

Jane kept her own gaze steady and told herself that this was no different from a hundred other situations she'd faced in Recoletta, with seething whitenails demanding explanations for crises she knew nothing about – incriminating stains on husbands' trousers, missing silver, empty brandy decanters. This was no different.

"I don't know what you're talking about," she said.

The woman considered her a moment longer, holding her chin with a strong but clammy hand. Finally, she released her and focused on Roman.

"But you are knowing precisely wass I am talking about," she said. "Look at me. Tell me."

But Roman kept his head down and his mouth clamped shut.

The woman wound back and hit him in the gut.

He doubled over, holding his stomach and gasping in pain. He was still bent forward when the woman spoke.

"Where is Geist?"

If their three captors hadn't been so intent on Roman, Jane was sure they would have seen the surprise on her own face. She remembered the name from the wanted poster – the man with a scar, who had stolen and crashed an airship.

What she didn't understand was why these people thought she and Roman had anything to do with it.

Roman must have heard the name, too. But still he said nothing, and the woman hit him again.

This time, he cried out with a sound that chilled Jane's blood. Knowing that he was still holding it back made it all the worse.

"You know something," the woman said. "Spreck."

Jane silently begged him to comply.

Instead, Roman gave the same noncommittal shrug she'd seen from him a thousand times before.

The woman hit him again. "We have many hours still to go before Nouvelle Paris. One way or another, you will talk." This time, she didn't wait for Roman to answer before punching him again.

The air left him in a pained groan. He retched and spat blood on the floor.

She socked him again.

Jane was aware of a voice yelling, "Stop! Stop!" She didn't realize until the others turned to stare at her that it was her own.

"You have remembered something?" the woman said.

Roman was still bent forward and coughing, a crimson-flecked pile of vomit at his feet. He couldn't – or wouldn't – speak, but Jane was aware of him shaking his head.

It didn't matter. She couldn't keep watching this. Besides, one way or another, they were already caught.

"He's Roman Arnault," Jane said. "He's Faraj Arnault's descendant. We don't have any documents because we just came from Salvage and the buried cities."

Roman heaved and threw up again. Whether it was at the sour smell of his vomit or the nagging sense that she'd just betrayed him, Jane felt as though she might be sick too.

The steward had a queasy look as well. The usher was hopping from foot to foot as though he might soil himself, saying, "I knew! So familiar, that face." His excitement curdled to horror as he realized what that meant, who he'd been complicit in assaulting.

The woman was quiet, studying Roman's downturned face. After several seconds, she knelt. "Forgive me. You have been gone for so long, I did not know–"

Roman coughed a final time and wiped his mouth. "There is nothing to forgive." Jane felt a twist in her gut as he regarded her.

"We will see that your wounds are swiftly tended to," the woman said, her eye twitching. "Anything you require, we shall provide."

Roman was tugging his shirt back into place and straightening his sleeves. Without even a glance of request, the steward snapped a silk handkerchief out of his jacket pocket and passed it to Roman, who dabbed at a spot on the embroidered cuffs.

"A finger of brandy and some privacy," he said. "You will allow us to return to our compartment, and you will not speak of my presence here. I desire to reach Nouvelle Paris with as little fuss as possible."

The woman bowed her head even lower. Her throat bobbed with an anxious swallow.

"Is there a problem?" Roman asked. His voice carried the razor-thin suggestion of a threat.

"We are making all possible haste for Nouvelle Paris, but we must signal the gendarmes to receive you, Senure."

Roman took a slow breath through his nose. For a man who had always dodged any appearance of authority, he now wore it surprisingly well. "I am not making myself clear."

"It is for your own security." The woman shook her head. "Forgive me, I thought you already knew. There was an attack weeks ago. On the palast at Versailles. Most of your relations passed."

Roman's shock was little more than a tightening around his jaw. "Most?"

"Your great-uncle was unexpectedly away. Julius Rothbauer."

Roman's face paled a shade. He pressed his lips into a hard, grim line. Something was different about him and the calm, determined authority with which he was receiving this. "Has the murderer been apprehended?"

The woman coughed to mask her surprise. "Senure, no. That is why we – why I was so eager to apprehend you. The culprit – Geist – he stole a top-of-the-line airship from the Nouvelle Paris moorings und evanoosed. But there are reports of him in the area. We can take no chances."

Watching Roman receive the news, watching his blue eyes frost over, Jane suddenly realized who this change reminded her of.

It was Augustus Ruthers. The man she had shot. Roman's other great-uncle.

CHAPTER TWENTY-THREE
NOUVELLE PARIS

Geist's network gave a new meaning to the term "organized crime." They'd stopped an eastbound train – what the Continentals called a "rail" – outside of Nantes-Neugeboren after nightfall by dragging a fallen tree across the tracks at a long straightaway. While the crew cleared the debris, Malone, Geist, and a handful of his followers had slipped into one of the cargo compartments at the back of the train. From their hidden passage to the forged identification, to the carefully timed arrival and departure of people whose names and roles she didn't know, Geist's operations put all of the petty smugglers and gangs she'd chased in Recoletta to shame.

Perhaps that professionalism made it feel less like she was working with the criminals now.

But as she watched them, she came to realize that this was not so much a testament to Geist's organizational genius as to the extent of his support. He had found a rift in the world around him – just as Sato had – and he had pried it wider and carved out a niche within it.

Still, none of the planning, organization, or discussion had prepared her for the chaotic grandeur of Nouvelle Paris.

Malone hadn't realized that cities could be so big. From her vantage point atop the Porte Nord mooring tower, all she could see were the tangled, migraine-inducing roofs and arches of the city stretching into the distance. Even that, Geist had told her, was only part of the sprawl.

Nouvelle Paris wasn't a city. It was several cities built on top of one another.

When she thought about it, the strangest part wasn't the jumbled architecture or the hybrid language or even the strangely opaque people. It was the way they inhabited their ruins – they built through them and around them, wove them into the strange fabric of their city.

Recolettans would have burrowed as far as possible from their relics.

And yet, for a people so comfortable resting among the bones of their dead, they were paranoid about the "Pesteland" and the warlike, diseased savages they assumed lived there. Already in her short time in the city, she'd seen street performers dressed as hairy, snaggletoothed villains; flimsy paperbacks imagining the adventures of Continental explorers across the sea; and posters bearing the images of men and women promising to protect good, honest people from the western menace.

Geist had told her that she had Sato to thank for resurgent obsessions about her homeland. But that wasn't even what concerned her the most.

The streets hummed with tension, much in the same way Recoletta's had in the months since Sato's takeover. Nouvelle Paris was a city divided and ripe for trouble – she saw it in the way strangers kept to their own side of the street and in the way they whispered and watched one another, as if everything were part of a conspiracy. She smelled it like the reek of nervous sweat.

She wondered how much of this Sato had instigated and how much he had merely accelerated.

Still, seeing the Continent's fear of the Pesteland gave Malone an understanding of the discomfort Geist's crew had displayed around her.

And now the startling view was giving her a new appreciation for her time aboard the *Glasauge*. At least it had inoculated her from her fear of heights.

Malone was stationed in a small cafe with a good view of the mooring platform. A headache scratched behind her eyes, and exhaustion numbed her fingers. She'd been awake and on the move since leaving the boat the day before, and now she was running on desperation and adrenaline. She'd been at the cafe for the better part of an hour, sipping tea that had long since gone cold. It was stronger and heavier than the stuff she was used to in Recoletta, but nonetheless a welcome change from the caffee.

The local police – the gendarmerie, Geist had called them – were milling about the berth, just as Geist had expected. Most of them were in plain clothes, but Malone would have recognized their alert postures and strategic placement anywhere.

She wondered if she'd ever been so easy to read. Arnault probably would have said so.

The thought of him brought a sudden and unexpected pang of guilt. She swallowed it back with another gulp of over-brewed tea.

She smelled a rich, familiar musk. As if someone were wearing Lachesse's perfume. She scanned the cafe crowd again and saw only the same set of strangers. Or maybe the many strangers here were starting to blend together.

But activity around the mooring station was picking up. The gendarmes passed by one another to exchange quick, hushed orders. Something was happening.

Malone shifted and squinted into the clouds. A dark shape was forming in the midst of them. The gendarmes were shuffling and fretting like anxious hens.

She couldn't shake the feeling she was missing something.

She passed a hand over her jacket pocket where a small electric lamp was tucked away. She had been selected for the dubious honor of signalman, both because none of the guards patrolling the mooring would recognize her in connection with Geist and because she was the one who could best recognize

Roman Arnault and Jane Lin.

And, more importantly, because she was the only person Jane and Arnault might be inclined to trust.

When she saw them step from the ship onto the tower, all she had to do was flash her lantern three times and one of Geist's people would trigger a riot on the tier below while another two would approach the guards. Meanwhile, she would approach Roman and Jane and guide them down the tower and through the hole Geist's men were supposed to leave.

Assuming everyone was in place. Assuming everyone pulled off their roles at just the right time. Assuming Jane and Arnault trusted her enough to follow.

And perhaps that was the part that bothered her the most. She'd already seen Geist's people pull off meticulously planned and spectacularly ambitious feats. But reaching out to Jane and Arnault, offering them a refuge only to betray them, felt wrong.

Still, if that was the price of safety for Recoletta and the buried cities, it was a fair trade. Even if it didn't feel like one. She supposed Lachesse would have agreed.

Malone finished her tea and rose to move into position, the amber-and-musk scent fading behind her.

By now the stiff, formal patter of the Continentals was familiar enough that she could snatch bits of conversation like hors d'oeuvres from passing trays. She listened for anything out of the ordinary, any sign the crowd around her knew what was happening. Instead, people talked about work, friends, loved ones. All the blessedly dull things that now felt distant.

The airship grew larger on the horizon. A part of her hoped it would sail on by.

Malone leaned against a support pillar and watched the crowd for several minutes. She'd seen one of Geist's people hanging around here earlier, but now the man was nowhere to be seen. She had to give them credit – they were professionals.

The minutes ticked by. The airship grew larger by the moment – what had started as a clenched fist had swelled to blot out a third of the sky. And it only grew faster, yet the minutes stretched on.

Malone felt as though she could hear her heartbeat tapping along beneath the murmur of conversation. She wanted this plan – this terrible, desperate plan that she had suggested to Geist – to be over and done with.

It didn't help that her headache was worsening. What had started as a blunt scratching had progressed into full-on pounding, a steady, painful rhythm that synced with her racing heart.

She took a deep breath. The heavy scents that clotted the air only added to the headache – machine smoke, unwashed bodies, overripe fruit.

Malone started, searching for Geist's other two people. They were still nowhere in sight. She circled around to the other side of the support. Still nothing.

Yet there, discarded at the base of the pillar, was a plain leather valise. Malone pried it open, already knowing what she would find.

Two dozen or so wrapped bundles of explosives, and attached to them a clockwork mechanism that ticked alongside Malone's own racing pulse. Geist's people must have brought these, set the timers when the airship appeared, and made their exit.

Malone looked. The approaching airship was banking, surrendering its ample flank to the tower. It couldn't be more than a couple of minutes away from docking. And there was no telling how many bombs had been placed on this platform or the others.

There was still time to run. All she had to do was make her exit, and Jane and Arnault – and the threat they posed to the buried cities – would be gone. She could disappear here or find her way back home, but this would all be over.

Maybe that was what Lachesse would have called "doing what was necessary."

Still, Malone couldn't. And if she acted quickly, she might just be fast enough to make a difference this time.

She ran toward the edge of the platform, waving one hand and holding the valise in the other. "Hey! Turn around, go! Run!"

People standing near backed away, blinking at her and murmuring to one another.

"Get away, fast!" she shouted. The crowd around her was dispersing with the rising song of panic. If only she could get the airship to do the same.

Rough hands gripped her arm. Malone sucked a breath through her teeth as someone snatched the valise away.

"Wass are you doing?" asked a man who was now inches from her face. One of the gendarmes.

"Turn them around," Malone said. "There's a bomb, probably several–"

But the gendarme was already addressing one of his fellows. "Move her away. She is crazy, probably–"

"Look in the bag!" Malone said.

But they weren't listening to her. And already a long, metal walkway was extending toward the hovering airship.

The gendarmes were still murmuring, as if she were a drunk party guest. "– will have my head if this is spoiled by some lunatic–"

The airship's main door opened. Any minute now.

"It's Roman Arnault," Malone said, as if suddenly remembering the magic words. "Geist knows he's here. He's trying to kill him, you idiots!"

The two men blinked at her, moving from annoyance to surprise.

And then alarm.

One of the gendarmes turned to the others. "Search the platform, now! Aral, signal that airship–"

Malone tried to pull away, but the first gendarme only tightened his grip.

"Oh, no," he said. "You will stay here."

CHAPTER TWENTY-FOUR
REUNION

Jane had spent the remainder of the airship trip in the berth, alone but for the steward standing guard outside. Since the ordeal, the airship's crew had smothered her with brittle courtesy – it was hard to know whether she was an honored guest or a pampered prisoner. They wouldn't allow her to see Roman, but they assured her the "senure" was enduring even more careful ministrations. They hesitated even to permit her out of her compartment, though they offered to bring her anything she might conceivably desire.

Yet the one thing she wanted right then – besides Roman's presence – was sleep, and neither she nor her dutiful guards could summon it.

But it wasn't long before the sun rose, and shortly after that they reached the outskirts of Nouvelle Paris.

It was everything the port town had been, but larger. Jane watched the maze of asymmetrical rooftops and winding streets below, waiting for them to end. It almost reminded her of looking out at the sea her first day on Salvage.

Then the motion of the airship – and the motion in it – changed. Footsteps pattered about in the hall and on the decks above and below. The rooftops rose like a tide. The steward waiting outside the curtain would tell her nothing, but it was obvious enough – they were docking.

At last, two women pulled back the curtain to escort her out.

"Where's Roman?" Jane asked.

The woman on her left stiffened and compressed her thin lips. "The senure will be accompanied out also. You will see him once the gendarmerie are assured of everyone's security."

Jane suppressed a sigh of exasperation.

They waited in front of the door. Jane heard the bump and scrape of the walkway being attached and the moorings cast and tied off. After opening the door, the two women held her arms all the more tightly. As if she had anywhere to go.

A small crowd of people was milling around on the mooring platform. Jane didn't take the time to scan their faces – her attention was pulled down.

Down, to the rooftops and spires that now seemed like blades and spears raised toward her. To streets like the grating in an abattoir floor.

She was only dimly aware of one of her escorts squeezing her shoulder. "We must go." The voice was barely more than a whisper over the blood rushing in her ears.

But she went. One foot after the other, staring at the slats in the walkway, not looking at – not even thinking about – the spaces between them. One foot and then the other. The gangway couldn't have been more than forty feet long, but she didn't dare glance up to see how far she had to go.

One of the guards was behind her, the other ahead. Jane timed her stride with theirs, following the regular motion of the gangplank, pairing every few steps with a deep breath.

Then the walkway began to shake.

She held to the railings. "Stop! Stop!" she yelled, but the shuddering continued. Someone was shouting.

Several someones. She looked up to see one of her escorts sprinting full bore toward the tower. The crowd on the platform was rushing around as if the place were on fire. A few were yelling and gesturing at the sky, waving their hands as if in farewell.

Away. Go. Flee. That's what they were saying.

Except for a discordant but familiar melody that rose above the rest.

"Jane. Jane. RUN." While everyone else waved and shouted at the ship, someone else was waving and shouting at her.

Jane looked back. Almost halfway down the gangplank, her other escort had just reached the outer hatch and was pulling it shut.

Suddenly, she found that she could move. Very, very fast.

She ran down the gangplank. Racing toward the tower even though some part of her animal brain recognized that it was a dangerous, hectic place to be, but knowing still that it would likely be the only solid ground in a matter of seconds.

As fast as she was moving, it still didn't feel fast enough.

She raced toward the figure and the sound of her name. Toward the platform and safety. Toward–

A heavy boom thudded through the air. The walkway shook, and Jane instinctively ducked and gripped the rails.

A second later, the ground fell away.

Jane held to the railings as tightly as she could while the gangplank swung toward the tower and screams raked furrows in her throat.

She slammed into the side of the tower. The force knocked the wind from her and nearly pried loose her grip. But she held on, steadying her feet against the uprights.

And held on, frozen, wishing now that she only had the clawing waves and endless deep beneath her.

Someone called her name again. Jane looked up and saw Liesl Malone.

She was both certain that it was her and that it couldn't possibly be her, because Malone was supposed to be back in Recoletta, doing whatever it was that people did when they weren't running for their lives and falling out of airships.

But the only thing that mattered was that the woman was there, shouting her name and reaching toward her.

So Jane climbed. Rung by rung, raising one hand toward the

next upright and then following with a foot, not thinking about what awaited her on the tower or why parts of it seemed to be aflame.

When she was at last within reach of Malone's improbably strong arms, she felt herself hoisted up and onto the platform. Only then did she realize how exhausted she was, how close her muscles were to total failure.

Jane was pulled away from the edge, and she felt Malone's lean-muscled limbs wrap around her back. "I've got you. I've got you," the woman said into her hair.

Jane shivered. She didn't know if it was an assurance or a threat.

CHAPTER TWENTY-FIVE
A COMMON ENEMY

It was the worst possible scenario for Malone – she and Jane Lin were in the custody of the Continentals, and Roman Arnault was still at large. The airship he'd been in had pulled away from the tower when the trouble started, bearing him and every other person onboard to parts unknown.

On the brighter side, the gendarmes had found and disarmed most of the bombs. Casualties had been minimal, she was told. Thinking back to Sundar, Lachesse, and the dead inspectors, it was a bittersweet relief to have figured things out in time to save so many. Still, no one would tell Malone much else.

But she was telling them plenty. About how Roman Arnault was a man of great importance, even in Recoletta. About how she had gone to retrieve him when she'd learned he'd been taken by the pirate city of Salvage.

Geist, as she explained it, had come to Recoletta as an envoy of the Continent, claiming a mission to escort Roman Arnault safely home. Malone had believed him and had followed in good faith. Even when their airship was shot down, even when they'd fled and snuck into Nouvelle Paris, Malone swore she'd believed his explanations that he was acting against rogue elements, trying to reach Arnault before they were alerted to his presence.

It wasn't until the mooring tower that her instincts had overruled Geist's deceit, and she had realized the attack he was planning.

Most of the events were technically true, and yet Malone was surprised at how easily the lies about their meaning rolled off her tongue.

And at how readily the gendarmes believed all of it.

But she was telling them what they wanted to hear – about Roman's prestige, the awe in which the yokels of the buried cities held his family, Geist's incomparable deceit. They were eating it up without even bothering to question aspects of her story that should have raised their doubts.

At first, she was quietly appalled at herself. But the deceit quickly became routine.

It reminded her of so many Cabinet meetings under Sato and of all the reasons she'd been so eager to leave politics. All the reasons she'd never wanted to be a part of them in the first place.

She felt as though she were getting whiplash from how many different sides she'd played over the last few weeks. From preparing to execute Arnault to letting him go, then chasing him and Lin across the sea only to inform on the people she'd been running with. And that wasn't even counting everything that had happened around Sato.

She liked things simple. She liked to know whose side she was on and what she was up against. Now, things were anything but simple, and none of the sides seemed to fit. All she knew was that she couldn't side with a bunch of people who would destroy a tower and an airship full of innocent people.

Though what that meant for the people of Recoletta and the other buried cities, she couldn't rightly say.

Perhaps Lachesse had been wrong about her and her willingness to do what was necessary. She was starting to think that maybe she was fine with that.

The gendarmes had taken her and Jane to a lavish apartment. Like everything on the Continent, it appeared to have been built from something else. The wide, cruciform halls and the balconies that lined them were ancient, the tile worn and cracked.

But the apartments that nestled within and branched off them were another matter entirely. Pale, uniform bricks looked as young and clean as an infant's flesh next to the blotchy, weathered gray of the old stonework. And the space inside was vast – much larger than she would have guessed from the modest entrance outside.

And this, she was told, was the temporary residence of Julius Rothbauer. She and Jane were introduced to him in the evening, the same day as their arrest.

Rothbauer did not appear to be in mourning for his family or his estate so much as for the world as a whole. He seemed exhausted – like he'd been worn out, used up, and left to harden. Malone suspected that if he had been present for Geist's attack, he would merely have withdrawn into his layers of finery like an irritated turtle retracting into its shell.

Even so, she could see the resemblance to Augustus Ruthers. The same energy that had been like a bonfire blaze in Ruthers was a graying ember in Rothbauer – dangerous, but in a way that was easy to disregard until it was too late.

Malone and Jane were seated at opposite ends of a long, narrow dining table when Rothbauer emerged to meet them. Malone hadn't had a chance to speak to Jane – they'd been separated since the events on the mooring tower. She looked unharmed, but had already retreated into herself in that unassuming, servant-in-the-background way she had.

But at the sight of Rothbauer, her eyes opened just a little wider, and her fingers spasmed into a fist on the polished table.

Rothbauer's attire was every bit as imposing and chaotic as the huge mishmash of a city around them. He was a big man – more like Arnault than Ruthers in that regard – and the wide ruff around his neck, the raised epaulets at his shoulders, and the heavy, flared cape at his back only made him loom larger.

Though it was hard to tell how he was supporting all that weighty regalia, or if it was really the other way around.

Rothbauer settled into the chair at the head of the table. His blue eyes – bright and cruel like Ruthers's – flickered between the two women.

"I am told that you arrived with my great-nephew," he said to Jane, "and that he is missing once again." His accent was lighter than most of the others she'd heard, or maybe she was just growing accustomed to them. He turned to Malone. "And I hear you traveled as the prisoner – or collaborator – of Geist, the man who killed the rest of my family. And then you disrupted his bombing plot at the Porte Nord mooring tower. Is that so?"

Malone nodded, relieved that at least this much could be straightforward. For now.

"But what I do not know," he said, his voice disconcertingly even, "is what has become of my younger brother."

Ruthers.

"He's dead," Malone said, hoping he would ask no more. As angry as she'd been with Jane, she couldn't really count Ruthers's death among her crimes, especially when it was one she would have gladly committed herself. Besides, given how the Continentals fawned and fretted over Arnault, it didn't bear thinking on how they'd treat his great-uncle's killer.

It was hard to read the emotion in Rothbauer's puffy face as he absorbed the news. "By what means?"

Malone kept her eyes on Rothbauer's as she tried to concoct a lie with just enough truth to be reasonable and just enough fiction to spare them both.

"I killed him," Jane said.

The laundress's knuckles were white around her clenched fist, and her gaze was locked on Rothbauer's. Malone felt both proud and sorry for the girl despite herself.

But Rothbauer burst out with a thick, phlegmy laugh. "Augustus always was a fool."

"He was a tyrant," Jane said, her voice tight. Malone was surprised by her vehemence.

"Is that why you killed him? Because he was cruel to you and all the other people with dirt under their fingernails?"

"I killed him because he wanted to use Roman," Jane said. Her eyes accused Rothbauer right back.

But he only smiled and leaned back in his chair. "Angry the old man was going to beat you to it?"

Jane recoiled. She said nothing, but her gaze burned with protest and affront. Malone found herself wondering why. After all, the girl only had to portray herself as Roman's deliverer from the buried cities. It wouldn't be a hard sell, and it would gain her all of the power and security she'd come to the Continent seeking.

A servant placed a cup like a tiny wineglass by Rothbauer's right hand. The old man picked it up with surprising delicacy and sipped from it. "Come now," he said, "what is it you want? Money, land, fame? You brought Roman back to us – I will forget the rest and see you well rewarded."

"I want nothing from you," Jane said. Malone willed herself into the background, wondering how this would play out.

Rothbauer smiled and wagged a finger. "Everyone desires something. But not all desires are reasonable." He watched her for a second. "You must know that Roman has certain responsibilities here. Responsibilities which you've no part in."

"You mean the vault," Jane said.

The baggy flesh around Rothbauer's eyes pulled back. "So you know of it. Its secrets are not for you, whatever Roman might have told you of it. What did he promise you?"

Jane flashed a bitter smile. "To destroy it."

Malone felt the shock of those words in her bones. After Jane's stunt at Maxwell Street Station, her parting act of sabotage, her flight across the sea – Malone had been certain her and Roman's trip to the Continent was all a gambit to seize the influence and security that had eluded them in Recoletta and Madina. That the buried cities that had abused them both were, at best, a casualty, and at worst, a calculated cost.

But perhaps she'd merely seen that story play out too many times from the likes of Sato, the Qadi, and the rest of Recoletta's powermongers.

Suddenly, Jane and Rothbauer were both looking at her.

"I take it your friend knows about the vault, too?" Rothbauer said.

"What do you want with us?" Malone asked.

"To find my great-nephew," he said. "My best men are searching for him, as are your erstwhile allies," he said with a contemptuous raise of his eyebrows. "But I am thinking one of you might know where he has gone."

Jane stiffened. The movement was little more than a straightening of her back, but Rothbauer caught it like a predator honing in on movement.

"The young lady remembers something."

"He's in an airship," Jane said, rubbing a thumbnail. It was as clear a tell as Malone had ever seen. "I don't know how you miss one of those."

Rothbauer swirled the liquid in his tiny glass. "Consider that a tower full of bombs was a considerable distraction. But Geist's people will waste no such opportunity. And if they find him, they will kill him."

Jane waited a long time before shaking her head. "I don't know where he is. And even if I did, I wouldn't help you put him in a cage," she said.

Rothbauer smiled. "Is that how he told it?" He folded his hands on the table. They were large and smooth, with close-trimmed nails and an assortment of iron-gray rings. "It is true, certain duties will be expected of him. He must produce an heir – several, ideally, given our family's recent longevity problems." He gave her a long, amused look. "And he must be prepared to open the vault."

"Why?" Malone asked. "You have everything here – flying ships, great cities, prosperous people. Why do you need to open the vault?"

He straightened. "What we have is history, and history comes with peculiar burdens. That is how we developed these advances of which you speak so highly – by drawing not only on the designs of the past, but on the impetus, as well."

Malone glanced from Rothbauer to Jane, whose lips were pursed in confusion. "What do you–"

"I mean that such developments are as much a matter of social investment as of capital or technological investment." He sipped his drink again, the glass looking absurdly small in his large hand. "How do you think you mobilize several million people after the near-total destruction of their civilization? How do you persuade them to rebuild cities instead of tearing one another apart?" He motioned toward the shadows, and a liveried attendant emerged to refill his glass. "And when you have a hundred million, already dividing according to custom and culture, how do you keep them working together? How do you stop them from building walls across their cities?"

"By building a wall across the Continent," Malone said.

"You understand perfectly," said Rothbauer. He sipped his drink and shivered with pleasure.

"So everything you've built – your cities, your airships, the rest of it – it's all been to defend against the buried cities?" Jane asked.

"Everything must have a purpose," Rothbauer said. "And no purpose is more unifying than a common enemy."

"Especially an enemy that brought a terrible plague to your shores," Jane said, scowling. The same story Malone had heard.

Rothbauer raised his glass.

"So all this – it's all over something our ancestors did generations ago?" Malone said.

Rothbauer opened his hands in apology. "As I said, with history comes peculiar burdens."

"This is mad," Jane said.

"You think I am happy about this? All we can do is keep our corner of the world moving forward for as long as possible. Authority is not supposed to be pleasant." He grimaced. "It certainly has not been of late."

Malone recalled something Geist had said. About Sato's sudden appearance and the trouble he had brought. "Did you ever meet a Recolettan named Jakkeb Sato?"

"Burning red hair and a spirit to match? I would not soon forget him." Rothbauer scowled, turning the tiny glass between his hands.

"Why did he come to you?" Malone asked.

"He desired to see how we work. What we remember." Rothbauer paused, frowning. "He was not happy with what we told him."

Malone thought back to Sato's fervent pursuit of the Library and its contents. She'd never understood what drove him to unearth an ancient trove of stories, studies, and histories, much less why he seemed to need the people of Recoletta to explore it alongside him, but she was starting to.

He'd learned the Continent's terrible history and how the ancestors of the buried cities had wrought the Pesteland. And he had wanted to find another version of events to refute it.

Malone remembered his descent and increasing desperation. He hadn't succeeded.

Jane smirked. "He made a mess in Recoletta, too. How badly did he stir up your people?"

"I told you Roman is in danger from unsettled elements. Is that not enough?" Rothbauer drank a final time from his glass and set it aside. "Whatever our enmity with your homeland, let it never be said that we are not gracious hosts. While you are my guests, you shall be housed comfortably and fed amply."

A servant appeared behind Rothbauer and pulled the chair back as he rose. Another bore the empty glass away on a shining silver tray.

"And in the meantime, I urge you to think very hard about what you might remember." Rothbauer aimed this remark at Jane. She was staring at her folded hands on the table, her eyes sharp with a private conundrum.

After the meeting, Rothbauer's attendants took Malone to a room with the most comfortable bed she'd ever lost sleep on.

The mattress and pillows were as soft and cool as cream. Malone was confident she would have noticed even if she hadn't spent the last few weeks sleeping on the hard, flat cot on the *Glasauge*. Yet she tossed and turned, trying to find a position that didn't leave her feeling as though she were being swallowed by the bed.

Even though Jane was the one who had been led away under guard, even though Malone had opened the door of her room to find it not only unlocked, but also unguarded, she felt trapped. By the lies she had told, by the lies she was still telling, and by the realization that she was probably going to have to keep lying before this was all over.

At least she wouldn't have to kill Roman herself – Geist would find him while Rothbauer fumbled and Jane sulked. Yet she didn't find as much solace in that as she should have.

When at last she grew bored of watching the ceiling, she got up and dressed. If she was doomed to stay awake, she might as well stretch her legs.

The tiled hallways of Rothbauer's apartment were cool and quiet – she doubted anyone else's wandering thoughts were keeping them awake. At dinner, Rothbauer, and even Jane herself, had sat fixed and firm with a kind of clarity Malone could only envy.

Before she realized what she was doing, she was heading down the corridor where she'd seen Rothbauer's men take Jane.

Malone didn't know what she'd say to Jane, and had even less of an idea of what the younger woman would possibly say to her, but suddenly the idea of talking to someone she'd known before, even briefly, felt like a beacon in a storm.

She met no one as she continued along the hall, passing one empty room after another. It seemed as though everyone in Rothbauer's household slept.

It also seemed as though what counted as an apartment on the Continent would have been a Vineyard mansion in Recoletta. If this was the temporary residence, she wondered where the family lived the rest of the time.

Had lived, she remembered.

At the end of the hall, moonlight spilled through the windows and fell on a single closed door. A key protruded from the lock.

Surely this was where they'd taken Jane. Yet Malone couldn't see any guards.

She pressed her ear to the door and heard muffled commotion. Like someone was making noise but trying not to.

Malone glanced down the hall a final time. There was no one in sight.

She turned the key and pushed the door open to find the room in disarray.

Jane had made up her mind the moment Julius Rothbauer walked into the room: she was going to get the hell out of there.

And then she was going to find Roman and get him far away from all the people who wanted to catch or kill him.

She was just working out how when Inspector Malone showed up.

She'd been granted a suite of rooms – a bedroom bigger than her entire apartment back in Recoletta, a bathroom, and a small sitting room. Once, so much space would have felt like a luxury, but after getting used to the tight quarters and packed crowds on Salvage, the openness only made her feel exposed.

And, as if to prove her point, Malone herself was now standing in the open doorway.

"Shut it, will you?" Jane asked. The last thing she needed was this woman with all the subtlety of a whitenail in the factory districts, drawing Rothbauer's people to her.

Malone retrieved the key and closed the door. "Jane, what are you doing?"

"What's it look like?" She'd already shifted most of the furniture and picked through every corner of the suite, searching for something – anything – useful. Now, she focused her attention on the windows. They were high off the ground, but climbing through them was probably a safer bet than trying to sneak out of the apartment and then the rest of the building.

The inspector paced, the carpet crunching under her feet. "Where will you go?" she asked.

"Away." The north-facing wall was broken up by windows. Most of them were barred, and the ones that weren't only swung open a few inches.

Malone sighed. "Do you know how big the Continent is?"

"Big enough to disappear in." Jane continued into the bedroom. It was full of big, wide windows.

Malone followed. "What you said back there, about the vault–"

"Forget the vault." Jane examined the window nearest the bed. It didn't open more than a sliver, either, but it measured a good three feet in width and rose three stories above a lamplit garden. It would have to do.

"You and Roman came all this way to destroy it."

"And then I realized the Continent has airships, civilization-ending diseases, and an old grudge against the buried cities." She found a pillow. It was oddly shaped, but it was just large enough. "Even if we could destroy the vault, these people would find another way."

Malone was silent for a while, which allowed Jane to focus on the task at hand. She needed something hard. Like the candelabra on the bedside table.

The inspector coughed in that artificial way of someone trying to make a point. "I didn't realize that was why you'd come."

Jane hefted the candelabra. It was heavier than it looked. Good. She turned to Malone, standing awkwardly just inside the bedroom. "It was Roman's idea." The garden was still dark and quiet below. Jane held the pillow over the glass with one hand and wielded the candelabra in the other. It was a clumsy operation, but after escaping Salvage and the airship she was certain she could manage this.

She was still trying to hold the pillow in place when Malone's ghost-pale hands steadied it for her.

"Just try not to hit my fingers," the inspector said.

"This doesn't mean we're going together," Jane said. "We're splitting up as soon as we hit the ground."

"You really want me falling back in with Rothbauer's people? Or Geist's? Besides," Malone said, "after getting me hanged, you owe me."

Jane was so taken aback that she nearly dropped the candelabra. She looked back at Malone and noticed the scar that rose across her neck, ending in a knot of puckered, ruined flesh just above her collar. Jane had glimpsed it earlier, as the gendarmes were packing them off for their interrogations and as they'd sat in Rothbauer's dim, carnivalesque dining room. But she'd been too focused on escape to give it much thought.

She suspected she was supposed to feel guilty, but she only felt annoyed.

"I didn't put that rope around your neck."

"No, but you stirred up the people who did," said Malone.

Jane shook her head and struck the pillow with the base of the candelabra. The pillow muffled most of the sound of cracking glass, but even so she'd hit it harder than she intended.

"I talked to a reporter. That's all," Jane said.

"You destroyed a peace," Malone said. "Between Recoletta, the other cities, and the communes."

"It was built on lies." Jane bashed the pillow again, feeling the satisfying crunch of glass. "How strong was it if it couldn't survive the truth? That Ruthers and the other whitenails were just trying to dig themselves back in?"

"It was the only one we had," Malone said. "A lot of people died to create it."

Her chiding tone rubbed a nerve in Jane. One that had already been worn raw by Rothbauer's pressing, Roman's disappearance, and the anxious, sleepless night that had preceded it.

Jane gave the pillow a final thwack and felt the last of the glass fall away behind it. She rounded on Malone. "You think you're the only one who tried to do anything? Or the only person who lost anyone?" She couldn't bring herself to mention

Freddie, or how he'd died aiding her. "I knew Ruthers planned to use Roman to get to the vault himself. I knew the Qadi was sending a train full of soldiers to pacify Recoletta." She couldn't bring herself to say what she'd done with that knowledge, either.

But Malone's posture stiffened, and Jane supposed she didn't have to.

Then the inspector cleared her throat, and Jane realized she was still raising the candelabra.

She held it out. "Clear off the sharp bits, will you?" She was too angry to look at the inspector and too afraid of dissolving into emotion when she most needed to keep her head clear. But after a moment, she felt the burden lifted from her arm.

She went to the bed and rubbed the linens between her fingers. It was a fine, high-quality fabric – the kind of thing whitenails would have slept on. It would almost be a shame to use it this way.

She was already tearing the top sheet into strips when Malone spoke again.

"It's easy to leave a mess when you're not staying around to clean it up."

Jane was tying the first of the bedding strips together. She gave the knot in her hands an especially fierce tug. "No one made you stay to clean up Recoletta."

"No one else was going to. Here, let me show you." Malone took a few of the strips and knotted them together with a few more loops and tucks. "Stronger this way," she said.

It did feel sturdier. Still, Jane wasn't ready to thank Malone for anything just yet. "You done this before?" she asked.

The inspector only grunted.

In a few quick minutes, they had a makeshift rope between them.

They tied one end to the window frame. The other hung just over the grass below.

"Think it'll hold us?" Malone asked, her head out the window.

Jane was privately wondering the same thing, but didn't want to say as much. "Let's just go one at a time."

"I'll go first," Malone said.

Jane peered out the window at the ground some thirty feet below. If Malone wanted to try, she wouldn't stop her.

She watched Malone hoist herself out the window and shimmy down the bedsheets. The fabric went taut, the knots bulging around the thinning, stretching strips, but everything held.

The garden below appeared to run the length of the building. It was laid out with thick shrubs trimmed into disconcertingly smooth rows and arches, stunted trees, and a few lamps. It abutted the river's edge roughly one hundred feet away. Jane guessed it was just after midnight – no one else was out wandering the garden, and the buildings across the river were too far away for anyone inside to see their escape under cover of night.

The bedsheets went slack. Jane gazed down at Malone whose pale face glowed up at her like a distant moon.

Jane crawled out of the window and started down, thinking how happy she'd be if she could just keep her feet on solid ground after this. She didn't dare look at the distance below her, so she kept her eyes on the sky above, watching the stars. Something about the dark expanse and its distant mysteries reminded her of watching the ocean from Salvage, catching flicks of movement beneath it.

The descent was going well enough until she heard a sharp hiss.

Her hands prickled with sweat as she risked a glance down at Malone, who was still an alarmingly long way below her. The inspector was waving her arms in small, urgent "hurry up" motions.

Jane looked up. Their bedsheet rope was elongating above her, one of the knots twitching as it was pulled to its limit.

She doubled her pace.

She didn't know exactly how far she'd gone, but her feet were still wrapped around the sheets and her eyes level with the wall when she started to fall.

It didn't last long. Her legs rang with pain as she landed, but Malone caught her about the shoulders, softening the impact.

They dusted themselves off and caught their breath. The sheets had come apart near the top, but the few tangled strips that still hung out of the window fluttered softly in the breeze, like a handkerchief waving at a train station.

"Where to now?" Malone asked.

Jane considered politely telling the inspector she was welcome to go wherever she pleased, but at the moment she wasn't in any position to stop her from following. It would be easier to lose her later. And until then, she might be useful.

Jane pointed across the river. "This way," she said.

They reached a bridge, which was also deserted. Jane wanted to find busy, crowded streets. Somewhere she could blend in.

Malone drew up beside her as they crossed the bridge. The waters below were almost impossibly still after the constant motion of the sea. They were smelly, too.

"I think Rothbauer let us get away too easily," Malone said.

"You're not the one who nearly broke a leg." Her left knee ached despite Malone's intervention.

"You know what I mean." The inspector glanced over her shoulder. "My guess is he let us go. To see if we lead him to Arnault."

She had a point. It was one Jane had been avoiding. Still, what else could they have done? "You're welcome to go back." The building containing Rothbauer's apartment – and who knew how many others – was now a long, low shape squatting over the river.

"Just let me keep an eye out," Malone said.

"As long as you don't slow us down." Perhaps the inspector was also using her to get to Roman. Or maybe she just wanted to buy Geist enough time to do the same. Either way, she'd have to make a break for it once they were clear of the city.

Malone gave her a sidelong glance but said nothing.

CHAPTER TWENTY-SIX

THE FRACTURED CITY

It was obvious to Malone that Jane didn't trust her. It was equally obvious that the laundress was hoping to leave her behind at the earliest opportunity.

Still, for now, they both needed to get out of Nouvelle Paris, and they needed to lose any tail Rothbauer might have set on them.

"I can find the rail station," Malone said. She remembered the one at which she and Geist's people had arrived late at night, and she'd been careful to build a mental image of the place – the way the streets widened around it, the sloped roofs that seemed to bend away from it, and the strange spire that rose just beyond it.

That spire, now glowing with lights, pierced the skyline to the west.

"Fine," Jane said. Her voice was tight with mistrust, but Malone was reasonably certain the young woman would stick with her at least until they reached the station.

After that, Malone would have to improvise. Not only to keep Jane close, but also to get aboard a train. After all, she didn't have the benefit of Geist's people to help her drag another tree across the tracks.

The distance to the spire couldn't have been much more than a mile and a half, but the twisting, unpredictable streets made the journey feel twice as long. Furthermore, bizarre architecture warped the patchy mental map Malone had assembled. More than once, she found herself following a street that appeared to lead directly to the spire, only for it to veer steadily away. Jane appeared to hold her suspicion and frustration between clenched teeth.

But after the third time they doubled back, the laundress spoke up. "You said you'd take us to the rail station."

"And I will," Malone said. "But if you know a better route, you're welcome to lead."

"I don't even know where it is," Jane said, eyeing her. "Or if that's really where you're taking us."

Hairs bristled along the back of Malone's neck. The day's trials and her lack of sleep weren't helping her temper any, but the worst part of it was bearing the contempt of this insolent laundress who had created so many of their problems in the first place. "If I wanted to lead you back to Rothbauer, I wouldn't have followed you out the window. And if you think I'm leading you to Geist – the man who tried to kill us both, let me remind you – then you're more of a fool than I thought."

Jane shot her a look of pure venom. "So it's fine if he only wants to kill me or Roman. Just as long as he doesn't go after you."

"You know that's not what I meant," Malone said.

Jane harrumphed. "I'm sure all of the people Sato–"

"Quiet," Malone said. "Do you hear anything?"

Jane broke off and frowned, listening.

The streets were empty and altogether too quiet. Malone didn't know much about Nouvelle Paris, but she knew enough about cities at midnight to suspect this was unusual. And all the detritus of urban living – discarded paper wrappers, scraps of food, cigarette butts – seemed to confirm this.

She remembered Geist's talk of recent unrest. The brooding, stewing city felt familiar.

"Jane, we need to be careful," she said.

The younger woman acknowledged with a vague hum of

assent. Jane just wanted to leave, and as quickly as possible – Malone saw that much in her hurried, stiff-legged pace.

Presently, a distant rumble arose ahead of them. Something about it reminded Malone of packed, tense crowds at train stations. She wanted to steer clear, but Jane kept going.

Malone cleared her throat. "We shouldn't–"

"If someone's following us, a crowd's the best place to lose them," Jane said. She didn't break her stride.

Malone sighed. Jane was her only chance of finding Roman and keeping him out of Rothbauer's hands, so she had no choice but to follow.

The noise of the crowd steadily rose. After several minutes, the two women emerged into a packed plaza. Hundreds of people gathered, arms and voices raised. They reminded her vaguely of Geist and his people. They were shouting about Rothbauer, about Arnault, about liberty. Malone couldn't make out most of their words, but their rage was clear enough, and it was burning hot enough to boil over.

And the idea of being trapped in the midst of another furious mob terrified Malone.

Jane, however, was still shouldering her way past and between people in a way that reminded Malone of an impatient child shoving through a buffet line. It was only a matter of time before she caused a ruckus.

Yet the younger woman pressed on, and the people she shoved past mostly seemed to ignore her. Whether it was her short stature, her general ability to blend in with her surroundings, or something else, Malone couldn't say. All she knew was that she had to use every sharp angle and hard surface in her body to part the crowd, and she was barely keeping up.

She hoped anyone following them was having at least as hard a time of it.

And then, before Malone could put her finger on what was wrong, alarm bells went off in her head. The crowd began to agitate and undulate in a way that reminded her of the food riot.

Maxwell Street Station. The stormy sea tossing Geist's lifeboats around.

Shots erupted from somewhere to the right. Screams echoed throughout the crowd. Jane ran, and Malone followed.

The clamor of shouts, gunshots, and stampeding feet rose around them. Jane, despite her shorter legs and injured knee, was pushing ahead with more desperate speed than Malone would have thought possible.

At least the throng around them was mostly headed in the same direction. Malone couldn't tell where it led except "away."

Suddenly, the movement ahead of Malone slowed, and the people behind her pressed into her back. Buildings rose around them; they were caught in a bottleneck where the streets branched from the plaza.

And Jane was nowhere to be seen.

Malone glanced around, searching the crowd for Jane's face or the familiar shape of her head with her dark hair gathered in a bun at her neck, all the while trying to stay upright and steady against the frantic horde.

Something grabbed at her ankle. Malone looked down just long enough to see a man curled on the ground and reaching out with one bloodied hand, and then the crowd swept her further ahead.

She fought the nauseated panic rising in her chest and kept scanning for Jane.

Finally she saw her. The laundress was a handful of people away, her head tilted back and her mouth open in a silent scream. She was being crushed by the people around her.

Malone shoved her way to the young woman's side and elbowed the person behind her, creating just enough room for Jane to slip free. Malone grabbed her shoulders before she could fall and suffer the same fate as the half-trampled man.

"Move diagonally," Malone shouted. "Lead with your shoulder."

Gasping, Jane nodded.

They pushed along through the crowd, and at last cross-streets opened up around them. Most of the panicked people were still moving blindly forward, so the two women had to angle their way to one of the open streets to reach it.

But they did, and it was as though the city had just expanded around them.

"If anyone was following, I'm hoping we lost them," Malone said.

Jane nodded, still sucking deep, ragged breaths. "We gotta get out of this city."

Malone scanned the skyline until she found the shape of a familiar spire. Less than half a mile to go. "This way," she said.

Jane was either too shaken or too exhausted to argue. When they finally reached the rail station, Malone could have whooped with relief. The wide, squat building bulged with mismatched terminals. Even at this hour, scores of people milled around it, fleeing the present unrest.

"What now?" Jane asked, ever alert and mistrustful.

When Malone had arrived with Geist early in the morning, they'd taken back routes and service passages in hopes of avoiding security. She thought back to their route. "There's an entrance for catering around the back," she said. "Then we can hop on any train we want." That was the idea, anyway. She'd snuck aboard a freight train in Recoletta months ago by finding the right opening – this shouldn't be any different.

Of course, she was also hoping Jane knew where Roman had gone. And that she would point them to the train that would take them to him.

More likely, of course, was that Jane would try to leave her behind as soon as they were inside the station.

"Just so we're clear," Malone said, "if you disappear once we're inside, I'm raising the alarm."

Jane gave her a calculating frown. "So that Rothbauer can lock us up again?"

"I don't want that, but neither do you. So we stick

together for now."

Malone couldn't tell if the laundress believed her bluff or not.

"Lead the way," Jane said, all false pleasantness.

Next to the catering entrance were crates of all weights and sizes which people were carrying into the station. Malone and Jane chose a box each and continued inside without trouble.

The mood in the station was tense, with passengers and guards keeping to themselves and watching one another carefully, but it was a welcome reprieve from the chaos of the riot.

Malone shifted the crate in her arms and scanned the posted signs with their ever-more-familiar words. "Northbound trains are straight ahead," she muttered to Jane. "Southbound and eastbound lines are that way."

After a pause, Jane spoke. "We're headed to Cologne-de-le-Kur." Her voice was tight and sullen.

Malone found the name – or what looked like it – on the board for northbound lines. "After you," she said.

Jane led them to a train surrounded by agitated people and puffing steam. Would-be passengers crowded the doors of the cars up ahead while the harried attendants checked their tickets one by one. The place was far more crowded than it had been when she and Geist had arrived – she wondered if the riots had something to do with so many people leaving. At any rate, she wasn't sure if anyone at the train station was searching for them yet – or if anyone here even knew what they looked like – but there was no sense in getting caught now.

Fortunately, the platform was busy enough that no one appeared to be paying any attention to two women carrying cargo amidst the nervous passengers and groggy crew.

"They're loading the freight cars down there," Malone said. "We'll take these." She hefted her crate.

"And then?"

She was making this up as she went along, but there was no sense in letting Jane know that. "Just follow me."

There were about a dozen freight cars. Malone guided them

toward one near the middle and slipped inside.

After several minutes, the whistle shrieked and the train began to move. The muscles in her jaw and shoulders relaxed, releasing tension she hadn't realized was there. Malone felt the rumbling of the train in the soles of her feet and the arch of her back, and she realized how exhausted she was. Across from her, the laundress was quiet and apparently lost in her own thoughts.

Malone felt her thoughts drifting back to the train she'd snuck aboard months ago, and the strange library to which it had taken her. She wondered where this journey would end.

For now, at least, there was nowhere to go. Malone let herself drift off to sleep. She had a feeling she'd need all her strength later.

As the train rumbled on, Jane watched the mottled blue and black of the sky through the open hatch in the ceiling. She was almost certain Roman had headed toward the vault in an attempt to destroy it – he'd been intent on doing that since their departure from Recoletta. She was equally certain that Malone would kill him if she got the chance, assuming she knew the danger the vault posed. In fact, she'd probably kill her too, if she realized she knew the code. And from all Rothbauer's men had said about Geist, she had to assume the revolutionary had told her all about the vault.

She was beginning to appreciate what Petrosian had meant about the danger of Malone's convictions.

She needed to get away from Malone at the earliest opportunity. The inspector had been asleep since departing Nouvelle Paris, but they were still moving too fast for Jane to risk a jump.

The sky overhead had begun to pale to violet when the train began to slow to a stop. Something about the moment seemed odd to Jane – she couldn't hear, see, or smell any signs of a nearby city. And the stop was far too sudden.

Jane glanced at Malone as the train decelerated to half-speed. The inspector was still asleep. This might be her best chance to slip away.

The hatch above yawned invitingly beyond the stacked crates. It would be a quieter and easier exit than the heavy door in the side of the car. Jane stood, and when she was confident of her balance in the rumbling car, she climbed.

The train had slowed to a crawl by the time Jane poked her head out of the hatch. A bracing wind pulled tears from her eyes as she looked at the rolling meadows and patchy forests just emerging from the twilight. Up ahead, she saw the cause of the trouble – a tree lay across the tracks.

Which seemed odd, because the tree line stopped a hundred yards away. But there was no time to consider it – Malone sounded like she was stirring in the car below, and if the stop didn't wake her, the commotion of the train crew clearing the tree away surely would.

She climbed down the side of the train and dropped onto the grass, stumbling. She was stiff, hungry, and not entirely sure where she was, but she was free.

She sprinted for the forest.

Her injured knee twinged with every other step, but the trees loomed larger and closer. She promised herself she would slow down once she reached cover.

So she swallowed her agony and threw all her energy into the last ten yards.

Jane kept running as the low wisps of branches swatted at her face. She sucked deep breaths of the cold, damp air. She registered the distant movement of a deer – or whatever the Continental equivalent was – from the corner of her eye.

Something collided with her from behind. She fell to the ground as strong arms wrapped around her waist.

She hit the grass, catching herself on her forearms. The cold earth knocked the wind from her, and over her own agonized groans she heard several voices around her whispering urgently.

"Move, schnell!"

"Wass does she do here? She flet–"

"Just bring her."

Jane was half-carried and half-dragged to a long stack of brush. There were more than a dozen armed people hiding behind it, and she glimpsed other such shelters between the trees. Now, it was hard to see how she'd missed them.

Rough hands held her in place, and something sharp poked her side.

"You will be tranquil, ya?" a man asked, showing her a knife as plainly as though it were nothing more than a harmless curiosity. Most of his expression was hidden behind a sandy beard, but his eyes were deadly calm.

She nodded, and her minder turned to watch the train.

With nothing else to do, Jane watched, too.

Twenty or so of the guerrillas loped alongside it in single file, their bodies close to the cars. They steadily made their way forward.

Meanwhile, the doors of the lead car slid open. Eight crew members tumbled out, trotting toward the tree blocking the track.

Jane realized she could scream, but she suspected that would only get her killed. She had no reason to believe it would make a difference, anyway.

A whistle like birdsong split the air, and scores of people – everyone but her minder, it seemed – burst from cover behind the trees, roaring as they rushed the train. One of the unlucky crew members fumbled for something at her belt; there was a loud crack, and she fell.

The other seven raised their hands.

While one contingent surrounded the seven crew members, the rest of the irregulars divided up and climbed aboard the train cars. Jane heard frightened shouts from the passengers and barked orders from the troops, but thankfully, nothing worse.

After several minutes of this, the train reached a kind of equilibrium, quiet and still but for the pacing guerrillas and their one-syllable shouts.

Jane glanced back toward the car she'd fled. The door was ajar, and one of the women peered inside, a rifle at the ready.

She felt another sharp poke in the ribs.

"You were in refuge there." Her minder nodded toward the car.

"Could not afford a ticket," Jane said, attempting the Continental accent again.

The man frowned, one plump lip ripening through his beard. "Wass others mit you?"

She had no love for Malone, but she wasn't prepared to turn the woman over to these bandits, insurrectionists, or whatever they were. "Just me," Jane said. "Sole."

He watched her a second as if giving her a chance to change her mind, then looked back toward Jane's abandoned freight car. Another man stood in the open door and shook his head.

Jane trapped the sigh of relief in her chest.

"You are picking a boocoo dangerous time to be voyaging alone," her minder said.

"Lucky I have you now," she said.

"Come," he said, leading her toward the troops gathering by the tracks. There was an anxious, jubilant energy amongst the crowd, as if they were thrilled with what they'd just pulled off but only half-believed their luck. A shorter man paced amongst them, exchanging words and cheek kisses with fraternal solemnity. From his posture and the way the others sought him out, Jane discerned that he was probably in charge of the group. There was something familiar about him that drew sweat from her brow despite the cool air.

He passed close enough that Jane could have touched him. Then he turned, and she saw the ragged scar along his cheek.

She remembered that face – that scar – from the posters at the airship station. It was Geist. Malone's ally, the man who wanted to kill Roman.

She lowered her head. If he was here, that could only mean he was still on Roman's trail. Though Jane couldn't yet be sure what he knew or what he – like her – had only guessed.

Jane allowed herself a brief moment of relief as she felt herself pushed past Geist and onto the train she'd just fled.

Malone had awoken to twilight in the train car. She'd been aware of something having changed without knowing quite what it was, and it was only after several groggy seconds that she realized the train had stopped and that Jane was gone.

But the sky through the hatch was the orange of a warning label, uncluttered by city or smoke.

Something had stopped them in the middle of nowhere, just like she and Geist had stopped the train to Nouvelle Paris the day before.

She'd awoken very quickly after that.

Exiting through the hatch or the great rolling doors seemed too conspicuous. Fortunately, there were doors on either end of the car, each opening toward the next. As long as there was no one with a clear line of sight toward her car, she wagered she'd be able to slip out unnoticed.

Better than waiting to get caught.

Moving quickly and quietly, Malone cleared the crates stacked near the forward door. She inched it open and squinted out of the sliver at a dark line of trees some one hundred feet away.

No sign of anyone yet.

Rhythmic patter broke the morning calm. It took Malone a moment to realize they sounded like footsteps, and a lot of them.

And they were drawing closer, approaching from the back of the train.

She could duck inside the car and hope they passed her by, but she needed to look for Jane, and she needed to know what was happening. The idea of being deaf and blind to whatever was underway seemed almost worse than getting caught.

Malone eased the door shut behind her and slid to the tracks below, scooting behind a row of massive wheels seconds before several pairs of feet – twenty on either side, she guessed – dashed by.

She scanned the space on either side of the train. No sign of Jane.

It was a tight squeeze beneath the cars, but there was just enough clearance for her to crawl forward so the enormous wheels shielded her from view. Between those wheels and the morning dimness, no one would spot her unless they were looking for her.

She'd begun working her way forward when she heard a whistle and saw scores of people dashing from the trees toward the train. She crawled behind another line of wheels.

Malone didn't recognize any of these people, but they looked like Geist's. And she suspected there weren't many other organized groups with a habit of stopping trains.

Whatever was happening, it was different from when she and Geist had slipped aboard the train outside of Nantes-Neugeboren.

A gunshot split the air. The men and women who had emerged from the forest were stomping through the freight cars, knocking over crates as they searched.

Malone peered between the wheels again. There, striding toward the train with a stiff-legged posture she'd come to recognize, was Geist. There was still no sign of Jane, but there was no way the laundress could have slipped past his men.

She was either being held somewhere in the woods, or she was already dead.

Yet even though Jane had been causing serious trouble for weeks now – and showed every sign of continuing to do so – Malone sincerely hoped the young laundress was alive somewhere and as well as circumstances permitted.

Meanwhile, she took advantage of the guerrillas' distraction with the train cars to crawl forward, slowly making her way toward the locomotive.

She'd only advanced a couple of cars when a pair of figures emerged from the trees. She quickly recognized Jane's outline and saw her being led toward the train.

Malone swallowed a curse. If Geist figured out who Jane was, he'd spare no effort in extracting Roman's whereabouts.

Given how poorly her luck seemed to be going, Malone had to assume that he'd succeed at both endeavors.

As she watched, Jane was pushed along to the front of the train, that stubborn, unreadable expression rigid on her face.

Not long after they disappeared, the train began to move.

Just as she had at the Porte Nord mooring tower, Malone realized that allowing Geist's plans to play out was the simplest, surest way of ensuring that any chance of opening the vault died with Roman. All she had to do was wait, and the train would roll past her.

It was a tempting prospect. But she'd never been any good at giving up on a case, even a hopeless one. Besides, Geist was reminding her entirely too much of Sato, and she would not make the mistake of elevating another firebrand.

Nor would she leave Jane to whatever tortures Geist might inflict on her.

She waited for the front of the next car to pass overhead. When it did, she grabbed at the coupling, pulling herself up while jogging madly backwards. She lifted herself free of the tracks just as the train began to pick up speed.

Malone climbed the ladder to the top of the car. She was near the middle of the train, and Geist, Jane, and most of the former's men had gone towards the front. She headed that way, moving as carefully and quietly as she could. She didn't know what she'd do when she got there, but she still had a dozen or so cars' worth of travel to figure it out.

CHAPTER TWENTY-SEVEN

THE TRAIN TO COLOGNE

As the train began to move once more, Jane was ushered into a service car just behind the locomotive. The lead passenger car, which was just behind that, was already overcrowded with its original passengers and the addition of Geist's troops. The narrow service car was spacious by comparison, even though it was constricted by shelves and cabinets and clogged with a handful of other prisoners. Crew, by the looks of their uniforms.

They all sat with their heads down and their hands clasped over their bent knees.

"Avant," said Jane's escort, prodding her in the back.

Stepping over the seated crew, she scanned the countertop for anything useful. Stemware hung from wire racks, and heavy pans clattered dangling from hooks.

And there, near the rear end of the counter, was a knife block. She made it a point not to stare as she was led past it.

"Setz," her escort said, pointing to a space between two of the seated crew. On the left was a man with graying hair, an elaborate crimson and blue uniform, and the kind of steely presence that made Jane think he'd been in a position of authority before people with guns had shown up. The man to her right looked barely older than her, with twitching eyes and lips that threatened tears and pleas.

She sat and watched her escort's curly ponytail as he retreated to the forward end of the car. Another guard with a shaggy mop of hair took up position at the rear, near the passenger car, and tapped an irregular rhythm with one foot.

Jane had encountered enough soldiers of various stripes to recognize that these two were not cut out for the job. They were soldiers by necessity, not profession, which could make them either more or less dangerous, depending on their temperament.

She couldn't face either of them right now, much less the rest of Geist's contingent. But she could, perhaps, learn something of where they were headed, and why.

Jane scooted toward the graying crewman, inch by agonizing inch, until the sudden stiffening of his shoulders told her he'd noticed her.

"Where are we going?" she whispered. She supposed they could still be headed to Cologne-de-le-Kur, but nothing was certain.

He angled his head toward her but said nothing. Maybe he hadn't understood her phrasing. Or maybe he didn't know.

"We... voyage?" she tried. "Where–"

"You will keep the silence," said the shaggy guard at the rear end of the car.

This set the younger crewman next to Jane into a blubbering fit of hysteria. "Pleece! Liberate me. I will spreck to no one!"

"Tranquil," said the ponytailed guard. "You will be staying here, und when we arrive to Cologne-de-le-Kur, then we shall liberate you all."

That answered one of Jane's questions, at any rate.

"You will arrive en tard," said a woman seated at the other end of the row. Her voice was sharp with defiance. "The senure returns und the people are knowing it."

"Silence," the shaggy guard repeated.

"Never," said the woman, her pitch rising. The younger crewman next to Jane began weeping; his older counterpart kept his face stony and still.

"You will keep silence or you will be dining on your dents," said the shaggy guard, taking the first slow steps toward the rebellious crewwoman. The promise of violence trailed him like a shadow.

Jane saw it unfolding in her mind's eye – another challenge from the prisoner, followed by a blow or a bullet from the guard. All because of the crewwoman's fealty to Roman, a man who had never desired anyone's allegiance.

She could not let that kind of violence happen for his sake even though he wasn't here to witness it.

"I must use the bathroom," Jane announced.

All heads turned toward her. Even the weeping crewman fell silent.

"Pleece," she added.

The ponytailed guard sighed and beckoned for her to rise. "Just keep it tranquil, ya?" he said with a scowl aimed at the other guard.

As Jane rose, the older crewman next to her lowered his head in a tiny nod.

The shaggy guard muttered something indistinct, backing toward his post.

"Come," Ponytail said, heading toward the rear of the car. Jane followed, casting a quick glance at the knife block.

The shaggy guard glowered at her as she squeezed past him.

"Prudence," he said, pushing the rear door open with a hard shove.

The roar of the tracks momentarily deafened her. For a moment, Jane stood frozen in the doorway, watching the ground blur by and thinking of the roaring, churning sea below Salvage.

She became aware of a nudge and an indistinct voice at her back. There was a small gap in the narrow walkway that connected the service car to the passenger car behind it. Two coupled bars of metal rattled below the gap, and Jane shuddered to think that this was all that connected them.

Then the door to the passenger car opened, and Jane hurried to safety.

Several dozen people were packed into a space intended for half their number. As Jane entered, most of them looked in her direction.

Just as quickly, they looked away and resumed furtive whispered conversations.

"The toilet," Ponytail said behind her, pointing over her shoulder and toward the far end of the car.

Even the open windows and ceiling vents did little to cool the overcrowded car. Jane stepped over people seated in the center aisle and maneuvered between others perched on the outer edges of the seats.

It was slow going, but it gave her a chance to hear something of what the passengers were whispering.

"– sole a rumor–"

"It is vert. I heard–"

"– cannot esteem them, what are they knowing?"

A sharp whistle pierced the air. A voice near the front of the car called out. "Silence, pleece!"

But the crowd had already discovered their captors' limits, or so it seemed. After a moment of quiet, the whispers resumed.

"– in an airship, ya–"

"But it is he? It is certain?"

Dread shivered through Jane's spine. She feared they were talking about Roman, but she needed to be sure.

"Pardon," she said, sidling past a man and a woman squeezed together in the aisle. "What is this everyone is sprecking?"

"You are not knowing?" the man asked.

"The senure appeared to Nouvelle Paris," the woman said, her expression beatific. "Und these brutes say his airship appeared aus of Cologne-de-le-Kur."

So Roman had continued on, presumably to destroy the vault on his own. The idea brought Jane a thrill of joy and a rush of nausea.

That certainly explained Geist's urgency. But if he'd caught wind of Roman's movements, then it was likely Rothbauer had, or soon would.

Leaving Roman trapped between two advancing forces, one of which would imprison him, and the other of which would kill him.

"Rasch, rasch," said the ponytailed guard, poking her in the back again.

Jane pressed forward. The bathroom was just a few crowded feet away.

She slipped inside, but as she pushed the door closed, a boot appeared in the gap.

Jane looked up at the ponytailed guard.

"You cannot be sole," he said, glancing at the floor between them.

She balked. "I won't do this."

He shrugged. "Then you will attend patient."

"Then you will have a very messy car on your hands," Jane said, summoning up all of her gravity.

Ponytail frowned.

"One minoot," Jane said.

"Und no more," he said, grudgingly withdrawing his foot.

The small washroom reminded her of her quarters on Salvage, except that it was actually larger. Jane relieved herself, washed up, and splashed water on her face. Even under the circumstances, it felt good to have a moment alone. A moment to think.

If the guards in the service car were telling the truth, all she needed to do was keep her head down until they reached Cologne-de-le-Kur.

But what if they weren't? She knew they'd left bombs on the mooring tower where she and Roman had been scheduled to land. What would people like that do to a train full of witnesses?

From what she'd heard, Geist didn't seem like the kind of man prone to wanton cruelty. But he didn't seem to have a problem with collateral damage, either.

After her original exile from Recoletta and her subsequent

manipulations at the hands of Lady Lachesse and the Qadi, Jane had decided that she would never again leave her fate in the hands of other people if she could help it.

She might be stuck on the train with Geist in the near term, but she'd prepare herself to escape when the opportunity presented itself.

There was a sharp knock at the door. "One minoot," said the guard.

Jane opened the door. She was ready.

Ponytail blinked as though he were surprised that she was still there. "Fini?"

"Ya," she said.

He frowned. "Your accent. I am noticing it is stark curious. Where are you from?"

Jane's veins turned to ice. But she remembered Roman's answer, or she thought she did. "Second Lichtenstein."

He nodded, still frowning. He seemed to believe her, but it was hard to tell. "Come mit," he said, gesturing back toward the service car.

Jane headed toward it, feeling a sudden stiffness in her legs.

Crossing the rattling walkway, Jane heard the commotion inside the service car before she saw it. Muffled shouts came from within, and Jane feared she'd made a mistake in leaving the temperamental guard alone with the others.

She pulled the door open. The shaggy guard and the defiant crewwoman were shouting at one another, both clearly beyond all reason. His hand was clenched around the grip of his pistol. The crewwoman either didn't notice or didn't care. She leaned forward, tension in every angle of her body, looking like she was ready to spring.

"Wass is this?!" roared the ponytailed guard from behind Jane. The shaggy guard and the crewwoman began talking at once.

And there, just to Jane's right, was the knife block. Close enough to grab, but not without being seen. Especially now that everyone was looking at the ponytailed guard behind her.

As she looked up, her eyes met those of the gray-haired crewman, and he gave her another barely perceptible nod.

Then he hollered at the top of his lungs.

The shaggy guard and the other prisoners turned to stare at him. Ponytail shoved past Jane, muttering angrily.

And for just a moment, everyone was turned away from her.

She grabbed at one of the shorter handles near the bottom of the block. A paring knife. Small enough to hide and sharp enough to matter.

She had it behind her back and was working it into the waistband of her trousers when a gunshot split the air. Ponytail was grimacing, his pistol held aloft.

"Tranquil und silence, pleece!" Ponytail said.

The others fell silent.

Ponytail pointed to her. "You. Setz."

Jane had the knife wedged awkwardly against her back. It felt secure, but it was also jabbing her in the buttocks.

She tried to keep the pain off her face as she returned to sit between the gray-haired crewman and the younger one. No sooner had she settled into place than the forward door burst open.

Geist stood in the threshold, a snarl of irritation on his lips.

"Wass is this?" he asked.

Ponytail lowered his head. "The voyagers became agitay. I–"

"You will make alles the voyagers agitay! Merde."

The rear door opened and another guard poked her head into the service car. Seeing Geist, she relaxed. "I heard–"

"Alles goot," Geist said, waving her off. "Go."

She ducked out of the service car.

"Now," Geist said. "You will explique the trouble." He looked between the two guards, his eyes hard with displeasure.

The ponytailed guard cleared his throat. "The defect is mine. I sortayed to escort her to the toilet." He pointed to Jane.

Geist's gaze fell on her, and Jane felt her stomach shrivel. "But she is not crew! Wass is she doing here?"

"She flet," Ponytail said. "When we halted the rail. She was refuging mit the cargo."

Geist's eyes glowed with intrigue. "Imposant," he said. He knelt, close enough that she could see the ripples in the scar along his cheek. His oiled hair was tangled in clumps, and his rumpled, dirty clothing looked – and smelled – as though he'd been on the run all day.

She resisted the urge to turn away. She was terrified that he'd somehow figure out who she was.

He cocked his head. "Regard me. Are you knowing who I am?"

It seemed like nearly everyone on the Continent – or at least the cities she'd visited – knew who Geist was.

Jane nodded.

He gave her a smile that appeared and vanished like steaming breath in winter air. "You are knowing we do not wish to harm you."

It wasn't clear whether this was a question or a statement.

"Why did you flet?" he asked.

She glanced at Ponytail's pistol and made a point of raising her eyebrows. The less she said, the better.

Geist chuckled. "But you are sprecking so little. Und I am not knowing who you are. Pleece." He opened a hand in invitation.

She waited, but it was clear he expected an answer. Unfortunately, she didn't know many Continental names, and if they were as distinct as the names on Salvage she couldn't expect to make one up.

"Ilse," she said, thinking of the first one that surfaced. She belatedly remembered where she'd heard it – it was the name of Roman's late mother.

She hoped it was common enough.

Geist nodded expectantly. "Ilse…?"

"Mueller." She'd heard that one recently, maybe among Rothbauer's staff, or maybe among the soldiers who'd arrested her back in Nouvelle Paris.

"Und why, Ilse Mueller, were you in refuge mit the cargo?" Geist's voice was low and dangerous, but his eyes gleamed with mirth.

"No ticket," she said, as quietly as she could.

"Wass regret." He leaned forward, perched on the balls of his feet. "But your accent. It is sounding familiar. Where have I known it?"

Again, Jane remembered Roman's answer. "Second Lichtenstein," she said, steeling her voice with more confidence than she felt.

The amusement vanished from Geist's face. "No. I am recognizing it now. You are a Pestelander. Und if you have come here…" He looked her up and down as if seeing her for the first time. "The waschergirl."

Jane would have denied it if she thought it would have done any good.

Instead, she took advantage of the momentary bewilderment to snatch the paring knife and drive it into Geist's thigh.

He screamed. Jane ran for the door at the forward end of the car.

Malone watched the scene play out from the roof of the service car, peering through an open ceiling vent. She couldn't make out the conversation between Geist and Jane, but she was almost certain it meant trouble.

Her suspicions were confirmed when the laundress plunged a knife into the man's leg, bless her.

She popped up and clambered to the forward end of the service car as the sounds of a fight broke out below her. Despite the odds, she was glad for the change in pace. Her hands and face had started to go numb from the wind.

Malone climbed down from the roof just in time to see Jane darting across the gap to the locomotive. The young woman tried the door, but to no avail. When she turned and saw Malone watching her on the opposite platform, her surprise was such that Malone was thankful she'd already disposed of her knife.

"You," Jane said, her face pale.

"I want to get us both out of here," said Malone. "So find a way in while I hold Geist off."

For the moment, it appeared to be enough. Jane tried the handle again, and Malone flattened herself next to the door of the service car and waited.

Seconds later, it slammed open. A guard with shaggy hair emerged onto the landing, gun drawn. Malone braced herself against the rail and planted a kick in the man's chest, fast enough that he didn't see it coming and she didn't have time to consider it.

He sailed over the opposite railing with a cry and disappeared.

Malone grabbed for the door. In the instant that she reached across the threshold, she caught Geist staring at her open-mouthed, an indistinct tableau of violence situated around him.

She pulled the door shut. "How's it coming?" she hollered to Jane.

"I'll tell you when I get there." The laundress was climbing up the ladder toward the roof of the locomotive. After a few moments, she disappeared over the lip of the roof, and Malone returned her focus to the door.

A gunshot rang from within the service car, and a hole appeared in the wood paneling a few feet away.

Whatever Jane was doing, Malone hoped she did it fast.

Presently, Geist's voice rose on the other side of the door. "Malone. It is not entirely dessplessant to be seeing you again."

"So come out and say hello," she shouted back, hoping he wouldn't call her bluff.

She could hear the smile in his voice. "I am not thinking you are armed, but I am not liking unnecessary hazard." He paused. "I am also comprending why you had such trouble with your waschergirl."

Malone felt herself grin.

"I am regretting the way of our parting," Geist said. "I had no desire to cause you mal."

Nor much of a desire to avoid it, apparently. "What about the rest of the people on the tower?" she asked.

"A catastrophe," he said. "But necessary to eliminate Roman Arnault. I was thinking you would comprend."

The door to the locomotive rasped open. Jane stood in the doorway, and behind her a balding man held a gun to her head.

"Capitulate, pleece," he said.

"Do not assassinat the waschergirl!" Geist roared. "She is utile!"

The balding man looked from Geist's direction to Malone's. He turned the gun toward her.

Jane drove her elbow straight back into the man's gut. He cried out and doubled over. The laundress began raining punches and kicks on him with amateurish technique but admirable vigor.

Malone crossed the gap to the struggling pair and kicked the man's right hand. He released the gun.

She scooped it up and spun around just in time to see Geist rushing at her. She squeezed off a shot. It went wide, and Geist dove back into the service car.

"We have one of yours now!" Jane yelled, nerves and defiance trembling in her voice.

"Assassinat him if you must," Geist said. "He comprends our cause."

The two women looked at each other.

"Don't move," Malone said to the man, pointing the gun at him. She jerked her head in the direction of the locomotive. She and Jane both ducked inside, leaving Geist's balding ally seated on the exposed platform.

"We can't hold them off all the way to Cologne," Jane said.

Nor could they afford to let Geist follow so close on their heels. But as Malone had made her way along the train cars, she'd noted the link-and-pin connections holding them together.

"We'll separate the cars," Malone said. "Leave them stranded and take the locomotive." Geist would eventually follow, no doubt, but the move would buy them precious hours. Maybe more, depending on how long it took him to find another transport.

Jane nodded. "You," she said to the balding man. "Reach into the gap and unhook the train cars."

He shook his head. "Boocoo risk."

Malone gestured to her gun. "More than this?"

He frowned and appeared to consider. "Do not be shooting me, pleece," he said, holding one hand up while he maneuvered himself to the edge of the platform and the gap between it and the service car. "The difficulty is tension," he said, reaching down. "You–"

A gunshot cracked, and the balding man fell in a spray of crimson and bone. Malone leaned out long enough to see another of Geist's troops – this one with a long ponytail whipping in the wind – kneeling on the roof of the service car.

She took a shot and heard a scream as she ducked back into the locomotive.

The balding man lay sprawled across the platform, his head a bloody ruin.

Malone held the gun out to Jane. "Cover me. I'll work that pin loose."

But Jane shook her head, her face pale as she looked at the gun. "I'll go. They won't risk shooting me."

Malone wasn't certain about that, but there was no point in arguing. She was undoubtedly the better shot, anyway.

"Work fast," she said.

The laundress darted onto the platform and, grimacing, dragged the corpse out of the way. The door of the service car swung as the train bounced along, flapping open to reveal an empty aisle. Geist must have retreated to get clear of her line of sight.

Or to muster more soldiers from the passenger car.

Jane, meanwhile, was perched at the edge of the platform, her arm darting in and out of the gap.

"How's it coming?" Malone asked.

"– stuck," Jane said, turning. "Too much tension between the cars."

Which was what the balding man had been telling them before he died. Malone took quick stock of the space inside the locomotive. There was a forbidding-looking control panel against the forward window. Surely one of the levers or knobs would slow the train enough to pull the pin.

"Back away from the edge," she called. "I'll try and slow us down."

The controls reminded her of the ones she'd seen on the *Glasauge* – there were a few large-handled levers, several rows of toggles, and an array of meters and dials with twitching needles and foreign text.

She found a red handle hanging near the window. Easy to see and easy to grab – that seemed like the kind of thing that would slow a train in a pinch. She pulled it.

A whistle shrieked from the roof of the locomotive.

"Malone!"

She looked back. Jane was still crouched on the platform, and beyond her several figures were advancing down the service car.

Malone took a shot at the middle of the group. One of the figures staggered, and the others backed to the rear of the car, dragging him along.

She could buy them time, but she couldn't hold them off forever. Especially not with four shots remaining in the cylinder.

She turned back to the control panel. There was another red handle, this one attached to a long lever. She pulled it.

The tracks below shrieked, and Malone was thrown against the control panel. The locomotive was slowing, much faster than she'd hoped.

She looked back. Jane had slid halfway through the door and was crawling back to the gap. A few of Geist's troops lay in a heap on the floor of the service car.

Then Jane reached into the gap and pulled out a long, metal bar.

"I've got it!" she shouted, pale but beaming.

"Great," Malone called. "Now take the gun and hold them off while I get us moving again."

Jane came over and took the gun. Malone could tell she was making a mighty effort to keep her hands from shaking.

"You can do this," Malone told her, realizing that was probably more of a comfort than 'you've done this before.'

The laundress nodded and scurried back to the doorway, and Malone returned to the control panel.

She raised the red lever, and the squealing noise and the deceleration stopped, but they weren't picking up any speed.

She scanned the meters and found one labeled "Rapidity." Its needle fluttered counterclockwise, winding slowly down to zero. Below it was a lever. She tried to push it up, but it was stuck.

A shot rang out. The troops had advanced halfway down the service car. Jane had fired and missed, and they were still coming.

She turned back to the controls. There had to be something nearby, she just had to stay calm enough to find it.

There. Just below the lever was a wheel – one that reminded her of a release valve she'd seen on the *Glasauge*. She spun it and felt a hissing in the machinery beneath her feet.

She tried the lever again. This time, it slid up easily. The needle on the meter twitched, then began ticking its way clockwise again.

They were picking up speed.

Another shot sounded. Jane had missed again, and Geist's people were stumbling toward the end of the service car.

They looked like they already knew they wouldn't make it.

As the locomotive pulled ahead, Geist appeared between his men, looking both furious and anguished. He shouted something, but by then Malone and Jane were too far ahead to hear.

Malone slammed the door and took a moment to enjoy the quiet, closing her eyes.

Her ears were still ringing from the shouting, the gunfire, and the noise of the tracks. But when she opened her eyes again, she saw the laundress staring at her, a look of expectation on her face.

"I said, 'thanks,'" Jane said, her arms crossed and the gun in one hand.

"You can thank me by sticking with me."

Jane gave her a careful stare. "What are you going to do when we find Roman?"

Malone sighed and nodded at the gun. "Are you going to shoot me if I tell you I'll arrest him?"

Jane looked surprised to see she still had it. After a brief hesitation, she handed it back.

"I've been making most of this up as I go along," Malone said, which was the truth. "I let him go because I didn't want to see him killed. I still don't. But I also don't want him used to unleash something awful." She didn't know how else to describe the threat of the vault, but Jane seemed to take her meaning.

"Then we've got to hurry. I heard people saying that his airship had been spotted outside of Cologne. Where we're headed."

"That's why Geist hijacked this train," Malone said.

Jane nodded.

"And that's where the vault is."

She nodded again. "And if Geist found out, then Rothbauer will, too."

"That's what I was thinking," Malone said. And he would bring his own forces and resources, which were likely many times greater than Geist's. "We've got to hurry," Malone agreed.

Jane cast a worried eye at the controls. "Can you... manage this?"

"Close enough," Malone said. "And I've got time to figure it out."

CHAPTER TWENTY-EIGHT
THE VAULT

After a few hours, another ragged skyline appeared on the horizon. To Jane, it looked even more chaotic than Nouvelle Paris's had, but then again the hours on the locomotive, waiting to arrive and wondering what she'd find, had worn her nerves raw.

Malone manipulated the various knobs and wheels and slowed the train well before they'd reached the outskirts of the city. "I'm not sure how long it'll take us to stop," she admitted. "Besides, I'd rather not have to answer to anyone at the station. Wherever that is."

Jane agreed.

They slid to a halt outside a jumble of low, tumbledown houses that reminded Jane of the factory districts back in Recoletta. No one came to see as they exited the locomotive.

"Where do you suppose everyone is?" she asked Malone.

The inspector pressed her lips into a hard line. "If what you heard is true – if Arnault made a scene on his way here – then maybe people went to watch. Or hide."

The thought tied knots in Jane's stomach. She and Malone hurried on, following the tallest towers like beacons.

The sky grew dim and gray with clouds as Cologne-de-le-Kur constricted around them. They were surrounded by domes, pyramids, and spires when they finally came to an open square and the rapt crowd packed within it.

Malone froze, tense and ready to bolt. Jane felt a buzz of alarm, too, but this group looked different from the one in Nouvelle Paris.

"I think it's okay," she said. "They don't seem agitated."

Malone frowned at her. "That can change fast."

"We don't even know where we're headed. Let me just see what's going on, all right?"

The inspector sighed. "Fine. Just keep to the fringe."

Jane found a man near the back of the crowd. He held a wide-brimmed hat in both hands and watched the sky with eyes full of reverence.

"Pardon," Jane said. "Wass is happening here?"

He kept his gaze fixed on the sky. "The guards obstruct the streets beyond. But it is just apparent." He pointed to a gap between the buildings. Amongst the low, gray clouds was the unmistakable bulk of an airship.

"The senure encurves there, the same plass, for many hours," the man continued.

"The same... plass?" Jane asked. "Wass is there?"

"Unter him is the Gran Platz. Mit the monument of the Kur, of course."

Jane looked at Malone. "The vault," she said. The inspector's eyes were wide with dread.

A woman standing near them turned to Jane. Hope and joy shone in her face. "He is attending patient. So that the people are gathering for his arrivage."

Another man turned, sniffing and shaking his head. "It is a crypted message. An hour for every yar of his absence."

Malone spoke up. "You said the guards are clearing the streets?"

"Ya. Ahead," the first man said. He had lost interest and was already staring back up at the airship.

Jane turned back to Malone. "We've got to find a way to reach him before the city officials do."

Malone nodded. "This way."

They sped through the streets, following the beacon of the airship as it vanished and reappeared amidst the buildings. It certainly looked like the one she and Roman had taken from the coast, but then again, most of them looked similar to her.

"Checkpoint ahead," Malone said, pointing to a line of guards standing across the road. A few other onlookers milled about, no doubt hoping for a closer glimpse of their savior.

"There has to be a way around," Jane said. "They can't have the whole city covered."

"Let's try a smaller street," Malone said.

Unfortunately, Cologne's streets were just as tortuous as those of Nouvelle Paris. When they finally found one that curved back in the direction of the airship, they found it also blocked with guards.

"Maybe the next one," Malone said. "There's got to be one that's open."

"We don't have time to keep going in circles," Jane said. It felt like whatever lead they'd gotten on Geist was evaporating. She considered the guards. There looked to be six or seven of them – enough to span the street with only a carriage's breadth between them. There were perhaps three or four score civilians loitering in the street ahead of them.

Enough to overwhelm the guards.

"I've got an idea," Jane said. "Give me the gun."

Malone started back. "You can't–"

"I'm not going to shoot anyone," Jane said.

Malone raised an eyebrow.

"I'm going to start a distraction." She held out her hand.

Sighing through her nose, Malone handed over the gun.

It felt heavy, but not as heavy as Jane had remembered it feeling before. She took a deep breath to steel herself, realizing that this could backfire very badly.

Malone was watching her through slitted eyes, every muscle in her body telegraphing tension. "Put your thumb on the hammer and–"

"I know what to do," Jane said, more peevishly than she'd

intended. "Just get ready to run." She pointed the gun into the sky and fired.

The crowd echoed the gunshot with a chorus of screams. Jane put the gun away and screamed, too, hoping to blend in amidst the general panic.

Malone just stood there, half-crouched, looking like she was ready to pounce on someone.

But that didn't seem to matter. The crowd was already surging forward, pushing past the guards shouting for calm.

"Let's go!" Jane said. She took off, threading her way through the panicking mass. She'd always had a knack for blending in and moving unseen, which served her well here. When she reached the head of the swarm, where the guards were still heroically waving and hollering, she darted past them, ducking between flailing arms and legs.

Over her shoulder, Malone, gangly and built for confrontation, was still struggling to the edge of the crowd. Nevertheless, Jane didn't dare stop until she'd reached a bend several dozen yards away.

She was still catching her breath when Malone joined her, panting raggedly.

"I don't think anyone was paying any attention to us," Malone said, jerking her head back toward the street, where others were still fleeing. "Still, let's take the rest of this more... slowly."

Jane nodded as she heaved another deep breath.

The streets of Cologne-de-le-Kur were eerily quiet. As they walked, Jane noticed flickers of movement behind windows and in the shadows of alleys, but everyone left seemed to be hiding.

And watching.

Above and about a mile away, Roman's airship was still circling.

"What do you suppose he's doing?" Jane asked. If this was a distraction, it was certainly an effective one. She wondered if perhaps that hadn't been the point after all – to keep people watching the airship while he fled.

"You're the one who said he came all this way to destroy the vault," Malone said.

She was right. Jane couldn't imagine Roman going through all this just to abandon it.

"We didn't get around to planning specifics," Jane said.

Malone gave her a look of quiet judgment.

Jane shrugged. "We didn't know what we'd find. Or what our options would be."

The inspector snorted. "You hoped you'd just stumble across a few sticks of explosives? Places like that are made to be indestructible. Even Geist said it couldn't be destroyed by normal means, not without–"

Malone broke off and stopped dead in her tracks.

Jane's mouth felt dry. "What is it?"

The inspector turned her cold, pale eyes on the airship. "I'm so sorry," she said.

Jane looked up, too, and saw the floating behemoth's nose angled sharply down.

With a drop in her stomach, she understood that Roman meant to crash it into the vault.

Malone's arms were around her before she could take off running. "Let me go!" Jane screamed. "Get off me!"

"I'm sorry," Malone said. "There's nothing we can do."

She knew the inspector was right even though she wasn't ready to accept it. "We can signal to him. We can get to the guards. We can..." But she trailed off as she watched the airship plummet, dipping below the skyline.

For a brief moment, it vanished entirely, and Jane could hope that it might resurface elsewhere, fading into the horizon.

Then there was a distant roaring, and a plume of flame rose in the sky.

The vision blurred, and Jane sobbed against Malone's sleeve.

After a while, she became aware of the other woman's voice. "You did everything you could, Jane."

But that wasn't entirely true. There was still one more thing she could do for Roman.

"We can make sure that damn vault doesn't outlive him," she said, brushing tears from her cheeks.

After a moment, Malone released her. "Okay. But careful. And quiet."

The previously calm streets had erupted in panic. The people who had been hiding now leaned out of windows or fled toward the blockades.

At least no one would be paying attention to them now.

They dashed through the winding streets, following the glow of the blaze. Jane tried to prepare herself for what it would look like. She tried to remind herself that whatever happened would have happened quickly.

Still, when they emerged into a broad square and saw the collapsed, burning scaffolding of the airship, she stopped.

Whatever had been beneath the airship was now a crushed, smoking ruin, as were the buildings to either side.

"He's definitely destroyed... something," Malone said.

A moderate crowd had gathered around the site, held back by the heat of the fire. They were talking animatedly among themselves, gesturing at the sky and the wreckage. Jane and Malone approached, and as they did, Jane noticed something strange.

They didn't seem to be panicking.

They were a strange assortment, red-eyed but energetic, dressed in the motley styles of the Continent. Scattered amongst the crowd were a few people in familiar uniforms. Not guards or police, Jane realized, but something else.

Airship crew.

Jane tapped the nearest crew member on the shoulder. "Pardon," she said. "Wass is happening here?"

"We must attend patient," the man said. "It–"

A uniformed woman standing next to him turned and noticed Jane. "Ach, I am recalling you," she said. "You were voyaging with him."

Suddenly, Jane recognized the other woman, too. She was

the crew member who had beaten Roman until Jane revealed his identity.

"He will be most joyous to see you," the crewwoman said. "So I am hoping." She turned back to the wreckage with a worried frown.

"What are you talking–" Jane began, but then Malone grabbed her arm.

"Look," the inspector said, pointing at something away from the wreckage.

Two figures were approaching from the other end of the plaza, talking and clapping each other on the back. One walked with a distinctive limp.

"Roman!" Jane ran toward him and found her own astonishment and joy mirrored on his face.

"Jane," he said, wrapping her up in his arms. He smelled like sweat, smoke, and machine oil, and at that moment, there was nothing so wonderful.

Jane sobbed, her eyes warm with tears of relief.

"I'm so sorry for leaving you behind," he said. "I was coming back, but I had to make sure the vault could never–"

She kissed him. She felt his surprise, and then his relief, in the movement of his hands on her face, his lips on hers. The truth was that she'd never been more proud of him. The man who had spent a lifetime running from his duty and legacy had finally accepted both on his own terms.

Jane stepped back and finally noticed the figure standing next to Roman, a man with a voluminous gray mustache. He was politely averting his eyes.

"Arnault." Malone's voice and rapid footsteps rose behind Jane. "I wasn't expecting to see you after that."

Roman blinked at her in shock, then looked to Jane. "Did you two…"

"We don't have a lot of time," Malone said. "Geist's on our trail, and your uncle's people won't be far behind." She jerked a thumb over her shoulder. "Is that the vault? Destroyed for good?"

Roman's eyes narrowed. "That was the vault. Now, it is slowly turning to slag and ash. But if you have any doubts, you're welcome to check yourself," Roman said with a wry smile.

"What exactly happened?" Jane asked.

"We pulled away after the explosions at the Porte Nord mooring. I saw that you were alive and being taken into custody. The crew assured me you would be looked after until I arrived. They were initially determined to take me to another mooring tower, but I convinced them against it." He hesitated. "I don't think they would have listened, but the bombs changed the circumstances considerably."

"What did you tell them?" Malone asked.

"I told them the truth," Roman said. "That the buried cities were no threat to them and that the vault was a great danger. Not all of them believed me, but enough of them did."

"The senure made a most impassioned argument," the mustachioed man said.

"Didn't realize you were one for speeches," Malone said, her arms crossed.

"I can do what needs doing," Roman said. "Anyway, I discussed a plan with Captain Vicenzo and his crew. We dropped off most of the passengers just outside the city – a tricky operation under the circumstances, but Vicenzo is an excellent pilot."

The mustachioed man bowed.

"But many of them insisted on coming." Roman nodded to the crowd, most of whom waited a respectful distance away. "Said they wanted to see history. And help out however they could afterwards." He paused, watching them with what seemed to be genuine affection. And perhaps a little guilt for allowing them to get caught up in his predicament.

"So they entered the city on foot while you came in by airship," Jane said.

Roman nodded. "And then we circled. The remaining crew parachuted away, but I had to give the city authorities time to clear the area. Not to mention that lining up the approach was challenging with just the two of us." He glanced to Vicenzo.

"The senure apprends most rasch," said the captain.

"Vicenzo gives me too much credit." Roman turned and contemplated the burning husk of the airship. In the pale gray morning, with the orange firelight flickering over his face, he looked younger than Jane had ever seen him. "Anyway, the vault is gone, and present company excluded, most people will think I am, too."

Vicenzo held a finger to his lips. "We will maintain the senure's secret."

"Perhaps now we can disappear. Enjoy as many years of quiet as we can manage." Roman looked at Jane as he spoke, and she felt a warmth that had nothing to do with the blaze nearby.

"This isn't over yet," Malone said. "Rothbauer's still going to take the Continent to war against the buried cities. Assuming Geist doesn't carve this place up first."

"What do you suggest?" Roman asked, frowning. "Because I'm not getting caught up in another revolution."

"This is about your family's dynasty," Malone said, color rising in her pale face. "You can't do nothing."

"I can't do anything," Roman snarled. "Rothbauer doesn't need me, he needs a war. An enemy. He'll attack the buried cities no matter what I say. And if you're suggesting I aid Geist," he said, giving her a measured stare, "well, I would hope we both learned our lesson with Sato."

"There's got to be someone else," Malone said, but even Jane could tell she was grasping at straws.

"The problem isn't with these people, it's with this place," Roman said, throwing his arms wide. "Their damn obsession with their history. They've spent generations building up their walls, sending spies across the sea, preparing themselves for the day when they either wipe out the remnant in the buried cities or are destroyed by it. They call us 'the Plaguelands,' Malone. This is the only story these people have ever known."

As Jane listened to Roman, her mind wandered back to all the stories she'd heard and told – about the dangers of pre-

Catastrophe knowledge, the reasons and ways leaders had seized and lost power – and the way those stories had shaped Recoletta, the farming communes, and the other buried cities.

It was a humbling thought, that something as simple as a story could change a way of life. But she'd seen it. And when she'd brought the story of Sato's revolt to the farmers, she'd made it happen.

She thought back to the book she'd taken from Salvage and its tales of the strange and wonderful things people had built. She still wasn't sure if it was true, but if it was…

"What if we gave them a different story?" Jane asked.

Roman and Malone fell silent, both turning to look at her.

"Roman, do you still have the book I gave you?" Dread prickled at her neck. She hoped it hadn't been left on the airship.

But Roman pulled the familiar volume from his back pocket and gave it to her. She brushed the grime off the cover with its field of stars and its short, simple title: *ESA*. Then she flipped to the middle, where pages showed pictures of enormous, unfathomable machines. Worlds that looked like marbles and dewdrops hanging against the night sky.

"What am I looking at?" Malone asked, squinting at the page.

"People built these things," Jane said.

"Why?"

"To go places. To see things."

Malone glanced up at her. "And?"

She suppressed a sigh of exasperation. "That's not – the point is, they built them. And they built them with our ancestors. Look." She flipped through a series of pictures that showed ancient people in strange suits laughing, talking, shaking hands.

Malone stopped her hand and leaned in closer. "I've seen that place," she said, tapping a picture that showed a happy ceremony in front of a tall, pointed pillar of some kind. "It's fallen over now. But it's near the Library. Near Recoletta."

Roman was only watching quietly, his lips pressed into a thoughtful line.

"So, what are you saying?" Malone asked. "That we tell people that we all used to get along?"

Jane gnawed her lip. This was the difficult part. "It's not just about the past. I'm saying we give people a new future. One in which we're building things like this. Not fighting old wars." She stole a glance at Roman out of the corner of her eye. "But it'll take leadership. Someone directing the Continent away from war and toward something more concrete. Constructive."

"A Gran Meisterwork," Roman muttered.

Jane nodded.

"I hate to tell you this," Malone said, "but you're going to need more than a book. For starters, you're going to need proof this stuff actually existed."

Jane flipped to a map in the back. "There were places all over the Continent. Maybe one of these sites would have something."

But Roman shook his head, and Jane felt her heart sink.

"Chances are anything useful would have been taken for scrap or built over a long time ago. We could look, but–"

Vicenzo cleared his throat. He was standing next to Roman, peering at one side of the map. "Pardon. But I am thinking maybe that one still exists." He tapped a dot with a most curious label: Noordwijk.

"What's special about that one?" Malone asked.

"It is in the Flooded Lands."

"How do we get there?" Jane asked.

"We will be needing an airship. There is a mooring tower on the nord of the city. I am certain none would refuse the senure if he wished to requisition one," Vicenzo said, eying Roman.

Roman nodded.

Malone crossed her arms, staring at the map. "Geist'll follow. Maybe Rothbauer, too."

"Then we hurry," Roman said. "The lead we've got now is our best hope."

CHAPTER TWENTY-NINE
THE FLOODED LANDS

The new airship was like the *Glasauge*, only larger and more lavish. They were speeding along as fast as it would allow. Even so, Malone was told their journey would take several hours. She supposed she should take the opportunity to rest, but she couldn't sit still for any length of time.

Most of the crew and passengers who had followed Arnault to Cologne-de-le-Kur had insisted on joining him for this journey, too. The remainder who had stayed behind had promised to spread word of the discovery in the Flooded Lands and his new Gran Meisterwork. Malone was surprised at the loyalty the man inspired, but at the moment it seemed useful enough.

Now she just hoped there was really something to find. And that it was enough for Rothbauer, Geist, and the hopeful multitudes of the Continent.

So, as the hours wore on, she paced between the cockpit and the aft lounge, watching the sky behind them for signs of pursuit and the land below them for anything else.

For a few hours, all she saw were gray skies and green fields.

She was in the cockpit with Captain Vicenzo when an expanse of water appeared on the horizon. Her skin prickled with cold.

"The place is Old Holland," Vicenzo said. "Once, it was a busy und prosperous nation."

Malone contemplated the flooded landscape through the

window. "What happened?"

"They used pumps und dams to keep their lands dry. But after the war and the great sickness – the one the senure's forefather cured – few people remained. They did not comprend the engines that kept their cities from sinking." He shrugged. "They flet. The sea took its tithe."

It was as likely as anything she'd learned about the pre-Catastrophe people in the last few days. "Seems like a bad spot for cities in the first place," she said.

Vicenzo considered the view. "If Dame Jane's book is vert, then the anciens left even grander things here."

Malone looked out the window, watching the still waters. Doubt gnawed at her even now, even after all she'd seen. Skepticism was a hard habit for a detective to break, and stories of airships that flew to the stars seemed too fantastical to be true.

"Do you think we'll find anything?" she finally asked.

"The senure does," Vicenzo said. "That is sufficient for me. Und for the others who have come."

It wasn't an answer, but hers had been a pointless question. One way or another, they were out of places to run.

The thought left her tired and a little relieved.

"I'm going to lie down," Malone said. "Wake me if anything happens."

She stretched out on a couch in the first-class deck, not particularly caring how unprofessional it appeared. She fell asleep almost instantly and dreamed of falling and crashing.

She dreamed of the *Glasauge*.

In her dream, Geist's crew were running around, trying futilely to keep the airship aloft. But it was plummeting, the world outside the windows looming closer and larger. Only Lachesse stood by, either unconcerned by their plight or else resigned to it.

Malone herself moved with the same clumsy torpor that afflicted her in every dream.

She tried to grab Lady Lachesse's arm, but she couldn't seem to move her own hands. "Run," Malone said, "We've got to get off this ship."

Lachesse looked at Malone with something between amusement and exasperation. "I wouldn't have thought the woman who survived her own hanging could be defeated so easily."

"The ship's crashing. We're going to die." *You're going to die.*

The whitenail shook her head. "You used every excuse you could find to go sleuthing around, avoiding the political responsibilities with which you'd been entrusted."

"Please," Malone said, wanting the dream to end even as she knew how it would play out. "I can't save you."

The woman laughed. "I know you'll do what's necessary."

The dream ended with a jolt. Someone was gripping Malone's shoulders and shaking her awake.

It was a young crewman; his face was rigid with panic.

"An airship follows. We must be landing, und quickly."

A strip of land had emerged from the water about an hour ago. Sitting next to Roman, his hand in hers, Jane watched it so intently, looking for any signs of the wondrous site from her book, that she nearly jumped when Captain Vicenzo approached, tense but composed.

"Senure, Dame Jane, we must begin debarking. An airship follows, und after the senure's... demonstration in Cologne-de-le-Kur, it is imprudent to descend on top of the site itself."

"But where is the site?" Jane asked. So far she had seen only rolling meadows, broken up occasionally by crumbling stone buildings and the bald spots of pre-Catastrophe roads. Certainly nothing that looked like a repository of miracles.

Vicenzo winced. "Comprend, the maps of this place are stark ancient. Und the land changes much. But I am thinking we are close. A few kilometers away at most."

"A brisk walk, then," Roman said.

Vicenzo bowed. "Assuredly."

"Do we know who's following us?"

Again, Vicenzo looked pained. "I regret there is no way to know until they are much closer."

"Thank you," Roman said. "Please make preparations to land. We'll be ready."

Vicenzo departed with another bow, and Roman gave Jane's hand a squeeze. She looked at him, hoping – as she suspected he was – that it was Rothbauer in pursuit. Rothbauer, at least, wanted to keep Roman alive. Jane suspected he could be reasoned with if they could find the site and convince him of its value. With the vault gone, the site and any ancient machines there could become a potent symbol for a united future.

Geist, on the other hand...

"Let's find the site first. We can worry about the rest later," Roman said, squeezing her hand again.

But the thought of coming so far and accomplishing so much only to lose him again was nearly unbearable.

The airship shuddered as they set down – Jane could see why tower moorings were preferable. By the time they'd all filed out and into the grass, the pursuing craft was the size of a saucer on the horizon.

Malone was pacing, watching the approaching ship and the open fields with a sleep-reddened but alert gaze. Captain Vicenzo was making a headcount of thirty or so passengers and crew and passing out small whistles that glinted in the late afternoon light. Each was strung on a cord. Jane slipped hers around her neck.

When Vicenzo was done, he clapped his hands for silence. "Pleece, we must proceed quickly. We space ourselves und continue west in formation. I will take one end und Lieutenant Yulia the other. Attempt to maintain some visual contact mit the person on either side." He held up the whistle around his neck. "One tone for something of interest, two for danger."

With that, they headed west, spreading out in a wide file. Jane was somewhere near the middle of the row, with Roman on one side and Malone on the other. The small comfort she felt at having them both close evaporated when she looked over her shoulder and saw the mysterious airship drawing closer still.

Before long, they came to the ruins of an old town, now overgrown with vegetation. The deteriorating buildings provided some cover, yet Jane quickly lost sight of Roman and Malone. Behind and above her, the climbing trees and tumbling walls blocked her view of the horizon. In the brief glimpses she caught, however, there was no sign of the airship.

Which likely meant it had landed, or was close to doing so.

She had just reached a break in the ruins when she heard two distant trills behind her and to her right.

Followed by gunfire.

Jane ran. The ruined buildings were receding back into the earth, replaced by scrubby trees and tall grass. Roman and Malone were still nowhere in sight – she supposed they'd lost each other amidst the ruins. In fact, they all probably had.

She found the callus of an old road and followed it. Two more whistle blasts sounded. Still behind her, but closer. She threw herself into another burst of speed.

Her legs were burning when she finally heard a single whistle tone. It was coming from a spot ahead of her and a little to the right. She pointed herself toward the sound, hoping to reach it before their pursuers did the same.

Three whistle blasts sounded from somewhere to her left. Three more distantly behind her. She didn't remember a signal for three blasts, unless –

Of course. The others were distracting the pursuers. Drawing them away so that she and Roman – and anyone else nearby – could converge upon the source of the single blast.

She was heaving for breath when she came upon Malone, standing next to a heavy cone that lay on its side. The former inspector was glaring at it as though she still weren't sure what to make of it.

"This looked like one of the things from your book," Malone said.

Jane reached out and felt the cold metal, rough with peeling paint. It was real. Her heart thudded in her chest.

Roman came dashing around the corner, his face glowing with exertion and surprise. "Is that–?"

A whistle shrieked twice from the woods that Jane had just emerged from.

"No time," Malone said. "Inside."

A building stood behind Malone. The glass panes along the front were either frosted with filth or shattered entirely.

The blocky letters above the entrance read: European Space Research and Technology Centre.

Jane followed the others inside, through one of the broken windows, her heart in her mouth.

They had entered a large room. It was dark but for the light coming through the broken windows. A broad hallway burrowed further into the shadows. Jane and the others followed it.

"Look," Malone said. "Light."

A wide set of double doors stood at the far end of the hall. A faint, grayish glow seeped out from beneath them.

Jane tried the handle, but it was stuck tight. "Locked," she said. "Or jammed just as good."

"Maybe there's another way around," Roman said. "We–"

Two whistle blasts. Not far from the shattered entrance, by the sound of it.

Roman aimed a kick at the door which shuddered but held fast. He tried another.

"Move," Malone said, barreling toward them. She was holding a bulky red canister, and she brought it down hard on the door handle as Roman jumped out of the way.

The handle fell away after another two blows. The door swung open, and for a moment no one said a word.

Jane, Malone, and Roman stared at a large, high room. Part of the ceiling had collapsed, leaving a pile of rubble in the center of the room and diffuse daylight that illuminated marvels.

A spindly apparatus lay on the floor, looking like two pairs of mated dragonflies, with long, tubular segments connected to iridescent, rectangular panels. Near it, on a bed of sand that had spilled and spread throughout the old room, was a clunky contraption with a body like a turtle shell set on wheels, topped by a long-necked head. In a different corner was another rounded cone, much like the one outside, only larger and still coated in paint. On it was an emblem – a blue and green planet, the dragonfly apparatus soaring triumphantly above it.

Malone swallowed. "Is that–?"

Jane could hardly contain herself. Everything she'd read, everything she'd hoped for, was true. "That one sent pictures from other worlds," she said, pointing to the turtle-like device. "And that was one of the airships that sailed beyond the clouds." She pointed to the cone. But it was the dragonfly apparatus that truly excited her. "That's where people lived. Pre-Catastrophe people from every part of the world, all watching the stars together."

From the other end of the hallway came the sound of breaking glass and tense, shouting voices.

"Hide," Malone said to Jane and Roman. "I'll handle this."

Malone watched as Jane and Arnault scurried into something that looked like a very large and very complex tin can.

From the sound and timbre of the voices in the hall, she'd realized that it was Geist who had followed them.

She felt naked standing in the open without a weapon, but she realized a gun would do her little good now. Killing Geist wouldn't be enough, just as deposing Ruthers and killing Sato hadn't been enough. Either she'd convince him to lay down his arms – Sundar's way – or she'd at least provide enough of a distraction for Jane and Arnault to run. Doing what was necessary, as Lachesse would have called it.

Geist emerged from the hall seconds later, leading a handful of his irregulars. His eyes widened as they fell on her.

"Still you are surprising me," he said. "Are you sole?"

"We split up," she said.

Geist nodded and turned to his companions. "Cherch."

"The question you should be asking," Malone said, "is why."

He cocked his head. His troops hesitated. "Why did you imagine you could hide Arnault? Or why are you aiding him?"

She took a deep breath, trying to imagine what Sundar would have said. "No one came here to hide. We came to show you something. To show everyone something." She waved a hand at the ancient contraptions and hoped they impressed Geist as much as they had Jane.

"I am not understanding," he said, keeping his eyes on her.

"You talk about a history in which our lands were at war," Malone said, thinking back to the way Sundar had talked down a drunk at a bar. She had to tell him something true, something he needed to hear. If she could convince him, they could convince the rest of the Continent easily. "But there was another history. One in which they built machines that took them to the stars."

Geist glanced around. "Und you are thinking Rothbauer will build these machines?"

"No," Malone said. "But Arnault will."

"Arnault," Geist said, scowling, "will be the last of his dynasty."

"Only if you murder him like the despots you despise," Malone said.

"It is different," he said, tapping his ragged lapels. "I am different."

But she knew better. She just had to get him to see it. "No. I've seen this history, Geist. I've seen it with Sato. If you defeat Rothbauer, you will become everything he was and more in order to maintain order. If he defeats you, then you will have given him all the license he needs to come down even harder."

History held rare sway over the Continentals, including Geist's people. The men and women who had come in with him were wavering, looking to their boss. Geist himself was harder to read.

What did he need to hear? What would Sundar have told him?

Malone remembered their conversation on the boat with

sudden clarity. Geist resented the iron grip of the past – what he'd always wanted was a brighter horizon. "You can't win this on your own," she said. "If you want to make the Continent better, you have to give your people something better to work towards. The question is, did you come to seize power or to find a better future?"

She watched him, waiting. Whatever happened now, she was sure Sundar couldn't have said anything more.

Geist smiled. "You are having a rare way with words, Malone. I am hoping you stick around to conclude what you have commenced."

He lay his gun on the floor and motioned for his soldiers to do the same.

CHAPTER THIRTY
EPILOGUE: A BETTER STORY

Jane shaded her eyes. It was a sunny day from the top of the lighthouse. Waves lapped at the remnants of the wall, now eroded and broken apart like old teeth wearing down to the gums.

Dismantling the wall had been one of Roman's first acts. Like so many things, it was a work in progress, and one that Jane did not expect to see completed in either of their lifetimes.

But that was all right. It was the progress that mattered.

The distant horizon blended into a pale blue line. The sprawl of Salvage was just visible a few miles offshore. It was smaller than when she'd known it, but formidable nonetheless.

Roman checked his pocket watch and grumbled. "She's late."

In Jane's biased opinion, her husband had aged very well. He still wore his hair long, but the black had frosted to iron gray. The years had softened some of his hard lines and angles, or maybe it just seemed that way because he smiled more.

The present moment notwithstanding.

"She's always hated these things," Jane said, giving him a peck on the cheek.

He smiled despite himself. "So have I," he muttered quietly.

As true as that was, he'd gotten quite good at them.

The lantern room was crowded with Jane, Roman, and pair of young capitans from Salvage, and various other dignitaries from the provinces of the Continent. Between the sunlight streaming through the glass and the press of overdressed bodies, the little room was quite stuffy. Yet by unspoken agreement, everyone stood with straight backs and shoulders for the benefit of the masses below.

Jane peered down over the crowds. There had to be several thousand people, maybe more. The nearby town of Renaissance du Rochelle had been overwhelmed with the influx, but people had come from all across the Continent to witness Roman's Gran Meisterwork. She supposed she should have been glad, but the sight of so many people still made her a little nervous.

She felt an affectionate squeeze on her arm.

"Don't worry," Roman said. "It'll work."

Presently, the sound of playful quarreling rose from the stairwell. Jane turned to look, though all of the other dignitaries were pretending – ever so politely – not to notice.

"– thousands of pounds of metal into the sky, but they can't put a lift in the lighthouse?"

Even over the panting and grunting, Jane recognized Liesl Malone's voice.

"You're always clambering around the wilderness with Salazar. You can handle a few stairs." That was Farrah, Malone's former secretary and constant companion.

"The stairs are not the problem," Malone panted. "The problem is these shoes."

Jane heard two hard clomping noises.

"Put them back on!" Farrah hissed. "You can't run around in front of a thousand people barefoot!"

"None of them can see my feet."

Jane stifled a laugh. Roman was still gazing toward the sea, but a smirk tugged at the corners of his mouth.

Moments later, the two women emerged from the stairwell. Malone seemed as uncomfortable as a trussed turkey in a suit of black and green with a long, brocaded jacket. Farrah trailed behind her, wearing a green dress and an expression of beautiful vexation. In Malone's hands were two orphaned shoes.

Jane glanced down long enough to note that Malone's feet were, indeed, bare.

As packed as the lantern room was, people squeezed together to make room for two more.

Malone's white hair was only a few shades lighter from the color Jane had always known it to be, and her pale eyes were just as sharp. She didn't look like she'd aged so much as she'd merely hardened.

Malone gestured to the throngs below. "Arnault, you've got to be insane, leaving yourself exposed to a crowd like this."

The other dignitaries blushed and cleared their throats. To nearly everyone else, Roman was "the senure."

He gave her a patient smile that Jane had seen him practice many, many times over the years. "I've got nothing to hide," he said.

"You mean nowhere to hide," said Malone. "If they get–"

"Liesl!" Farrah snapped. She gave the former inspector a glare that would have melted butter, then turned to Roman and Jane with a more gracious smile. The years hadn't dimmed her beauty or her bright red hair. "It's an honor to be here," she said, exchanging kisses with them both in the local style.

"Thank you for coming," Jane said. "It seemed right that we should all witness this together."

"Next time, the buried cities are hosting," Malone said, swooping in to Jane's cheek. Despite the woman's pallor, her face was feverishly hot.

As Malone leaned toward Roman, Farrah frowned an apology at Jane.

Still hates flying, she mouthed over the pale woman's shoulder.

"Geist sends his regards," Malone whispered, just loudly enough for Jane and Roman to hear. The scarred revolutionary had put them all in a difficult spot. They couldn't let him run free after committing so much bloodshed, but he'd been instrumental in uniting his followers under Roman's vision.

In the end, he and his closest associates had "escaped" with

Malone to the buried cities and led peaceful lives there.

Roman nodded his acknowledgment.

"We are all ready, ya?" called a voice from the other end of the lantern room. Some minister whose name Jane couldn't recall at the moment.

"Ready," Roman said.

There was a pause, then a hum of electricity in the floor below them. Jane watched the sea beyond. The lamp behind them glowed to life, flashing across the windows as it made a few lazy circles.

Roman squeezed her hand. To her right, Jane saw Farrah stroking Malone's arm with a quiet, familiar tenderness, drawing the tension out of her lover's shoulders.

Malone whispered something to the redhead. She smiled.

A collective gasp echoed in the lantern room. A plume of flame had sprouted from the decks of Salvage, just beneath a long, narrow cone. It was tiny at this distance, but Jane had seen it close enough to know how big it was. Excitement – and a little fear – sped her heart.

"I'd hate to be the one riding in that thing," Malone said.

"It's just metal and wires this time," Farrah said.

Roman squeezed Jane's hand.

As they watched, the shooting flames lifted the rocket into the sky, pushing it higher and higher. They followed it sail through the clouds and recede into a bright spark until it disappeared completely. At last, all that was left was a gray trail through the blue.

The lantern room erupted in cheers. Jane embraced Roman, Malone, Farrah – everyone within reach, her cheeks wet with her tears and theirs. Below, the crowd was a writhing, joyful mass.

Only Malone looked uncertain, gazing up at the sky as if waiting for the whole thing to come back down. "That was it?" she whispered.

"That," Roman said, "was only the beginning."

ACKNOWLEDGMENTS

Looking back from the end of Book Three, I'm delighted to have had the opportunity to tell – and finish – the story of Jane, Malone, Roman, and Recoletta, and I'm grateful to the many people who have made it possible.

First of all, thank you to Angry Robot's current and former staff, especially Marc Gascoigne, Lee Harris, Phil Jourdan, Paul Simpson, Mike Underwood, Penny Reeve, and Caroline Lambe for supporting these books, and to artist extraordinaire John Coulthart for dressing them up so nicely.

Next, thank you to my agent, Jennie Goloboy, and to the rest of the Red Sofa Literary team, including Dawn Frederick, Laura Zats, and Liz Rahn for championing the series.

Over the years, I've had the privilege to get to know some wonderful writers who have become good friends as well as invaluable sources of encouragement and feedback. Thank you to Jacqui Talbot, Michael Robertson, and Bill Stiteler, who have provided insightful critiques and heartening support from *The Buried Life* onwards.

Thank you to the Freeway Dragons (and the Orange County Dragons) for writerly camaraderie and advice over many write-ins and hangouts. That's Remy Nakamura, Tracie Welser, S B

Divya, David Kammerzelt, Nicole Feldringer, Jenn Reese, Chris East, Andrew Romine, and Megan Starks. Special thanks to Megan for insisting on resolving the vault!

A big thanks as well to the Unclean Synod (Dan Bensen, Tex Thompson, and Kim Moravec) for Friday morning critiques and catch-up. Especially Dan for his invaluable thoughts on language.

Also, thank you to Lieutenant Commander Sean Purdy, USN, and Lieutenant Raza Beg, USN, for their service and for their generosity in providing a tour of the USS Essex and many helpful explanations of shipboard life. Any inaccuracies in this book are my own. Thanks as well to Hiral Beg for warm hospitality and cold Moscow mules.

I couldn't have written this without the loving support of so many wonderful friends and family members. Thanks most of all to Hiren Patel, Julie Lytle, Sydney Thompson, and Ryan Thompson – I love you all.

Finally, thanks to you for reading, sharing, and dreaming.

ABOUT THE AUTHOR

Carrie Patel was born and raised in Houston, Texas, in the USA. An avid traveller, she studied abroad in Granada, Spain and Buenos Aires, Argentina. She completed her bachelor's and master's degrees at Texas A&M University and worked in transfer pricing at Ernst & Young for two years.

She now works as a narrative designer at Obsidian Entertainment in Irvine, California, where the only season is Always Perfect. She has written for *Pillars of Eternity* and its expansions, *The White March Parts I* and *II*. She is currently working on the sequel, *Pillars of Eternity II: Deadfire*.

electronicinkblog.com • *twitter.com/carrie_patel*

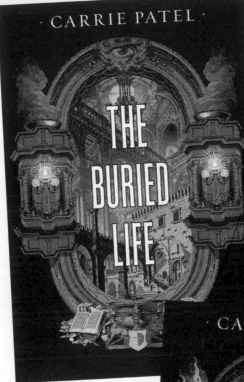

· ONE ·

THE
BURIED
LIFE

· TWO ·

CITIES
AND
THRONES